Published in Great Britain by
L.R. Price Publications Ltd, 2021
27 Old Gloucester Street,
London, WC1N 3AX
www.lrpricepublications.com

ISBN: 978-1-7398052-0-3

THE LAST POACHER

Peter Thompson

Dedicated to my best friend Johnny Mason.

Contents

Author's Note

Behind the scenic hills, lochs and rivers of Scotland lies a little-known twilight world, inhabited by lawless, ruthless, vicious and highly-organized gangs, intent on making a killing. Their prize: fresh, wild salmon, for which there is an endless demand on the black market, where one night's work can yield eight-thousand pounds tax-free profit.

Poaching, a word so often used to describe the lonely old codger living in a croft and snatching "one for the pot", has now become the second most profitable criminal activity after drug trafficking in Scotland.

Unfortunately for the salmon, the bad news doesn't stop there. In the British Isles, wild salmon are now threatened by a lethal new peril: a tiny, parasitic fluke which could spell disaster; across northern and western Europe, the salmon industry has already been totally devastated. Although not harmful to humans, the parasite is deadly to salmon. The U.K. has escaped this threat so far...

In writing this novel, based on real facts, the author has drawn on his own experience of salmon fishing in Scotland. He decided to combine forces with a ghost writer to develop the intriguing storyline, and provide a unique, fictionalized account of the many dangers which beset the world of the wild salmon.

CHAPTER 1

Johnny's secret

JOHNNY MASON STEPPED outside his back door, glanced upward at the night sky and noticed the dark, fleecy clouds sweeping across it, getting broken up and scattered by the fierce wind high above. Tearing through the narrow street, the biting easterly gust seemed far stronger – colder too, he thought – and he turned up the collar on his long army greatcoat, glad of the protection it gave, and pulled down the rim of his battered, shapeless old trilby.

The night was not ideal for the task he had in mind, but having no control over the weather he decided it would have to do, strolling the short distance along a gravel path to the gate which, like himself, was clearly showing signs of age. The hinges creaked more often than not and badly needed oiling – like his joints in the morning, crying out for Ralgex heat spray, to soothe away the sore stiffness and dull ache.

After slamming the gate behind him, he shrugged then turned westward, ambling along with a stoop which made him appear far older and less agile than he really was. He stuffed both hands into the deep pockets on either side of his old army coat, which he'd owned for more years than he cared to remember.

His greatcoat was like an old friend that never let him down. Unlike the naval duffel coats, it didn't soak up water like a sponge, then weigh twice as much after a sudden downpour. He'd never managed to work out why the Navy issued such garments to the sailors. Neither could he imagine why duffel coats had caught on with teenagers in recent years. Still, they had a hood; maybe that was the attraction.

The items he'd stashed in the pockets before setting out provided some degree of assurance. In the left pocket, his fingers wound about a tightly-rolled, plastic bin liner. In the right, he felt two stubby candles and a box of matches. If searched, nothing would connect him with his intended pursuit, and the thought never failed to bring a smile to his long, slender face.

Should that night – or on any other when about his seemingly honest business, which others might deem shady – a small child observe him passing in the gloomy street, they would have not slept well, suffering nightmares filled with devils and demons; his dishevelled appearance showed him as such.

Without hesitation, he scrambled through a wire fence at the end of the street, and entered the first of two fields which needed crossing before reaching his destination, and possibly safety. The fields were sopping wet, too, but being an ex-soldier, he knew how to cross such terrain without leaving a trace of having passed through. To thwart any prying eyes which might be watching his every move, Johnny never looked left or right, up or down, and gave the appearance of a man with nothing to fear or hide; a figure who knew exactly where he was going.

He soon crossed the two fields and entered a long, narrow wood, where he stopped for several minutes and observed the way he had come. Johnny was always dead careful when out on a mission. "Comes from S.A.S. training," he used to mutter to himself.

Satisfied that nobody was trailing him, he set out through the rest of the wood until he reached the far end, where a large ash tree stood. Standing with his back against the broad trunk of the ash tree, his eyes by now used to the darkness, Johnny could see across fifty yards of open ground, the narrow track alongside the riverbank made by the trampling hooves of sheep and the boots of fishermen.

The river provided a bountiful harvest, if one had the skill to catch the life which swam in its waters, and one was not too greedy. Yes, the generous river – with water clear and bubbly, like Champagne – would always provide. Johnny could hear the water gush over and between the boulders and rocks, in a noisy, cascading flow, before finding peace and quiet in the large, deep pool which lay farther down the river.

Across the river, stone walls divided the hilly landscape into large and small fields, where sheep and cattle, forever on the move, never seemed to satisfy their appetites, always chewing grass and perhaps coarser herbage, rich, luscious and nutritious. On the hill stood an ancient house, now derelict and abandoned a lifetime ago; a standing lone sentinel, silent, its bleak, dark windows forever watching the valley below. Who had lived in that house, and what sort of lifestyle the occupants had led, Johnny could only dimly guess at. He vaguely thought that the place was Victorian, maybe a gamekeeper's lodge, left over from the days when the old queen herself went grouse-shooting on the moors. Then again, it could have belonged to a country doctor in the 1930s. In fact, it might have served both. But now the place was silent – as silent as a grave, almost. Empty, perhaps, but sanctuary for whichever creature needed it: a place to hide, or to shelter and watch from. Surrounding the house, a large belt of coniferous woodland, appearing as a black patch on the hillside, also made a hideaway, or a viewing stage to observe the valley below, while remaining concealed. It was dark and very secret.

The heavy scent of damp pine needles reassured Johnny, and made him feel that what he was doing was part of nature; a sustainable activity. Totally appropriate in a world gone mad, where politicians cared not about dead soldiers, and even shook hands with terrorists. Johnny inhaled deeply, and the pine odour was still there: deep, sharp, yet sweet and comforting.

Happy with things so far, Johnny walked ten paces back into the wood, to a small mound he knew very well. He swept aside the top layer of fallen autumn leaves, removed an inch or more of topsoil and uncovered a small, black, tin box. He opened the container and withdrew a soft cloth bundle containing a telescope. Placing the wrapping cloth and box on the mound, Johnny returned to the ash tree, clutching his precious telescope. Sitting with his back resting on the trunk, he brought the telescope into focus, while bearing on the old house upon the far hill.

After watching for a few minutes, he panned across to where the fir tree wood came to a point roughly three-hundred yards from the river, then began sweeping along the riverbank in both directions. Seeing no trace of any activity, and glad of it, he placed his telescope on the ground beside him.

While he sat in the dark, eyes still watching and ears listening, his mind wandered. Back to when he was with the Black Watch, a long time ago in a distant land: a battle; a war in Korea. Hordes of screaming Chinese soldiers, some blowing bugles, came charging up the hill toward him and his battalion, while his best mate and number two on the Bren gun, Angus McGregor, lay dead in a pool of blood beside him, now unable to change barrels. His Bren gun got so hot that he couldn't see the enemy target for smoke. Afterwards, the gun jammed; he never fired the weapon again.

The major's voice bellowed above the raging battle: "Hold them, lads! Hold the yellow bastards, my bonnie laddies!" All while a piper played in the lea of a huge boulder.

But it was hopeless: there were far too many of the Chinese – too many by far.

The long months of incarceration which followed, in the hands of a cruel and sadistic enemy, forever haunted Johnny; he still shivered at the very thought of it. As prisoners of war, they suffered horrific treatment, with beatings, forced labour, endless marches and starvation. The "yellow bastards", as the Chinese were dubbed, played malicious tricks, too. Sometimes, but not often, they'd hand out gut-destroying, raw corn to the starving soldiers. Johnny had wondered what sort of people could inflict such misery. Barbarians, he'd concluded.

But, worst of all was the chronic dysentery, humiliating and strength-sapping. Some of his fellow prisoners were so weakened they couldn't lift their head, even to nod. Johnny was one of the lucky few: his plucky and canny outlook got him through the ordeal.

But only just.

With his release, he re-joined his regiment, stayed with them to complete his service and, during that time, met a wonderful woman, Annie, who eventually fell to his charm and they married. He liked to think that he'd rescued her from the open sewer of life in rundown Glasgow.

Annie had a hard life. Born and raised in the rough district of the city, she lived with her family in a pink-brick tenement slum, not fit for a rat to live in, let alone humans. She had two sisters and four brothers; seven children in all, her mother had brought into the world – positively Victorian, many neighbours had commented. And, like a Victorian, her father ruled the family with a rod of iron, and he used it – or, rather, his thick, black belt.

The teachers, wielding draconian discipline, made her childhood – at a school plagued by pestilences like nits and other infectious ailments – more miserable. To get to school, she had to cross the local park, packed out with winos exposing their manhood to every pretty, young girl – and the not so pretty girls, too; anything in a skirt was fair game, as far as they were concerned.

Then, at seventeen, one of her older brothers, Alun, raped her. For some strange reason, they were alone in the house, she scrubbing the filthy linoleum floor in the kitchen, he with nothing much on his mind, other than a bit of fun. He just knocked her to the floor, then raped her. Straining away among the soapsuds on the tatty linoleum, he had no compassion for her at all; it was simply self-gratification. It was a sad way for a girl to lose her virginity. And worse, he was committing incest without batting an eyelid.

He'd sunk to the bottom rung of the ladder, already frequenting one of the hundreds of bedbug-infested brothels which proliferated across Glasgow's red-light district. But this time, with his sister, it was free. Annie didn't fall pregnant, and for that she was glad, but kept quiet about the incident. If her father had known, Alun would have been despatched to the undertaker faster than being struck by lightning.

Of course, when she met Johnny, she was naturally at first cautious, but eventually realized that not all men were bastards. Besides, he was respectable: an Army sergeant, and perhaps a gentleman. After Alun, any man seemed gentle. Johnny was, too.

To Johnny, Annie was his saviour. She bore him two children, both boys: Hamish and Ewan. He really adored her, and she helped him overcome the trauma left over from his days of internment at the mercy of the Chinese.

After holding the rank of Company Sergeant Major, he served for a short spell with the Glasgow Police Force. That wasn't too bad; it brought in the money – not a vast fortune, but enough to keep his family housed, fed and clothed. Unfortunately for him, there was a downside: Detective Inspector McTavish.

No matter how Johnny tried, they just didn't hit it off. At C.I.D., McTavish threw his weight around; he forever bullied the younger constables, and was given to sporadic outbursts of violence, even while questioning suspects. But McTavish always got away with it; he'd contacts in high places. They simply turned a blind eye to his less customary techniques which, although questionable, brought results in solving crimes, petty or otherwise. McTavish, he thought, should have been with them in Korea, then perhaps they might have won that dire battle and never suffered the endless torment.

Eventually, when his two sons were able to fend for themselves, he retired from the police force and was glad to. With retirement, Johnny and Annie moved back to the village where he was born, to look after his ailing mother. On the first year back, his father passed away, after a lifetime of chronic boozing, followed a year later by his mother, largely through illness, or the strain of living with an alcoholic.

Misfortune always came in threes; only two years later, his wife Annie died from cancer. He thought it a horrible, slow, degrading way to go, and remembered with deep sorrow all the long vigils by her bedside in the hospital – then the waits in the gloomy hospital lobby when she deteriorated. How the hospital stank of death. Very different from that of the battlefield, but death, nonetheless.

Almost as though to rub salt into an open wound, many of the N.H.S. staff – the nurses, attendants and young, inexperienced doctors – were Oriental. Worse, Chinese. That Johnny found awfully difficult to swallow, even though the young immigrants would never have been so much as a twinkle in their parents' eye when he was in Korea.

Although the yellow peril had receded, the communists were only then to be replaced by Islamic militants. Both his sons had joined the Army, partly to follow his footsteps and perhaps win his approval, or prove themselves – Johnny could never be quite sure which. Hamish and Ewan were now serving with the British forces in Afghanistan, hell-bent on defeating the Taliban.

Now he was alone. Totally alone, except for… that feeling of being at one with nature while in the field. Savouring the isolation. Acceptance of being part of the great outdoor order of things, just like the owl that he sometimes saw in the pine forest. *A survivor; a hanger-on,* he thought. *That's what I am: a hanger-on.*

He was about to move on when he heard the flutter of wings, looked up and saw the small owl he often thought of as a survivor – a natural one. The owl landed on a branch just above his head, its form a dark silhouette against the night sky, visible through a gap among the branches of the tree. He couldn't see its bright yellow eyes, but instinctively knew the owl was watching him, perhaps trying to make out what he was. Or perhaps the wild bird already knew, and wondered why he was there in the first place. Of course, he was intruding on the owl's home territory, sitting in the bird's larder, almost. He hoped the little owl didn't think he was after its food, hunting for moles, bank voles or mice and other little rodents, high on the menu of predatory birds.

Such thoughts made him feel even more aware of the wild world around him, but he respected it, too. He knew what to leave and what to take, showing consideration for all things wild and free; never taking or destroying untamed, feral creatures or their resources simply for the sake of it. Reverence, he felt, was mutual between him and wild creatures. Besides, he had already decided that the owl was far too big to shoo off; to do so would be disrespectful, anyhow. Maybe the little owl already knew this, as it flew off moments afterward, leaving Johnny alone to speculate on the wisdom of leaving wild, untamed things. Of working alongside nature, instead of trying to brow-beat it, like the politicians… or the mega-buck consumer corporations.

For a brief moment, Johnny thought about reincarnation. Perhaps the little owl was one of his mates in the Army, and had flown into the tree, drawn by his musings or his presence there. He decided the idea was rather whimsical, far-fetched and too removed from reality.

Then, he realized time was running away and there was so much still to do, so fixed his mind on the task ahead.

He rose to his feet again, returned to the mound and wrapped the cloth around the telescope, then slid it back into the box and buried it. He carefully camouflaged signs of disturbance by brushing more leaves and twigs over the soil. *No point in taking chances, or let them sassenach bastards in on my little secret.*

He moved to the opposite side of the mound, to a smaller, similar hummock, also hidden under heaps of leaves. He cleared them away and, from a hole, removed a small box – a wooden one; he also extracted a gaff and a camouflaged net. Johnny was dead proud of the camouflage net, which had taken several weeks to perfect, weaving into it the colours and materials associated with such a riverbank as this: the dull greens, browns and russet hues all blended in, along with bits of twig, leaves and dry grass stems.

Johnny carefully placed the wooden box in a deep pocket on the inside of his greatcoat – a pocket specially made for the purpose of carrying the box, gaff and net. He returned to the ash tree, and for a spell stood under it, looking around and listening for anything untoward. Satisfied that there was nobody about, he decided to make a move. Even if there was a person wandering around, if he could not see them, he hoped the same applied in reverse, and that others could not locate him.

Johnny never left things to chance; he was better than that. He always thought chancing it was for amateurs, or inexperienced kids trying to grab whatever they could find in the woods. He'd heard often enough that local kids grew dope plants among the dense undergrowth, but he doubted it; the bleak, cold climate was far too inclement for cultivating cannabis sativa.

Johnny sniffed, peered around again, then covered himself with the net. It gave him the appearance of a tall heap of living and dead grasses – a walking heap, too. He stepped out of the wood and slowly sauntered across the open ground, toward the river.

He remained ever watchful, ready to stand stock-still and not move a muscle or hunker down, so as to blend more into the background. Seeing nobody around near the river, he pressed on, cautious and alert, straining his ears for any signs of human footfalls: the crunch of leaves or the snap of a dried twig. He heard no such sounds and sidled onward, reflecting on the procedure he'd adopted.

Should the ghost of some former, long-departed poacher have witnessed Johnny's tactics, they would have surely thought his methods eccentric, to say the least. But no ghosts ever turned up, that he could see. Johnny knew his technique was unusual, perhaps unique, but he had no qualms, and had always been successful on his nocturnal forays; not once had he returned empty-handed, or ever got caught. Maybe it was the net. On the other hand, it could have been the little owl, keeping an eye open on his behalf. Or perhaps just plain old luck.

Of course, the ex-soldier knew his methods weren't completely infallible: there was always the risk; it came with the activity. More than once, the men who hunt down wanderers in the night had walked past, unaware of his presence, concealed beneath his net. The camouflage was so good that, on occasions, the hunters had almost stepped onto his hidden body, while discussing what they would do with the wily thieving bastards, as they branded people like himself.

On reaching the riverbank, he took stock. He'd frequented this place many times before, and the terrain was almost as familiar as the back of his hand. Johnny was almost tempted to think of the place near the pool as his own back garden. But he knew that was a dangerous notion: it could easily lead him to a sense of false security, and to becoming careless. "Familiarity breeds contempt," he had heard somewhere, long ago, and that was true. Out here in the wild, the land belonged to everybody, not just the elitists, or the folk who held no respect for the fertile ground and nature.

The riverbank proved ideal for the purpose he had in mind. On the bank side, he sat down next to an old bush. From his trouser pocket he pulled out four thin metal pegs, then lay under the net and pegged down each of the corners, making it taut. Reaching into his coat pocket, he removed the wooden box and the two stubby, home-made candles. The wicks had been made thicker to give them a brighter light, and less chance of being blown out by the night wind, which could often be blustery along the river.

Johnny smiled. Yes, the candles: a special innovation; an occupation to while away the wet afternoons indoors. In fact, he was proud of his idea. Almost looked upon the candle-making as a form of alchemy – a bit like turning lead into gold, almost. First, he melted down ordinary candles in an old milk saucepan on the hob, careful not to scorch the wax. Then, he extracted the wicks from the molten liquid, cut them to roughly an inch or so in length; to make a thicker wick, he spun two or three of the existing wicks together. Afterward, he reheated the wax so that it was liquid and smeared a dab of lard around the inside of aluminium nightlight holders. He'd bought a pack of six nightlights from the local supermarket, as he usually made the candles in batches of six. He poured the molten wax into the holders, right up to the rim. As the wax cooled and gradually solidified, he stuck the thickened wicks in the middle of each holder, and left the improvised candles to set. When cold, he tapped the base of each little holder and out popped a perfect stubby candle, lubricated by the lard. Johnny knew preparation was vital to the success of his missions, as he thought of them.

Next, he checked the wooden box, made sure the narrow slats he'd cut into the four sides were clear of muck and mud, then he took the stubby candles and pressed them onto two sharp tacks nailed through from the base. Sure that the candles were secure, he struck a match and lit them, then gently eased down the box lid, careful to avoid snuffing out the small flames. Then, he tied a short length of string to a fastening on the side of the box.

Leaning out of his net hide, he placed the box onto the calm river surface, then tied the other end of the string to an iron peg. As the box floated over a small, calm backwater, candlelight from the slats flickered over the water's clear surface. Gaff firmly in his hand,

Johnny waited.

He got to thinking why, during the hours of darkness, salmon ware attracted to light – especially a flickering light like that from a candle – and knew not; if asked, he couldn't even make a guess of it. Johnny had absolutely no idea that most fish were attracted to lights in the night, especially green lights, often used by anglers at sea. But he found the candles worked, and was mighty glad of the seemingly foolproof method of luring the fish; he knew that at the evening's end there would be a nice financial reward for all the effort, which he regarded as a sport more than anything. A healthy and profitable activity, which enabled him to go out most nights during the week to his favourite watering hole, a local pub called "The Leaping Salmon". At the pub, he relished the company of his friends, and chattered about all manner of topics that took their fancy, though usually conversation turned to salmon fishing, passing on tips and ideas.

Johnny Mason, like all the other villagers who indulged in such nocturnal expeditions, never regarded himself as a thief, not for a minute. To Johnny and most villagers, the real thieves were the duke, and others of a similar standing: the landowners, the lairds and rich entrepreneurs, with big houses and fancy hotels swallowing acres of land. The villagers' feelings were: who gave these aristocratic oppressors the right to take as their own the mountains, fields, rivers and all that God had seen fit to put into them? What right had the so-called gentry to claim the fish in the rivers, and to profit from the exclusive right to fish from them? The duke and his family neither reared nor fed the fish. In fact, he did very little for the river and its stock of salmon, trout, carp, mullet or any other which inhabited the waters.

Instead, the duke policed the rivers with fanatical zeal, and his estate raked in the fat-cat revenue that these beautiful, river-dwelling creatures attracted, simply by swimming the clear waters in the first place.

Feeling ran high among the villagers. Why should they, born and living there, be deprived of the free right to fish in the river that passed through their homeland, without facing duress, while the moneyed folk from afar did?

Johnny vaguely guessed it was a ploy endorsed and encouraged by Britain's first and so far only woman prime minister, Maggie Thatcher. Yes, she had indeed brought victory of sorts over the Falklands, he thought, but few knew the full horror that conflict entailed. Johnny only found out the details from his eldest, Hamish, then a raw recruit.

With victory over Argentina, everyone thought Maggie was the saviour – the new Messiah, almost. What's more, she encouraged free-market enterprise. In her eyes, accountability had become the key word, at expense of all else; if a venture didn't generate revenue, it was cast aside. And, thousands of up and coming youngsters embraced her philosophy – those from affluent backgrounds, that is. Hence, people like the duke joined in the great moneymaking crusade, capitalizing on all that lay to hand, or whatever he could snatch. For the duke, that meant the river and the lands around. Almost like a city racketeer, he pounced on natural resources across the valley, charging exorbitant prices for fishing weekends, letting out refurbished cottages on his estate as holiday homes for small fortunes, and generally hobnobbing with neighbouring landowners of the same mind.

It was round about that time that many local landlords set up hotels upon the hillsides. Scotland had gained in popularity as a retreat for the wealthy, no doubt inspired by the long-running T.V. serial *Monarch of the Glen*, thought Johnny.

He also realized that local people had been priced out of the housing market, as property across the region had escalated. Johnny knew it was unjust; that Maggie's dream of a home-owning democracy amounted to little more than cynical mockery.

Then, a funny thing happened. A strange quirk of fate, perhaps, Johnny often thought. A nasty little upstart called Saddam Hussein invaded Kuwait. On the eve of the first Gulf War, the Iron Lady suddenly lost her mettle, though her departure from Number Ten was, at the time, largely accredited to her stance against Brussels over retaining British Sovereignty. The damage had been done: she was gone, and eventually so was Saddam.

Unfortunately, the idea of making money didn't fade away; if anything, it spiralled out of control. Property prices leapt up, and quite suddenly everybody wanted the means to live in extravagance and comfort. Houses were no longer somewhere to live, but an asset to capitalize on. Huge extensions were built, gardens became outdoor rooms and a new rash of greedy estate agents sprang up like a rampant social disease. And, like a disease, the idea of catering for the elite, for the sake of profit, expanded into every corner of the land. The duke was no exception.

During the last few months, the duke and his lackeys had tried to find different ways to rid the riverbanks of fishermen from the village who, over the years, got into the habit of purchasing seasonal fishing permits at vastly reduced prices. The reason behind wanting to bar these people was dead simple: the duke wanted to sell daily fishing permits and weekly permits to the rich English sassenachs, who arrived in their spanking new 4x4s, sported flashy waxed jackets, wore green Wellington boots and couldn't catch a cold in a snowstorm. They were amateurs: city boys playing at being sovereign of the glens. And, the really funny thing which amused Johnny was the fact that they still clung onto their iPods and mobile phones. Some even sent text messages while waiting for a bite, instead of watching the river for tell-tale signs of movement beneath the water's surface. *Yeah, that's city-boys alright: probably couldn't tell the difference between a trout and a carp,* he thought, contemptuously.

Johnny had been lying in position for no more than twenty minutes when the fish appeared, rising gradually from the depths of the pool, its mouth slowly opening and closing. Hardly daring to breathe, Johnny saw its eyes, cold and still, gold ringed, with the dark beads for pupils unmoving, but clearly entranced by the flickering light. Whether the fish realized what the lights were nobody could guess, not even Johnny, but for a few minutes it nosed the box forward. Like a surfaced shark with its back out of the water, influenced by the light, the salmon nudged the box along, slowly pushing it gently through the still backwater.

Until this very moment, every move Johnny made that night had been slow and deliberate. Now he moved with surprising speed and agility for a man of his age: in what appeared to be one movement, the sharp point of the gaff entered the fish just behind the gills, and it was wrenched from the water onto the bank, where its exit was immediately concealed from sight under the camouflage net.

Johnny quickly and expertly dispatched the salmon to its maker with one swift blow from the gaff handle; the box he pushed under the water, to douse the two candles. Then, in the near complete dark, he dropped everything, including the fifteen-pound salmon, into the net, slung it over his shoulders and slowly made his way back to the wood.

After hiding the net, the four metal pegs, wooden box and gaff, in the hollow of the second mound, and covering the surface with leaves, he put the salmon in the plastic bag. Then, he slung his prize in the bag down his back, under the greatcoat, and headed for home. *Yep,* he thought, *this has been one hell of a profitable night.*

He didn't dare sigh with relief, lest anyone should hear. Silence was the key to getting home undetected, especially while carrying the booty. He suddenly remembered a wartime film he'd watched in another age: *Run Silent, Run Deep* it was called. He grimly smiled; true enough: silent and deep, like the fish in the river that he'd just returned from. Still, prize gained, Johnny knew there would be plenty of evenings in The Leaping Salmon. He also knew that this was not the last night-run by a long chalk; while he had strength left to hike across fields and through woods, Johnny Mason would strike again, then maybe yet again after that.

Johnny returned across the two fields, and in spite of his extra burden, left no tracks behind him – not so much as a bent blade of grass. But then he was used to traversing enemy territory, where snipers might lie in wait, and snares or even mines had been laid around every corner. His current adversaries weren't gunmen or bombers, but ordinary civvies; folk corrupted by greed, ambition and power over others.

Before he knew it, he'd reached the wire fence. He quickly bent down, slipped through the gap and stepped onto the tarmac road leading to the village. Although Johnny felt safe now, a pressing need for urgency quickened his step. The salmon in the black plastic bag under his greatcoat kept bumping into his backside, the weighty bag was gradually slipping downward. The *thump, thump, thump* at the top of his buttocks also warned him to slow down, as he realized that anyone watching, even a casual glance from a passer-by, might wonder why he was walking so awkwardly, and ponder on the weird swinging movement above the tail of his greatcoat. *Heh, dinna sod things up at this stage,* he thought, while wiping his brow and trying to appear casual.

He rubbed his hand down the outside of the deep pocket of his coat. Then, he looked around to make sure nobody was around, especially those who might suspect where he'd been. Or, even worse, someone harbouring a grudge and ready to point an accusing finger: *"Aye, that's the thievin' bastard, alright. Walking all over the duke's land and helpin' himself to the stock, like he was liftin' a pack o' fish fingers outta MacCready's Supermarket, if ye please."*

He was glad to see nobody about on the narrow, poorly-lit street, but the euphoria of gaining the prize gradually filtered away to angst, while carrying the precious cargo. He suspected drug runners must feel the same way when passing through an airport security arch, carrying a gut full of condoms packed with heroin.

Johnny didn't do the drugs thing. He'd thought about it often enough, but somehow couldn't work up any enthusiasm for it, even though the money would have been useful. Drugs killed kids and brought untold grief to families – Johnny didn't want to be any part of that. The drug barons, he thought, were little better than murderers. He knew that his trade, even though furtive, wouldn't involve innocent folk suffering. What's more, he felt on safer ground doing what he'd become highly skilled at and, at the same time, in harmony with nature – that was most important. Johnny got the idea that if he respected the natural world, nature or the Supreme Being would forever provide bountiful reward from the river.

The bagged salmon slipped downward another inch and, glancing around, he drew a breath. *Easy does it. Take it steady. The Leaping Salmon won't be closed for another hour or so.*

After another five minutes' walk, he'd almost reached his goal and turned left into an unlit, narrow alleyway. He turned again, slipped into a small yard, then sidled up to a little outhouse. Careful to avoid making noise, he gently unlatched the ancient, wooden door, entered a dark room and felt around a beam set into the wall above the doorway. His fingers located a square nail and snatched the key hanging from it.

Padding across the flagstone floor, he stopped beside an old chest freezer left over from the1980s, unlocked it, lifted the heavy lid and placed the salmon inside. Having locked the lid again, he replaced the key on its peg. He slipped his greatcoat off, hung it on the nail over the key and, through a second doorway, entered the noisy, well-lit public bar of The Leaping Salmon, in Glenstone village.

Feeling mighty relieved; Johnny walked over to the bar.

"Make it a pint of heavy there, landlord," he requested, while glancing around the room, taking note of the folk present.

"Pint of heavy coming right up," replied the publican, Reg McGuire.

Having pulled the pint with expertise, Reg set the glass of dark, slightly gassy beer on the polished wooden bar. Then, he plucked the soiled, creased five-pound note from Johnny's grubby right hand.

"Everything alright with you then, Johnny?" he asked, with a glint in his eye.

"Aye, a right grand night, indeed," he replied, palming the change – all one-pound-forty of it. Grasping his pint, he turned away from the bar and muttered: "A grand night, indeed."

Johnny saw his cluster of friends sitting in their usual places, over in the far corner. Landlord Reg grinned knowingly, and swaggered into the lounge bar, happy that wild, fresh salmon would be on tomorrow's pub menu, once more.

After the usual chorus of greetings, and before Johnny could so much as sip from the pint, old, pipe-smoking Tom Stuart suddenly blurted out: "Have you heard the bad news of the day, Johnny? Did ye ken the big yen lost his permit today?"

"No, I ruddy well didn't," replied Johnny, morosely. "How come?"

Tom fiddled with the pipe, then sneered, displaying a mouthful of broken, yellow, tobacco-stained teeth. "That brown-nosed bastard, McGee! You know him: the duke's head bailiff. I saw him talking to Bell down on the riverbank," interrupted Ben Thompson.

Johnny snorted, then pulled on the pint before speaking. "Well, he knew the score. He'd been warned often enough."

"True, but did McAlease have to report him? After all, he's from the village and one of us: a Scotsman! De ye no agree? It's not right. Not right at all," grumbled Ben.

Johnny took another sip and thought about Bell. Dinger Bell, as he liked to be known, Johnny regarded as a right pugnacious bastard, well known for beating up his wife, and any drunken old men in his path, too. Bell could often be seen wandering around the village with his few cronies, and their intended purpose was dead obvious to many.

CHAPTER 2

Dinger Bell

ALTHOUGH FOREVER UNEMPLOYED, Dinger Bell never wasted any time standing at the riverside with rod and line, nor was he content to poach the odd salmon or two – not Dinger. He went in for bigger things, and cared little about who or what suffered.

Johnny remembered one night, about two years ago, Dinger and four of his cronies from the city came and poisoned the river, using some kind of noxious gas which took the oxygen out of the water. Just to get a dozen or more salmon, they'd killed every living creature in the river for miles downstream.

Due to Bell's previous gas poisoning activities, on arrival the police knew exactly where to look. Having obtained a search warrant from the local judge, A.G. Buchannan – who just happened to own part of the gassed river – the police searched his house. The evidence they found upstairs, in his white enamel bathtub, the spoils of an illegal night's work – ten beautiful silver salmon – was more than enough to get him booked. At his trial, Judge Buchannan ordered a Crown hearing, and Dinger went down for two years.

On return to the village after his stay in prison, Dinger was barred from holding a fishing permit for life. Wily as ever, the ban didn't stop him from walking along the banks of the river. Any local fisherman caught conversing with him on or near the river also had their fishing permit revoked for life.

Dinger, along with many of his kindred across Scotland and elsewhere, simply bided their time, awaiting the social revolution that would surely come. He realized it might not happen today, but sensed that change would take place one day, in the not too distant future. During the ensuing time, he nursed grandiose aspirations, planned and plotted. Then, when that special day arrived, he and his good comrades would storm the castle and murder the duke and his family in cold blood – quite how, he had yet to determine; perhaps make him suffer a little bit first, then put a gun to his head, or a butcher's knife through the nobleman's vile, black, selfish heart.

Then, in that near-future date, he'd turn the castle and its grounds into a paradise for all the fishermen of Scotland, and his great deed would be done in the name of the people, for the good of the common masses. He'd be free to poison the river where and when he wished, hunt deer with dogs, shoot pheasant without restrictions and snare rabbits into the bargain, and all would be well in his paradise. While the duke's corpse hung from the ramparts, and crows pecked away at the bloody eye sockets, he'd sit in the nobleman's study, drinking his best port wine or brandy.

Savouring his ill-gotten gains, he'd then contemplate on the fate of the castle, and probably decide to leave things as they are. "Why change it? Nobody would thank me for doing so." From then on, he decided, he would become known as the "grand duke", and be even greedier.

Thus, he and his comrades would be just like Napoleon and the other socialist pigs from Orwell's story, *Animal Farm*. Except that, in the end, the new duke would be no better than the present one, and maybe far worse.

Hunched over their pints of heavy, snug inside the tavern, the five old men of Glenstone concluded that if nothing were done soon, the duke would achieve his aim of ridding the riverbank of local fishermen, and not have to worry about replacing them, either. There'd be no room left for them, anyway.

Each season, hundreds of English folk crossed over the border, eager for a spot of salmon fishing, and were willing to pay any amount for the privilege. In some cases entire families came, for a sort of fishing holiday. The duke relied on these successive waves of English punters to fill the beds, bars and dining rooms, in his large, opulent hotel, aptly named "The Grouse in The Heather". It was the kind of place where visitors always found fresh salmon on the menu and, naturally, the duke's head bailiff McGee informed people, right or wrong, of the best places to fish along the river.

In Scotland, the salmon fishing season was a long one, lasting all the way from early February through to late October, which made a nice, lengthy period for the nobleman to rake in plenty of money from those so willing to spend it. But, the duke had another string to his fishing permit racket: the river also contained rainbow trout which, being an indigenous species, could legally be fished for at any time of year. So, even during the scantest days in December and January, some unsuspecting, eager would-be fisherman handed over money for a permit, even if he hooked nothing more than clumps of waterweed out of the river with his rod and line. Of course, Johnny knew the duke wouldn't be in the least concerned about that little problem.

Johnny's group of friends all sighed, sipped, mused and eventually Tom Stuart got his pipe going again. Little clouds of smoke spiralled up toward the ceiling. Although the ban on smoking was supposed to be in force since November 2006, Reg kind of overlooked his locals lighting up, especially in the hours after dark.

Tom waved his pipe. "Obvious he's going to drive us ordinary folks right off the river."

"Aye, we already know that, ye twat," remarked Ben.

"Shame someone don't come along an' knock yon bogger off his perch," added Arthur Cormack, "then we'd all be spared this grief."

"Right enough," muttered Tom, "and ah reckon Mr. Bell might be the chappie to oblige us, eh?"

Johnny's eyes narrowed down to slits. "Aye, an' whose side d'yer thinks that slinkin' parasite's on? Hellfire, he ain't got any respect fer us, anymore than he has fer that bastard duke!"

Old Tom suddenly smiled. "Right. Situation's just like the old agricultural tripartite system of the nineteenth century, ain't it? The landlord, the farmer and penniless labourer, all at odds wi' each other and all desperate ter make a few bob."

"Never mind a few shillings, what's to be done about this fishing problem? If we dinna find an answer soon, none of us will be able to get within five miles of the river," stated Johnny, flatly.

Everyone knew he was right. The little problem of the duke was fast snowballing into a major headache for the villagers.

Tom shrugged, said nothing and continued sucking on the pipe stem.

All five men unanimously agreed that they were too old, tired and, above all, wise to start thinking along the same lines as Dinger Bell and his cohorts. However, the old men realized that, given time, an opportunity might arise for Dinger to take on the duke and his minions, without risk to themselves. But, as Johnny already stated, there'd be no real advantage to them, unless of course something also happened to Dinger, too. Maybe a careless driver on the dark lanes one night might... Alas, Dinger was too clever and wary.

The old men's musings were suddenly brought to an abrupt end. "Time, time, time, gentlemen, please! Drink up now!" bellowed Reg.

Johnny glanced at the brass clock on the brick wall and saw it was getting late. They'd been chatting away far longer than he had thought. "Aye, best make tracks," he stated, rising from his chair, having drained the last of the heavy from his glass.

Tom tapped his pipe on the tin ashtray, a dark-green thing from the 1950s. "True enough," he replied, stashing the pipe in his baggy tweed jacket and carefully arranging his tartan scarf, to keep cool night air from his chest.

"Right, see you tomorrow, then," commented Arthur, with a wink and nod. Arthur had also lost his wife, ten years ago. She'd had a dicey heart, forever in and out of hospital, so he identified with Johnny.

"Yeah, an' you take care now," warned Ben. "Keep yer eyes peeled fer that Dinger bastard, too."

Arthur nodded. "Heh! The day that one catches up wi' me, he won't half cop it. I dinna go round village wi' this fer no good reason." From the publican's narrow wooden stand, used to hold wet brollies, he withdrew a hefty walking stick of polished yew. Upon the end of the stick, a carved ram's head made for a really good club. Ben smiled at the wily old man's resolve. Dinger and his mates had never set upon Arthur, and clearly the old man had no intention of ever getting into that kind of difficulty.

Johnny sniffed and glanced at Arthur for a moment. "Aye, that's a deterrent, right enough. But, I would nay use it unless really pushed; you could get charged wi' manslaughter usin' a weapon like that." Johnny suddenly envisioned the club smashing down on Dinger's head, perhaps fracturing his skull, or worse.

"Self-defence," remarked Arthur. "We'll see, we'll see. Bet the police would be glad to see the back o' that rogue, anyhow. Besides, I'm in with Buchannan; he'd get me off any trumped-up charge."

Johnny stared at the floor for a moment, wondering what Arthur's statement meant. He'd never known his friend mention being pals with the local judge, and found it slightly disconcerting.

Arthur defiantly waved the yew stick. "Until the morrow, then." He departed through the doorway and was gone.

Ben hastily swilled a last mouthful of heavy and slipped his ragged anorak on. "Don't worry, I'll track the old man; mek sure he gets home safely." In fact, Ben lived in the same road as Arthur, a little farther along. He gave the thumbs-up, then flitted out of the doorway.

"What an evening," muttered Tom, easing himself into a second-hand mohair coat which was far too long for him. It looked almost as lengthy as Johnny's greatcoat.

"Aye, a grand night," Johnny stated.

Then, he stepped through the back door into the outhouse, to retrieve his greatcoat, hanging over the freezer key. "A rare old grand night," he repeated softly, thinking of the cash Reg would hand over the following morning.

He left the outhouse, crossed the yard, slipped down the alleyway and headed for home. Johnny liked to enter and leave the pub via the outhouse, partly to conceal his tracks and remain anonymous, and also to evade any risk of bumping into Dinger. Not that Johnny felt afraid of Dinger, but he didn't fancy running into him and his mates, end up with a broken arm and be unable to go poaching for several months.

While strolling along the dark lane, he thought about the river situation, and how things seemed to be changing in ways he didn't really care for. In Johnny's opinion, there were three main problems threatening his poaching activities. Firstly, the avaricious duke, with his endless succession of moneymaking schemes, robbed local folk of their liberty, and did very little for the future of the river he claimed as his own. Secondly, the roving gangs of poachers from the city, who were highly organized, utterly ruthless and endangering everything, simply for profit. Violent men they were, too; Johnny had read in the papers of a River Fisheries director being threatened with a hunting knife, after confronting a gang of poachers. Fortunately, they spared him and, though relieved, the official expressed dismay at these gangs spreading a reign of terror along the riverbanks. Thirdly, Dinger Bell and his cohorts – another menace the villagers could do well without. Like the city gangs, he was only poaching indiscriminately for the money, at the expense of all else. *Shame someone don't ding his bell for him, and save us a load of aggro,* thought Johnny, miserably.

Johnny cared little for rod-fishing and never had, always happy to gain a share in what the bountiful river provided by using his own resourceful technique: candles, box and all. Besides, a ban on the sale of rod-caught salmon had been in force since October 2002; there was no ban on the sale of salmon snagged from the water, lured by a flickering candle. Not yet, anyway. Johnny smiled at the irony: although poaching, his unusual method meant he didn't have to break the law regarding the ban.

Johnny was concerned for the younger men of the village, especially those who had gone off to fight for Queen and Country. One day they'd return, but would there still be a village left, if things continued as they were? *Sure as a pile of pigshit, the duke's squeezing the very lifeblood outa the village, strangling the inhabitant's hopes, and also their trust,* Johnny cogitated to himself. *Yes, what are we to do? Before long it's going to be a right pressing problem!*

Johnny Mason was not a greedy man, nor did he ever boast to others about his many successful trips alongside the river, under cover of darkness. He also kept silent about the failures: the nights of returning empty-handed, or having to call off his foray, due to the duke's men out hunting for prowlers in the night. He knew other poachers were often keen to brag about their escapades, to any folk who cared to listen, and decided it was a foolish move. Johnny felt dead certain that holding his tongue regarding his nocturnal expeditions had contributed to his success as a lone poacher, and also averted trouble or detection from the duke's lackeys, and others who might be tempted to muscle in on his activities. After all, so far he'd never been caught, and assumed nobody suspected him of being a poacher; to most villagers, he appeared as just a clapped-out old soldier, traipsing around in his greatcoat, minding his own business. And that was exactly how Johnny wanted to keep things.

Except, there was one villager who knew him better than any: the publican, Reg. Thankfully, he was a good friend; an ally, in a quiet, unspoken way. Though he, too, had aspirations to rake in the money; pub lunches and dinners were a really good earner, especially when he could serve up fresh, wild salmon. Reg knew very well where the supply of fish came from and, being a shrewd man, had many other little ventures on the go. He'd oblige regular customers with takeaways for a little extra payment, as the village had little in the way of restaurants. That, sadly, was another of the duke's doings: forcing local restaurateurs out of business.

The Tartan Platter, farther down the road, could hardly be called competition and, although licensed, they didn't serve beer, only wines. It was really the sort of place that toffee-nosed snobs went – people who regarded The Salmon as a watering hole for the local proletariat. Besides, The Platter would never dish up real wild salmon – not the kind Johnny supplied.

Around the corner, Glenside Tea Rooms – a tiny place occupying the front of a revamped cottage – remained in business. Although chintzy, it was mainly frequented by the local wrinklies, who indulged in delicacies like tea and scones, toasted teacakes and similar dainties. They were no competition to The Salmon at all. Besides, the Tea Rooms had gained the reputation of being a bit Godly, as the Church Committee held their meetings there. So, Reg wasn't too cut up about that. Nor was Johnny; he didn't frequent the Tea Rooms, ever. Johnny only went out to catch what his sole customer and publican friend, Reg McGuire, could use.

He fully realized that, by working alone, his or anyone else's safety was not jeopardized in such a risky venture.

On the nights when he caught a good fish – anything over ten pounds – he felt content to pack it in and, with burdened net, return to the mounds in the woods, stash away his gear and get back to the village. However, when he only snagged a six or seven-pound fish from the water, the temptation to linger by the river was incredibly strong, in the hope that another fish of similar size would make up the shortfall, so to speak.

Alas, times and the nature of poaching were fast-changing, more than ever. Gone were the days when most poachers were only interested in "one for the pot, back at home". These days, roving gangs of poachers were out with battery-powered stun guns, canisters of numbing chemicals, gases and other toxic agents, to kill or stun the fish on an industrial scale. Others systematically set up illegal netting schemes by waterfalls, to trap those salmon battling upstream to spawn. Consequently, the fish weren't nearly half as numerous as they had been in years gone by. Now, during some weeks, if fresh salmon was on the menu of local pubs, it got served on a first-come-first-served basis. One or two of the more unscrupulous publicans even had the audacity to dish up frozen salmon fillets from Wilson's Cash and Carry in the city. Once thawed and cooked, who was to know or argue – or, come to that, even care?

Johnny was old enough to remember when salmon, along with other fish such as trout and carp, were commonplace in the river. He recalled his father and grandfather, and even older members of the village, tell of the time when fish were so plentiful a person could cross the river using their backs as stepping-stones, and avoid getting wet feet. Naturally, Johnny knew that claim was a wild exaggeration, but he also recognized that the old men liked to spice up their anecdotes a wee bit, in order to entice the younger folk to listen. One thing Johnny knew was certain: all the older folk really believed that life in the past was far better than the present.

Sadly, the facts were around for all to see: during the past ten years or so, the numbers of fish caught and observed swimming upstream had tapered away dramatically. A fisherman would consider it lucky to catch one fish during an entire week, having fully paid up for a permit.

Unfortunately for all concerned, the salmon had scores of enemies – far too many of them. Wild Atlantic salmon, intent on spawning far upstream in the Highlands, had to run three gauntlets. To survive in the open ocean, the salmon – poor things – had to evade the blood-sucking lampreys, voracious jaws of sharks and, funnily enough, the cod, which also found salmon a right tasty morsel. Then, approaching near the coast, overhead attack from sea birds – tern, cormorant and gulls – decimated their numbers, not to mention hungry seals swimming offshore. Entering the estuaries and swimming upstream to fresh water, osprey and otter were also partial to salmon.

Apart from predators, natural obstructions impeded their journey, too. Long stretches of water, along some of the smaller streams, often had water so shallow they barely managed to slip through to deeper pools. Fallen trees lying on the riverbank were another occasional hazard. More regular were the frequent waterfalls which called for monumental effort, leaping up to the next pool above. In some places, artificial waterfalls, too: eel traps.

But, worst of all, the salmon had to face the most cunning of all their adversaries: mankind. The eel trappers, not so far removed from Johnny and his poacher friends, found their activity highly profitable. From the thousands of seafood vendors across the Midlands, takeaways along the South Coast and the rash of trendy new pie and mash shops in London's East End, there was a perpetual demand for jellied eels; they were big business and the eel trappers knew it. Most eel trappers weren't concerned about the salmon, though few turned their nose up at bagging the odd salmon which got caught in their traps.

The illegal netting of salmon was a far greater problem, and one which was fast-growing, too. The netters and the half-netters – fishermen who lined the riverbanks on both sides, where the watercourse ran straight – also did the same on every bend or deep pool. They operated at any spot they thought a salmon might stop to rest up. To lure the fish, they threw flies, minnows, spinners, worms and even prawns, in the hope that the salmon would snatch these offerings and regard them as the tastiest morsels.

Although illegal, netters often worked in small groups, for the rewards were huge. Like the eel catchers, the outlets for fresh salmon were endless, and most of the catches ended up in London's restaurants and eating-houses. But the netters were highly organized.

Then, some poachers, men like Johnny Mason, were quite content in taking the odd fish every so often; they usually worked alone and furtively. Other men, who liked to be known as poachers, used dastardly methods to snare their quarry, applying the same sort of unsavoury techniques adopted by Dinger Bell and his ilk. Those men were destroyers of natural resources and environmental saboteurs.

A week later, Johnny set about making a fire in the open hearth. He shoved some screwed-up newspaper into the grate then added a handful of broken twigs. Finally, he carefully laid a couple of small logs on top – that was another little resource Johnny helped himself to every now and then. He didn't regard lifting a bit of dead wood from the scrubby belt of land at the bottom of the hillside as thieving; more like clearing up litter – even though it was not exactly paper or Styrofoam food containers. *Recycling what nature doesn't want,* he thought. Besides, along the public footpath on the edge of that heath, everyone was free to come and go as they pleased; not even the duke could stop people walking there. But the surrounding ground was so poor and useless anyway, it had no commercial value.

Reflecting on that, he lit the fire, then threw a sprinkling of sugar onto the ignited paper, to get the blaze roaring faster. Settled in his favourite armchair, watching his small T.V. set, he soon dozed off.

Quite suddenly, he woke with a start, hours later, to the voice of the lady presenter announcing the local weather forecast.

Johnny perked up and leant forward, eager to find out what the weather held in store. Alas, the presenter told of heavy rain due in the next few days. The weather chart for Scotland was awash with little cartoon clouds, each bearing a black raindrop hanging beneath. *Not good news,* Johnny decided, rubbing his now stubbly chin. He knew only too well that heavy rain would raise the water level in the local river, and that would make his kind of fishing quite impossible.

He sighed deeply, then glanced at the oak mantelpiece and the jar where he stashed his ill-gotten income. The jar still held a few pounds, left over from the money that Reg had given him the morning after his last nocturnal foray: a sum of fifty pounds. Of course, Johnny realized that was far below the value for such a fish; on the black market, a fifteen-pound salmon would fetch at least seventy-five pounds, if not more. Sums like that would solve his money problems, alright.

Johnny knew that many poachers who worked in gangs had good connections in the fish trade. Consequently, they got a good price for their illegal harvest, which from that point was sold legitimately. Most of the salmon ended up at Billingsgate Fish Market for sale, or got smoked or exported. But, working alone, with hauls of only one or sometimes two fish a night, he had absolutely no idea how to go about such a venture. Who would he sell to? Who could he approach? He'd no contacts in the black market for salmon, and wasn't sure that such connections would be a good thing, anyway; they might just blow his cover. He stroked his chin thoughtfully and then looked at the jar again.

There was only one thing for it: tonight, he would have to pay another visit to his secret hunting spot, before the rains came; when the river swelled with floodwater, he'd be unable to continue supplying salmon. With funds running low, he felt it was rather imperative, needing the money to see him through the next few weeks. At times like this, Johnny wished he'd a second occupation to bring in the dough.

That evening, having decided to venture forth, he peeked out the front door to find the sky was overcast, though not yet dropping the promised deluge, and he was glad. Then, he checked over his poaching gear: two candles as usual, tightly rolled bin liner and length of string, wound round in a loop.

Suddenly, he snapped his fingers. "Matches, ye silly old sod, won't get anywhere wi'out any blinkin' matches!"

Grabbing his greatcoat off the hat-rack stand, he slipped it on then, from the pinewood kitchen table, scooped up the candles, matches and bin liner. As always, he dropped the plastic bag into the left pocket, candles and matches into the right. He felt it was a ritual – maybe a "good luck" rite or formula to follow.

Knowing it would probably be windy, he pulled the battered old trilby down tight over his head and, having flipped off the light switch in the hall, stepped out the front door, into night. Once again, he appeared to be just an ordinary villager going about his daily business.

Eventually, he reached his lookout post beneath the old ash tree, in the strip of woodland, and glanced around to make sure he'd not been followed. After going through his well-tried routine drill, he lay concealed beneath the net hide, while the flickering light from inside the wooden box reflected over the calm surface of the pool.

Johnny kept an eye on the box and thought: *This is my river. Stuff the blasted duke and his lousy cronies.*

Gradually, his feeling of deep apprehension gave way to calm confidence, reinforced by his knowledge of the local terrain and of the thing he sought. He hoped to snag a nice, fat, weighty salmon – a fish of around eighteen pounds would be ideal.

Then, he thought about the old parachuting school at Abingdon, Oxfordshire, where he had done his eight jumps, which earned him the privilege of wearing parachute wings. Their motto was *"Knowledge Dispels Fear"*. Johnny grinned. *Aye, never was a statement so bloody true!*

An uncle of Johnny's had passed the place where he now lay, hiding, onto him many years before. Nowadays, his uncle was far too old to make further use of it. Besides, he had rheumatic joints. His poaching days were over.

In a funny way, his Uncle Furgus had been forced to find and use this spot for exactly the same purpose as Johnny. Back in the lean, post-war years of the late 1940s, food, especially meat, was scarce, and still on the ration coupons, even though the war had long finished. Goodies like salmon, unless fished out of the river, were unobtainable. Even spuds ended up being rationed in 1947: three pounds per person, each week, were all. Hence, Furgus fished in that rewarding spot mostly to feed his own family. On occasions, he'd barter a choice fish with a neighbour for a cut of meat, or maybe a chicken and no questions asked. Poaching of game was rife, too, but in a localized way. Everybody kept mum in those hungry, drab days, when the idea of ever being able to buy plenty of meat or fish in the shops seemed like a faraway dream. But, eventually things did get better.

Johnny remembered rationing ending in 1954, only one or two years after the trouble in Korea flared up. It made him think how there was always trouble or strife in one place or another. While the war in Korea ground on and on, life for the villagers of Glenstone improved; in general, people were earning better money than ever before, had more time for leisure and, in rural areas, fishing became a popular pastime. In Glenstone, the situation was no different: for those who could afford to buy a rod and line, fishing became a regular event, especially on Saturdays.

Then, the present duke's father started issuing fishing permits, thus putting a price on fishing in the river. Not surprisingly, many locals adopted alternative methods, instead: illegal ones. They had no choice. Some local villagers found the fishing tariff far beyond their means, while others refused to pay up through obstinacy or out of resentment.

Even if Furgus could have afforded the permit price, he would have been unable to use it anyway, as he worked six days a week. And in Scotland fishing wasn't permitted on his only day off, being Sunday.

For centuries, the river had yielded its treasure to the villagers in the form of water, food and money for those who sold their catch. Then, all of a sudden, only one generation back, the priceless joy and freedom to fish the waters was snatched away, and became the duke's personal property.

CHAPTER 3

River fight

THE SOUND OF low, muttering voices and the pounding of walking feet along the riverbank drew Johnny back to the present, with a start. Fearing the very worst, his heart thumped away. Cautiously, he peeked out of the hide, glanced around, then leant over the bank and pushed the box beneath the water surface, and drew it under the net. A fish that had been lying on the surface, just outside the box, disappeared in a swirl of water.

"Did yee heer that, Daad? Did ye heer that fish jump?" whispered the voice of a young boy, so close that Johnny feared he would be stepped on.

"Shut yer mouth or yee'l no come again. Wee'r after fish, so no go makin' any fucken' splashes," replied an older voice, clearly that of an adult.

The hollow where Johnny lay was a good hideaway, in so many respects. It had a proven past of being good for poaching fish; this special bank happened to lie alongside the largest and deepest pool along the river, where the salmon always rested on their journey upstream. And, in this particular pool, fish could always be found, no matter how low the river level fell.

For these very reasons, it was also a very dangerous part of the riverside to frequent. From time to time, gangs of poachers descended on that part of the river. And, just as bad meat draws in the flies, bad men drew in the duke's lackeys, who kept their eye on that section of the river. Since Johnny was near the head of the pool, close to the tumbling white water, he found it hard to hear above the continual gushing roar.

When he thought the strange adult and the boy had walked on a fair distance, Johnny lifted the corner of the hide and peered downstream. He saw several figures silhouetted against the pale sheen of slow-moving water, at the lower end of the pool, and could hardly believe his eyes.

The group of men at the far end of the pool were not poachers, but bailiffs, accompanied by an officer from the Scottish Environmental Protection Agency and the police. A sudden, chilling shiver ran down his spine on seeing the uniformed figures approaching. He didn't like this dire situation at all, even though the group was still some way off. Where the boy and his dad had got to, he couldn't make out, but he guessed their freedom was to be short-lived.

Johnny flapped the corner of the net back in place, and cupped hands over his chin and nose, almost as though to cancel out the sound of breathing, yet warm his chilled fingers. *Hell, a right ruddy mess if ever, an' ah canna see a way out.* He couldn't decide if the bailiffs were onto him, or the boy and his dad.

A new thought alarmed Johnny even more: were the police working in co-operation with the duke's lackeys, or on information gained from another source? If so, then an officer from the Scottish Environmental Protection Agency, or SEPA, as the organization was locally known, might have brought in the water bailiffs. Even worse, if bailiffs appointed by the District Salmon Fisheries Board were involved, Johnny knew big trouble would result. Big trouble.

Johnny sighed, softly. His little profitable enterprise was suddenly threatened from all quarters. The quiet calm of less than an hour ago had given way to this frightful and perilous situation. With so many unknown factors, he fretted and pressed his brow, desperate to think of a way out of his dangerous position.

Then, above the gush of the waterfall, he heard other voices in the opposite direction. They had a rough, broad dialect, too: heavy Scot's accent. Johnny suddenly realized that the water bailiffs and the policemen must be searching for a gang of poachers, farther upstream; they wouldn't turn out in such numbers for the sake of one boy and his dad, prowling along the riverbank – that much he was sure of. Maybe they were part of that gang. Johnny couldn't be certain, though.

He risked another quick glance from under his net, saw nothing, but heard a few more shouts, farther along the river. His worst fears had been confirmed: another gang was conducting their dirty work along the river, maybe netters, too. He already knew from their voices that they were not men from Glenstone. He just hoped these poachers were from a neighbouring village; rural poaching groups just tended to be less vicious than the organized gangs from the city. *Yes, indeed, far less violent,* he recalled.

For a brief moment, he considered whether to grab his gear and chance a run for it – or, at his age, a fast hike – and hope his presence went undetected.

To run or stay put? Hell, I canna figure a way out o' this!

Johnny felt dead scared by this awful new predicament. Never, in all his years of poaching along his patch, had he ever encountered such a ticklish situation. Here he was, hemmed in by two opposing groups which might end up clashing. In the ensuing struggle, would he be discovered? He dared to snatch another peek, heard more angry voices in the distance, then withdrew under the net and contemplated his dire circumstance.

He imagined making a dash for it, with both water bailiffs and the angry mob chasing him. If he got caught, one of the other strange poachers or, worse, the bailiffs, just might recognize who he was and, sure as eggs are eggs, spill the beans to the authorities or SEPA. Then, Johnny Mason's days as a poacher would be finished forever, unable to use or visit the river pool again. And, if those involved inhabited the duke's pocket, they'd inform their paymaster without a qualm, which would also permanently squash his riverside escapades. *Damn, never has there been such a vile choice! Best keep calm. Think clearly now.*

If, as he feared, this band of poachers came from a town or the city, they'd be dangerous, bad men to encounter. These ruthless men, who came in gangs to net the rivers and snatch salmon by the score, had one philosophy: attack is the best method of defence. That phrase Johnny knew only too well.

His military training instinctively told him to stay put. The camouflaged net had worked for years, concealing him from prying eyes, on occasions too numerous to remember. *Besides, being an old fart, I'd never manage to outrun younger men, especially those half my age,* he thought, nodding to himself in agreement.

Deciding to lie low, he hoped that the poaching gang would remain at the far end of the pool, and not take too long about their business. Unable to do anything but wait, he felt isolated, in spite of the bunch of poachers nearby.

Johnny watched from under his hide with growing interest, as the poachers, who grew in numbers over the past years, went about their unlawful act of netting the river.

Although loathing and even fearing these wild men, Johnny also had to admire their cheek. Not that he wanted them on his beloved patch of riverside, pinching fish from his pool in such an unlawful and merciless way, while folk in the village, wanting to fish legally, were denied that right. It really wasn't fair, and Johnny smarted at the injustice of it all. Yet, for some unknown reason, he wished the poachers no harm, and certainly didn't want them to get caught by the duke's men, to end up being punished by the Justice of the Peace, who shared the same interests as the nobleman. He just wanted those rogues to stay away from his river.

From his hiding place, Johnny could see the outlines of the men as they moved back and forth with complete assurance. Experienced, knowledgeable and certainly canny, they'd carried out this kind of work many times before. In a legal trade, they'd have gained a reputation as "old hands".

He watched the wild poachers as they dragged out the net, onto the riverbank, while others gathered around to dispatch their illegal catch and shove the fish into empty sacks.

While rounding up their illegal booty, out of the darkness many black-clad figures suddenly descended on them. The police and the water bailiffs had skirted around the edge of the wood and moved in, rather than simply charge along the riverbank from where they first approached. Johnny already knew the outcome: they were doomed. Would he also be apprehended? A lone, almost respectable poacher by comparison to those outlaws, could still end up branded a thief.

The tranquillity of earlier had been replaced by an explosive riot of noisy confrontation, as battles raged between the law and the lawless. Johnny heard the sounds of scuffles, running feet and much cursing and bellowing. Some poachers tried to escape across the river, only to get dragged back onto the bank, while bawling an endless string of obscenities. Other poachers fought the policemen with whatever they could lay their hands on: gaffs, stout sticks, stones, nets and lengths of cord. It was all to no avail as, armed with batons, the bailiffs and police moved in for the kill.

Unfortunately for all concerned, Detective Sergeant Doherty was running the show, in conjunction with the officer from SEPA. Doherty was determined to return to base, as he called the police station, with a maximum number of arrests. He was greedy, too, but greedy for promotion, not river fish or salmon.

Heavily outnumbered, the poachers were getting felled by the constant flurry of kicks, punches and thumping with batons. A few of the wild men vainly attempted to fight back. One wielding a gaff struck a young constable, the hook tearing open his cheek and leaving a deep, red gash, oozing blood which dripped onto his padded black riot vest. The poacher sneered, knowing his opponent was scarred for life. The constable fell to his knees, clasping his cheek, while a colleague delivered a blow to the poacher's neck. He fell right over and, while momentarily stunned, a third policeman moved in and dragged the man to his feet.

Another poacher threw one of the nets over a policeman, and sent him crashing to the ground. Grabbing a huge flint, the lawbreaker was about to smash the man's skull, when a second officer whacked the poacher's back with enough force to make him stagger and topple over his netted victim. The officer delivered another savage blow to the fallen man's shoulder, possibly shattering the bone, before reaching for the cuffs.

The water bailiffs, many carrying sturdy hazel rods, also lashed out at the poachers. One whacked the back of a poacher's legs, just behind the knee joint, and sent him collapsing onto the bank. Constables moved in and grabbed him, while another of the bailiffs struck a younger poacher on his upper arm. He wailed out in agony, cursing and holding his injured arm.

Doherty smiled; things were going his way. He rubbed his hands, eager to chalk up his victory and await untold praise, perhaps from the chief superintendent, if he was lucky.

Besieged on all sides, the vicious poaching gang's numbers fell away, as the remaining few fought back and cursed the policemen, with every colourful suggestion and threat known under the sun.

From his hideaway, Johnny watched and prayed like never before to remain undiscovered when, out of the turmoil, a young lad bolted along the path. Desperate to escape the law, he sped along, legs pumping up and down, almost as though pedalling away on a bicycle. In one hand he held a large salmon, almost as big as himself.

Johnny quickly dropped the corner of his net hide and clasped his head, fearful of discovery. He had worried for nothing. As the lad passed the hide, he tripped over one of the corner pegs and went flying over the net, to end up headfirst in the centre of the river. Spluttering and gasping for air on surfacing, the fast current rapidly swept him away downstream, right back to the battle scene from where he'd fled. Without ado, one of the constables waded into the river, grabbed his jacket and hauled him to the shore, to join his elder fellow poachers, now in captivity. Johnny grinned, and thought he was a lad of spirit, if nothing else.

Lying beneath the hide, Johnny prayed again to the Supreme Being, or whoever was in charge of such things, for deliverance from this awkward situation, and for his unknown hideaway to last a bit longer.

Afterward, he gingerly lifted the corner of his hide and peeped out. No more than a few inches from his face lay a huge salmon. He also saw the dark figures striding along the track toward him. Fearing they would notice the fish and, whilst picking it up, detect his hide, he reached out. With the speed and action of a starving tunnel spider, Johnny grabbed the fish and hauled it into his hide. To ensure it was dispatched, he gave the fish a rap with the gaff handle. Then he remained motionless, not daring even to breathe.

He realized the violent skirmish was now over, the outcome crystal clear: all the poachers had been arrested. Even so, Johnny still heard an endless tirade of verbal abuse uttered from the lips of the noisy band of poachers. Both of Johnny's enemies now passed along the narrow track, only a few feet from where he was hiding. Shouts and threats of retaliation, among endless curses, reverberated across the valley, flushing out snipe from their grassy depressions under overhanging vegetation, and water rail from the thick reeds. Johnny heard angry voices making statements as clearly as if listening to a wireless:

"Yef broken me nose, ye stinkin' bastard!"

"Yer lucky I did nay break yer fucken' neck!"

"Ye wedney say that if ye weer on yer own."

"Shat yer bastard mouth! Yel regret comin' utinnite, yewait."

The seemingly endless harangue of crude banter lasted for ages, until their voices receded into the distance. Then Johnny once again heard the water tumbling over the falls, and it sounded like music to his ears.

As an added bonus, alongside him lay the unexpected salmon. He estimated it to weigh around twenty pounds. His eyes narrowed, calculating a new move: *Perhaps I might be able ter screw Reg for eighty pounds. Make up fer all this extra hassle, eh?*

Johnny waited another hour for things to quieten down, before emerging from his hide. With the swiftness of a news reporter, jotting down shorthand notes, he whipped out the pegs from the ground, bundled his goods and chattels into the net, and made a speedy exit to the nearby woods and safety.

He felt exhilarated, but also very scared. Having pulled through the precarious situation, Johnny was now mighty glad that his military profession had given him the skill to survive.

By the second, smaller mound, he stashed away the net, box and pegs as before, following his well-tried routine. Then, he unfurled the black bin liner and dropped the salmon inside, smiled and bent down to sweep leaves over the top of the mound. *Mission accomplished,* he thought, proudly.

He stood up, almost patting himself on the back, when the night silence was pierced by the sound of a twig breaking.

Johnny's hackles rose. He spun around, glared at the surrounding woodland, but saw nobody. He strained to catch any sound in the still night, but heard nothing. He frowned, trying to convince himself that the twig snap had been nothing more than a fox passing through on its nightly foray.

He glanced at the black bag, barely visible in the gloom. He remained stock-still, listening for further movement. Silently, he sidled over to his lookout post under the ash tree, peered toward the riverbank and saw no evidence of anyone prowling around. All was dead quiet; silent as a graveyard at midnight.

Deciding to chance the return journey to the village, he grabbed the bag, slid it down his back under the greatcoat and made off for the edge of the fields, now desperate to reach the tarmac road.

Calmly does it, he thought. *Dinna rush now. Dinna panic.*

Things didn't feel right; the atmosphere in the night felt odd: different; menacing. The huge salmon was unexpectedly heavy, too – far weightier than he had calculated.

While trudging along his route through the field, he kept hearing the sound of that twig snapping. It almost took on the menace of a crack of thunder rolling across the heavens. *I canna a' been tracked, surely? Nobody knows I weer out there.*

Johnny scowled, partly with the effort of lugging the salmon, but also the uncertainty of everything. The dark, unknown factors were downright nerve-jangling. *Ah tell yer, it weer a fox,* he kept thinking, trying to work up a bit of light-hearted positive thinking. But the element of doubt remained. Surely foxes were too canny to tread on dry, crispy twigs while foraging through the woods?

On reaching the tarmac road he ambled along, the salmon getting heavier by the minute. Then, a new worry filtered through his mind: would the bin liner be strong enough to cope with the unexpected burden? In a split second, he imagined the bag tearing open and the huge fish spilling onto the road, right in the village near the alleyway. *Aw, hell! Dinna even think it.*

Hoisting the bag up under his coat, he cursed softly. *Getting trickier by the day, this little lark.*

On reaching the familiar alleyway, he cast a quick glance around to make sure nobody saw him enter, then sidled along to the turning which led to the small yard.

Inside the outhouse he sighed with relief, dropped the fish into the ancient freezer, wiped his brow and slipped out of the greatcoat.

CHAPTER 4

S.S.S.T.F. on the scene

ENTERING THE PUBLIC bar, Johnny saw his four friends Tom, Ben, Bobby and Arthur, huddled around their little table. He stepped over to the bar, just as Reg entered from the lounge bar.

"Ah! An' how's things wi' you, then?" he asked, following the usual encrypted enquiry regarding the illicit haul.

"A grand if not tricky night," replied Johnny. "Very grand indeed, in an unexpected way. Make it a pint o' the heavy."

Reg grinned, then pulled the pint. "Aye, there ye go."

Johnny slipped a well-worn fiver across the beermat lying on the bar. "Earned this tonight, I tell yer." He grabbed the pint and strode to the four old men. He sagged in the empty chair his friends had kept for him.

"Ya look right dun in," commented Ben, wryly.

"Is that a fact?" replied Johnny. "An' you'd be too, after..." He stopped speaking, remembering his unbroken stance on discussing matters relating to his little illegal excursions. It hardly mattered, as Ben was bursting to tell the group a new trinket of news, having delayed until Johnny's arrival.

"Ya'll nay guess, but this mornin' there weer a right shindig up at river," Ben announced.

"Aye, bastard duke throwing a tea party out there, were he?"

commented Tom, acidly.

Ben glared at him. "Aw, nay, it's far worse. S.S. were out along riverbank. Like they were lookin' out fer signs o' summat."

Johnny's right eyebrow shot up in alarm. "Really?" He knew all about the "S.S.", as the villagers had dubbed them. Not Hitler's stormtroopers, though they came close, the Scottish Salmon Strategy Task Force, or S.S.S.T.F., was determined to stamp out poaching, right down to the last man, woman or child. Far more ruthless and efficient even than SEPA, who were more concerned with the environmental angle, and regarded salmon as a species to conserve. Whereas SEPA were keen to prosecute the river polluters and flytippers who damaged the water quality, the S.S.S.T.F. rigorously enforced the ruling on poaching set down by The District Salmon Fisheries Board.

On hearing Ben's story, Johnny took a hearty, greedy gulp at the heavy, placed the glass on the table and ruminated: *If the S.S. were out there this morning, they must have got a tip-off about tonight's illicit fishing expedition. The S.S. must have been casing the place, planning their method of attack. No wonder the coppers nabbed that mob.*

He stared at the grainy pattern on the wooden tabletop, deep in thought, only vaguely aware of the others chattering. *Obviously, someone got wind of where that mob planned to net the fish.* He gnawed on his right forefinger knuckle, considering the implications. *Who could have known? Who did the dirty and grassed? That blasted duke, perhaps? Or, on the other hand, would it have been Bell? Hardly likely,* Johnny considered; *he'd be more likely try to muscle in on the activity, grab a share in the illegal harvest.*

Johnny was now dead certain the wild fishermen out that night must have come from the neighbouring village, Ravencroft. No poachers from Glenstone would have been stupid enough to try a venture like that, if Ben and possibly others knew the S.S. had been within half a mile of the river that morning. Then again, he hadn't known about their prowling around, either.

He sighed quietly, sipped the heavy and returned to the mysterious informant. Then, the twig snapping in the still woods also had possible sinister implications. He shuddered at the thought of it.

"Yer quiet tonight," remarked Tom, lighting his pipe.

Johnny glanced at him. "Aye, bit under the weather, I guess."

He desperately wanted to tell his friends about the harrowing evening, the clash and how near he came to being discovered. He also wanted to recall the twig snapping in the silent woods, afterward. Instead, he choked it back, keeping to his maxim. He knew silence on such matters was the key to success, and evading detection so far.

Another little factor niggled away: Arthur, God bless him, had let it slip the other night about having favour with the local judge, Buchannan. Johnny didn't think any less of his friend, whom he'd known for years, but the link was there, and it stood out like a sore thumb, for which he cared not an ounce. Arthur could easily get him over a barrel, should too many illicit facts come to light. He wasn't sure if Arthur suspected his nocturnal trips to the river – if he did, so far he'd made no moves regarding extortion.

For the first time in years, Johnny was rather glad when Reg called last orders. All in all, the night had been nerve-wracking, and he longed to sleep off the fatigue. Having crouched under the net for far longer than usual, Johnny felt his joints getting stiff. He supped the last of the heavy, nodded knowingly at Reg, then made for the outhouse. Afterward, he crossed the yard then sidled out of the alley, watching out for anyone tracking him, or for Dinger and his cronies. Nobody was around, and for that Johnny was grateful.

Shutting his front door, he threw the bolt, just in case. It had been a weird night. Even now, Johnny wasn't entirely sure if all the wild Ravencroft men had been rounded up. If so, maybe the twig snapping resulted from the footfall of another poacher watching his every move.

Feeling exhausted, yet highly agitated, Johnny went to bed, but found it difficult to drift away. He kept hearing the sound of that snapping twig.

Hell, it was a fox, he answered mentally, for the umpteenth time.

Eventually, he dozed off with an uneasy feeling.

CHAPTER 5

Johnny's nightmare

HE FOUND THE morning arrived far sooner than anticipated, and heard someone rapping loudly at his front door. On opening the door, he saw D.S. Doherty and his minion, D.C. Turner, standing behind it. The detective held out his warrant.

"Mr. Mason?" Doherty smirked.

Johnny frowned. "Aye? What exactly is the trouble?"

The detective slid the warrant into his coat pocket. "We've reason to believe—"

Johnny woke with a start, bathed in sweat.

His chest felt numb and tight, like an iron fist was squeezing his heart. Clutching his side, he fought for breath, wondering if the fright had brought on a heart attack. He lay for a few minutes, while the squeezing pain slowly subsided. He mopped his brow with a dirty rag which had once been a handkerchief, then got up, feeling a desperate need to visit the toilet.

Downstairs again, leaving the lights off, he felt around in the kitchen cupboard for a bottle of whisky, kept for such emergencies; Johnny knew sleep would be impossible without heavy anaesthetic. He sloshed a liberal quantity of whisky into a cracked mug and swilled, savouring the scalding sensation searing his gullet. He deliberately swilled a second and felt quite light-headed.

Keen to avoid another nightmare, he was unsure whether sleep held appeal, but also realized it was badly needed after his long vigil at the riverside. Grasping the mug, he padded into the living room and saw that the fire hadn't quite died out. He placed another log onto the embers, hoping the fire would flare up again, and wrapped an old tartan picnic blanket over his shoulders. He sank into his favourite armchair by the fire, drinking from the mug and savouring warmth within and from the fire.

He got to thinking about the kid who had tripped over the peg holding down a corner of the net. Would the kid have noticed the peg, or thought it a root or stump that he'd tripped on? And, since he flew over the net, had he noticed it and told someone? He sipped another of the spirit. *There's nay end to this. Nay end to it.*

With the mug empty, it fell from his hand, as he slipped over the edge, into unconsciousness.

Next morning, Johnny felt downcast on glaring out of the rain-spattered window at the sky, now the colour of slate.

Just as the lady weather forecaster had predicted, the rain came on time, but lasted for much longer. For days it swept across the hills in great sheets, stair rods bashing down rank vegetation. Unable to soak up the excess volume, the water ran off the hillsides, into the streams feeding the river, which rose alarmingly. The clear water of the river turned into an angry, clay-coloured, raging, muddy torrent. Not even the rod fishermen could gain a bite.

Visitors who did not return home stayed for most of the time indoors, and spent a great deal of money in The Grouse in The Heather, which cheered the duke no end. Naturally, the villagers who had permits wisely left their rods aside, knowing how futile fishing would be in that wild weather.

During the miserable, sodden days which followed, while at home or in The Leaping Salmon, Johnny was told or overheard many different versions of the event he'd witnessed. The number of poachers involved in the clash grew or diminished, as did the injuries they sustained, depending on who told the story, and the quantity of beer the storyteller had drunk. Johnny listened to all those who wished him to do so, and to other folk who cared neither way, but all the time said nothing. Except for his friend and patron the landlord, as far as he knew nobody suspected that he'd been present at the riverside that night, and knew more about it than folk who claimed to know it all, and more.

Amid the stories emerged one which Johnny could not confirm or deny, since it was the first he'd heard of it. Some folk claimed that the duke had engaged a new man, for the sole purpose of taking on the poachers, wherever they came from. He was a big man – a hard man with a callous streak and, worst of all, an Englishman. He'd been hired to prevent those who came from the towns and cities to steal the duke's fish. The move also included protecting his deer, pheasants, grouse, sheep and cattle – anything the poachers could lay their thieving hands on that was edible. All the duke's minions agreed that these poachers were like a disease, and had to be stopped.

Since the new man hadn't been working for the duke for very

long, that was all the villagers knew about him. But, soon, Johnny would know and be told all, by the very man who knew all.

"Look who just walked in," commented Arthur Cormac, nodding toward the bar.

Johnny turned around to see, standing at the bar, with his back turned toward them, his cousin Chuck McGee, the duke's new head bailiff, scourge of the village.

"What's that bastard doing here?" Tom Stuart asked.

Johnny took little notice of Tom's exclamation, being too busy studying his cousin's smart outfit, and speculating on who paid for it all, the duke or himself? He sported brown boots, green stockings, green tweed knee britches and a jacket to match, and perched on his round bullhead was a green tweed deerstalker. He certainly looked the part and played it, thought Johnny.

After buying two pints of heavy, Mr. McGee, as he preferred to be known to the English fishermen, found an empty table in a corner. He placed the drinks on the tabletop and, without hesitation, strode over to Johnny and his friends. He smiled, but showed little sign of pleasantry.

"Join me for a drink, Johnny? There're a few things I'd like to talk over with you."

"Dinna sup with the devil," advised Ben.

McGee glared at Ben Furness, like he was something nasty he'd stepped onto while walking along the main street. He declined to pass comment.

"What's this about?" asked Johnny, suddenly feeling unnerved.

"Alone, Johnny," his cousin replied.

Johnny glanced at his friends, shrugged his shoulders and drained his beer in one swallow. Then, he followed his cousin to the corner table, dreading the outcome of their talk, wondering if he'd finally been rumbled by a foe, so far unknown.

Totally mystified and rather unnerved, Johnny sank onto the chair at McGee's table, and looked at the man he'd despised for years. Had anyone asked Johnny why he suddenly accepted his cousin's invite for a drink and chat, if choosing to be totally honest about it, he would have replied: "Curiosity." But, above all, it was fear: the deep-seated fear of not knowing.

After hearing the twig snap in the wood that night, he felt incredibly wary. And, the more he thought about it, the more certain he was of being tracked from the river to the woods.

Had his cousin uncovered his furtive nocturnal expeditions? If so, was there a possibility that McGee already shopped him to the duke? Johnny had his doubts, but could be certain of nothing. Then again, if a person had stepped onto that twig, it could have been anyone, not necessarily McGee or any of the duke's other minions.

Johnny took a slow, deliberate sip from the glass of heavy, placed it on the cardboard beermat and looked again at his cousin. Time had flown past, and now the loathing he bore him had given way to mild disdain, and he no longer really gave a fig about his cousin's aspirations, one way or the other.

Among Johnny's mixed-up feelings, there was a slight hint of snobbery about sitting at the same table as his dapper dressed cousin, now the duke's head bailiff, to be seen talking to him on equal terms. Of course, he'd never have admitted this strange sentiment to anyone.

CHAPTER 6

Benjy is killed

JOHNNY'S EYES NARROWED and the past flashed through his mind.

When he and his wife Annie had returned to Glenstone, they brought with them a Border Collie pup. Johnny harboured high hopes of training the pup to become a sheepdog, with the vague notion of getting a job as a shepherd, a profession he'd taken up before joining the Army. In that job, he'd be free, to a certain extent, to wander the hills and glens, drinking in the glory of the great outdoors, and have regular money coming in, too. In those days, with two fast-growing sons, money had always been something of a problem.

Then, if the shepherding proved successful and he got really good at it, there might have been the opportunity to enter regional then maybe national sheepdog trials, too, and win prizes: possibly cups and cash, or at least a fat cheque. In fact, he had often thought of the Collie pup as a fork on a road, with two options to choose from: the right hand-turn leads to a satisfying career as a shepherd, and he becomes renowned for his craft; the left-hand turning... well, Johnny already knew that: the trail to a life of nocturnal spoliation, on a lesser scale than some wily rogues. He also knew that perhaps the Supreme Being, or nature, made those choices for different people on the highway of life. So it was for Johnny; he was, by chance, forced to take the left turning.

Not so long after settling in Glenstone, when the Collie became a young dog, the animal went missing. Distraught by the disappearance, he and his two sons, Hamish and Ewan, searched everywhere, across fields and hillside, the heath and the woods, but to no avail. The dog, it seemed, had vanished from the face of the Earth.

Early next morning, Chuck McGee, who was then one of the duke's many gamekeepers, happened to be out shooting vermin, and by accident found the dog in the water meadows, doing what it supposed was right: rounding up the sheep. Naturally, being an inexperienced young dog, things got out of hand. Unfortunately for Johnny, not only were they the duke's sheep, but also being looked after by a tenant farmer. With three ewes lying dead in the grass, and another seven ewes having aborted their lambs, brought on by the fear and worry of being chased by the dog, although McGee recognized the sheep worrier as Johnny's dog, he ruthlessly shot it dead. He didn't kill the dog out of malice toward Johnny, but simply to guard his own position among the duke's staff. McGee was no fool; he realized the tenant farmer would have done exactly the same thing, had he a gun on him at the time.

Sadly, the damage was done, but the thing that angered Johnny most of all was the fact that McGee, his own cousin, hadn't even bothered to pay a call and explain what had happened. In fact, Johnny and Annie hadn't found out what happened to the dog they adored and loved until many days later. For that dastardly and, in

Annie's opinion, needless deed, she never forgave him or spoke to the man ever again.

Thus arose a long-standing, simmering feud between the two cousins, and simmer it did, year in and year out. Then, eventually, like a hot casserole taken from an oven, the simmering hatred between them cooled to a mutual indifference toward each other.

Until now, that is, thought Johnny, brought to the present with a jolt.

CHAPTER 7

A Gypsy's warning

"HAVE A DRINK, Johnny. It's heavy you drink, isn't it?"

"Aye. What have you to say to me?"

Ignoring him, McGee took his time looking around the bar, before replying: "It's been a long time since I had a drink in here."

Johnny scrunched his forehead. "Be that as it may, what do you want to see me about?"

"Okay, Johnny, if that's the way you want it, that's the way you shall have it."

"That's exactly the way I want it."

"You know, of course, that the duke brought in a new man, to put an end to all this poaching that's been going on just lately?"

"Aye, I've heard it mentioned. Isn't he happy with you, then?"

"It's nothing to do with that. I've got enough work cut out, without having to lie around among the heather all day, hoping to catch these bastards."

"Is that so? I heard one of your daytime jobs is to get rid of the local fishermen."

"Be fair, Johnny. These 'local fishermen', as you call them, could get away with some of the things they got up to years ago, but not today. Not in front of the visiting fishermen, for Christ's sake, or we'll have them all doing it."

"Doing what, exactly?" Johnny asked.

"Foul-hooking, for a start. These rogues know every place where the salmon lie, and they are not satisfied with fishing for them; they are snatch, snatch and snatch, all day long, trying to foul-hook them. I don't believe they've hooked a fish by its mouth for years. I have warned some and begged others to stop, but as soon as my back is turned, they are at it again. I have a job. It's a job I like, and if I lose it, then I also lose my pay-house, vehicle and an awful lot of perks that go with the job."

Johnny sniffed. "What's all this got to do with me? I don't fish."

McGee leant back in his chair and sneered at him. " '*What's it got to do with me?* ' That's really rich. I want you to stop poaching, Johnny."

Taken totally by surprise, Johnny was left shocked, speechless and McGee knew it, having never taken his eyes off the old soldier for a minute.

"Me, a poacher? Whatever gives ye that daft idea?"

"I've known for quite some time, Johnny. I have been told, and since found out for myself, that you've been taking far more salmon from the duke's river in a season than any fisherman paying for the privilege of trying could ever hope to catch. I also know what you do with them."

Both men glared at each other for a moment, without saying a further word.

"Who told you all this?" Johnny asked quietly, now feeling very uncertain of where he stood with his cousin.

"No one person in particular. You see, the thing is, when

someone has a secret, that for some reason they must share with a friend they can or must trust, and in turn the friend tells it to his friend, so it goes on, until lots of people know the secret. Then, among all who know, there is always the odd one who will, for some reason, inform, as was done in your case."

"If you know so much, why haven't you done something about it?"

"You're my cousin. And, anyway, I owe you one."

"So, what you're saying is if I were taking a fish now and then, you are going to stop me?"

"I'll tell you this much, Johnny: it's not the duke or me who is tightening up on things; it's his damned steward. He's the one who ordered the clampdown on the local fishermen. He's the one who brought in this ex-soldier and his mate. By the way, they were the ones who caught that gang from Ravencroft the other night. That particular gang has been a thorn in the duke's side for years."

"What's going to happen to them?"

"Who, those bloody poachers? I'm not sure yet. There was a young lad of about fourteen with them. He was let off with a warning, after accusing our lads of trying to drown them. The rest are out on bail. I expect they'll get a heavy fine. We've confiscated two cars and lots of gear."

Johnny took a deep breath, slowly exhaled, then sipped the heavy. "You think I'm a poacher?"

"I don't know when, where or how you do it, but I know you are. I'll tell you this: if you don't stop, they will get you. They can hide away in a hole in the ground for weeks. If you were standing next to them, you'd not know they were there. And, with all the fancy gear they have, they can see around for miles, anything that moves, day or night."

McGee drained his glass, stared at the old man, shook his finger and smiled, almost like a warning gesture. Johnny watched him get up, straighten his tweed jacket and grab the deerstalker. He whacked the hat heartily on his left palm, then bent over and whispered in Johnny's left ear: "Heed my words, cousin; you beware." Then, he spun on his heel and was out of the doorway in a flash.

Johnny sat back in the chair for a moment, contemplating his cousin's advice. *So, my little venture's been discovered, eh? Well, what's to do now?*

Slowly, he got up and wandered over to his cluster of friends, all looking at him, eager to hear the news.

"What'd yon bogger have to say, then?" asked Bobby, anxiously.

Johnny sagged onto the seat he'd vacated what seemed a year ago. "Aye, wheer do I begin? Alas, the duke's brought in a hard case ter cracks down on them poaching gangs."

"Tell us, who? Did he say?" clamoured Bobby.

"Some ex-army type. English, too."

"Figures," muttered Tom, fiddling with his pipe. "He'll end up driving away all the local fishermen, whether they've permits or nay."

Johnny sucked his teeth. "True, but he hinted that the duke dinna want his paying visitor fishermen ter go gettin' ideas, like a wee spot o' extra illegal fishin' on the side."

"Bastard duke's gonna finish this village. Yer realize that, dinnya?" declared Bobby.

Johnny stared at him. "Aye, I know. But far bigger bastards are out doing their dirty deeds, too. Much bigger," muttered the old man, thinking of the newly recruited bruiser. The battle along the riverside flashed through his mind. He felt sure that the men taking on the poachers hadn't been anything to do with the duke. How could he have mistaken that fact? Then again, he'd been under duress, frightened and might have misconstrued events that took place. The fourteen-year-old lad who ended up in the river was another factor to consider. Had the kid noticed the net peg? Was that how McGee clicked that he'd been poaching?

The unexpected chat with McGee had swallowed up more time than Johnny realized, and suddenly Reg bawled his closing time recital. He briefly recalled other bits of the discussion to his friends, careful to leave out any mention of being caught out as a poacher himself.

Tom stuffed his pipe away in his pocket and got up. "Blasted duke," he muttered, under his breath.

Johnny suddenly felt incredibly weary, simply nodded and sidled out to the outhouse for his greatcoat.

He ambled home, his mind a whirl of different ideas and suspicions. It seemed that nobody at all could be trusted. Had Reg blabbed to someone about the source of his wild salmon? Johnny didn't think so.

He shuffled along to his gate, slipped along the gravel path and fumbled the key into the lock. Glad to be home, he threw the door bolt and sat by the fire. He didn't fancy going to bed, either; far too many revelations had come to light that evening. Besides, by the comforting glow of the log fire, he could think things out. And he did, too, until eventually sleep overtook him, while in his favourite chair.

CHAPTER 8

Johnny confides in Reg

THE BOUT OF wild, stormy weather gradually eased off. The torrential downpours gave way to light drizzle, then faded out altogether. The sullen, dusky clouds which had swept overhead for many days drifted westward, leaving behind a clear, blue sky. But, the bright, sunny sky of daytime was of little consolation to Johnny Mason.

A few days after speaking with McGee, he felt anything but confident. While standing on the little stone bridge, he gazed down on the clear water of the river that he loved so much. The river that willingly gave to those, like himself, who knew it, respected it and took just a little.

While he watched, a fisherman had hooked a fish. The young man, although clearly an English visitor, obviously knew what he was doing. Within ten minutes, without fuss or bother, the fish – a large, clean salmon – was in his landing net and on the bank. His friends and spectators alike all clapped their hands and congratulated him on a job well done.

Johnny smiled meekly at the jogging of another half-forgotten memory. Once, long ago, he'd enjoyed rod fishing, but the declining number of salmon heading upstream made the pastime nothing more than a wearisome chore, and often the results were very disappointing. So, he called it a day, having discovered far more entertaining and profitable ways to catch a salmon. And much of his knowledge passed down from his Uncle Furgus.

From nearby, the hearty roar of laughter erupted from an open window of the duke's hotel, The Grouse in The Heather. Inside, those revelling in such mirth were fishermen, too – of that Johnny had no doubt – telling each other true exaggerations and downright lies as part of the fishing fun.

While he stood there listening, he speculated on just how much his cousin really knew about his nocturnal activities, if anything. Had he been all that honest when declaring that he knew all? Or was he grasping at straws, guessing at clues carried on the wind? Was it possible he knew something at all, or did he just suspect? He'd no way of knowing for sure.

Johnny told his friend, the landlord of The Leaping Salmon, what McGee had told him. But Johnny also made it clear to Reg that he'd never mentioned his poaching activity to another soul, ever. Of course, Reg seemed sympathetic, and must have wondered if his supply of wild, fresh salmon from the river would be forthcoming quite so regularly in the near future. If not, maybe another villager in Glenstone would be ready to earn a few extra tax-free pounds during the course of a dark evening, he thought.

That night, Johnny looked out of his kitchen window, to see the dark shadows of the approaching night begin to fill the sky. It would be a perfect night to go fishing, as the floodwaters had brought fresh, clean fish to the large pool. And, just perhaps that windfall included Johnny's share. Those wonderful, healthy salmon were already there and waiting.

Johnny was a stout-hearted man, not easily put off or frightened by those turning to intimidation. Plenty of folks in the past, had they still been alive, would have vouched for that.

He still really couldn't come to terms with the duke's bold assumptions. Why should one man claim as his own so much that was not his? The hills, the glens and rivers, and all that God or nature put into them, was for everyone, not one selfish tyrant. Why should men like himself, born of the village, on the banks of the river, who had fished it long before the duke or any of his henchmen were even born, be denied the right to fish?

Yet, Johnny realized the precious benefit of doing so was sold, simply to profit from visitors arriving from another country: England. It wasn't right, and he desperately wanted, by any means, fair or foul, to smash the duke's little empire to smithereens. He felt like kicking the duke all the way down his main flight of stairs inside the opulent castle. Then, he'd probably boot the rotten nobleman into the moat for good measure, afterward. That night, he really detested the duke more than ever.

Later, Johnny stepped outside his front door and glanced at the night sky. He found it clear, except for the trillions of stars glinting like a box of sequins, which could have been spilt upon a black velvet curtain.

After closing the gate behind, he hesitated for a moment and thought what might lie ahead. With a deep breath and bold shrug, he dismissed the shilly-shallying, turning westward and hiking along, with the stiff march of the old soldier that he was. Striding along, he felt defiant, his confidence renewed, or maybe fuelled by resentment of the duke.

Almost as a ritual, he felt in the deep pockets of his greatcoat and fondled the tightly-wound plastic bag. In the other, he felt the two stubby candles. If stopped and searched, he felt certain that absolutely nothing would link these items to the purpose he had in mind. As ever, a smile spread across his long, thin face.

On this particular night, Johnny took extra precautions and skirted around the edge of the two fields, kept to the shadows and stopped every so often, to watch and listen. Happy that nothing untoward appeared to be taking place, he stepped on for another good twenty minutes before checking again. Peering round, having grown accustomed to night vision, his ears strained for the sound of footfalls or voices. On hearing nothing, he entered the woods.

Then, all at once, a strange odour carried on a gust of wind assailed his nostrils – an aroma which had no place in a Scottish woodland – near the river. It was a foreign odour, obviously from a kitchen: that of burnt meat or a spoiled dinner, a casserole perhaps, which had spent too long in the oven. Even so, the odour Johnny thought delectable. His stomach churned, not in revulsion but hunger. For the first time in a long while, Johnny wished he'd still a wife to cook for him; to serve proper meals, instead of his munching the endless round of cold sandwiches, beans on toast, bits of chicken or the odd tin of soup. *Aye, how different everything might have been,* he mused. He caught a further waft of the savoury odour, then it was gone. It was not really a smell which aroused his suspicion; probably blown across from one of the houses, their lights at times visible far downwind from him, as he skirted the field.

Eventually, he entered the woods and, with the telescope, took up position beneath the ash tree, but this time took far longer to peruse the riverside. He'd got a strong gut feeling something wasn't quite right, but couldn't place his finger on it. The sense of assurance that all was okay, he realized, was distinctly missing. He got the same reaction while in enemy territory, during his Army career. The sense of danger was all around, behind every bush, or thick tree trunk. Who, if anyone, was out there tonight, he wondered?

Unnerved, on two occasions he felt like calling it a night, packing up his gear and going home empty-handed. He'd done so before, on nights when he'd noticed movement along the river: little shadows creeping along the sheep-worn path. Tonight he saw no tell-tale furtive movements, but remained unsure if anyone was lurking around, watching.

After a spell standing alone under the tree, and seeing nothing untoward, he put the burst of paranoia down to reaction brought on by hearing McGee's words. Almost for reassurance, he looked around for the little owl, but it was not there. He hoped it might appear, but it remained absent, and didn't always turn up on every visit. Johnny wasn't really sure how extensive the owl's territory was, but assumed it was on the hunt elsewhere for water voles, mice and little furtive creatures of the night. That made Johnny think he was furtive, too – a furtive sneak, poaching fish like some frightened animal. *Aw, hell. Damn ye, bastard cousin. Why could ye nay let things alone? Damn ye,* thought Johnny, angrily.

The anger made Johnny feel more confident again. He returned to the second, smaller mound and retrieved his net, box and gaff, having buried the telescope. Then, he set out across the open stretch of land toward the river, ever watchful for anyone sidling around. The merest tell-tale sign of another's presence and he was off, he decided.

After setting up the net hide and going through the candle-lighting ritual, he settled. While the little wooden box gently bobbed up and down on the water's surface, occasionally tugging against the string tether, the yellow light flickered over the surface of the clear water. Grasping his gaff, he lay under the hide. Whatever fears or doubts he had were now gone, to wherever such emotions go when no longer present.

He heard the combined splashes, as several wild ducks landed near the centre of the pool. He smiled at their quacking conversation with each other. He also heard individual splashes, as both large and smaller fish broke the water's surface, for a snatch of air perhaps, or maybe an unwary midge.

The harsh *ke-wick* of an owl echoed across the river, and Johnny wondered if it was his little night caller, who no doubt thought of him as an enemy; a trespasser who might deprive it of a tasty morsel.

At first, Johnny found it rather difficult to judge the size or weight of a fish while it remained under the water at night, even if only below the surface. His experience gained through years of poaching usually enabled him to roughly gauge the weight of a fish, and be right within a pound or so, either way. The first fish to appear that night Johnny judged to be eight or nine pounds, and decided to snag it.

With one swift, effortless motion, the gaff entered the fish's side and, once hauled under the net, a quick rap with the gaff handle left the salmon dead. "Fifty ye owe me, Reg, that's fer sure."

Later, two more fish appeared, followed by a third. He was never greedy while hooking in the goodies, but tonight he regretted not taking the lot, thus depriving those who were out to dispossess him. After gaffing the largest of the three fish, he now had all he could carry.

A chill breeze suddenly swept across the water, and made Johnny eager to leave. Having extinguished the candles, he dropped all his gear into the net and sidled away, back to the relative safety of the woods.

He looked across the stretch of open ground between the river and the woods, wary of being seen or, worse, caught carrying not one but two salmon. Entering the edge of the woods, the doubt and anxiety returned, stronger than before. He felt troubled, but failed to reason why, having seen nothing untoward so far. Still, the unsettled sense remained.

Without messing about, he buried the gaff, net and pegs in the tin box, did the leaves trick for camouflage and stood up. With two salmon in the bag, he was certain that eyes were watching him, taking stock of his every move, yet nobody appeared to be lurking around in the dark woodland.

Without running, but with an urgency in his step, he skirted the edge of the two fields again, eager to reach the tarmac road once more. Even then he could possibly be accosted there. After slipping through the wire fence, he sped down the road, but the fish hanging awkwardly beneath his greatcoat made speed difficult. He kept going, glanced around and entered the dark alleyway.

Inside the outhouse of The Leaping Salmon pub, Johnny almost wallowed in the relief, while dropping the two salmon in the old freezer. He mopped his brow, left his coat hanging on the peg, as usual, and stepped into the comforting, well-lit public bar.

CHAPTER 8

Rona arrives in Glenstone

"AYE, HOW GOES it wi' ye tonight, eh?" Reg asked, while wiping a pint pot with a stained cloth.

"Make it a pint o' heavy, as usual. Grand two-fold, some might say, on this fine night," he replied.

Reg's eyebrows shot up. "Really? That's miraculous, under the rather trying circumstances."

"Trying? I'd say that's a wee understatement, if ever. Things are getting a tad tricky out there, ye know."

Reg nodded in commiseration and plonked the glass of heavy on the bar. "Aye, I'll nay doubt it. On the house, Johnny; I owe ye. Otherwise, I'd ha' tay send Sally away ter Wilson's Cash and Carry, fer the you-know-what."

Johnny gave the landlord a knowing nod, wiped his nose and grabbed the pint. He crept over to the usual corner occupied by Ben, Tom and Bobby, then sagged into his reserved chair.

Inside the bar of The Leaping Salmon, Johnny appeared to all patrons as a happy, contented old man, enjoying a pint of heavy with his friends. While savouring the familiar surroundings, Johnny wondered why on Earth he'd ever thought things were different. Tonight, he'd not got the kick the heavy usually brought on, and felt the need for another pint. He sidled over to the bar and ordered from the landlord a second jar. Then, while Reg pulled the pint, Johnny glanced around the room.

In the corner, he noticed a young woman sitting alone at a little, round table, fiddling on a laptop, occasionally taking a sip from a glass of the house red. Johnny had never before seen such a machine, but had heard about them. Those miniature computers were portable, too.

To Johnny, the world of computers was a profound mystery. His sons, Hamish and Ewan, had one long ago – a second-hand Dell processor – and often did their homework on it, to pass their A-level exams and hence gain acceptable qualifications to get into the Army.

Trying not to appear intrusive, or like a dirty old man, he glanced at her again. He noticed her petite figure, dressed in a burgundy sweater, black corduroy trousers and a tartan scarf around her shoulders. She sipped from the wineglass, obviously deeply ensconced with something on the laptop screen, which was hidden from Johnny's view. She shook her head, and the mass of short, frizzy, blonde curls flew about, like warm afternoon sunshine.

She looked up and smiled at Johnny. He noticed her hazel eyes: vivid hazel, just like Annie's, long before she fell to the illness. Feeling self-conscious of his rather unkempt appearance, he flushed slightly and nodded at her.

"There ye go, Johnny," said Reg, "that'll be three-pound-sixty."

Almost in a trance, Johnny chucked a moth-eaten fiver onto the bar, awestruck by the girl's eyes. If he'd believed in reincarnation, he would have sworn the girl typing away was his long-departed Annie. But he didn't believe such things.

"Who's our friend over there?" Johnny whispered.

The landlord grinned. "Ah, ya dirty old fart! She's young enough ter be yer daughter."

Johnny smiled. "Aye, right pretty little thing, ter be sure. But, ya have nay answered me question."

The landlord shrugged. "To be perfectly honest wi' ye, I have nay the slightest idea. She was in here for the past two or three nights, as a matter o' fact, in the lounge bar."

"Ya dinna say. Maybe she's just visitin', eh? Maybe one o' them secret gourmet spies that pounce on unsuspecting publicans," joked the old soldier. "Ye better watch out: she might report ya serving up…" He stopped short, not even daring to mention the words "poached" or "salmon".

Reg nodded, cynically. "Then I'll be big news all over the tabloids. That should pull the punters in, duke or no ruddy duke."

Johnny grabbed the glass and, out of curiosity, wandered over to the round table. "Excuse me, missy, I, er… yer kinda reminded me o' someone I knew a while ago."

The girl looked up, her hazel eyes almost like marbles. She smiled again. "My, that's an original chat-up line," she replied, still smiling.

"Oche nay, I didnay mean ter infer…" Johnny stopped speaking, wishing he'd gone straight back to his friends.

She gestured him to sit. He did so, not wanting to offend her. "I mean, it's real unusual ter see a lassie all alone, sitting in a pub in these parts."

She looked at him, a hint of mild amusement sparking in her

eyes. "Really? When was the last time ye went to Glasgow?"

From her accent, Johnny knew that she was Scottish, though from where exactly, he couldn't tell. "A right tidy while ago," he muttered.

"Obviously," she replied, while fingering the mousepad. She stopped, sipped her drink and looked at Johnny. "Are you local?"

Johnny sipped from his pint. "As local as yer can get; I was born in this village."

"It's nice to meet local people; gain an insight into their outlook on life. More important, what they think about their environment."

"Aye, ya mean the woods, hills and river? I could tell ye all about that, especially the—" Johnny quickly stopped, realizing he'd reached the borderline of never speaking about salmon or poaching to anyone but Reg.

She looked at him, those hazel eyes filled with intrigue. "I bet you're a mine of information."

"What's yer name?" Johnny asked, hoping to change the subject.

"Rona. Rona Cullen."

"Aye. Er, Johnny Mason, by the way."

She smiled. "I think your friends over there are getting curious. They keep nodding and nudging each other."

"Aye, I bet. Sorry, I didna mean to intrude, like."

"No intrusion. It's good to meet new folk."

"Aye, that it is," agreed Johnny. "Best get back. I, er... glad I met you, anyway."

Rona smiled again, but said no more.

Johnny grabbed the pint and sidled back to the corner table, unsure what to say. He plonked his pint on the table.

"She's a bit young fer you," Bobby joked.

Johnny waved his finger at him, stopped, then supped from the glass.

"Who is that bonnie lass?" asked Tom, lighting up his ancient pipe.

"Rona Cullen, apparently," replied Johnny, casting a furtive glance at the far corner. She didn't look up.

"What's she doing wi' that laptop? Casin' this place?" asked Bobby.

Tom blew a plume of smoke toward the ceiling. "Yer probably hit the nail on the head there. Strangers turn up in pubs, then before yer know it, poor landlord gets an unexpected visit from the local health people."

"I knew it: she's a spy," Bobby blurted out.

"Rubbish!" snapped Ben. "If you must know, she happens to be an ecologist."

All glared at Ben, astonished by his sweeping statement.

"Aye, ye'd know all about her, eh?" Bobby teased.

Ben shifted in his chair. "I bloody well should do: she's staying with me for a while."

"Hey, can yer believe this?" exclaimed Bobby, in amazement.

Johnny gazed at his friend, unable to grasp what he'd just heard and, at the same time, felt a tiny stab of jealousy. "Yer a right sly old bod, I give yer that."

Ben suddenly chortled. "If only. She's me niece, you simpletons. With two empty spare rooms, it seemed daft to cough up for hotel accommodation. Anyway, that duke charges a small fortune."

"Ecologist, yer say? What's she here fer, then?" Johnny asked.

"Didn't I mention that? The boss at SEPA has assigned her the task of investigating the water purity, among other things. By all accounts, there's been a flood of complaints about pollutants in the river."

"SEPA?" Bobby quizzed.

Ben nodded, patiently. "That's right: the Scottish Environmental Protection Agency. Me niece is brainy – studied at Edinburgh University, no less; gained a PhD in Aquatic Bioscience. So, she got a good job doing what she loves: monitoring environmental hazards."

"Right, but there is nay any hazard round these parts," commented Tom, skeptically.

"Wrong on all counts. Remember two years ago, that bastard Dinger gassed the river? Well, SEPA want to determine how long the effects last, and whether the wildlife is still in danger."

Johnny gazed at the tabletop, unable to add anything, and listened.

"Surely the floodwater washed it all away by now?" stated Les.

"Maybe," replied Ben, "but other pollutants have also been found. It's got something to do with that huge salmon farm downstream."

"What kinda pollutants?" Bobby asked.

"I'm not really sure about that, but an investigation is underway."

"So, that's what all them S.S. folk were doing out by the river the other morning?"

Ben nodded. "Seemingly, they were looking for traces of pollution, maybe. On the other hand, they could have been tracking regions frequented by poaching gangs."

"All a bit of a dark mystery, ain't it?" Bobby declared.

Johnny leant back in his chair. Environmental pollution was something he knew very little about, but he had often heard local folk grumbling about agricultural pesticides in farming regions, getting washed off the hillsides, into the streams and rivers, turning the water cloudy and driving the fish away. He suddenly felt afraid for his beloved river, under threat from another quarter – nothing to do with the duke or his heavies, but a faceless sort of enemy: that of intensive commerce.

Speculation suddenly came to an abrupt halt, with Reg's nightly proclamation of closing up. The five friends drained their glasses, slipped coats and anoraks on, and made ready to return home.

Rona strode over to the group. She smiled at Johnny again. "Hi. Enjoy the evening?"

"Certainly did," he replied, then frowned. "Canna ask yer something?"

"Fire away."

"Is it true the river's under threat from all this so-called pollution?"

Rona's eyes suddenly widened. "Quite possibly. Things are still being examined. All part of a larger monitoring strategy, actually."

"Sounds heavy stuff," replied Johnny. "Monitoring what, ter be precise?"

She sighed. "Look I shouldn't say this – my boss doesn't like blabbing – it's just possible that the entire salmon industry is in danger. *Real* danger, far more widespread and devastating than anyone could imagine. That's partly why I'm here. I really can't say more." She clasped the closed laptop to her chest. "Coming, Uncle?"

Ben slipped his coat on. "Yes, let's get going, my dear." He turned to the others: "Tomorrow it is then." They slipped out of the bar.

Johnny blew breath, staggered slightly with the ominous news, and made for the outhouse to retrieve his greatcoat. As he ambled along the dark lane, he ruminated on the unusual evening in his familiar bar. The apprehensive tension he'd felt lately was now replaced by deepening intrigue.

What had the girl meant by "devastating"? He couldn't imagine. And why should this SEPA organization decide to turn up now, just as the duke's head man had called in this heavyweight to smash the poaching gangs? Was it all coincidence, or was some dark conspiracy afoot? He wasn't sure if a man like the duke would want anything to do with an official organization, especially when he'd neglected the river for years.

Johnny sighed. Everything had suddenly become incredibly complex.

CHAPTER 10

Caught out

HE REACHED HIS gate, strode to the front door and, once inside, drew the bolt across, as usual. He'd never worried much about it before, but now, after witnessing the Ravencroft poachers at work, then hearing his cousin's threat and fearing an unknown watcher in the woods, he took more precautions than usual.

In the living room, he dropped another log onto the embers, deciding to catch the late-night news and weather forecast – quite why, he didn't know. Perhaps just planning ahead, for another wee trip to the river? He wasn't sure how long the calm spell would last. In many respects, as a poacher, the weather forecast was more important than the news.

With the log blazing away, he settled into the favoured chair, warm and safe. He thought about the SEPA girl, Rona. Her striking resemblance to Annie of thirty or more years ago he thought too uncanny, almost supernatural. Johnny couldn't quite believe what she'd said, either.

She obviously knows a hell of a lot more about salmon than I do. Maybe she's clicked about the poaching, too. Johnny shook the thought away, dead certain that she'd know little of that activity.

He started to feel drowsy, but perked up just as the weather presenter appeared on the screen. He grabbed the remote and zapped up the volume, to catch every scrap of information. He need not have worried: the forecaster spoke of more fine weather to come, lasting into the middle of next week at the very least. Johnny thought the map of Scotland looked somewhat sparse without the usual array of cartoon clouds, but he was glad.

Aye, I reckon another little trip is on the cards, while the good weather holds. Bastard duke will never miss another salmon or two.

With that thought, Johnny drifted away into oblivion.

The following day being a Saturday meant open market day in Rosstown, twenty-six miles away from Glenstone. Since it opened many years ago, and word spread about the neighbourhood of the bargains and diverse range of goods available there, most villagers in Glenstone looked forward to a day at the market. Some even regarded it as good as a holiday.

Every Saturday morning, at ten-thirty precisely – or so most trippers hoped – the old, single-decker bus turned up to ferry those without their own transport. Trundling along the narrow lanes, the battered bus, crammed with jubilant children bawling away and waving from every window, was followed by an assorted convoy of cars, the odd van and a handful of individuals pedalling away on bikes.

Villagers who couldn't go, or had no wish to do so, gave money to friends or neighbours, to purchase badly needed items on their behalf. Everybody found something at the market, even things like the odd pair of shoes, a new washing up bowl, a woolly shawl to keep off the winter wind, and a whole array of items unavailable in the village stores and small shops. Wives dragged their reluctant husbands around, and girls their future husbands – men who would gladly have spent the time and money in the local pub, instead. Children cared little about who took them to the market, as long as they went, eager for the cheap toys, puzzles and games often available for only a pound each.

For precisely that reason, Johnny relished Saturdays, too. Having no need of cheap, brightly-coloured household items, goodies or worries over clothes, he gave the market a miss. And, with no wife or even a daughter to drag him away, Johnny relished the enjoyable task of spending his ill-earned income in the near-deserted bar of The Leaping Salmon. Besides, he also rather fancied another encounter with Rona, and was pretty certain a rural market twenty-six miles away would hold little attraction for her. Inside the pub, he looked for her, but she was not around that morning.

While standing at the bar, Reg the landlord, who knew the whole salmon-poaching picture, attempted to restore Johnny's shattered confidence, after his fracas with McGee.

"I told yer that bastard knew nothing. I think you'll find he's saying the same thing ter anyone who doesn't hold a fishing permit, or those who don't buy him a drink or two at The Grouse," stated Reg, cheerfully.

"Aye, you could well be right there," replied Johnny.

While supping and talking, he still wasn't entirely convinced by his friend's explanation, but he awaited the fourth pint of heavy, the round of free beers part-payment for his effort in supplying the illicit hauls of wild, fresh salmon which appeared on the pub menu.

Reg plonked the glass on the bar. "Dinna fret so, Johnny. You'll worry yerself to an early grave."

Johnny grabbed the pint and took a good, long pull from the glass, when the bar door suddenly flew open and in strode McGee. Johnny saw from the stern expression on his face that he'd not come to pay a social call, or stop for a drink.

"I'd like a word with you, Johnny. Not in here; outside."

Without a chance to utter one syllable, Johnny followed his cousin through the doorway, his mind once again racked with doubt. For a fleeting second, he thought all was okay. Then, McGee introduced him to a well-built man of about thirty, who stood beside his Land Rover. McGee took a deep breath and waved his hand toward his sturdy, thickset colleague. "This is Ken Davidson, the man the duke has hired to stop the poaching."

Johnny said nothing, but nodded at the stranger, who returned the gesture likewise. Then he spoke: "I have something of yours in the back of my Land Rover. I'd like you to take a look at it."

Johnny edged toward the rear of the vehicle, and panic struck him like a blow to the forehead. There he saw, lying on the floor, all his gear, net, gaff and small boxes. His eyes narrowed, but he felt neither self-pity nor defeat, just a burning hatred for the two men present.

Davidson wasn't finished. "Because of his position, and my friendship with your cousin, Mr. McGee, I am willing to forget all this and everything I saw last night. But, if I ever catch you again —"

Davidson never finished issuing his threat, as Johnny spun on McGee, pointing at him with his right forefinger. "I guess this makes you a very happy man now, eh? Got one over me at last, yer weaslin' bastard!"

Before McGee could answer, he turned back to Davison, still waving his forefinger. "Have nay fear, ya'll never catch me again. Bu I'll poach here once more, long after your master gets rid o' you, be sure about that."

As Johnny stalked back to the doorway of the pub, he stopped suddenly, struck by an afterthought, and turned to face the two men. He spoke again to Davidson. "Do you or your friends ever eat curry?"

Davidson frowned, and for a moment didn't answer, then he smiled for the first time. "Yes, all the time. Why?"

"Ah just wondered, that's all," replied Johnny, sneering; "just a passing thought – nay more."

Johnny walked to the rear of the Land Rover, followed by Davidson. He stopped, turned to the new man on the block and said: "What squadron were you with?"

Taken aback, Davidson then realized that Johnny was ex-Regiment. "Why? What squadron were you?"

Johnny replied: "B-Squadron. B for 'best'."

"I was with A-Squadron," said Davidson.

"A for 'arseholes'! The smell of curry told me you were no ordinary steward," said Johnny.

The bond was immediate. Johnny gave his mobile number to his now brother in arms; they were to communicate later. The old man then turned his back on them and entered the pub, a smile spread across his thin face, cheered by the curry question. *I'll get the bastards, yet – too right! Curry, eh? Eh? Then curry they'll bloody well get!*

Inside the bar again, he supped on the heavy and knew he had the time; the ways of the river would not vanish, ever. Besides, there were plenty of other pools, deep pools, where an abundance of salmon lay waiting.

CHAPTER 11

Cousin Will

WILL SOAKED UP the action, excitement and drama taking place before his very eyes, just yards from where he stood. He knew very well what was happening, and on many occasions felt the urge to bawl out advice to those taking part in this win-or-lose venture, even though he was far from qualified to dispense it. To be perfectly honest, he'd never participated in their stimulating and rewarding activity; just watched and admired his friends. Although longing to join in, he knew that if his luck didn't change before very long, an envious spectator he'd remain.

Although the final outcome of the event was of little personal interest to him, Will observed his two friends' every movement, and now and then snatched a glance of their quarry. Oh yes, indeed: quarry slipping through the water with more ease than a hot knife cutting a block of butter.

When things looked far from winding up, he drifted away, back to the past, a vague and hazy recollection of times past, people he'd known and places far away.

Will remembered that five years had passed since his cousin, Johnny, had returned to his home village in Glenstone, Dumfriesshire, some twenty miles east of Stranraer. Will had visited that village many times to see Johnny and Annie, along with his uncle and aunt, Johnny's parents. Of course, he was really cut up when his aunt and uncle passed away, every bit as much as Johnny was at losing his parents.

What made it worse, though, was that only a couple of years later Annie went, which he found a right shock, it being so unexpected. What Will didn't know was that Johnny had deliberately kept the cancer business in the dark, after promising Annie, as she didn't want everyone in the village to know about her suffering. Will realized that Johnny was now living up at Glenstone all on his own – or so he assumed. Will knew little about his cousin in many respects, except that he liked to go for a pint at the local pub with his mates in the evening, and of course that other little evening venture, too – the profitable but furtive one.

Will was totally ignorant about the duke, or how McGee had recently threatened Johnny. Neither could he possibly imagine a lethal menace currently sweeping across the rivers and watercourses in mainland Europe – a deadly hazard, which could blow away the very resource which provided endless hours of pleasure to him and his friends.

Will had also retired, five years ago to this day, he reminded himself, though he didn't need to, but felt proud on doing so. He'd been an agricultural advisor and relished the job as, among other things, it took him away from home for long periods. He wasn't sorry about that, since his wife never lost any opportunity to make his life a misery. Will didn't really hate Dorothy – or Dot, as she was locally known – but sadly, during the last ten years of their childless marriage, he realized that she'd become a wretched woman, forever ranting and raving over the tiniest thing, for no apparent reason.

Many of his friends often asked him why he put up with it all. He invariably replied that he was simply too old to start a new life elsewhere. Although, given half a chance, he would have seized the opportunity to do so.

He'd somehow acquired the name of "Old Will", not on account of his age, but simply because his friends held him in high regard and thought it commanded respect, of sorts. Others living in the village thought he had one remarkable honourable quality, often lacking in rural agricultural areas: he never spread gossip, malicious or otherwise. Neither did he have a bad word to say about anyone, not even regarding his nagging wife. For that, and out of commiseration for putting up with her, he gained this respect.

Many of Will's friends, and even other villagers, had at some stage faced Dot's wrath. After an encounter with her, they'd shake their heads; some of the elders wrung their hands and the younger folk, usually the teenagers, thought nothing of giving her the finger behind her back.

A few villagers even thought the harridan would hound her decent, uncomplaining husband toward a premature heart attack, or a stroke. In fact, quite a few of Will's friends tentatively suggested he seek divorce, on the grounds of unreasonable behaviour. Unlike former decades, when divorce was looked upon as a disgrace, the procedure had become regarded as socially acceptable. One of his closest friends even told him it was dead easy to apply for a "quickie divorce petition", available online, all for the grand sum of forty pounds, thus cutting out vast expense and lots of legal formalities in the high street solicitor's. "And, for just sixty-five pounds, you get all necessary forms required for the court completed for you. Couldn't be simpler," the man implied.

Will shook his head and decided against it. After all, what would Dot do? How would she survive, being too old to work and with no money of her own?

As in all the other small villages in the rural districts, inhabitants of Droitwich Spa, where Will lived, spent rather a lot of time worrying and talking about other people's business, instead of minding their own. Apart from killing time, small talk and local gossip among wives and some of the menfolk coloured their lives – rather like a T.V. soap, but for real. Juicy titbits of information the villagers found irresistible, like what Mr. Jones down the road was up to on the allotments at the midnight hour, and so on. In fact, it was local hearsay that he was shagging the local harlot inside his large allotment shed – the wooden shack was certainly big enough to accommodate a bed. "Love among the flowerpots," many neighbours commented, wryly shaking their heads. Of course, the gossips wanted everyone to believe it.

Will never joined in their debates, malicious or otherwise, nor wanted to know the private affairs of other folk. Instead, he just listened, or made the excuse that he'd got a chore which desperately needed seeing to.

In the course of their discussions, many villagers, in jest, implied that it would come as no surprise to find out Will had been arrested, charged with the unlawful killing of Dot. Some folk even thought that their dark mutterings might give him ideas. Will ignored the banter and carried on about his daily business, preferring to stick to his band of trusty friends.

Will was lucky enough to have four really good pals in the village, and they always met up in the local pub, The Badger Inn. Les Hopkins, the landlord, looked after the four friends, too: Andy Thompson, Tom Richards, George Martin and Old Will. The very minute they entered the pub, there would be four pints ready and waiting for them. The foursome was the engine that kept the pub in business.

Will Mason was a man of few vices – the only ones Dot accused him of were that he smoked a pipe, thus reeking the house out with the stench of tobacco, and drank too much. Not surprisingly, Will relished meeting his mates, especially at Sunday lunchtime. Without fail, Les would have a special with real ale for his regular customers. He never missed a Sunday get-together.

His friends were loosely described by the local folk as sportsmen, as at every opportunity they'd go off on a shooting or fishing expedition. For Will, these events were a no-go area, but he got used to it. *Maybe one day,* he often thought. They invited him to join in, but he always declined; he knew absolutely nothing about fishing or shooting, nor did those pastimes really captivate him. Besides, taking up any pursuit, like fishing, would invariably lead to more trouble and aggravation at home. Dot didn't like him hanging around in the house, but she also didn't want him to go gallivanting around the neighbourhood with his mates. It was a strange contradictory situation, but that was the way things were, and the way they stayed.

Until, one night, an incident in The Badger Inn occurred, which changed the course of Will's life forever.

It was a bleak September night – a Sunday, as he remembered. Above, a dark, cloud-filled sky threatened heavy rain, and a chill wind blew down the narrow street, pushing Will along faster than his normal pace. He felt glad on reaching The Badger Inn.

On entering the bar, Andy Thompson, the retired blacksmith, thrust a pint of finest ale into Will's hand, saying: "Cheers, Will – I saw you coming. What a bloody day! Let's go and join the others. Take this one for Tom."

Carrying a pint of best bitter for Tom Richards, the local butcher, Will pushed his way through the crowded, noisy lounge until he came to a long, rectangular wooden table. He sat down, joining the other two men already seated: the landlord Les Hopkins and young George Martin, the farmer's son. That morning, they had returned from one of their many fishing trips to Scotland and, judging by their conversation, it had been very successful. As usual, Will had been invited, but he'd declined.

"Aw, you should have come with us, Will. We had a great time," Tom stated.

"I'll show you something," remarked Les, the landlord. He got up and disappeared amid the crowd which packed out the lounge. A few moments later he returned, sporting a satisfied grin on his large, round face. In his right hand, he grasped by its tail an enormous, silver-coloured fish. He slapped it down onto the centre of the table.

"What do you think of that, eh Will? Isn't it a beauty? We

caught two, but that's the biggest; young George took the smaller one home. This one's going on the pub menu."

With enthusiasm, Les said much more, as did the others, but Will heard none of them. For some reason, he couldn't take his eyes off the fish; it fascinated him! Never before had he seen such a beautiful creature. Staring at that cold, lifeless body, he imagined the power it once held, the strength that would have taken it many miles, over any obstacle, as it made its way from the sea to its spawning bed.

Will listened many times to the tales these four fishermen recalled. All four pals frequently left their village on such fishing trips filled with high hopes, only to return, more often than not, empty-handed. Their excuses were rich and varied: due to lack of a certain fly, minnow or worm, they failed to bag any salmon. Now looking at that great fish – which they told Will weighed in at nearly thirty pounds – he believed all their stories of battles on the riverbank, mostly lost; of broken lines and straightened hooks.

"Were on the banks of the river, at a large pool called Johns Burn," explained Andy.

Will looked at the fish once more, and thought about his constantly badgering wife, and how his friends all relished a pastime he had never known. Something in the dead fish's unseeing eye suddenly made him wonder why on Earth he denied himself the same happiness. Time and again he declined their generous offer to go along, join in and become part of their jolly escapades.

He sighed, and secretly wished he'd long ago taken up their offer to go with them. It was rapidly apparent that Dot was never going to change – not ever. And, if he continued to refuse his friends' offers, they might grow weary of his continually turning down the chance to go on such trips. Dot would never thank him for that, either. At that moment, something suddenly snapped inside him. For years, he'd tried to please and placate his miserable wife, only to be continually rebuffed by her snide comments.

"Hey, Will, you really ought to come along. You'd really enjoy it," Tom said. "Give it a go, for Christ's sake! What have you got to lose? You're free to come and go as you please; you have no work shackles or kid commitments."

"You're bloody right there. When do you plan the next trip? I'm game, if you'll have me along," he stated, suddenly not caring an ounce for Dot's sarcastic and endless commentary on his doings. Perhaps the real ale fuelled his sudden resolve, or maybe, for the first time, he'd finally decided that enough was enough. "Be no damned good at it, mind," he added afterward.

His friends laughed and clapped him on the back.

Less than two weeks after the talk in the pub, Andy Thompson received a call from Scotland, informing him that there had been much rain, making the river conditions perfect for fishing, and salmon were showing in every pool. Early the following morning, Will and his three pals were speeding up the M6, heading for Scotland.

Having just passed Carlisle, they turned west on the A75, the road to Dumfries. By nine-thirty they had crossed the border, and

Will speculated on what lay in store on their great adventure.

CHAPTER 12

Rona's riverside discovery

AS WILL AND his friends crossed the border, Bobby Burgess strolled along the riverbank, with nothing much to do on a sunny morning. He liked walking, and often went for tramps across the hills and moor. But today, for some reason, he decided the river was ideal.

After twenty minutes ambling along, he saw a figure hunched by the bank, fiddling with something right at the edge of the river. What's more, this person was obviously not averse to being seen, wearing a bright, dayglow-yellow, plastic jacket. He paused for a moment and watched. Then, out of curiosity, he paced along the bank to find out what the person might be doing. *Obviously they wouldn't be poaching fish! Not in daylight,* he thought.

Then, Bobby recognized the figure: the blonde girl in the pub the other night. Whatever she was doing, it looked sort of official. He noticed her rucksack farther along the bank.

In order not to startle the girl, he coughed deliberately. She turned round, peered at him for a moment then smiled, while wiping off the funny looking instrument with a tissue.

"A right morning fer a bit of dabbling in the water," commented Bobby.

She stood up. "Dabbling? I hardly think so. Checking, but definitely not dabbling. You're one of Uncle Ben's friends, aren't you?"

"Aye, fancied a ramble. Nice weather."

She nodded, then grabbed a little glass vial and, using a teat pipette, siphoned off a tiny water sample from the river and filled the receptacle.

"What are yer doin', if you dinna mind me askin'?"

With a squeeze bottle, she washed off the pipette and, in a second vial repeated the exercise, to clean the inside of the narrow tube. "Humdrum water samples," she remarked, scribbling notes down in a small logbook. "I'm also checking the water quality for signs of pollutants; there's been scores of complaints about contamination."

Bobby frowned. "How come? There's nay heavy industry out here in these parts."

Rona blew breath. "I know that, but pollutants can still turn up. The farming districts are the worst: run-off from fields sprayed with herbicides are a major headache – environmentally speaking, that is. Sometimes, the residue is so heavy the river water turns cloudy. And the fish farms aren't helping much, either."

"I kinda get the message," muttered Bobby. "How can yer tell where it's polluted?"

"Basic checks first of all: collect samples and take pH readings."

Bobby stuttered: "Right. What's a pH?"

She smiled again. "It's a value on a scale measuring the acidity and alkalinity of water or soil. At pH7, the water is neutral, perfect for living organisms. Any reading between pH1 to pH7 is on the acid side, while the other end of the scale gets increasingly alkaline. In fact, most fish and aquatic insects are missing in rivers if the water is below pH4 or above pH10."

"All sounds a bit technical, like."

"Not at all; it's dead simple. Are you familiar with this river?"

"Known it all me life," replied Bobby. "Used ter be the lifeblood of the village at one time, before the duke moved in, robbin' villagers o' the right ter fish."

"Duke? You've lost me," commented Rona.

"He's a right bastard – pardon me French. Doesn't give a fig about the river or the fish, just gets the punters in, issues fishing permits and makes a right packet out o' all the English visitors."

Rona frowned. "He sounds like a right typical eighteenth-century aristocrat."

Bobby laughed. "Aye. So, how can yer tell the pH, then?"

"I'll show you, if you've time."

"Not doing anythin' in particular."

"Okay, let's go downstream. I've to take samples and readings every kilometre, to get an idea of what might be happening."

They stopped farther along the river, and Rona withdrew the funny gadget, which Bobby thought looked like a mobile phone, with a wire affixed to a pencil-like rod. "Reading first," she said.

Rona slipped the rod into the water, and Bobby saw numbers appear on a tiny window, at the top of the box. She wriggled the rod in the water, and he saw the numbers stop at 6.5. "Is that bad?" he asked.

Rona took note of the reading and cleaned off the rod. "It's not brilliant; slightly on the acid side. Obviously, something's present in the river. You probably know the river was gassed around two years ago. It's highly possible that other poachers might have slipped something nasty into the river, too. Finding out is all part of my job."

"Most gangs from the other villages use nets," commented Bobby. "It's only the heavyweights seem ter bother wi' chemicals."

"I know. Poaching is rife in these hills. The Scottish Salmon Strategy Taskforce is all too aware how it's increased over the past few years. Trouble is, Dumfries and Galloway, being near the border, is tempting for gangs of English poachers. Like the open door of a sweetshop to a hungry kid, dying to pinch the goodies."

"Do yer reckon many English folks are grabbing the fish, then?"

"Difficult to say. There's an awful lot of unemployment in the north of England; people down there have lots of time on their hands and are desperate to gain much-needed capital."

"Aye, true. Endless problem, ain't it?"

Rona nodded: "Yes, but it's not my job to police the rivers; I simply monitor threats to the environment. Of course, if we find clear evidence of illegal activity, enforcement action will be taken, whether the culprits are polluters or poachers."

"Can this SEPA outfit do that?"

"Yes, definitely. In fact, it's vital right now. Poachers are often, without knowing it, spreading harmful agents along the river."

"Don't say?" Bobby replied. "What kind of things do yer mean?"

"Could be traces of chemicals or just polluted water. On the other hand, poachers could easily transfer organic parasites from A to B and never realize it. Sea lice, for instance, are deadly to salmon. Incidence rates of infestation have also shot up over the past decade."

"I've never heard o' them."

"I guess you haven't. Nasty little devils; aquatic equivalent to sheep ticks. They cling onto the side of the salmon and rasp away at the skin; that's what they feed on. It's really the juvenile salmon that are mainly at risk, though: their skin is thinner, and really young fish don't have protective scales."

"Yeah, but I thought young salmon lived in the sea?"

Rona shook her head in agreement. "Yes, but the fry have to travel downstream, first of all. And, juvenile fish near a fish farm are seventy times more likely to suffer from the lice than those not near a farm."

"I dinna understand why the fish farms are a problem?"

Rona took a deep breath. "Okay, here it is: a tank the size of a suburban house could hold twenty-thousand young farmed fish, creating a hotbed of infectious diseases among the livestock. Under those conditions, sea lice thrive in profusion. In order to eradicate lice infestation, some of the less savoury farms have administered a chemical called Deosect to the water in the tanks, and that's illegal. Deosect was developed to treat ticks and flies on horses and poultry, not fish. It contains cypermethrin, which is often used in agriculture and if it enters the rivers and streams, the water acidity is raised. Under acid conditions, cypermethrin is stable; it doesn't break down like it would in neutral water."

"Right, then the fish farms ain't good news fer anyone?"

Rona sighed. "They're not what could be classed as environmentally sound. Bear in mind that cypermethrin is highly toxic to wild fish and aquatic invertebrates. These farmers are playing with a timebomb, and one day—"

"Ain't a very sunny picture, is it?" interrupted Bobby.

Bobby and Rona came to a bend in the river, where a shingle bank lay at the corner. Rona took another reading and found the pH slightly on the acid side.

She was cleaning up her equipment, when Bobby spotted an object, lying on the pebbles near the water's edge. "Hey, over here," he called.

She packed the meter away and strove over the shingle bank, toward him. He pointed to the corpse of a ravaged fish: a salmon, which had its side pecked away.

"Kinda looks like it were snatched by an osprey or falcon," stated Bobby. "An' then it abandoned the fish, for some reason."

She tugged a pair of latex gloves from an inside pocket, slipped them on, then bent down and turned the corpse over. The fish looked far from healthy; most of the skin had flaked away, exposing dull, grey flesh.

"Sweet Jesus," she mumbled, pulling a stout polypropylene bag from the jacket pocket. "I'll have to get this analyzed." Carefully sliding the fish into the bag, she then labelled up the find. "Keep your eye open for anything else."

He scowled at her. "Like what? Another fish?"

"Anything," she replied, taking the bagged specimen to her

rucksack.

Bobby perused over the shingle, but found no other fish. She returned from the grassy bank, then scrutinized the shore, searching thoroughly.

"What we lookin' fer?" he asked.

"Another salmon, or any discarded tackle: fishing line, float, whatever."

More mystified than ever, Bobby scoured over the shingle but saw nothing.

Having investigated the stony strand and found nothing, Rona sighed. He noticed her troubled expression; "What's up?"

"It's that fish – the way the skin seemed to have dissolved away. I might be wrong. I hope I am."

"Right, then why worry about discarded fishing gear? Apart from it being litter, like?"

"You won't believe me."

"Get away. What do yer think happened?"

Rona shrugged. "You've seen the fish, so I might as well explain. I could lose my job telling you this, but here goes: all salmon in the U.K. could be under threat from a super-parasite."

"Yer jokin', ain't yer?"

"No way! Have you ever heard of a salmon pest called Gyrodactylus salaris?"

Bobby shook his head from side to side and remained quiet.

"Right, I won't go into a science lesson but, in short, the 'G.S. fluke', as it's commonly known, has already devastated the salmon industry in Norway, Sweden and Russia. The parasite has since turned up in Germany, Denmark, France, Spain and Portugal. So far, the British Isles has been unaffected."

Bobby's face clouded over. "You reckon it's spread here, then?"

"It's why I bagged that dead fish: we have to find out why the thing had no skin. You see, this G.S. fluke is tiny – only half a millimetre long – but if seen under a high-power microscope it would resemble a leech. At the rear end, it has a flange with sixteen razor-sharp barbs, to hook onto the host fish. At the front end, it has special glands to fix onto the fish, and through the mouth releases a digestive enzyme that dissolves the salmon's skin. The resulting mucus is then sucked into the fluke's gut."

Bobby glared at the girl. "Sounds a right wee charmer, eh?"

She nodded in agreement. "But that's not the worst part. Like aphids, the flukes give birth to live young, and the offspring are already carrying the third generation, so they multiply rapidly. Furthermore, the flukes can survive for up to seven days without a host, in damp places like anglers' clothing, waders, wet reels or landing nets. That's why I wanted to see if any discarded gear was lying around."

"Now I see what yer mean. Is there any safeguard against these fluke things?"

"Only if anglers and fishermen make sure equipment is dried off properly. Or, alternatively, exposure to heat above sixty degrees for an hour kills them. Fishing stuff left in a freezer for a day also destroys them. Immersion in G.S.-killing solution for ten minutes is also effective. I don't go for that option, though; it's not eco-friendly."

"What's going ter happen if it turns up?" asked Bobby.

"Obviously, stringent measures will have to be set in force. It's all too obvious that poaching has to be stamped out. Imagine if the fluke got established in their nets and other equipment. Apart from stealing fish, they'd spread the fluke far and wide."

Bobby stroked his jaw, thoughtful of the implications. "Aye. Alarming, ain't it?"

"Yes, and the first thing to do is get that dead fish examined. Come on, I'll give you a lift back to the village if you like. I left my car near the bridge."

"Okay, I'd like that; make it ter the pub fer a quickie. I kind of need it, after all this news."

Bobby and Rona strolled back along the riverbank. Admiring the seemingly tranquil scene, he could hardly take in Rona's account of this new and deadly threat hanging over the rivers and glens – far more pressing than the duke and his henchman's aspirations could ever be. *Ye wait, Johnny; have I got stuff ter say tonight?* he thought, turning over all the things Rona had said.

Totally unaware of the potentially devastating discovery Rona had made that morning, Will and his friends drove out from Dumfries, after many hours on the road, eventually arriving at his cousin Johnny's home village of Glenstone.

For a brief moment, he thought about Johnny and how he was coping without Annie, but said nothing to the others. Skirting around the village, they headed up the twisting hillside road and finally reached a wooden fishing hut – more of a cabin, actually – close to a pool called Johns Burn.

Will knew next to nothing of river conditions, or whether they were good or distinctly unfavourable. Judging by the remarks his four pals made that morning, he guessed the state of the river was just perfect.

Every so often. in the different pools along the river, the fish showed, some leaping clear of the water, in much the same way as young lambs on a spring morning, while other, heavier fish made their presence known with a sudden splash.

As Will knew very little about fishing, having only gained insight as a spectator, he admired the scene around him, while the others set about preparing their gear for the day's angling ahead. He noticed, on the far bank, a small herd of cattle watched them, almost as if awaiting results. No doubt they'd witnessed many a catch hauled in by the fishermen, and maybe wondered what all the fuss was about.

A burly, bearded fellow fishing nearby glared at them every so often – that was the only time his eyes left the water surface. Will had a sneaky feeling the large man resented them being there. Upon the shingle behind him lay a small salmon and, around its gills, fresh, red blood. He wished they'd arrived earlier, in order to witness the big man land the fish.

Will noticed the trees everywhere, covering the slopes, which in places ran almost at the water's edge, lining the fields and meadows on both sides of the river. Some of their leaves already showed signs of turning golden, edged with a russet hue, giving the seasonal warning that winter was not far away.

At the head of the pool, the water rushed around between rocks and large boulders, causing it to turn into white foam, which noisily tumbled far below into the deep water, then swirl around until gradually slowing down. At the tail end of the pool, the water looked as smooth as polished plate-glass, the surface broken now and then, as if raindrops were falling on it, when fish rose to snap up stranded insects.

Will sighed quietly and, for the first time in many years, felt free and contented. Everything around gave him pleasure. Simply just being in this wonderful haven of tranquillity was more than enough. He thought the Scottish countryside all looked so incredibly beautiful – far better than photos on the calendars or chintzy chocolate boxes.

A small salmon jumped clear of the water, just a few feet from where Will stood, at the edge of the shingle shore. He could have sworn the fish had looked at him, before it returned from whence it came. Seeing it, Tom Richards rushed over and bet anyone that he could catch it. Brazen, bold and foolish, perhaps, he failed. The salmon, for some deep, instinctive reason, chose to ignore the worms. Even the yellow and green minnows proffered by young George held no attraction to it.

"Don't just stand there like a dummy, Will," remarked Andy, acidly, "make yourself useful and get that blasted frying pan sizzling."

Drawn from the wonderful reverie of drinking, in the spectacular and tranquil scene, Will scowled at his friend. "For Pete's sake, don't take it out on me, just because you lost your lousy bet."

After a little coaxing, Will sauntered back to the car, parked on the roadside. He opened the boot, retrieved all the camping gear and brought it back to the riverside. On the small, bottle-fed gas stove, he cooked up the breakfast of free-range eggs, smoked bacon and fried potato bread, purchased from a local shop that morning. Scoffing their well-cooked, though somewhat greasy breakfast, they chatted amicably about the one that got away.

While the others finished their meal, Andy took Will to one side and showed him how to put a fresh bunch of worms onto the hook, suggesting that he try his luck, since it appeared to have deserted them for the moment.

After clearing away the breakfast things, the four friends made their way back down the track to the deep pool. As Will strode along the path behind them, he realized what must be done, and that was catching a salmon.

During the next two and a half hours, Will watched his fishing friends, eager on trying his luck. Standing next to Tom, he watched his every move, wanting to understand how it was done. Tom showed him how the fixed spool reel worked and how to use it. Then, he explained where he thought the best salmon might lie and why he'd reached that deduction.

Shortly afterward, Andy joined them and handed Will his rod. Thinking it was going to be dead easy, he took the rod, but on his first cast he forgot to release the line, and the hook simply landed close to where he stood. His second cast landed on the shingle bank, on the far side of the river. Naturally, his efforts evoked howls of laughter, mixed with shouts and calls providing advice and encouragement. Even so, Will felt mighty glad the burly, bearded fisherman had departed, knowing it was only his friends who were laughing at him and his abortive attempts at fishing.

Then, at long last, he managed to get a cast right, and the small bunch of red worms landed upstream in the fast water. Following Andy's example, he held the rod high, keeping the thin, nylon line taut all the time, while observing the line where it entered the water. At times, he found that a difficult enough task, as it rushed downstream toward the deep pool, where it came to rest among the still water.

During the line's journey downstream, the bait often came to a halt, and in that short spell he waited for the salmon to swallow the worm. His heart missed a beat or two as he waited, hoping and praying that a salmon would take the bait. Alas, it always turned out to be a snagged hook on the riverbed.

Will had just cast upstream, when from behind he heard the sound of the others approaching. Glancing around, he saw them pass through the open gateway. As this was to be his last cast, he decided to make the most of it. Turning back to the water, he noticed the line appeared to be moving slowly upstream, the tip of the rod bent downward and moving in small jerks. If he'd not been so ignorant of this situation, and realized what was causing it, his heart would have missed many beats. From close behind, Will heard someone bawl: "Strike! Will, strike it! You have to hang on."

Very unsure of things, Will did not strike, and simply stood watching his rod and hearing the reel creaking away, as the gears slipped. The thing which affected him most was the power and strength of what was pulling the rod from his hands. It was the power he'd thought of while admiring the fish in The Badger Inn. Now, he realized he might have underestimated the strength the fish had.

"So, you reckon you can land it, or do you want me to?" asked Andy, now standing beside him.

Will dithered, unsure how to handle the situation. "Here, you know what you're doing."

He handed the rod to Andy, who immediately struck, sending the hook deep into the fish. Instantly, it turned and, with unbelievable speed, made for the deep water in the pool. With landing net in hand, Tom dashed over, ready to haul the fish to shore. On reaching the centre of the pool, the fish jumped clear of the surface, turned over once, before crashing to the water with a mighty splash. The fish circled, broke the surface several times, turned and twisted, in an attempt to escape. All watched spellbound, hoping that a successful netting and landing by Tom would see Will's fish lying on the shingle shore.

The fish rushed toward the tail end of the pool but, before getting there it turned and, with equal speed, returned to the fast water at the spot where Will stood. There it stayed, and ignored all attempts to get it to move again.

"It's come home," laughed young George. Will had absolutely no way of telling whether the fish had returned to its domain, but it was most reluctant to leave the post.

For a few minutes, the party stood gazing into the water, trying to work out the best move to force the fish out of its sanctuary. After a few unsuccessful attempts at dislodging the fish, they began to bombard it with large stones and rocks off the shore. Will got the impression the amount of rocks they'd chucked into the pool had made the water level rise an inch or more.

Without warning, the fish moved again, suddenly and unexpectedly, taking everyone by surprise. It raced back to the deeper water in the pool and, as far as Will could tell, it was still there. The last they saw of it was the large tail fin which broke the surface, almost as though to wave goodbye, and then it was gone.

"Awfully sorry, Will; I've lost it," grumbled Andy.

"That's alright, Andy. You did your best," answered Will. He couldn't think of anything else to say.

Will had already decided that he'd like to come fishing again and knew that he would, whenever and as often as possible. He also made up his mind, there and then, never to hand his rod to anyone; in future, he would land or lose his own fish.

Although many fish made their presence known in different parts of the river pool, splashing, circling and showing their dorsal fins, they didn't appear to be remotely interested in the worm bait. Nor did they seem attracted to the yellow and green Devon minnow, thrown to them every few minutes by young George, the only member of their party tempted to try other bait instead of worms.

By late afternoon, the weather started to deteriorate; it rained soft at first, then in heavier showers. By that time, the fishing team decided they'd had enough, and mutually agreed to have an early start the following morning.

That night, in a small, cosy hotel not far from the river, the group reflected on their day's fruitless fishing, and spent time working out the strategy to adopt the next day. Having worked up an appetite in the fresh Scottish air, they enjoyed a hearty supper: chargrilled steak with all the trimmings – mushrooms, peas, chips and oodles of fried tomatoes – washed down with beers and chasers of Scotch whisky. While dining they toasted each other's efforts and, even more important, for better results the next day. Afterward, they reminisced about previous expeditions, recalling tales of the one that got away, and how Scotland seemed so much better for salmon fishing than Droitwich Spa.

That evening, Will came to realize, for the first time since his retirement, that he'd found enjoyment and freedom to savour the splendour of life – available to those willing to accept such things.

After bidding his friends goodnight, Will carefully stalked up the narrow, creaking, wooden staircase leading to his small but adequately furnished room. He stifled a yawn brought on by plenty of clean, fresh, pine-scented air, exercise and good food. Almost tearing his clothes off, he slipped into bed, briefly looked at the room and, as his head crashed onto the soft, downy pillow, before slipping into a deep, untroubled sleep, the word "paradise" flashed through his mind.

George, being younger than the others, had stayed up later and, during the festivities, almost came to blows with an equally young Scotsman, who bragged on and on about being the very successful local poacher. George had nothing whatsoever against poaching and, with his mates back in Droitwich Spa, had often engaged in that illicit activity. He looked upon it as a form of sport, more than anything else.

The thing that rankled with George was not the young Scot being a poacher, but the amount of fish he claimed to have snagged. Unwisely, he said so, too: "You bloody liar! You'd need a fuckin' trawler to catch that amount of fish."

"Who yer callin' a liar, ya English bastard?!" the Scot snarled back.

"You, you stupid moron. Who d'you think?"

"Aye, so you know all abert poaching' do yer, eh? Yer could nay poach a bloody egg and yer knows it."

George sneered. "Wouldn't waste me time with eggs; I go in for bigger things back home."

"Yer, then why come up 'ere? Yer English are all the same; flit o'er the border like a pack o' thievin' bastards, that's what yer lot is: thievin', stinkin' sassenach bastards, and yer knows that, tew." In contempt, the Scot spat on the floor, missing George's Nike trainers by half an inch, and stormed out of the bar in a rage. The door slammed shut behind him, almost caving inward with the impact.

While George glared at the doorway, he heard a voice call out: "I want a word wi yer, sonny."

He turned and saw the pub landlord beckon, then strode over to the bar. "Yeah, what's the problem?"

"You, fer a start. I'll nay have me guests go rattlin' the locals, do yer get the message?"

"He started it, bragging on about—" George didn't get a chance to finish.

"You listen here, sonny, yer bloody lucky he dinna give yer a Glasgow kiss. He's expert dispensin' them, and usually ends his arguments that way."

"What the shit's a Glasgow kiss?"

"Yer dinna want ter find out. But I'll tell yer, then ya know ter steer clear of the likes o' him."

"Ah, go on then. I'm just pissin' me jeans to hear about it."

"Ya'd be doin more than that if he'd struck. It's like a headbutt, but far more effective. He brings that thick skull on his crashin' down atop the bridge of his opponent's nose. Done properly, the result's… well, devastating is too mild a word. Blood everywhere, shattered bone and, heh, yer'd be breathin' through yer mouth fer the next six months. Mind out fer that one'. Ya might have rattled him somethin' rotten."

On that word, George hit the sack, too, in the tiniest room, right in the attic – after first visiting the toilet and peeing for an eternity.

CHAPTER 13

Bob's learning

NEXT MORNING, JUST before first light, the four fishermen were back on the riverbank of the same deep pool, fired with enthusiasm and hope of a rewarding time. Like the others, Will looked forward to a good day's fishing, had borrowed a rod and purchased a one-day fishing permit. As this was their last day, he was determined to enjoy it and thought that, if luck was on his side, he just might stand a better chance of catching something.

He recalled hearing another fisherman once say that Hell would be a place where, on every cast, a fish would be hooked. He reflected on the quote and thought the speaker was a true sportsman. He knew that his friends would all agree to spend a pleasant hour in Hell before the devil knew of their presence.

Before long, the bailiff called on the party from Droitwich Spa, soon after they had arrived on the bank. He always checked the permits of everyone fishing along the river. Being totally new to the game, Will whipped his permit out first and proudly flashed it before the officer.

"Me first day of fishing ever, this is," he declared, like a kid with a new toy. "I'm just hoping for beginner's luck to kick off."

The officer smiled, wryly. "Really? Well, you can't do any worse than your mates here." Then, he whispered into Will's left ear: "Ye want to try over there." The bailiff pointed to a spot he knew the salmon were laying. Will suddenly thought that he'd gained an advantage over the others. Little did he realize that the officer was merely playing a mischievous prank at his expense.

Andy Thompson was soon into a fish, but lost it almost immediately. Tom Richards also hooked a fish that morning, but it escaped after a brief but exciting contest. Tension and frustration started to build up among the small group, now gripped by a sense of failure. It was their last day, only three fish had been hooked and none landed. Will reached the conclusion that good fortune, or whatever else helped in catching fish, was absent, and if it didn't arrive before long they'd be leaving empty-handed, as half their day was already over.

Just after midday, a fisherman accompanied by a young girl appeared on the far bank. Down by the tail end of the pool, they stood together and, for several moments, looked into the water, as though trying to determine their next move. While fishing, Will glanced at them every so often, and assumed they were father and daughter. The father was about to teach his daughter, of about fifteen or sixteen, how to fish using a fly.

Will guessed he was right about the relationship between the two, but he could clearly see that she was no beginner when they started to fish. She stared at the tail end of the pool and worked her way upstream, toward Will's party. He was in absolutely no doubt that she knew exactly what she was doing.

Her long, slender rod waved back and forth, behind and ahead. The heavy line grew longer until it reached the place where she wanted it, then the fly dropped gently on the water's surface. Using her left hand, she drew the line, pulling the fly slowly toward her.

Will gained a feeling of subtle pleasure at watching her, and within an hour she was into a fish. Without fuss or bother she played it and, with a little help from her father, a good-sized salmon lay on the bank. The pair, with their fresh salmon, waved goodbye and they were gone.

Bereft of his poaching gear, Johnny Mason ambled into the public bar of The Leaping Salmon, where Reg pulled him a pint of heavy. He looked around to see Bobby, Ben and Tom already sitting in their usual corner. Bobby looked kind of flushed, had obviously been drinking rather a lot, and seemed very agitated. He kept waving his hand, wildly.

"What's eating Bobby, do yer reckon?" Johnny asked.

Reg plonked the brimming glass of heavy onto the bar. "I have nay idea, but he was in here at lunchtime. Packed away more than was really good fer him, too. At about one-forty-five he dashed in, face white as a sheet o' blinkin' paper when he arrived."

"Odd. He's not one ter get the jitters."

"He's obviously got wind of somethin'. He downed the first pint in eight minutes flat. It was heavy, too – not just ale, but heavy. Well, I mean…"

Johnny's eyes narrowed. "Like he deliberately wanted ter get pissed as fast as possible, eh?"

"Can't think what brought it on. Do yer reckon he was set

upon?"

"What'd be the motive, and who would have attacked him? Dinger? He's been absent fer days now. Good riddance, too." Johnny was about to sidle over to the corner and turned back to the landlord. "On second thoughts, I'll have a bag of crisps – the thick, crunchy ones. I guess our friend needs a little something ter soak up the excess, otherwise stand by wi' the mop."

Reg grinned and chucked a thick foil pack of crinkle-cut chips on the bar. "Aw, take 'em on the house if it stops that idiot heaving up all over me floor."

With crisps and heavy, Johnny strode across to the others. Bobby reeked like a brewery.

"Phew! Ye certainly made an early start o' it today," stated Johnny, calmly.

Bobby lolled about in the seat. "Early start? Had an early start, thanks. Needed it, too. Boy, I needed it."

Tom and Johnny glanced at each other. "Someone had a go at yer?" Johnny asked.

Bobby shook his head from side to side. "Nay, not me."

Johnny tore the crisp bag open and proffered it to Bobby. "Get some o' these down yer. Eat somethin', fer Christ's sake."

Bleary-eyed, he stared at the bag of crisps like they were a jar of caviar, then nibbled the edge of one. "Cheers, Johnny, yer a good un. Yer knows that, eh?"

Tom lit his pipe and blew a little smoke gently toward the partially drunken friend, to help him sober up. Bobby didn't smoke, but Tom reckoned the smoke would help.

He nibbled another crisp like it was a canapé. "Ye'll never, ever guess what I know."

Tom and Johnny glanced at each other again, as much as to say: "'Ere it comes."

Tom spoke quietly: "Okay, what's the big mystery, then?"

Bobby munched away at another crisp before answering: "Wow, yer ain't going ter believe this. Whole of yer salmon across the country is doomed."

Johnny and Tom gazed at their friend like he was mad.

"How come ye think that?" asked Johnny.

"She said so – that blonde bit. Er… Rona."

Johnny sniffed. "Right, yer gonna have ter explain a bit more. Why should she say that?"

Bobby shoved a handful of crisps into his mouth, chewed and racked his brain to say the right words. "I met her out by the river this mornin'. Doin' lotsa funny tests, she were."

"Aye, probably just doing her job," muttered Tom.

Bobby nodded. "Then we found this dead salmon on a shingle bank. Weird, it looked: all sort o' grey and skinless. Made her scared, it did."

"Wouldn't be a pretty sight," replied Johnny, grinning.

"Nay, ya dinna understand. Fish didn't scare her; it were reason behind it bein' in that condition. She said it were done by a fluke."

"Fluke?" Johnny repeated, like it was a new word. "Ye mean some kinda worm?"

Bobby nodded again, and chewed through another handful of crisps. "Yeah, and it's wiped out the salmon in Norway an' other places. She said could be a threat to salmon here, too. She got the dead fish, bagged it up and taken it somewhere."

Johnny and Tom stared at each other, unable to decide whether to believe the story.

"Aye, I reckon they'll sort it, then," said Johnny, thinking of his gaff and net lying in the back of Davidson's Land Rover.

That was another pressing little problem: how was he going to supply Reg with the goodies from the river? *God alone knows the answer to that.*

CHAPTER 14

Rona goes to H.Q.

IN HER NISSAN Almera, Rona tore along the A75, desperate to reach Dumfries and SEPA's regional H.Q. It was nearly dark and the rain had come on. She kept her eyes on the road ahead, irritated by the windscreen wipers swishing away, occasionally glancing down at the empty front passenger seat, where the bagged fish lay.

The traffic was not too bad and she found that a blessing, but the rain came down heavier. Up ahead, a juggernaut trundled along, impeding her progress. She frowned and contemplated overtaking, when suddenly a driver from the rear swerved out and sped past, tyres swishing water off the tarmac. She pursed her lips, looked in the rain-spattered mirror and saw that all was clear behind. "Well, if he can do it, here goes." She pulled out and zipped past the juggernaut, then pulled over to the left lane again.

Up ahead, she made out the skyline of Dumfries amid the gloom. Low slate clouds scurried across the sky southward, and rain continued falling. "Shit! Just get there in one piece."

Twenty minutes later, after wending through the town, she parked the Nissan outside H.Q. in Irongray Road. The rain eased up slightly. Grabbing the plastic bag and its contents, she dashed into the foyer and saw Jill on reception.

"Liam in?" she asked.

The girl nodded yes, but was busy with a caller on the switchboard.

Rona spurted across the foyer, to a door with a plate-glass window, ran her I.D. swatch card through the slot of the lock and hurried down the corridor. She barged into her boss Liam Findlater's office – he happened to be SEPA's chief environmental officer.

Busy checking data on a spreadsheet at the workstation, he twisted round, startled by the sudden intrusion. "Hi. Back so soon?" he joked, then noticed her serious expression. He got up and sauntered toward his desk.

She dropped the bagged fish onto his desktop. "I'd no option. That's probably the start of a major ecological disaster. Hope I'm wrong."

Liam peered at the bag. "Salmon?" he asked.

Rona shed her coat and pulled up a chair. "Dead right. I found it this morning, along the river at Glenstone. It was just lying on a shingle bank. If that's what I think it is, then bye-bye salmon in the U.K."

He turned the bag over. "Bugger all in the way of skin left, ain't there?"

"That's what got me down here. I just couldn't take the chance. Hell, do you reckon this is G.S., arrived on our doorstep?"

Liam shrugged and fingered the bag. "I don't even want to think about the implications. Jesus, one angler could spread the parasite far and wide. The entire salmon stock across Dumfries and Galloway could be wiped out. Thing is, it won't stop there."

Rona blanched. "Christ, are you talking about one legitimate angler? Poaching is rife up there, by all accounts. Illicit fishermen would spread the fluke all over the place."

Liam switched the desk lamp on and examined the bag. "Yeah, I know. If this is an infected fish, poachers could already have spread the fluke. They probably wouldn't know it, either. Salmon stocks worth seventy-five-million pounds might be wiped out, including all those in the fish farms. Think about it: that's three-thousand jobs in Scotland at risk. That's a hell of a price to pay through a handful of lowlife poachers doing the dirty."

Rona rubbed her temples. "I checked with the Environmental Agency in England. So far they've not had any reports of the fluke turning up."

"Right. Doesn't mean to say Scottish rivers are any safer. If it is the fluke, and it spreads across Scotland, the salmon industry stands to lose roughly thirty-million a year."

Rona glared at him. "Some pretty picture, that is."

Liam bit his thumb while thinking. "Yeah. Trouble is G.S. can affect other fish, apart from salmon."

"I know that much, eels included; I studied a report from a Russian ecologist: Ivan Vladilin, I think it was."

Liam laughed. "You don't half pick 'em. He's a big noise in Eastern Europe regarding environmental hazards. Still, if Vladilin says as much, it's got to be true."

"What in God's name are we going to do? This infestation would equate to an aquatic equivalent of the foot and mouth epidemic a few years ago."

Liam blew breath. "Okay, let's not jump to hasty conclusions; we don't actually know it's the fluke. Did any other dead fish turn up along that river?"

"No, that's the only one I found."

"Let's take a look at it, then, if you're okay."

"I've no qualms. Actually, I'd rather know for certain, like now."

She followed him along the corridor, to another wooden door with a small, plate-glass window. He tapped a sequence of buttons on the security lock and pulled the door open. They entered a small, well-equipped lab. He unsealed the bag and tipped the badly pecked salmon onto a stainless-steel tray. "Holy shit! No wonder you were in a hurry to get back! Just look at this thing."

She peered at the fish. In the stark laboratory light, the salmon looked more grisly than ever, the grey flesh glistening with a sickly sheen. Liam grabbed a surgical probe and scraped the salmon's flank.

"There's hardly any skin left at all. Was anything harmful present in the water?"

"Readings indicated a pH of 6.0 to 6.5, so obviously something's entered the watercourse."

"Cypermethrin?"

"Could be. There's a large fish farm up there, near Rosstown."

"Yeah, right. It's possible those bastards might have drained wastewater from the tanks into the river."

"This morning I was dead certain that fish was affected with G.S."

Liam snatched a high-power, bifocal hand-lens and examined the dead fish. "Skin looks as though it's been rasped away."

"Then I'm wrong."

"Maybe; let's not get hasty. I don't like the look of that lustre: it kind of suggests traces of mucus – perhaps residue of a digestive enzyme."

Rona drew breath. "Okay, there are three possible suspects: G.S., sea lice or an unknown chemical. Christ, I just thought: that river is the same one that got gassed by poachers, two years ago."

"That figures. Was the BOD count under par?"

"The oxygen consumption level seemed normal enough. I brought the water samples down, too. We might as well give Kay something to work on."

Liam stood upright and dropped the lens on the bench. "Buggered if I see any trace of G.S. That's not to say it isn't present, though. Analysis of the mucus should provide clues."

"If this is the result of G.S., we'll have to get the S.S.S.T.F. in. There are simply too many bonafide fishermen, not to mention poachers wandering all over the place."

"Those wily bastard poachers won't give a damn about spreading G.S., or anything else."

"Tell me about it. That particular river's an ideal spot, too: loads of pools and nearby tree cover. Ah, yes, and there's some local magnate running a kind of fishing resort. He charges the Earth for fishing permits, apparently."

Liam sneered. "He won't be for long, if this turns out to be G.S. I reckon that fish farm is behind this."

Rona sighed. "There's something about that river, too. I can't quite put my finger on it."

"Like what?"

"I'm not sure. Anyway, I have to go back; I've not finished. I'll set out again tomorrow. All I want now is a good meal and a hot bath."

Liam stroked his beard. "Fancy a Mexican?"

"Heaven! Restaurants are few and far between up there. Besides, staying with my uncle is rather like living in the 1950s: pretty basic."

Liam grinned. "Sounds just like my old dad." He glanced at his wristwatch. "Come on, let's put this on ice. We'll get a table at Fernando's." He shoved the stainless-steel tray into the lab freezer.

CHAPTER 15

George Martin from Droitwich

WHILE RONA and Liam contemplated the dire threat hanging over British salmon, young George Martin had other ideas: he planned another illicit fishing expedition in his hometown of Droitwich Spa. He'd found the perfect place for poaching, one he guessed other folk knew nothing of.

George, being a farmer's son, was wise to the furtive ways of rural life, and reaped the rewards it brought, which included successful poaching of river fish. He'd never been caught and had a very successful technique – one which Johnny Mason might have envied. All he carried on him was a coiled rabbit snare, a marble-sized lead shot, a six-inch-high tripod and a bicycle lamp – that last was the clever bit, for he'd replaced the bulb inside with a green one.

That night, with his best mate Richie Baines, he set out along the footpath through the river meadows, a popular haunt for local fishermen – those who had a permit, that is. George wasn't worried about fishing there; he wanted the patch where the river ran through a belt of woodland. At that location, the bank almost overhung a deep pool where the fish rested up.

The two youngsters hiked along the path, silent as ghosts passing through a graveyard. They both knew keeping quiet was vitally important to avoid detection. As a further measure, both wore black clothing to melt into the inky dark of the night. George looked up at the sky, now partially overcast, and his eyes got used to night vision. They could see ahead the jet-black outline of the woods against the night sky, and sidled through the ancient wooden gate.

The main public footpath veered away to the right, and they followed a muddy lesser track which ran alongside the river. It was a secret, little-used path, perhaps only known to those intent on a spot of erroneous sport.

George felt a tingling thrill of doing something naughty. It was the same sort of kick he'd got when pinching sweeties from the confectioner as a kid. Getting something for nothing, he thought, was almost – but not quite – as good as sex. Besides, if they had a successful night, they'd be quids in; Richie knew a man who would give them a good price for their booty, and he desperately needed the money. Richie had – quite by accident, as he put it – got his girlfriend Fiona pregnant. And, being a Catholic girl, she wasn't prepared to have an abortion. So, with a baby on the way, every pound counted.

George, on the other hand, didn't need the money, but found his electrifying ventures too stimulating to miss out on.

At the end of the narrow path, they reached the grassy bank, and carefully George withdrew the coiled-wire snare. Yes, he was going tickling the fish with his bicycle lamp.

He loosened the noose, wide enough for a football to pass through, then weighed the lower part of the loop with the small lead shot, to anchor the base to the riverbank. With the noose set up in the river, he wound the other end of the trailing length of wire to a small stick lying on the bank. Then, he withdrew the small photographer's tripod from his deep anorak pocket, set it up and slipped the bicycle lamp onto the camera fitting. With a nod to Richie, he flipped the bicycle lamp on and directed its green beam through the centre of the noose. It shone through the water, powerful yet also subtle.

Like all brilliant ideas, George discovered the technique quite by accident. One evening, George and a bunch of his fishing mates were invited by a friend to indulge in a spot of mackerel fishing in the Irish Sea, aboard a small trawler, at night. The opportunity was too good to miss, so he went, and was glad to have done so. Having weighed anchor, while the anglers got their rods ready, the skipper slung a tethered marker float over the side; on top of the large float was a flashing green light. The skipper explained that the green light drew in the fish, and they found out he was dead right. With eight of them angling away, in the course of the evening they'd landed in excess of a hundred mackerel and nearly half as many herring. It had been a right profitable venture. Of course, the skipper took the lot, but gave each lad thirty pounds apiece on leaving the boat.

So, George adopted the same idea on his riverside exploits, and it worked, too.

Before ten minutes were out, a large rainbow trout wriggled through the water, drawn by the almost unearthly beam. It slowly swam through the noose toward the centre of the beam, as though mesmerized. Without a second's hesitation, George tugged the wire and the noose drew fast over the fish, slipped down its flank and held the fish tight above its tail fin. It wriggled and splashed, but to no avail. Hauled onto the bank, George gave the struggling fish a quick whack with a sturdy hazel stick and it lay there: one perfect catch, and perhaps the first of many. He judged it to weigh around seven or eight pounds. Rainbow trout were usually anything from three to seven pounds as a rule, but occasionally real whoppers turned up. Without speaking, but in mutual co-operation, Richie stuffed the trout into a black pedal-bin liner.

George set up the noose once again, and he and Richie waited, hunched on the riverbank, like the two concrete gnomes which adorned the vicarage garden.

The night was almost silent, and they heard the river water slowly gurgle as it passed over some deep, sunken obstruction – maybe a tree trunk, long submerged.

Before long, a second trout appeared and, like the first, it seemed hypnotized by the green beam. Gradually, it advanced toward the noose and George could see, in the green glow, its mouth slowly opening and closing. Hardly daring to breathe, he willed the fish to move in toward the light. *Come on, fishy, there's this lovely green for you,* he thought. *Easy does it. Just think of the green glow.*

Almost as though following his mental command, the fish edged forward, entranced. George stared at the fish and saw its speckled flanks. It was slightly smaller than the previous fish – probably a four-pounder – but still worth snagging, if he could. The trout swam slowly forward, through the noose. As before, George tugged the length of wire at the other end and snared the fish. The noose caught tight above the tail fin and it suddenly splashed. With a quick flip, George hauled it onto the bank and, with the same sturdy stick, dispatched the trout. With a deft hand, he released the noose and set it up in the river once more.

Meanwhile, and without uttering a word, Richie snatched and bagged the fish, then hunkered over the bin liner, peering at the green beam.

Ten minutes later, another trout showed up. In due course, it too slowly swam toward the centre of the green beam of light. With right hand hovering just above the wire on the bank, George got ready to snare the prize. As soon as the fish slipped through the loop George tugged the wire: a third fish snared.

George thought it was turning out to be a fantastic night, with three trout caught already; usually he'd only caught two or three in an entire evening. Deciding to chance their luck, he set up again and they caught two more fish, all of them so far trout. George couldn't fathom that little point. Some nights, all he caught were trout; on other occasions he'd snared a salmon or two. There was really no telling what was going to turn up.

For the sixth time that evening, George placed the noose back in the river, feeling ecstatic. Five in the bag. One more would cap it.

They didn't have too long to wait, and George couldn't believe his eyes: a sixth trout, far larger than all the others, turned up. It swam up alongside the wire noose, almost as though investigating the terrain, and wondering what a green light was doing in the dark river. With breath held, George really wanted to snare this large fish.

Slowly, it turned around, seemingly more cautious than the other fish that night. Had it detected something untoward? Or, being larger, was it simply more wary than the smaller fish? George had no way of telling, but he kept his eyes on the trout. Slowly, it swam forward, nose through the noose, but in no great hurry to move toward the light. George made ready to grab the wire, hardly daring to hope his luck would hold. The big trout slipped forward another inch or so; he waited for it to edge forward. The trout was almost halfway through the wire loop, when George tugged the wire with a quick jerk; the noose suddenly snagged the big fish. It thrashed wildly with a splash, and George hiked the huge trophy from the water with one swift movement. Without thinking, he walloped the huge trout with the stick and it lay there, dead. He couldn't believe his luck. It must have weighed all of ten pounds, if not more.

George glanced at his wristwatch by the light of the bicycle lamp, and saw it was gone one a.m. He tapped Richie on the shoulder, then pointed to his watch and indicated the time. Without speaking, Richie bagged the last fish in another bin liner, and shoved the catches in two deep pockets inside his parka.

George prised the lead weight off the wire loop, coiled it up and flipped off the bicycle lamp. They stood stock-still for a few moments, to get accustomed to the inky black night, then the two young men sidled along the path, quietly but speedily, keeping their eyes and ears open for the slightest sign of anyone about. At one a.m., they rarely saw anybody out along the river.

George kept thinking of the six trout. It had been a spectacular evening, one he couldn't envision Will believing for a moment.

George reckoned the biggest fish would bring in at least twenty or thirty pounds. For the smaller fish, he thought they'd get ten or fifteen pounds apiece. Perhaps Richie's contact would give them a special deal: one hundred for the lot.

Richie and George always split the cash right down the middle, fifty-fifty, and never argued about money. That's why George only ever took Richie on these expeditions. He'd tried once with another mate, who wanted a bigger cut.

Neither spoke until they had reached the outskirts of town again, where Richie lived. That was another trait that George admired in his mate: he knew when to keep quiet. Never once had he felt tempted to speak out, while in the woods. They made their way to Richie's tiny, squalid flat, so George could retrieve his bike and get back to the farm.

He still lived with his dad and knew that, being the only son, he would eventually inherit it. So, he felt little inclination to move out of the family home. Besides, his dad was always glad of his help, especially at harvest time, and saved him the trouble and expense of hiring some extra farmhand, or taking on casual labourers.

George bade his friend goodnight, knowing that the six trout would remain safe in Richie's fridge until the following day, ready for sale to his contact in the fish trade.

George kept thinking of the wild, electrifying evening, and of the possible fifty tax-free pounds to come. He knew it would provide a bit of spending power for the next fishing trip to Scotland, in a couple of days' time.

CHAPTER 16

Johnny restocks

JOHNNY MASON WAS not a man to give in easily, and that applied to his plan to continue supplying Reg with choice sweetmeats from the river.

Early next morning, he caught the bus to Rosstown for a special shopping expedition. Rosstown, being a fair size, had scores of shops, where things unavailable in Glenstone could be purchased, without having to face the hurly-burly of the Saturday market. In fact, Johnny preferred to travel to town on a weekday, as it was much quieter. He'd one purpose in mind: to find replacements for his confiscated gear.

First, he scoured all the thrift shops in town, and there were quite a few to choose from. He looked over them all. Thrift shops had, over the past few years, proliferated across the town, probably due to the recession, he mused.

Eventually, he found what he was looking for: two sturdy but lightweight wooden boxes, slightly smaller than the average cigar box, but deep enough to accommodate two burning stubby candles. One of the boxes had been carved and really seemed quite elaborate, possibly used as a jewellery box at one time; the carved box cost Johnny three pounds and fifty pence. The other plain effort he got for one pound. Satisfied that part of his task was over, he moved onto the next port of call: the fishing tackle shop, which was aptly dubbed 'Reel Stuff'.

He strode over to the unassuming, somewhat tatty shopfront, painted in blue and brown, stared through the window at the array of equipment, then pushed the door and barged in. He'd been there before – many times, in fact, since he'd taken an interest in illicit fishing.

Inside Johnny looked around, eyed up the range of fishing tackle and strolled over to the counter. The thing he sought lay under the glass counter, at the rear of the premises. *Perfect,* he thought, gazing at the six-inch deep-sea angler's hook. He purchased the item and enquired with the shopkeeper about a net, a large one.

"Ah dinna want a heavy net, mind," explained Johnny. "Me old one got torn. Fine it was, too. Those over there look a tad too cumbersome." Indeed, he noticed some nets which looked as though they weighed a ton.

The angling storekeeper smiled. "Yes, what you really want is a lightweight mono-filament job. I've the ideal thing: how about this one, sir?" He held up a net almost the size of a small tent. "Now, you won't believe this, but it can be stowed away in a jacket pocket. They're very popular round these parts. In fact, that's the last one I have in stock."

Johnny grinned and purchased the net.

There was one last small item on Johnny's shopping list: a gardening hand-fork. He nipped along the high street to the garden centre, where he found a wonderful fork with a shapely handle, comfortable to hold and easy to grip.

Johnny also wanted to replace his telescope, but at the moment, with funds running low, that was beyond his means. He made up his mind to get one at the earliest opportunity.

Content with his shopping trip, Johnny caught the bus home again. But, instead of going to The Leaping Salmon that afternoon, he stayed indoors to put his plan into operation. He'd a fair bit of work still to do.

In his kitchen, which had, since Annie's death, gradually become more of a multipurpose workshop than anything, he cleared a bit of space on the kitchen table. Johnny wasn't worried about the unkempt den. First, he stashed the net in a plastic bag and shoved it in the cupboard under the sink. Then, he hid the angler's hook in another cupboard and left the garden fork in a corner. The two boxes he placed on the kitchen table.

He then decided on a spot of light lunch; something for the energy, but not stodgy. He decided two boiled eggs and toast were quite enough. He swilled half a mug of Scotch, then put the kettle on the gas-stove hob.

He took a deep breath and, for the first time in days, felt really good about himself. In fact, he'd not been so pleased since cracking the curry joke, outside the pub with his cousin and Davidson.

"Aye, Cousin McGee, I'll show yer what I'm about, ya bastard," he muttered, while buttering his toast.

However, over the past day or so, a new idea filtered through his mind, and it was one that he didn't like very much. Just maybe his English cousin wasn't such a bastard, after all. He couldn't understand why he began to feel that way.

After eating, Johnny dumped the lunch crocks in the sink and commenced. First, he drilled three holes through each side of the wooden boxes, and with a fret-saw cut away more of the wood to make slits. The sawing took a fair amount of time, but Johnny wanted to do the job properly and not hash it. He ended up with two boxes, each with three parallel horizontal slits on each side. Happy with the results, he then carefully nailed two thin tacks through each box from the base; the tacks would enable him to secure the candles inside. The last chore he saved until after a break, and made a mug of tea. Johnny didn't often drink tea, but today of all days he wanted to save the boozing until later in the evening.

After sweeping up all the sawdust, and having filed down the rough edges along the slits, he set about making the outside of the boxes waterproof. First, he rubbed in a mixture of beeswax and varnish, let it dry, then applied a further coat of varnish on top.

By six p.m. he was done, and proudly gazed at his day's handiwork. All he had to do now was screw a little eyehook in the side for the tether string.

Johnny was brought to with a sudden start, as someone rapped his front door knocker, and loudly, too. Before answering the door, Johnny whipped the two wooden boxes into the cupboard alongside the angling hook, and did the same with the pot of varnish. Making sure there was nothing lying around to betray his activity, he strolled along the hallway, just as another round of heavy rapping reverberated through the passage.

He opened his door and saw his cousin McGee standing there.

Johnny felt the blood drain away to his feet. Not since he'd shot the collie had McGee ever set foot in the house; Annie had forbidden it. McGee stared at him.

"Johnny, I'd like a little word with you in private."

Totally flabbergasted, Johnny said nothing.

"It'd be to your advantage," McGee added.

"Since when have yer had my best interests at heart?"

McGee rubbed his right eyebrow. "Look, Johnny, I know things between us in the past have not been ideal, but I have to speak. Please listen to me."

Johnny's eyes narrowed to slits. "Aye, right. In the kitchen wi' ye. I were just about ter put kettle on."

Johnny followed his cousin down the hall, noticing he was still dressed in his tweed outfit, deerstalker and all. This time he also carried a khaki hessian knapsack.

None too pleased to see his cousin in Annie's kitchen, he slapped two mugs onto the wooden table, as much as to say: "Let's have it and no messing."

"Why have yer come round here? Ya know I'll be at The Leaping Salmon later on. Ya could have talked to me there."

McGee fingered the side of his nose. "I didn't want anyone to see me speaking to you on this occasion."

"Is that a fact? Well, ye surprise me."

"Can't we put aside past differences for ten minutes, Johnny?"

"Why should I? Because o' you I lost all me gear."

McGee nodded, sadly. "Yes, but it was for the best. You're my cousin and I don't want Davidson to get you. But if you continue, as I said before, he will eventually. I strongly advise you to stop."

"What if I choose not to?" Johnny asked.

McGee drew breath. "I've a proposition to make that might be mutually beneficial."

Johnny frowned at the man. "Aye, have ye now? And, just what might that be?"

McGee stared at his cousin. "If you stop poaching, I'll make sure you can still supply your friend, the landlord, with fresh salmon."

"Ye'll do what?" exclaimed Johnny, amazed.

McGee drummed the edge of the kitchen table. "Look here, Johnny, I'm not going to beat about the bush. Believe me, I have no empathy for Davidson, any more than you have; I simply go along with him, to keep the job that I love doing."

He reached out for his rucksack, withdrew a package wrapped in a black polythene bag, and chucked it onto Johnny's kitchen table. "Go on, open it."

Johnny reached out and undid the bag; out slipped two silver salmon. He gazed at McGee for an explanation.

McGee crossed his legs and leant back on the chair. "I confiscated that off another poacher this morning. As one of the perks of the job, I get to keep such fish, unless of course the duke wants it. I can keep you supplied every so often, you deliver to your innkeeper friend, he pays you and everyone is happy. Got the picture at last, Johnny?"

Johnny stared at the gamekeeper, incredulously. "Got everything worked out ter the last detail, haven't yer? Ya conniving bastard."

"Family trait, isn't it, Johnny?" McGee sneered. "What's it to be? Have we got a deal? I'll feed you fish if you stop poaching."

Johnny cupped his chin, deep in thought, totally taken by surprise.

"Considering the recent turn of events, I see there's nay choice in the matter; that Davidson bastard confiscated me stuff. What options have I?"

McGee leant forward and clapped his hands, then smiled. "Good, that's all settled then. What a weight off my mind. Now, how about a nice cup of tea, as you'd put the kettle on?"

He and McGee sat at the table and drank the tea in silence, Johnny's mind a whirl of different ideas. He was unable to work out the implications behind the new set-up. He'd now the opportunity to earn money from Reg with no risk to himself. It seemed almost too good to be true. There had to be a snag somewhere, but he couldn't find one.

McGee drained the mug. "Good stuff, this tea – better than you get at the gamekeepers' mess lodge, I tell you that. Right, one last little word," McGee wagged a forefinger at him: "nobody ever gets to hear a word of this, understand? It's our private little arrangement."

"Aye, ya dinna need ter worry about that," muttered Johnny.

The dapper gamekeeper snatched his rucksack off the floor, grinned and strode down the hall. He said nothing more, then opened the door, walked quickly across the path and was gone, leaving Johnny wondering about the latest turn of events.

CHAPTER 17

Another catch

THAT EVENING, JOHNNY slipped the two salmon into a large, plastic carrier bag and slung it over his shoulder, under his greatcoat, as usual. He sighed, unsure quite what McGee had in mind. But, he couldn't bear to waste the salmon, and having seen the funds jar on the mantelpiece beginning to ebb, decided there was nothing else for it. He'd not been fishing since Davidson had confiscated his gear, or been anywhere near the pool, either.

He peeked out of the front door, almost expecting to see Davidson pop up from behind a hedge, sporting flash binoculars. Such an apparition was not to be seen. He sniffed at the night air; it felt damp, clammy like a wet flannel.

Happy that nobody was about, he slammed the front door and strode down the dark lane, intent on delivering the booty as he would normally. Except he felt really strange, having missed lying under the net that evening.

He suddenly mused about the poacher from whom McGee had seized the fish he was carrying. Who had he been, and what made him turn to poaching in the first place? The answers, Johnny realized, he would never know, unless McGee chose to tell him. He smiled at the thought. *No way is that bastard going to tell me.*

For once, Johnny felt light of mind, in spite of being unable to fathom his cousin's motive for supplying the fish. It was risky for him: if the duke, Davidson or anyone else found out he'd handed over fish to a man caught poaching, even a solitary individual such as himself, surely he risked losing his job. That fact alone made Johnny suspicious and apprehensive. What had made McGee have this sudden change of heart? Johnny had no idea, but was suspicious of his cousin's motives.

Eventually, Johnny saw the dark alleyway, cast a furtive glance around to make sure he wasn't followed, and took the turning into the small yard. Inside the outhouse, he dumped the fish in the old freezer, locked it and hung both the fridge key and his greatcoat on the nail. He took a deep breath and strolled into the public bar.

Tom, Ben and Bobby were in the usual corner. Johnny sidled over to the bar, when Reg appeared from the lounge.

"Same as ever?" he asked.

Johnny nodded.

Reg plonked the pint of heavy on the bar and rang it up.

"Beer gone up?" Johnny asked.

"Yes, bloody brewery," replied Reg.

A well-worn fiver found its way from Johnny's pocket to the sodden beermat on the bar; the landlord snatched up the note. "I guess life isn't quite so grand these days," he commented, with quiet commiseration.

Johnny looked at his publican friend and smiled. "Now, ain't that a strange thing? Funny you should say that. Tonight, life was grand: twofold grand, as a matter of fact." Johnny tapped the side of his nose.

Reg gawped at him, his mouth hanging open. "Don't say?"

Johnny nodded. "A right little quirk of fate, or whatever brings about such events, has seen fit to keep a dainty on yer menu for some time, by the look of things."

Reg's face clouded, not fully understanding Johnny's statement. "Surely…"

"Let's not question the will of the gods – not tonight, at least," Johnny warned. "Such things are best discussed when the sun shines, eh?"

He grabbed the pint of heavy and ambled across to the others.

"Evening, Johnny," muttered Tom. "Earlier than usual; you generally get in later."

Johnny supped on the heavy and stared at his friend for a moment. "Aye, well, there seems to have been a change or two to my daily routine, like it or not."

Tom lit his pipe and exhaled before answering. "Is that your doing or someone else's?"

"I've been messed around by a less discerning relation."

"Are we speaking of that cousin of yours?"

"I'm nay referring ter a lump o' Gorgonzola cheese." Then, he smirked. "On the other hand, I just might be; he's stinky enough."

Ben chortled at the joke. "He'd have ter be, working fer that bastard duke."

"Never mind all that crap," commented Bobby. "I heard a lot o' complaints about that new chap. Apparently, that thug's out to squash all forms o' poachin' on the duke's land."

Johnny's hackles rose. "What sort o' complaints?"

"He's tryin' ter get folks to inform on their mates that go poachin', and such."

"With bribes, yer mean?" asked Johnny.

Bobby shook his head. "Not the way Davidson puts it."

Tom tapped his pipe on the green ashtray. "Money talks, as they say. It's true."

A new thought suddenly struck Johnny. Had somebody informed on him? Was that how Davidson found out about his expeditions to his pool? And, come to that, how had McGee discovered his little secret in the first place?

Johnny suddenly felt the public bar of The Leaping Salmon turn into a hostile place, full of intrusive busybodies, ready to shop their friends and neighbours for the price of a drink.

Tom cleaned the inside of his pipe. "Plain obvious this Davidson chappie turns to the dirty tricks department. What makes him so keen to clear the river of poachers?"

"Perhaps the duke's got something on him, eh?" suggested Ben, sporting a wily grin.

Tom glanced at him. "Like what?"

Ben shrugged. "In the Army, weren't he? Maybe he did something he shouldn't have, and somehow the duke found out."

Johnny had heard stories of this sort before. Cases like dishonourable discharge for malarkey among other soldiers, indecent assault of enemy prisoners, selling inside information to foreign powers – this list was endless. If Davidson had done any of those things, Johnny felt somehow that the duke would surely know of it. And, with such knowledge he could apply duress to Davidson, or any of his other employees.

Then, Johnny suddenly heard the sound of a thunderclap; everything suddenly appeared to fall into place! Was that the reason McGee had suddenly changed tack?

But, Johnny knew his cousin hadn't been in the Army, so it would have to be something else. He tried to recall his cousin's life history, but was unable to concentrate in the busy bar.

"How about another pint then, Johnny?" Bobby asked.

Johnny came to with a start. "Aye, definitely."

He looked around the room, wondering who the mystery spy might be. He saw a few casual acquaintances, but nobody who could possibly know about his riverside forays.

Bobby returned with the drinks. "Get that down yer."

Johnny smiled. "Like you did the other day, yer mean?"

Bobby flinched. "Aye, that day I got a right shock. Could nay help myself."

Bobby's words made Johnny glance over to the far corner of the bar, at the round table. The girl with the laptop wasn't there.

"Where's... er... Rona? Has she departed this realm o' ours?"

Ben sniffed. "Nay, she had urgent business in Dumfries. Flew in and out the house sudden, like, grasping a plastic bag, then drove off in that car o' hers, the day Bobby got pissed."

"I was nay pissed," Bobby retorted.

"Not much! Reeling blind, yer was."

"So would you be on seein' that skinless horror."

"Is that why she's gone there?" asked Johnny.

"Aye, she should be back tomorrow night, or soon after."

Johnny felt glad on hearing that news. He fancied another encounter with her, even though she must have been almost half his age. Still, was it Rona he wanted to see, or Annie as she was in her heyday? Johnny couldn't be quite sure. He suddenly wasn't sure about anything anymore, except he'd a longing to go fishing again. And that meant more work tomorrow; he was still missing a gaff.

After Reg uttered those daily words, "Drink up, please," Johnny retrieved his greatcoat from the outhouse, then sidled across the yard and strode down the road homeward, while musing over the payment to come.

The following morning, a slight drizzle blew in from the northeast, but Johnny was not in the least bothered.

After a leisurely breakfast of tea and toast, he inspected the wooden boxes, just recently varnished. *Ha! Perfect,* he thought, and added the little eyehooks to the side of each. He gave both boxes an affectionate pat and slipped them back into the cupboard.

By ten-thirty, Johnny was pacing down the road. He'd some pressing issues to discuss with Reg, and wanted to do so before the bar filled with lunchtime regulars.

He entered the bar to see Sally, Reg's daughter, stacking up bottles on the shelves opposite the bar. She saw him, too. "Hi, Johnny. You're very early this morning."

Johnny stared at her for a moment, before Reg spurted into the bar on hearing his name.

"Sally, love, go and help Mum in the kitchen, would you?

There's a good girl." Reg turned to the old soldier; "What you say to a free pint then, eh?"

Johnny nodded in affirmation: "Aye, ya guessed right."

Reg placed the full glass on the bar. He also dropped a wad of ten-pound notes beside the glass. "Call it ninety for last night's little delivery, eh?"

Johnny immediately scooped up the notes and stuffed them into the inside pocket of his greatcoat. "That'll do very well."

"I have ter say, I thought those days were done when that bastard snatched your gear."

Johnny scratched his chin. "So did I, fer a wee while. But I did nay poach those particular goodies."

Reg scowled and leant over the bar. "Really? How'd ye come by them, then?"

Johnny fingered the top of the pint glass. "This is goin' ter sound weird – unbelievable, in fact – but last night I had a caller: McGee. What's more, he brought round a free gift, on the understanding I stopped poaching from the river."

"Where the hell did he get the fish?"

"Confiscated them from another poacher. What else?"

"What's his aim in all this?" asked Reg, scratching his ear. "It doesn't make sense for him to give you fish, in order to keep me supplied. What's he getting out of it, for Christ's sake?"

Johnny smiled at his friend and rubbed his chin. "If I knew that, I might find a way out o' this bleedin' mess."

"Are ye going to keep accepting these deliveries, then?"

"Aye, fer the minute I will. If I refuse, that bastard will think I'm up ter something. But, taking the fish off him, he might think I've given up the old night trade."

Reg smiled, deviously. "You aren't planning to, though, are you?"

"What do yer think? I been playing the river fer too long to give it up just 'cos that bastard says so."

"True enough. If you're okay with it, I'll take the fish if you've a mind to sell them. Wild, fresh salmon is always a popular dish on my menu – one of the most requested, that is."

"Fine by me," replied Johnny. "When I get back in operation, I just might be able to supply double helpings, too. If I'm fishing and my cousin drops other fish round, too, you'll end up with plenty."

"The more the merrier. Then, if I end up with too many… well, the odd off-sale under the counter, eh?" Both friends laughed at the idea. "Have another, Johnny? On the house?"

"Aye, okay then, but I wanna get back; I've yet to finish preparing all me new gear."

Half an hour later, Johnny strode up to his gate. He was eager to put the next phase of his plan into operation, knowing it would be impossible to go out on his nocturnal ventures without a gaff.

That afternoon he began work and, first off, with a hacksaw cut away the end loop on the deep-sea angling hook. Afterward, he filed it down smooth. Satisfied with the result, he grabbed the garden fork. He unscrewed the metal fork from the wooden handle and slung the pronged implement on the floor. Then, he drilled a long hole through the wooden handle for about five inches. Making sure all traces of sawdust were blown away, he squeezed industrial strength glue into the hole, then slipped the filed end of the angling hook into it. He tapped the handle to make sure it was properly secure.

The final stage involved making sure the tool was going to last in all weathers. Around the end of the wooden handle, where the hook emerged, he packed down a small wad of pitch and, with a decorator's blowtorch, melted the tarry resin down to a liquid, then let it set. The end result would be a sturdy hook, capable of withstanding a bit of rough treatment.

Johnny suddenly laughed at his cousin's daft idea. "Aye, you wait, yer lousy bastard. No way am I givin' up me uncle's and my riverside patch just ter keep you happy. I'll get ye and that bastard duke yet. You'll see."

CHAPTER 18

Will the fisherman

AFTER RETURNING FROM Scotland, Will acquired all the fishing tackle he needed and, armed with advice, tuition and practice gained from his friends, thought he could now claim to be a fisherman. What amazed him most was the short space of time in which he'd managed to gain these new skills.

When able to cast a fly properly or spin a minnow, he'd managed to catch many trout, but failed to land a salmon, while those around him did so with seeming aplomb. Thus, Will felt he now had a target to meet, if only to prove something to himself. He often said hope was with him, and knew that one day a fish would be his – a fish which, at this very moment, may only be an egg hidden among the gravel of the riverbed, far upstream. As a smolt, that fish would one day become a leaping salmon, which first had to make the lengthy but dangerous journey to the sea, filled with yet more perils. Then, after two years, the grilse would return for the first time, to the freshwater of its birth, to lay her eggs among gravel in the shallows. And the male fish would almost immediately shed his cloudy milk over them, fertilization completing the endless cycle.

Will realized the cycle was perhaps as old as the river itself. Even when hooked, the salmon had unseen tactics to free it, and spurt upstream to achieve its purpose – perhaps the last act the fish would perform. The salmon he began to regard as a true titan among fish, and a splendid adversary.

Naturally, the thrills of seeing a large salmon leap clear of the water was known only to those with rod and line, casting a fly or worm-baited hook in the still, clear waters, hoping that, with luck and skill, the fish would be theirs. Yet, revelling in this new ability, Will felt competent enough to bawl out advice to less experienced fishermen making a complete hash of things.

The next day, Will decided to take a walk down to the banks of the Upton on Severn, to watch the local fishermen perform. He now felt that he was a professional fisherman – one who could give advice, whether wanted or not.

Not long after he arrived at the popular fishing pool, he saw two men blundering about on the shore, totally unsure of what to do and looking foolish. They'd hooked a fish, and Will wished they'd either land or lose the thing. The man with the rod held the fish, like a mad dog on a leash. The fish's only freedom came from the yielding line on the long, slender rod, and at times the tip of the rod even touched the water's surface. The chap with the landing net had absolutely no idea how to catch the fish, and made three unsuccessful attempts.

Will really felt an overpowering urge to call out: "Let it run, you fools! Give it some slack before it breaks the line, you stupid imbecile! You, yes you with the net, stay back until he tires it. If the fish sees you it's going to run, and there's nothing that foolish mate of yours will be able to do about it."

Wisely, he held his tongue.

Apart from the fact that he'd yet to land a salmon, there were other fishermen who knew this, and fishermen shouting advice to others – especially to people they didn't know – was not the done thing. Will doubted if those two clowns would have heeded his advice anyway, and if they had a violent temperament, just might have strode across and chucked him in the river. Instead, he kept silent and watched.

The long rod shot upright. The line with its three lead weights, which a moment ago had been in the water, shot high into the air.

"Agh, blast it!" cried the rod man. Will knew it was obvious that the fish was gone.

His mate slung the landing net aside in disgust, before glaring at his discouraged and dejected comrade.

Shortly afterward, they, like their salmon, went away, perhaps to try again in another place, at another time.

Although Will had already hooked several small fish, he'd yet to experience the exhilaration and sense of esteem on landing a large, silver, fresh-run fish. He imagined the sense of esteem when friends and others came round to gaze upon and admire a large, newly-caught salmon, and congratulate the fisher of the prize. Over the years, he'd seen many fishermen hook salmon, but for some inexplicable reason, far more fish escaped than those landed. Naturally, Will couldn't envision what took place under the water, but he didn't think the salmon's success was due to the inexperience or impatience of the fishermen. He guessed it was largely down to the salmon being a powerful creature, yet also resourceful and perhaps wise. Truly a noble fish, if ever!

CHAPTER 19

Back in Scotland

ALMOST THREE DAYS had passed since they'd arrived near Glenstone, for a week's fishing on the river. This time, Will's party had rented a small farm cottage. His friends had done so previously over the years, when it was available, and they wanted to stay for longer than a couple of days. The cottage accommodation was far superior and worked out much cheaper than the hotel. As a bonus, they had more freedom, and came and went without any worries. Andy, being a brilliant cook, had dished up suppers and snacks that could have rivalled the fare on offer at the hotel, or indeed any of the local pubs in the vicinity, and at virtually no cost. Pubs, hotels and bed-and-breakfast places were these days none too cheap, a large outlay being needed for lengthy stays.

Andy's menu that night would be fresh-caught salmon, probably with new potatoes and broccoli, as George Martin had landed a small, seven-pound fish the same morning. The cottage also had plenty of beer, wine and whisky in stock, as much refreshment would be needed, and more besides.

Shortly after midday, Will tried a third cast after returning from the car, where the party had a snack of ham and egg pie, washed down with plenty of bottled beer. They felt the respite gave them and the river a break from each other's company, trials and efforts.

They'd return to the waterside feeling refreshed, and perhaps more inspired, too.

For bait, Will used a small bunch of four red worms dug out of Andy's dad's manure heap, the morning before they left Droitwich Spa. Being of a soft texture, the worms needed replacing frequently, to provide a fresh, tasty morsel for the salmon. He'd heard a fisherman claim that salmon ate nothing while in fresh water. He couldn't fathom the reasoning behind that theory, as the fish never failed to take the bait.

Will had cast upstream and, as usual, kept the line tight and watched it, as the fast-moving water washed it downstream, toward the deep, calm water of the pool. When slightly downstream from where he stood, it suddenly came to a halt. Although he couldn't see the bottom of the river, having fished in the same spot frequently, he knew the places to avoid getting his line snagged.

On the riverbed, green waterweeds waited like greedy vultures, ready to grasp his hooks, weights and, if he were not careful, even his line. He had never encountered a snag in that particular area, where his bait came to rest; he was unable to tell if it was a snag or whether he'd hooked a fish. All he knew for sure was that something had caused the bait to stop moving downstream.

In the past, Will had lost fish through being impatient. Now he decided to wait, and allow the fish time to swallow the bait, and have less chance of losing it.

After a wait of half a minute, he noticed the tip of his rod slowly bending downward, toward the water's surface. It was the first sign he was into a fish.

He struck hard, hoping to send the hook deep and permanent into the hard bone and cartilage of the fish's mouth. For a split second, Will thought he'd been mistaken as, usually when the fish feels the hook, it will immediately run with such speed and vigour, and if taken by surprise can snap any line like a strand of thread.

At first, Will thought he'd hooked a tree branch, a large clump of weed or another submerged object. Whatever the reason, his line hadn't been taken slowly downstream, and could do nothing about it. Speculating on what he was into and keeping level with the line, he followed it downstream, until it stopped at the head of the pool.

"Are you into one?" asked young Andy, having stopped fishing and joined him.

"I'm not really sure," Will admitted, "but if this is a fish, it's not got much life in it. The line just drifted down here and stopped."

"Give your line a jerk and see what happens."

Before Will could do anything, his line moved slowly away from them.

"You are into one, Will," declared Andy, turning to shout for all to hear: "Will's into a fish. I think it's a big one."

For over an hour, the fish went wherever it wanted, without showing itself. From all directions, Will got inundated with advice that he thought was not needed. The suggestions and tips flooded in, regardless:

"Let it run."

"Give it more line, Will."

"Try and bring it in."

The successive hints went on and on, but Will didn't mind in the least; they were all his friends and had his interest at heart. Besides, they were successful fishermen and he, until now, was not.

Unable to do anything else, Will followed the fish up and down the pool. It never once appeared, either. He hoped and prayed the fish would not try to escape by rushing from the pool with the speed of a runaway express train – that much he knew a salmon was capable of. Instead, all this fish appeared to want was to swim around in circles, like a goldfish in a bowl.

Will was suddenly reminded of the grumbling of a Scottish fisherman he met once. The Scot professed to have hooked a thirty-five-pound salmon, and stated it was like having a railway sleeper hooked to his line. And, while that huge fish swam around where it wanted, he could do nothing but follow it.

Will sighed. *I just hope that it makes a run out of the pool, and the way is clear for me to keep up.* He knew there would be no stopping it. *Be patient, and perhaps it will come close enough to be netted by one with the skill to land it at the first attempt.*

Will became so engrossed in his efforts, he completely forgot the presence of the other fishermen, who now stood on both banks, patiently waiting for him to land or lose the fish. They did this to avoid snagging his line, causing him to lose the fish. The other fishermen standing around the shore were obviously sportsmen, but also proved to be tolerant gentlemen, too, and at times shouted words of encouragement.

Will found his present situation just as the Scottish fisherman had said: the only useful factor was knowing where it swam, and that its possible capture lay in keeping the line taut.

Just before coming into the bank, where George waited, net in hand, its large tail fin broke the surface, and everyone gained an indication of the fish's size. With the skill and confidence of a man who knew exactly what he was doing, George, with one deft sweep, had the fish in the net and dragged it onto the shingle, where it was landed. Hardly daring to believe it, he peeped at the net and saw the fish: an enormous salmon.

"Must be all of eighteen pounds!" declared George. He handed Will the polished stout stick to dispatch the fish. "It's your first – unless you'd rather not do the deed."

Will felt proud, but uncertain. "You landed the thing for me. Show me how it's done properly."

George whacked the fish, just behind the eyes. It lay still, while scores of anglers drew round to admire the catch and congratulate Will. He received many a hearty slap on the back and countless praises. He took a deep breath and savoured the moment. Will could now call himself a true fisherman, at last.

Gradually, the other anglers drifted away, back to their posts, possibly inspired by Will's catch, and hoping that they too would land such a prize. Tom and Andy stood beside him, jubilant.

"Guess tonight's cause for a real celebration, eh?" commented Andy, while snapping a picture of Will holding his first salmon, on his digital camera.

Afterward, Will put the fish down and stared across the river, revelling in the glory. Right there and then, he suddenly wanted to tell his cousin Johnny all about his amazing first proper catch.

He turned to face his three friends. "I reckon so, but let's do it in style, eh, at The Leaping Salmon – make a right night of it? I reckon it's time you met me cousin."

CHAPTER 20

Party time

THAT EVENING, ANDY Thompson drove the Ford Fiesta up the winding road toward Glenstone. All were looking forward to meeting Will's cousin and having a good night. Will's friends had never been to The Leaping Salmon before, or met Johnny. They entered the village, drove past Johnny's house and made for the pub. "Hope there's somewhere to park," muttered Andy. He knew he'd have to remember not to overdo the booze that night, having to drive them back to their holiday cottage in the small hours.

Will spoke: "Don't worry; they got a car park round at the side, so Johnny tells me."

Andy nodded while admiring the scenery. Dusk hadn't quite fallen and he tried to memorize the route. He envisioned getting lost somewhere along the dark lanes on the return journey, and the four of them spending the night in the Fiesta, parked at the edge of a field, if they were lucky enough to find one with an open gate.

Will pointed ahead to a red-brick building: "There it is."

Andy slowed and drove into the car park. They got out.

"He frequents the public bar. Christ, he's in for a shock, I'll bet; I haven't seen him for around five years."

"How come?" asked Andy.

"Dunno, I just kind of stopped visiting when me uncle and auntie died; had no reason to call upon him. Maybe I should have done. By the way, his wife Annie died two years later, so whatever you do, don't mention her. Don't think the old bod ever got over it. Okay? Everyone agrees?"

"Not half," the three friends answered.

Having parked the Fiesta, they entered the public bar to find a thronging crowd of regulars, some standing and others sitting, hunched around small wooden tables.

"Where is he, then?" asked Tom.

Will looked around the room, then saw a familiar figure sitting in the far corner with two old men, and one rather younger. He smiled. "Hey, Johnny," he called.

Johnny Mason stared at the figure who hailed the greeting, for a moment completely stymied. Then, recognition slowly set in: was it his cousin from England? Will looked older, somewhat plumper than he remembered.

"Who's that?" asked Ben Furness, frowning at the group of strangers.

Johnny's eyebrows rose and he smiled. "Well, I'll be damned. It's me cousin."

Ben scratched his sideburn. "I thought that bastard McGee was your cousin."

Johnny nodded irritably. "Aye, he is, alas. But God saw fit ter endow me wi' two cousins."

"Ya never mentioned another cousin before," uttered Ben.

"Had no reason to; thought he was part and parcel of the past.

Seemingly not. Now, what can have brought him up here, I wonder?" Johnny waved to his cousin.

Will strode over to the table and the two cousins stared at each other for a moment. Will thought Johnny looked healthy enough, but seemed somehow gaunter? Without speaking, Johnny slowly rose to his feet. Then, the two men briefly embraced.

Johnny patted his cousin on the shoulders. "Been a long, long time," he said.

"How are you doing, Johnny?" Will asked.

"I'm still here, ticking along, like a clock far past its useful life."

Will laughed, remembering his cousin often came out with the cynical witticisms. "Good to see you again, really."

Will suddenly remembered his friends standing behind him, looking lost and rather sheepish. "Ah, Johnny, meet me mates. This is Andy Thomson, Tom Richards and the young one's George Martin." The old man shook their hands.

"What's good fer one is good fer the other; here's me drinkin' pals," said Johnny, waving his hand at the table: "Tom Stuart, Ben Furness and Bobby Burgess – our little heavy-drinking club." Johnny chortled at his wry comment.

"Heavy?" exclaimed Will. "Don't follow you?"

"Yer surprise me, cousin. Heavy – it's beer. Have yer nay heard o' it?"

Will shook his head, then clapped his hands. "Look, let's get crackin' with the ice breakers, eh? What's everyone drinking? First round's on me; I got something to celebrate."

Johnny smiled. "Make it four pints o' heavy, fer a start. What do yer drink?"

"Usually best bitter," Will replied.

"Aye, yer want ter try the heavy. You'll be surprised."

Will faced his friends. "What do you reckon? Shall we try this heavy?"

"I'm in," said George, with no hesitation.

"Eight heavies it is, then. George, you help ferry the drinks over." The two men strode to the bar.

"Hey, barman, make it eight pints of heavy. And, have you got a menu? We'd like to order food later."

Reg looked astonished, then smiled. "Glory be, it's Will Mason! Am I right?"

"You got it," replied Will. "Paying a flying visit to me cousin, Johnny."

Reg beamed. "Right, eight heavy it is. I'll send the menu over. Where are you sitting?"

"Johnny's corner, I guess," said Will, looking around the busy room.

Reg turned to Sally: "Get me a couple of trays, would you, love?" He placed the brimming pints onto the bar. "Long time since you been here. What's the occasion?"

Will took a deep breath. "Got something special to celebrate. But I want Johnny to be the first to know, like."

Reg nodded and took the trays from Sally. "Thanks, love. There you go; that'll be twelve-pounds-fifty." Will handed over a twenty-pound note like it was toytown money.

Will and George, each carrying a tray, returned to the corner.

Conveniently, another party vacated the circular table beside Johnny's group.

"There's timing. Draw that table closer over," said Johnny.

As the eight sat around the two tables, Will sipped the heavy, surprised by its distinctive tang. Johnny leant back in his chair. "So, cousin, what brings yer ter this part o' the world, eh?"

Will sat up. "Without bragging, I can honestly say I'm now a fully-fledged fisherman. This morning I landed an eighteen-pounder, me first salmon ever."

Johnny's brow furrowed slightly. "Really? Remarkable! Yer were never into fishing much before."

"I know, but it's great, isn't it? I reckon I'll fish to the last of my days now. It's almost like a drug, in a funny way. Hey, Andy, you got that camera?"

Andy smiled and brought the digital camera from his jacket pocket. Will flipped on the last image button; the image of him holding the catch flipped onto the screen. He handed the camera to Johnny.

"See? Living proof: fisherman of the year. All the anglers down the river were envious, too."

Johnny smiled wryly at his cousin's enthusiasm. "Fine picture, ter be sure." He handed the camera to his friends and all agreed the fish was a prize to be proud of landing. Bobby handed it back to Andy. He flipped it off and slid it back in his pocket.

"You all go fishin', then?" Johnny asked.

Will's friends all nodded. "Come up here quite regular," commented Andy, "but Will's new to the game. Done really well, though. Fast learner, he is."

Johnny's eyes narrowed. "Aye, yer can say that again."

"You used to fish at one time, didn't you?" Will stated.

"Still do, on and off," remarked Johnny. "In me own quiet way, that is."

George stared at the old man, realizing what he meant. "Blimey, you go poaching—"

Andy suddenly elbowed his young friend in the ribs, as much as to say shut up. George rubbed his side, flushed and squirmed.

Johnny stared at the youngster, and wondered how much he knew about foul-hooking, as his other cousin called it. To change the subject, he turned to Will: "And, how is Dot?"

Will shuddered on hearing the name. "Acrimonious as ever, I no tell a lie – more than ever. Partly why I come up here to fish."

Johnny smiled again, realizing how lucky he'd been to end up with Annie. He looked around the room intently for a moment, hoping Rona would show up, then turned back to the group.

"Therapeutic, fishing is," stated Johnny, "and very profitable, too, I might add."

Young George stared at the old man; he kept dropping these hints. George felt dead certain that Will's cousin was a poacher – a lone one working as an individual, just like he did in Droitwich Spa.

Bobby perked up when Sally brought four menu cards over to the table. "Here we are, gents. Oh yes, Dad says fresh, local-caught salmon is also on the menu again."

On hearing that, Johnny smiled quietly to himself, knowing exactly where the salmon had come from.

Bobby wasn't interested in the salmon, and watched her glide back toward the bar. Just recently he'd taken a shine to her. *If only,* he thought.

Andy broke the brief silence. "Okay, shall we give the salmon a go or have a steakhouse grill?"

Will sighed. "Much as I love it, we've kinda been feasting on salmon nearly all week, thanks to your culinary skills. Besides, we got that whopper in the fridge, too."

Andy smiled. "Right, I take it that remark means it's a steak, then?"

Will nodded and turned to Johnny. "What about you, cousin?"

"Generous ter offer, but up here us local folk scoff at home first; save the cash fer the beer. You carry on, though; seems your lot are starvin', anyhow."

Will grinned. "Understatement. Okay, lads, four steaks with all the trimmings, eh?"

"You said it," added Andy.

"Not half," replied Tom.

At the mention of food, Bobby felt his bowel heave unceremoniously. "Er, I gotta visit the bog. See yer in a tick."

Tom Stuart lit his pipe. "Don't forget to wash your hands."

Bobby scowled at him. "As if."

•

CHAPTER 21

Dinger's plan

BOBBY DASHED TO the corridor leading to the public toilets and dived into the gents. Glancing around, he saw nobody there and entered one of two cubicles; he slammed the door and sank onto the seat.

He heard somebody else enter the toilet – two people, in fact. He reached for the paper dispenser, wiped his rear off and was about to flush the toilet, when he recognized one of the speakers, and his blood curdled. It was Dinger Bell, he felt dead certain. Quiet as a mouse, he flipped the lid down and sat silent, listening.

Yeah, thought Bob, *that's Dinger alright, but who's he talking to?* He waited and listened, but couldn't make out the other person's voice.

"Listen, ye wee runt, in three nights' time we do the job, got it?" said Dinger's voice.

"Aye. Why wait ter then?"

"Weather's just right: be a clear sky but nay moon."

The furtive sound of shuffling footsteps echoed in the passage, alongside the washbasin near the window. It sounded as though the other man was nervous.

"Ye got the stuff, right?" the cowardly voice asked.

"Course I got the bloody stuff: a seven-pound tin o' that cymag.

Heh, it should knock all hell out o' that river!"

"Is nay dangerous, is it?"

"Nah, all we gotta do is punch several holes in tin and drop it in the water, a little after dusk. Four hours or so later we scoop up all the fish, dead easy. Get the others ter bring landin' nets and loads o' sacks; it's goin' ter be a big job."

"Yer planned it well, I gi' yer that."

"Ain't fucken' stupid, yer thicko."

"Where do we dump the tin?"

"Near that wee bridge: the one far downstream, away from the village. Got it?"

"Aye, that I have," replied the nervous man.

"I dinna want any fucken' mistakes. Cock this one up an' I'll bash yer brains inter wallpaper paste."

"No sweat."

"Better not be. I got a bloke in that supplies them bastards down at Billingsgate Fish Market. Once that cymag gets ter work, we'll clear every goddamned pool fer a mile downstream."

"Ain't doing it by halves, are yer?"

"Listen, yer weasel: get it right an' we'll end up wi' eight grand. That's two grand apiece."

"Jesus, canna wait."

"An' that's the way we work it: going downstream. This bloke's goin' ter wait in a black, unmarked van by the woods outside Ravencroft."

"Aye. Fucken' brilliant."

"Bloody better had be. Doin' it this way, we steer clear o' that bastard duke an' all his stinkin' bailiffs."

"Aye, ter be sure."

The sound of hands being washed ended all further conversation.

Bobby sat tight on the pan, hardly daring to breathe, and hoped Dinger hadn't noticed the closed door of his cubicle, as footsteps padded toward the door. A brief flurry of sounds from the bar echoed down the passage, before the toilet door closed again. Then, silence reigned in the gents'.

"Fucken' hell, that bloody maniac's gonna poison the river."

Almost in a panic, Bobby got up from the bowl, flushed the toilet and sped to the sink to wash his hands. Then, he made his way toward the bar.

●

CHAPTER 22

Rona's return

WHILE BOBBY PLAYED spies, eavesdropping on Dinger's conversation, Will and his friends got stuck into the steaks, washed down with plenty of beer. Andy decided to switch from the heavy to halves of light ale, as he was driving them back that night. He suddenly wished they were getting plastered in a hotel bar, so he could also go the whole hog. Still, it was Will's celebratory party, so they fell in with his plan.

George went to the bar for refills, when all of a sudden Rona dashed into the room, stared at the crowded scene and for a moment hesitated. Then, she saw Ben sitting with his friends and hurried over to him.

"Hi Uncle, back again – at least for a while." She kissed him upon the cheek. "What's everybody celebrating?"

Johnny smiled, "Me cousin here's just landed catch of the year: Moby Dick, no less."

"Spare me; whales don't swim up Scottish streams."

"Aye, well, who wants ter munch whale meat when there's plenty o' fresh salmon available, eh?"

Rona looked at him, puzzled. "Have I missed something here?"

"My cousin's being sarcastic, as usual," stated Will.

"Pull up a pew and join us," suggested Ben. "No point in sittin' all by yerself, unless you want to."

She smiled. "Right, will do. God, I need a drink first." Rona strutted off to the bar for a glass of house red.

George leant across to Andy; "She ain't half a right cracker."

Ben glanced at the pair and wagged a finger at them. "That's my niece you're leering over."

George blushed. "Sorry, old chap, no offence. She's real pretty, though."

Johnny agreed and watched her, too, but in reality was probably reminiscing over Annie, as she was before the demise of flower power.

While waiting for Reg to serve her, Rona saw Bobby dash out of the corridor from the toilets. He stared at her, unable to believe his eyes; she'd turned up at the vital minute.

Rona smiled. "Hi. You look like you've seen a ghost."

"Far from it. Er, Jesus, how do I say it?"

"Say what?" she replied, handing Reg a fiver on being served.

"Drink first, then I'll tell you."

She sipped the wine. "What's going on?"

"Okay, I... er... overheard a conversation in bo— er, toilet. A local poacher's goin' ter poison the river."

"What?! When, for God's sake?"

Bobby flustered and held his temples, desperately not wanting to fluff it. "In three nights' time, I think he said."

Rona frowned, working out the implications.

"Come on, miss, we gotta tell the others." He dashed back to the corner.

Tom tapped his pipe on the tin ashtray. "Wash your hands, did you?"

Bobby glared at him. "Yeah, funnily enough; small wonder I dinna forget. He was here in this place. Have ye nay seen him?"

Tom fiddled with the pipe. "Seen who?"

"That bastard Dinger Bell – he and a crony o' his."

Johnny cupped his chin. "All bad apples eventually turn up. I thought the peace was too good ter last."

Bobby hurriedly gulped a quart of heavy to calm his jangled nerves, then spoke. "Ya don't understand: I overheard him, while in the bog. He's plannin' ter poison the river, in three nights' time."

Rona sat down next to Ben and stared at the shaking man. "How's he going to achieve that?"

"Er, he'd got hold of a tin of something." Bobby struggled to remember the name of the chemical he heard Dinger mention. "He said it were a seven-pound tin of... cymer... or somethin' like that."

Rona's eyes widened, almost to the size of dinner plates. "You mean cymag?"

"Yer got it; that's the word: cymag."

Rona took a good, hard gulp of the wine, then raked around in her shoulder bag. "Hellfire! Where the hell is it?" She finally located her mobile phone and sped to the doorway of the bar.

Johnny glanced around the room for any sign of Dinger. If he'd been in, maybe he and his cronies had decided to hang around in the beer garden, as they usually do.

"Who exactly is this Dinger Bell person?" asked Will.

"Don't ask questions like that, cousin, and you'll live long enough ter see yer eightieth birthday."

Will drew a sharp breath. "That bad, eh?"

Johnny nodded, slowly.

George spoke up: "Hey, there's eight of us; we could do the bastard over."

"Aye, then some dark night, far from help, you'd run into a bunch o' his cronies. Nay thanks, laddie. He's best left well alone."

George smirked. "Not scared of him, are you?"

"No, I just got a wee bit more common sense than ter kick an angry savage beast. A crazed, demented one he is, too."

His last remark made George certain, more than ever, that the old man was a poacher. Without realizing it, he began to admire Will's mysterious cousin, whom he'd only known for just over two hours.

By the doorway, Rona dialled frantically, desperate to speak with Liam. Eventually she got through.

"Hi, Liam. Look, things are getting a bit heavy down here... Yeah, not half. Might be a cymag-poisoning scenario on the horizon... No, don't get the S.S.S.T.F. out just yet; it still might all be a hoax. I desperately need some help, though: can you send Adam down here? ... Great, and get the S.S.S.T.F. on possible standby, just in case. Okay, love you." She hung up.

Two hours later, being unused to the heavy, Will felt his head swim. But he was happy; the night had been a great success. He'd had his catch admired by all, then he, Johnny and the others spoke of great fishing victories, Andy and Tom Richards adding a few whopping lies into the bargain.

"One fer the road, then?" asked Ben Furness.

Will glanced at his watch and had difficulty focusing on the time, thought it was around midnight. Fortunately, on Saturday nights Reg had applied for an extension. And he got it, too.

"Aye, definitely," replied Johnny.

Will was really amazed by the amount of beer his cousin could sink, without appearing so much as tiddly. Then, he realized he knew little about his cousin, or what he got up to in the village.

George, on the other hand, strongly suspected that Johnny went out poaching. An old hand at the task, too. Perhaps the last of the loveable old rogues, so often portrayed in romanticized, nostalgic reminiscences of rural life. He speculated on his technique: perhaps he went "howking", with a huge, treble sea-angler's hook on his line, and dragged anything from the deep pools, the fish snagged on their side to be hauled ashore. Right then, George really would have loved to talk to the old man, but would he have reciprocated in kind? The years between them were two generations apart.

Ben and Tom trundled over with two more trays, loaded with pints of heavy and half a light ale for Andy. Will swigged from the pint, but really felt he couldn't cope with much more of the dark, tangy, slightly gassy liquid on top of the steaks, trimmings and packets of crinkle-cut chips, to soak up the wooziness which swept over him from time to time. He just hoped to avoid heaving up inside the Fiesta and spoiling the evening.

It was dead obvious that Bobby had had more than enough to drink, and toward the end of the evening tried the chatter patter with

Rona, partly due to the fact that he fancied her in his current state, and also to try and make Sally jealous. Every so often he glanced around to see if Sally was watching him. If she was, she wasn't falling for his little shenanigan. Nor was Rona; she knew he was pissed and merely played him along.

But, Rona *was* concerned about the tin of cymag.

"If that canister ends up in the river, the water will be ruined for years afterward. All aquatic life, not just the salmon, will be killed off," she warned the party.

Tom fiddled with his pipe. "What exactly is this cymag?"

"It's a mixture of sodium cyanide and magnesium sulphate. It looks like a white powder, generally used to kill vermin. But, when dropped in the water, cymag soaks up all the oxygen, killing everything."

Johnny stared at her, but saw Annie speaking. "Aye, but surely the winter floodwaters will wash away the stuff?"

She flinched. "Traces of cymag will still be left behind. Really, I mean it: that chemical is lethal. Oh, sorry; here I am ranting on, souring your cousin's celebration."

Rona suddenly hugged Ben's arm. "Uncle, could you put up with having another guest? I've got a colleague arriving to help me out. By the sound of things, I'm going to need it."

Ben smiled at his niece. "At this rate, I might open up a bed and breakfast. Of course it's alright. Who is he?"

"Adam Burk, assistant environmental officer. Young, but brilliant at his job."

"Heh! Yes, no worries."

"Thanks, Uncle." She pecked him on the cheek, making Bobby squirm with envy.

"Time, gentlemen and ladies, please," bellowed Reg. "Empty yer glasses now; it's long past my bedtime."

Sally flitted around the tables collecting the empties, flirting mildly with one or two of the local lads, and casting a glance at Bobby, to make sure he got the message.

Johnny sighed. "Aye, time ter make tracks, I guess. Well, cousin Will, what a right surprise you turnin' up, an' no mistakin' it. How long are yer up here fer?"

Will had lost all track of time; wasn't even sure where he was. He peered at Johnny. "Lordy buggered if I can remember! I think we got one more morning up here. Rented a cottage down the hillside somewhere."

Johnny smiled at his cousin, and could see he'd had a happy evening – though, by the look of it, the heavy had hit home. "Aye, yer probably wake up wi' a rare stinker in the mornin', I reckon."

Will gave him a bleary glance and smiled back. "Hope not; I was looking forward to landing another salmon." Will patted Johnny on the shoulder, once again. "Maybe one day we'll get together again, eh? Even go fishin', like."

Johnny smiled. "Fishin', eh? Heh! We'll see. But drop in anytime; I'm always here."

With a hearty round of handshaking, everyone said their goodbyes. George even squeezed Rona's hand, though in reality he wanted to give her a great, juicy smack on the lips, but thought better of it, with Ben present.

Will remembered very little about the journey back to the holiday cottage. When stepping out of the bar to get to the car park, the fresh air hit him and made the wooziness ten times worse. Andy grinned, but feared for the inside of the Fiesta. He drove them down the hillside, but in the pitch-black took a wrong turn, backtracked and by two o'clock they saw the familiar, single-storey cottage.

Will couldn't believe they'd been to see Johnny, and how he looked so gaunt. Having shed their coats, everyone decided to hit the sack, as they described it. Will was glad to have a proper bed that night. He slid under the duvet and sank back, his mind a kaleidoscopic whirl of emotion, before darkness overcame him.

As Johnny had predicted, the first thing that struck Will next morning was a dull, searing throb along the base of his brain. The back of his eyeballs ached and his mouth felt like the inside of a parrot's cage. He turned over, which made him feel dizzy, and groaned. He shifted onto his back again and, even with the duvet, felt rather chilled. He swore there and then never to touch another drop of booze, and concentrated on that thought. For another half-hour he lay in torpor, then felt a pressing need for the toilet.

Having spent what seemed like twenty minutes peeing, he rinsed his hands and face, took a deep breath and thought some fresh air might clear away the fuzziness. The idea of brushing his teeth at that moment was repugnant.

He slipped his corduroys and anorak on and slipped out of the door. The morning was fresh, bright, invigorating and reassuring.

At the base of the hillside, the river glinted invitingly. Olive-green trees hemmed in fields, and the hills in the distance looked emerald. He wanted the last morning of their break to be a good one. He sat on the low brick wall to admire the spectacular scenery, and took slow, deep breaths to clear the stale odour of beer from his lungs.

From behind, he heard the sound of gravel scrunching and turned. He saw George approaching, grinning. "Hi, Will. You didn't half get plastered last night."

Will scowled. "That bloody beer was a trite powerful. Don't reckon I'll go for that stuff again."

"Weren't light ale, that's for sure. Head hurt, does it?"

"Feel right fuzzy and nauseous. Weak in the knees, too."

George grinned again and withdrew a tin of Coca Cola from his anorak pocket. He pulled the ring and its sweet, fizzy scent hit Will's nostrils. He handed the can to Will. "Here, get some of that down you – slowly does it, at first. It'll clear your head and settle the stomach."

Will looked at the can, dubiously. "Are you sure?"

"Bloody know it." He took a second can out of his pocket, tugged the ring and sipped away. "Ah, that's better already. I reckon I could face one of Andy's breakfast specials now."

Will sipped more of the sweet, sugary liquid, and did indeed feel better for it. "Odd, isn't it? I'd have thought the gassy drink would have made me want to spew."

"Mate of mine told me about it; he found out by accident. Funny, ain't it, how most good things come about by chance?"

Will took another sip. "Say it again. This stuff made me feel a ton better already."

George laughed. "Yeah, little things fall out of the woodwork now and then. Bits of info mentioned in conversation, that you'd never dream possible."

Will looked at his young friend. "Are you making a point here, or what?"

He grinned at Will. "Kind of. That cousin of yours goes fishing, don't he?"

Will tried to recall Johnny's past activities. "At one time he started fishing with line and rod. Didn't like it much; he gave up."

"I reckon he still does. Not with a rod, though."

Will suddenly felt confused. "What are you saying?"

"I reckon he's a poacher. All night long he kept passing odd comments. If he didn't fish, how would he know it was a profitable venture, eh?"

Will frowned, rubbed his forehead and glared at George. "Johnny, a poacher? Don't talk rot."

"I ain't. I'm bloody certain he's got a little racket going."

Will realized he knew very little about his cousin, apart from the fact that his parents and wife were dead. He'd no idea how Johnny filled in his days. He appeared to have no hobbies or pastimes, save for frequenting the pub with his friends each evening, and that was it! Where did he get the money to pay for the drinks? He dismissed the thought. "Aw, rubbish! I suppose you know all about poaching?"

"Actually, I do. Back home, I go tickling trout with a green light and a rabbit snare."

Will almost dropped the can of Coke in amazement. "What?!"

George grinned. "Dead easy; never been caught. Never plan to be, either."

"Bloody hell, I'm gobsmacked! What made you start?"

George shrugged. "Accidental discovery, really. Went sea-angling one night and the skipper dropped a green light on a float over the side; drew in the fish. So, I guessed the same trick would work on the river. It does, too. Dunno why, but green seems right attractive to fish – any fish."

"Do the others know?"

George shrugged again. "Who knows? Even if they suspected, I don't reckon they'd shop me. What would they gain, except losing me friendship?"

Will blew his breath. "This fishing trip's certainly been an eye-opener. Do you reckon, if Johnny does go poaching, he uses a green light, then?"

"Probably has a similar technique. I just know he goes out and snags the odd fish now and then, like I do. Nothing on a large scale, mind. Kind of takes a fisherman to know a fisherman, if you see what I mean."

Will didn't know what to think. He couldn't imagine Johnny poaching, yet he couldn't argue with anything that young George had said. He suddenly felt very intrigued by his cousin. Before he knew it, he'd finished the Coke and felt much better for it. Then, maybe he'd suddenly sobered up on hearing George's speculation.

"The others should be awake now. Come on, let's get some brekkies. We still got a morning left to land another catch."

The two men walked back up to the cottage.

On that last morning, the fine weather held. Andy dished up a hearty, pan-fried breakfast of smoked bacon, eggs and potato bread, along with button mushrooms, to use up their supplies.

Afterward, they paraded along to the river, cast their lines, baited with the last of the worms, and hoped for a catch. Andy landed a small, four-pound salmon and everyone cheered.

Then, at around eleven o'clock, Will felt his line being snagged, the tip bent toward the water. The line moved downstream and he followed it, playing the fish he knew must be hooked below the water. Then the fish moved back upstream, to more or less the same spot where he'd cast. Tom and Andy saw he was into a fish and raced over.

"George, get that net over here," Tom called.

Quite suddenly, the fish splashed out of the surface. They saw it was a medium-sized specimen. Will kept the line taut and reeled in, while George stood by the water's edge, ready to land the fish. Will couldn't believe it: his second catch! What a finish to the week! Desperate not to lose the fish, he cautiously reeled in. George scooped the net into the water, landed the fish and brought it ashore. Will gazed at the salmon and judged it to be around ten pounds.

"Your go this time; one last task to master: you gotta learn to dispatch them," stated Tom, handing him the stout, polished stick made for the job. Will took a deep breath, snatched the stick and whacked the fish, just behind the eyes. It fell back, motionless.

Tom clapped him on the back. "Now you're a true fisherman."

Will grasped the dead salmon, realizing he'd reached a new point in his life. "Couldn't have done it without your help, though," he told his three friends. "Without sounding a tad corny, I'm hooked for life, I really am. When are we making the next trip up here? I can't wait."

"Hark at him! Master fisherman now, eh?" Andy chortled.

Tom spoke up: "We still got that whopper Will landed, too." He turned to face Will. "I reckon landlord of The Badger, Les Hopkins, will be happy to give you a fair price for those two fish. Then he's got salmon on the menu forevermore."

"Do you think so?" Will remarked.

George smiled. "Bloody certain. You'll get eighty pounds, at least. Maybe a bit more."

Will felt overwhelmed. Surrounded by his friends, and with two fish in the bag, he realized his life was never going to be the same again. He was inspired and had gained a new confidence. Even the thought of returning home to face Dot paled to insignificance.

He nodded and smiled. "Come on, lads, let's pack up and get home."

•

CHAPTER 23

Adam's demise

ADAM BURK WAS deep in thought, as he drove along the A75 toward Glenstone from Dumfries, intrigued by the new mission and eager to help Rona. He was very enthusiastic indeed. He adored her – almost worshipped the ground that she trod on. He also wanted to impress his boss Liam, and gain a better post in the organization he relished working for.

He took the turning for Glenstone and drove along the hillside lanes. He felt proud that anyone seeing his white Ford Transit van, with SEPA's blue and green logo on the side, would be aware he worked for an important outfit. The pollution hotline number emblazoned on the side also increased his sense of status.

Adam knew this was a special chance, a make-or-break situation, to change the outcome of his life. At twenty-six years of age, he felt it was time to get somewhere. He wanted to purchase a little flat in Dumfries, get settled and gain a pay rise, yet remain dedicated to the aims of SEPA.

And, just maybe... He didn't dare think that he could possibly win Rona over; she was five years his senior. But he often thought: *What the hell; nothing ventured...* He kind of got the idea that, if he impressed her enough, anything might be possible.

Adam hated folk who had a disregard for nature, people with no qualms about poisoning the land or the rivers. This outlook was the main reason why he chose to become an environmental officer in the first place. He'd been through college and university, studied the relevant subjects, passed the qualifications and become an environmental scientist, which led him to his present position. Of course, he often worked long hours for no extra pay, but he didn't mind; it was all part of the job he loved and enjoyed.

He peered through the windscreen, having to slow down periodically, for the tricky business of negotiating the winding country lanes. He wasn't too familiar with the countryside in this district.

Okay, he thought, *must keep an eye open for The Leaping Salmon.* That was the pub Rona had arranged to meet him in, rather than get him to try and find the home of her uncle Ben, one of the villagers.

He saw the hedges on both sides of the narrow roads were in full bloom, filled with berries of all kind: haws, blackberries, sloe, holly, rowan and guelder rose. The leaves were tinged with the gold and tan hues of a deepening autumn. He liked autumn, in as much as he liked spring: the ever-changing cycle of the seasons. It was a joy that came with the job, even though many a day was spent sitting in the office, checking data on spreadsheets, updating records, filing and archiving documents. All part of the job to ensure that nature would remain untarnished.

He drove along the hillside road leading toward Glenstone and, before long, saw the village up ahead, with a scattering of cottages on the outskirts. He kept a sharp lookout for the red-brick pub.

Then he saw the building, with a swinging sign bearing an image of a salmon jumping over river rapids, in its bid to get to the breeding grounds. This truly was The Leaping Salmon. He drew up in the pub's car park.

As he got out of the car, he noticed Rona coming out of the pub's door. She waved at him. "Hi. Made it, then?"

"Yeah, no problem."

"Glad you got here."

"What's going on? Liam hinted about some kind of poisoning scam," said Adam, wanting to sound all knowledgeable about the reason for coming.

"Come on, let's grab a coffee; the landlord does hot beverages and brekkies. Have you eaten?"

"Yeah, I had breakfast. But, after that drive, I wouldn't mind a toastie."

Rona smiled. "I'll bet."

At her usual corner table, she explained all about Bobby overhearing the conversation, and of the grisly, almost skinless salmon she'd found a few days ago.

"Liam filled me in with the details about G.S. I guessed it might turn up," stated Adam.

"We're not dead certain it is G.S.; I'm still awaiting the results from Kay. Meanwhile, if this poacher drops that can of cymag in the river…"

"Gonna be curtains, ain't it? Shit, who'd think of doing anything like that? How could they?"

Rona frowned. "Some pretty despicable types live out here.

They're desperate to make money; there are not many jobs, and the opportunities in a village like this are few and far between."

"Kind of seems rather obvious."

Reg entered the bar, placed a tray on the counter and called out: "Coffee for two and a toasted bacon sandwich."

Rona walked over to the bar. "Thanks, it's much needed."

Reg glanced at the young man. "Not seen him in here before."

"Don't worry, he's a colleague, come to help."

Reg's eyebrows rose. "Really? Is something going on that I don't know about?"

Rona replied: "We are here as environmental officers, to carry out water tests, which I've been doing for the last few days. Unfortunately for us – or fortunately, as this is a beautiful village – the river is far bigger than estimated, so more tests are needed. Should be finished in a few days."

Reg nodded and returned to the pub's kitchen.

Adam looked around, noticing the room was empty, except for one soul standing at the bar with a pint. "Hardly doing a roaring trade, are they?"

"It's early in the day yet. They get packed out in the evenings."

Adam ate the toasted sandwich and mused over the bad news. "Why choose cymag, of all things?"

"Stuff's easy enough to get hold of, and it's very effective in the water, too. Jesus, if that tin ends up in the river, it could become lifeless for almost two years, if not longer. This community will simply fall apart; everyone here depends on salmon for a living, one way or another."

Adam wiped his lips with the napkin. "Yeah, what a bleak prospect."

"Understatement. And the impact on—"

"Don't even mention it; I read up previous reports about poachers messing around with cymag. Shit, what a mess. Who's the person planning to use the stuff?"

"A local low-life dropout called Dinger Bell, apparently. He's been unemployed for years."

"Figures. I guess he'd have contacts for his catch. It sounds as though he plans to clear the entire river, or a large chunk of it."

"That's not the only thing wrong. There's a large salmon farm upriver, near Rosstown – it seems they've been discharging wastewater from their tanks, into the river. Liam says Kay has found high levels of cypermethrin in the water samples I took back."

"Unbelievable. They must have been adding Deosect, or a similar substance, to knock back lice infestation."

"I know, and that dead fish just might have been infected with lice."

"But you said it was G.S."

Rona sipped from the cup. "I can't be certain until Kay finds out; it could be either. I'd rather it wasn't G.S., otherwise widespread poverty and destitution are going to devastate communities like this one, and not just in Scotland."

"G.S. could affect the whole of the U.K., couldn't it?"

"In a way we've never before known. It's terrifying to think about."

"As I see it, we're facing a two-prong adversity here: one, we've got G.S. hanging over us; second, the possibility of a river catastrophe, if it does get poisoned. Which do we tackle first?"

"Both together, if possible, and as we come to them. He isn't going to move for another two days. But he's a thug; even most local folk seem dead terrified of him."

"Do we know where he's going to strike?"

"About four miles downstream, I've been told. I've alerted the S.S.S.T.F. I found out this poacher is going to start shortly after dusk. The S.S.S.T.F. are going to send a party of water bailiffs and a couple of coppers along to the bridge, where they plant to start. I just hope this isn't going to turn out to be a hoax."

"What makes you think that?"

"I got all this information off the village idiot. Well, actually he's not that bad, but a bit on the simple side. But, on his word alone, I'm setting up a task force to tackle this threat. Unfortunately, I'll never hear the last of it should this operation come to nothing."

"Yeah, but what about the cymag?"

"We still don't know for certain that anyone has a tin of cymag."

Adam scowled. "I don't like this one jot. Too much is left to chance."

Rona smiled. "That's life, isn't it? Things are never cut and dried outright. Come on, let's get the van shifted before this place fills up with regulars. You can also meet my uncle Ben; he's agreed to put you up."

"Sounds great."

For the next two days, Adam got into a new routine and, after breakfast at Ben's, he and Rona set about taking more water samples and pH readings, to complete the task. Most of all, he loved driving around in the Transit van, to different parts of the river, and admired the scenery, which by now looked pretty spectacular; many of the trees were already turning deep cerise, especially the sycamores dotted here and there.

There was the odd surprise, too. While tramping along the riverside paths, many times pheasants would break cover from the thick vegetation, running and flying across the open ground, to find sanctuary in the next bit of cover. In the distance, foxes could be seen skulking around the edges of a field, probably on the hunt or patrolling their territorial boundaries. He'd found in recent years that foxes were becoming increasingly active during daytime, but had little idea why.

Tiny things were a delight to find, too. In the mild, sunny weather, hosts of dragonflies flew along the watercourses, hovering over the still pools and, on the odd occasion, getting snapped up by a trout or salmon. This particular river did seem incredibly rich in wildlife, and he decided it needed to be preserved.

Adam was surprised by the number of fishermen along the banks, either side of the stone bridge at Glenstone. He knew nothing of the duke, or of The Grouse in the Heather.

He sighed, softly. "This stretch of the river is fantastic. Scottish Natural Heritage should be managing this site for its ecological interest. Jesus, think of it! They could have a field study centre, observation platform, and facilities where parties of schoolkids and students could come and learn about our natural heritage."

Rona smiled at him. "It's a gorgeous idea, but for one thing."

"What? I reckon it's worth doing."

"So do I, but it's not a moneymaker. Besides, a certain land magnate holds sway over a large tract of this river. Few oppose him and even the local judge curries his favour, as I've recently found out."

"All the same old crap, isn't it? For hundreds of years the elitists have run roughshod over the rest of us, and they're still at it. Why should those rich bastards decide who can walk across the land, or seek to enjoy what nature has to offer? One day, ordinary folk are going to have to challenge them. What they're doing isn't sustainable."

"I realize that, but who is going to argue?" she replied.

"Dunno, but it ain't fair. It really can't be a just system. We're supposed to be living in a democracy, goddammit. These land-grabbing elitists just make that word sound like a sour joke."

Rona grinned. "You should have been a political activist."

"No thanks, I prefer working with nature. But, I guess what we're doing is pretty much the best we can achieve right now."

"That's exactly how I feel. That's why I joined SEPA."

"Me too. I just wish things were on a more equal footing. Not difficult to see why some local folk turn to poaching, is it? They've been robbed of their right to natural resources, just so the wealthy can fill their coffers."

"Depends how they go about it, I suppose. Poaching has become a national menace. It's not the odd villager snatching a fish or two that's the problem; it's the organized crime syndicates in the cities, getting in on the act. And they do it wholesale, too; make thousands in one night! The countryside is under threat."

"Yeah, and it's down to people like us to stop them, I guess."

Adam glanced toward the west and noticed the sun beginning to set. "It's getting late. We'd best make tracks back to the van."

That evening, in The Leaping Salmon, he and Rona sat at her table, updating the pH records on the laptop. Clear indications showed the river water was far too acidic to be beneficial to fish or other aquatic wildlife.

While standing at the bar, to order a pint of ale and a glass of house red, Adam realized it was the night he must set out to achieve his aim. He'd formulated a plan to gain incriminating evidence against the man calling himself Dinger, and put a stop to the cymag venture. He also desperately wanted to make a big impression on Rona. He took the drinks over, then bided his time.

He saw four men in a far corner, one of them Rona's uncle Ben, and another old man smoking a pipe. Obviously, they were all friends and the village pub regulars. One looked a little younger than the others.

"Is that your uncle and his cronies over there?"

Rona looked up from the laptop. "Cronies? Not a word I'd like to use. Friends, yes, not cronies."

"Sorry, I didn't mean to—"

"Forget it."

Adam felt tense. Tonight was his big chance; he needed an excuse to leave. By now, he saw the public bar getting busier with regular patrons. A fair crowd milled around the bar.

"I fancy some crisps," he stated, trying to sound casual. Rona nodded, while ensconced fingering the mousepad.

He sidled around to the far side of the crowd, then slipped out the back door, into the night air.

Once aboard the van, he drove off toward the large stone bridge. Adam decided he would walk the distance along the riverside, to the little bridge downstream, where the Dinger felon was supposed to be planning his dirty escapade. Driving down the lane in the near pitch-black was difficult enough, and twice he brushed heavily against the thick hawthorn hedge. Soon, he recognized the slight hump of the small stone bridge ahead, and saw a gap in the hedgerow on the southern side. He decided it was wide enough to drive through, but entering the field he scraped the van's sides on bushes. He parked the van under some trees alongside the smooth-running river.

He got out, changed his yellow day-glow jacket to a black duffel coat and made sure he had a torch, and his digital camera with infra-red enhancement. He quietly closed the van door, locked it and strode along the path, savouring the cool night air, confident, yet also highly aware of the danger which may lie ahead. He'd been on a couple of field survival training exercises, though not with the ambition of doing anything remotely connected with the military;

he'd simply assumed that, one day, when the Earth's resources were depleted, the only survivors would be people who could live off the land.

Surefooted and alert, he walked quickly along the riverside path. The night was clear; the stars shone like a smattering of diamonds on black velvet. Every so often he heard the splash of a fish in the water – a trout, no doubt – finding its supper. Now and again he would hear the barking of dogs, far away in the distance. How far, he could not say, but in the still night it seemed pretty near.

Then, Adam stopped briefly for a rest, took stock of where he was, and reckoned he'd covered half the distance.

He knew exactly what he was going to do: get a shot or two of the felons carrying the cymag tin. He wanted evidence that could be used in a court of law; an exhibit that would get the Dinger man slammed behind bars for a long time, or at the very least a hefty fine of two- or maybe even three-thousand pounds. With a bit of luck, the local rag or village newsletter would publicize the arrest. He hoped and prayed the four water bailiffs from the S.S.S.T.F. would turn up at the arranged time.

He set out again along the next part of the path, aware now of the danger he was approaching. That was partly why he'd also chosen to wear sneakers that night, instead of his sturdy field boots. Silence was the key to successful stalking in the countryside, as anywhere else, he guessed.

He knew the men might be dangerous, maybe armed with knives or other weapons. It wasn't even unknown for poachers from the cities, working in big gangs, to use sawn-off shotguns. They were vile, highly organized, and often involved in working for drug barons. These men were dangerous. On one occasion, he'd spoken to the superintendent of Dumfries and Galloway Fisheries Board, and been told that poaching was the second most profitable illegal activity in the region, after drugs. He didn't doubt those words. He found out that city thugs usually operated in gangs of eight, were dressed in camouflage gear and used lightweight mono-filament nets, which could easily be fitted into a jacket pocket. Netting was the favourite method they used. Some gangs refused to turn out unless they were guaranteed to snare a hundred or more salmon in one night. Even the clumsiest gang could clear a pool of ten or more beautiful salmon in minutes. He shuddered at the thought.

He'd heard about cymag poachers, the most debased of all: indiscriminate killers, and usually men that nobody would employ. That description, Adam thought, seemed to fit everyone's idea of this Dinger Bell person. He detested anyone defiling the natural world for short-term gain, and was feeling a deep loathing for the Dinger character, as he pressed on along the path.

He noticed the waterside vegetation around this part of the river was particularly thick. Lush, tall reeds and other waterside herbage, now spent, were rank and rusted in colour.

A moorhen suddenly flew out from the thick foliage and, flying low over the river surface, soon found safety on the far bank. This small incident added more stress to Adam's already tense and alert body. He stopped and listened, but could detect no other sound than the occasional gurgle of the water passing over a boulder. All was, so far, as he'd planned.

He continued his journey toward the smaller bridge, some two miles south of Glenstone, ever wary, and also feeling his pulse begin to race. He gulped and glared at the river: it looked dark; a ribbon which occasionally glinted, reflecting the starlight.

For the first time, he began to have reservations. Was he doing the right thing? Had the rush to impress Rona gone to his head? Was the Dinger man as dastardly as some folk might have cracked him up to be? He'd never met Dinger, and had no way of telling. But Rona had arranged for the party of water bailiffs to arrive, so maybe he was pretty safe, providing they arrived on time.

Up ahead, he saw the shape of the small bridge, which was much lower than the main one at Glenstone. Careful to remain silent, he stepped forward, but gradually began to feel a vague unease. He'd not been this apprehensive in a long while. For the first time that evening, he contemplated backtracking along the path, to the safety of his van, thinking that there would be enough officials to take on the poachers; after all was said and done, they would be armed and able to tackle the poachers easily.

He looked back over his shoulder and saw the distance he'd covered. It would be a waste of effort and time to retreat now, and he'd go back no better off than he was now. Rona would be proud of him, should he succeed now. He took a deep breath and made his way along the track, toward the small bridge.

He took out his small telescope, focused it and, in the gloom, could make out the shapes of three men standing in the middle of the bridge talking, one resting on the parapet, holding what looked like a tin – he guessed it might be the tin of cymag. Adam cautiously edged forward along the path, careful not to make any sound. He thought the men looked furtive, and noticed that the shorter chap kept glancing around, obviously on the watch for any unwanted strangers.

Adam took his camera out of his coat pocket and focused on the group, hoping the infra-red would show enough detail. He took three or four shots, then slipped the camera back into his duffel coat. "Done it. Got them."

Feeling bolder, he decided to try and get closer still, to ensure the pictures would be clear enough when he got them back to the lab. He crept along the path until he could hear their voices. Adam then reached for the camera again.

Out of the darkness, from behind, he suddenly felt a rough hand grab the back of his duffel coat's collar.

Before he knew it, the man's other hand gripped his upper arm tighter than a vice, and dragged him along the path. Unable to see who had attacked him, Adam struggled to break free, but the man held on, bellowing out: "Ya fucken' shite! Ya said it were all safe doon 'ere'!"

His angry remonstration drew the other men's attention, as he dragged Adam along to the bridge. "Then 'ow come this fucken' bastard's snoopin' round, eh? Yer pissed this up ternite, ain't yer?" On the bridge, the enraged man shoved Adam to the ground.

Dinger glared at the speaker. "Fuck! I dinnae believe this. Wheer'd 'at bastard come from?"

"Found 'im snoopin' among bushes yonder," snapped the aggravated man, pointing his filthy thumb at the path. "Ye promised nothin' wus gonna go wrong. Ye pigshit thickhead."

Dinger shook his fist at the speaker. "Watch yer fucken' mouth!" He spun on Adam; "Whit yer see? Tell us or I'll kick yer fucken' face in."

Adam trembled and felt sick. He was dead certain he had just made the biggest mistake of his life in coming here on his own, knowing he could have had backup catching these wild men. He prayed the police would turn up now. He came to realize that these weren't humans, but wild, savage beasts, primordial and far beyond rationality. "Nothing. Honest."

"Lyin' bastard! Ye were takin' shots o' us." The rough handler snatched the camera from his coat pocket. "See? A fucken' spy, workin' fer bailiees."

Dinger rubbed his stubbly chin, unsure what to do.

"We been fucken' rumbled," the other snarled.

Dinger grasped Adam's coat lapels and hauled him to his feet. "Who else is oot 'ere, eh?"

Adam flinched away from Bell, sickened by his rancid, stinking breath and mouthful of rotted, smashed teeth. "Answer me, ya bas'!"

"No one," Adam whispered, hoping and praying for the bailiffs to turn up.

"Liar!" snapped Dinger. "Who sent ya? Where's yer soddin' cow-son cronies?"

Struggling to quell the fear and steel his voice, he answered: "Nobody sent me, really. Honest to God, man, listen."

Dinger shoved him aside, paced around on the bridge, appearing uncertain what to do next.

The little weasel man barged forward. "He'll git the law doon on us fer sure. Bastard's seen us, he has. We've 'ad it."

Dinger spun on his miserable accomplice; "Shut yer trap, O'Shaig, or ah'll shut it fer ye. We dun nuffin' yet – nuffin' 'em bastard pollis can stick on us."

"Aye, nothin', and 'at's just it. Dinna ferget 'at fish dealer bloke's waitin' fer us, too."

On hearing O'Shaig's words, Dinger exploded in rage. "Ya dinna need ter remind me!" He grabbed Adam and shoved him forward. "Gi' off ye bridge, bastard."

Another of Dinger's associates hauled him onto the riverside path. Then, he shoved Adam toward Dinger. Adam held out his hands to stop toppling to the ground, and smelt the wild man's greasy, foetid coat. Dinger kicked him away.

"Whit wi' gonna doo? Cannae let ye sod go," one of the cronies whined.

Dinger glared at the speaker, then drew a baseball bat from his inside coat pocket, and brought it crashing into the back of Adam's skull, with a sickening crunch. Adam fell face down into the wet grass and lay still. Dinger sneered: "That's whit we'll dae; see 'ere. Nay, let's get on wi' it."

One of the strange men backed away. "Nae, I'll nae be part o' this."

"Ye dare back oot noo an' I'll finish ye."

The other man slowly backed away. "Yer a mad fucker, ya knoo."

Enraged, Dinger glared at the fallen, motionless man again. "Bastard!" he spat. "Bastard!" He smashed the baseball bat down on the back of Adam's head, again and again. "Ye fucken' bastard! Ye shit up ma plan. Bastard!" On the seventh blow, the tall crony grabbed Dinger's arm.

"Ye fucken' killed 'im, ya mad bastard. Ya fucken' killed 'im."

Dinger took a deep breath, focused on the target of his rage, and saw the bloody, smashed skull; in the half-light he could make out the blood flowing from the terrible wounds inflicted. He didn't care. He was Dinger, the toughest man in the village, and no one crossed him.

"Ya dun it this time. Yer fucken' dunnit!" cried the other wild man. "Jesus, yer a soddin' maniac, yer know 'at?"

Dinger dropped the bat and swayed, drew a half bottle of Scotch from the other pocket and swigged, greedily. He shoved the bottle back into his pocket and rubbed his dirty hands down his cheeks, trying to think.

"Chuck 'im in river. Get rid o' 'im, ya mug."

"No way! Am nae being accomplice ter this. Yer way out o' line. I'll nae touch 'im, yer hear." The tall man backed away.

The fourth crony spoke up: "Aye, he be right, an' all, yer stupid, crazed butcher! Ah'm nae goin' down wi' ya."

"Yer a fucken' spineless coward, are ye? Do it me fucken' sel', then." He grabbed the bloodied duffel coat of the dead man and dragged it toward the river's edge. Then, he rolled the corpse over the edge.

Slowly, Adam's inert body floated away downstream. No more

would the young environmental officer strive to protect the wonder of the natural world he so revered.

While the corpse drifted away on the swift current, Dinger and his associates stood on the riverbank, bickering.

The tall felon stepped forward; "Ah'm fucken' getting ootae here, an' if ah ever sees yae again, ya best watch oot. Ah'm nae goin' doon wi' ya fer being accomplice ter murder." He turned to his mate from Ravencroft: "Whit say yae?"

"Aye, I never wannae get in wi' that 'un, ever. Best make plans tae clear oot, noo, afore bailiees come."

The two wild men sloped off across the bridge, to the footpath leading up the hillside toward Ravencroft village. Dinger and O'Shaig were left alone, his grand plan shattered, like the battered skull of Adam Burk.

The weasel rubbed his hands. "Whit the fuck are we gonna doo the noo?"

Dinger glared at him, then glanced down at the blood-spattered baseball bat. He began to experience the shakes, with the full impact of knowing that his temper had finally got him into deep, deep trouble. He snatched the bottle and drank the last dregs of Scotch.

"Quit fartin' aboot." O'Shaig pointed to the bloody bat. "Pollis get one swatch o' that an' weer done fer. All they need's a murder weapon, ye noo."

Dinger snatched the bat and stared at it. "Ah'll hae ter burn it; make sure they dinnae find it." He rammed the bat inside his internal coat pocket, then walked over to the bridge, grabbed the cymag tin and turned to O'Shaig.

"Dinnae hang aboot; best get back ter Glenstone the noo."

Dinger and his weasel cohort tramped along the river path, desperate to leave. All the while, O'Shaig heard the wild, angry man muttering under his breath: "Eight stinkin' grand up the fucken' spout. Eight grand! That fucken' bastard!"

Dinger was desperate to get home, hoping that his wife hadn't let the fire die down. O'Shaig also lived in Glenstone, in a squalid shack at the far end of the village, a place shunned by all local inhabitants.

They'd got halfway toward the stone bridge at Glenstone, when O'Shaig spoke: "Whit yer gonnae do wi' that tin? Ya cannae keep it: evidence wi' planned ter poison yon river."

Dinger glared at the tin like it was a lump of plutonium. "Aye, yer right fer once."

Hastily, he wiped the tin with his coat tail, hoping all trace of fingerprints was erased. He tore off his ragged neck scarf and lifted the tin, then slung it among the rank, weed-infested thicket alongside the path.

O'Shaig looked dubious. "Cannae be sure it's hidden away fer good?"

Dinger turned on the weasel; "Nae fucken' time ter argue. Any poacher coulda dropped it, eh? Now let's gi' the fuck oot ah here."

They strode along the path. It was now gone one o'clock, and Dinger felt desperate and also very scared. He got the impression that something wasn't quite right.

On approaching the gap to the road, at the stone bridge, they both saw the white Transit van. For a moment, O'Shaig stood stock-still.

"Whit the hell's that?"

Dinger paced forward, unable to believe it. "How the fuck should ah' knoo?"

The little man followed him toward the van and saw the SEPA logo and pollution hotline on the vehicle's side. The full realization of events crashed down on him.

"Holy mother o' shite! Yer really dun it! Yer duns in some clown workin' fer that outfit. Jesus wept, man!"

Dinger stared at the van. "Fuck! That bas' must o' been trackin' us."

"Aye, an' his workmates are goin' ter come lookin' fer 'im, an' all."

Dinger suddenly grabbed the little man by his jacket lapels; "Shut it, ya wee bastard! An' nae a word aboot this ter anyone, or God ah'll dae fer ya an' all."

"Dinnae take it oot on me."

He let go of the small man. "Aye, yer right; ah' is nae thinkin' straight. Scoot afore anyone turns up."

The two men walked past the van then, quickening their stride, they made their way down the dark lane, toward their homes. Dinger Bell was now a worried man. Had he actually bumped off an employee working for a large organization? He suddenly detested the bat swinging in his coat pocket.

Approaching Glenstone, O'Shaig took a side turning, to skirt around the village and avoid being seen. Dinger threw caution to the wind, desperate for home and the burning hearth. The baseball bat was the thing that weighed on his mind. It was the one thing which would surely incriminate him. At that late hour nobody seemed to be around, and had any villager seen him approaching, they would suddenly have found an alternative route far preferable. He saw his run-down cottage and dashed for the gate.

Slamming the front door closed, he felt a sudden flush of relief. He shut out the vile event for a few moments.

Then the hall light went on, and his wife Morag stood there in her dressing gown. "Wheer ya been?"

Dinger ignored her, bolted into the kitchen and slung the bloody bat into a cupboard. Then, from another cupboard, he snatched a full bottle of Scotch and, still shaking, unscrewed the cap. He swilled greedily, eager for the blurry fuzziness of hard liquor to blot out the night's evil deed he'd committed. Then, he saw the blood on his hands.

Morag followed him into the kitchen. She saw the blood, too. "What's goin' on?"

"Shut ya face, woman."

He made his way into the dilapidated hovel they called a dining room, and saw the fire had almost died down. He then walked quickly back to the kitchen. "Get that fucken' fire blazin', fer Christ's sake. Hurry."

"What's wi' doin' a fire the noo?"

Morag's nagging made Dinger feel his temples throb. He took another swig at the Scotch bottle, then his temper exploded. With a clenched fist, he struck her squarely on the jaw and sent her sprawling onto the tacky linoleum floor. "Just fucken' do it!" He pulled on the bottle again, while she scurried away to make the fire.

Dinger stood for a moment, shed his coat, then at the kitchen sink scrubbed his rough, gnarled hands, for the first time in years, desperate to rid himself of the bloodstains. Satisfied he'd cleaned up sufficiently, he swigged more of the Scotch.

Afterward, he raked around in the tool cupboard and took out a saw. He glared at the cupboard door, then drew the bloodied bat and sawed it into three pieces. The effort made him pant. *Fuck,* he thought, *fuck the lot o' them.*

Morag managed to get a fire blazing away, having lit some screwed-up paper and a couple of rags doused with methylated spirit, then a few bits of wood and a log. Dinger entered with the sawn-up bat and chucked the three pieces onto the blaze.

He watched the murder weapon slowly burn away. Then he laughed for the first time, and felt free of the oppressive weight that hung over him, ever since his mate found the officer near the bridge.

Morag watched, too, but knew well to keep silent. What he'd done that night, she couldn't guess. She hoped the blood was from a slaughtered deer or some poached game.

Dinger sank onto a grimy, worn armchair, bottle in hand. He drank another mouthful of liquor, then suddenly another thought struck him. He got up and went back into the kitchen, looking over his coat. Was there any blood on it? Morag followed him, like the timid, frightened rabbit that she was.

He slung the coat to the floor. "Fucken' wash it first thing tomorra', ye hear?"

She nodded and stood there, shaking. "Dinna fret; I'll see tae it."

"See yer do."

Dinger returned to the fireside chair and stared at the hearth, the last of the bat burning away. He wasn't happy, though; a tiny doubt nagged away in his mind. He began to suspect that an insignificant detail had been overlooked, and the more he thought about it, the more convinced he was. While watching the last of the bat smoulder away and swilling the Scotch, he racked his brain, desperate to detect the missing element – the one thing which might give him away.

CHAPTER 24

Police investigation

DETECTIVE SERGEANT DOHERTY stood in the gents' at Lochbridge Road Police Station in Rosstown, combing his jet-black, crew-cut hair. Then, he wiped his equally black, clipped moustache – a slender affair, the type which went out with Hitler.

He'd got an all-important though suddenly unexpected interview with the detective superintendent from Dumfries. What it was all about, he'd no idea; he drew a deep breath and speculated.

Doherty wasn't a vain man, but he was ambitious. At forty years of age, he was frustrated at still being a measly detective sergeant, as he put it, and forever nursed a desire for promotion. *Perhaps this is it,* he thought. He glanced at his wristwatch and saw it was almost nine o'clock. *Let's bloody well find out.*

He braced himself and rapped at the currently unused office door.

"Come," an official voice beckoned.

Doherty entered and saw Detective Superintendent Wallace, a big noise in both Dumfries and Galloway Divisions, and head of the Crime Management Services.

"Ah, Doherty, do sit down."

He did as requested, and slyly glanced at his superior.

"Early this morning, a body was found in the river, four miles south of Glenstone."

"Is that a fact, sir?"

"Yes, and what's more, the victim had been savagely beaten about the head. And I don't under-emphasize the word 'savage'; it was particularly brutal."

"Who found the body? Was it a rape, or…"

"A local farmer's wife did, while out walking the dogs. Poor woman's now under sedation for shock. No, the victim wasn't a woman; it was a young man, actually."

Doherty stared at him and declined to comment.

"I've made a special journey over here to, shall we say, organize an investigation. As you're probably aware, Galloway Division – as most departments – is chronically short-staffed and working with next to no funds."

"Yes, sir, and a sad state of affairs it is, especially as we've no detective inspector."

Wallace brushed away his comment. "Savage though it might be, we've neither the manpower nor resources to investigate one pissing little felony."

"Indeed, sir."

"I'm assigning this murder inquiry over to you. Now, you find the culprit that committed this vile slaying and I'll make bloody sure you get to be detective inspector. Is everything clear?"

Doherty glanced at his boss. "Yes, very much, sir."

"Good. I want this cleared up and soon. Galloway and Dumfries have come under severe criticism for failing to stem the increasing trend in poaching, and salmon poaching in particular; there's far too much of it."

"Yes, sir. Do I have total jurisdiction to conduct this inquiry?"

"Absolutely. But I cannot, apart from Detective Constable Turner, afford to appoint any other staff to this affair. Got it?"

"I have indeed."

"Then our little interview is over. I suggest you get over to Glenstone this morning, gain a feel for the case."

Doherty got up. "Yes, sir. I should like to thank you for this opportunity."

He strode to the doorway, when Wallace called out: "By the way, Doherty, have you ever considered a sales career in double glazing?"

Doherty stopped, amazed by the question and puzzled by its inference. "No, sir, I haven't. Why?"

Wallace sat back and smirked. "Fail me on this case and it'll be an option to consider, that's all."

An hour and a half later, Doherty and his assistant, D.C. Turner, stood on the bank of the river, taking in the scene, now cordoned off with blue and white tape.

"Has the police surgeon arrived?" asked Doherty.

"Not yet, sir," replied Constable Abbot.

Doherty looked over at the corpse, now beached and lying face down on a shingle bank. "Don't look a pretty sight, does it?" he muttered to Turner.

"Do you reckon this guy fell foul of poachers, or is it a city murder that got dumped out here?" Turner asked.

"How the bloody hell should I know? Forensic will soon put us in the picture, providing the police surgeon turns up. The minute he's through, get the body down to Rosstown morgue."

"Right, sir. Er, Doc Storie has agreed to do the autopsy."

"Bloody great! That dithering old fart's going to be a fat lot of help!"

Doherty paced around, anxious to get the body shifted and for the forensic team to arrive. "I want the riverbank scoured on both sides, from here to Glenstone, got it?"

Turner nodded: "Right, sir. What are we hoping to find?"

Doherty sniffed. "Anything. Anything at all. And I want it done and dusted before nightfall."

Turner glared at the shingle bank. "Wonder how long the poor sod's been lying there?"

"Storie should be able to tell us. Before we get his report, let's stick with the forensics team. If they unearth something, we might gain insight on where to start; no point in buggering about willy-nilly. That'd just be wasting valuable police department time."

Turner grinned and, as always, admired his boss's sarcastic comments.

CHAPTER 25

Johnny's new pool

JOHNNY MASON REALIZED the salmon fishing season was nearing a close, when all good fishermen stashed their reels away until spring, and left the salmon and other fish to go about their business in peace, follow the course of nature and spawn the next generations. During that time, he wanted to put another plan into operation.

Although he'd now got a new box and gaff, he'd still nowhere to stash his gear, having no desire to wander around the countryside carrying such implements. He decided to reconnoitre a different stretch of the river, north of Glenstone, far from the duke's domain, and hopefully away from the prying eyes of Davidson and McGee. Johnny knew the river there had loads of deep pools where salmon and trout congregated, and decided it was worth trying.

A little after midday, he set out along the river path, having taken a secret, little-used trail from the village, via the local allotments, then through an overgrown paddock swamped with brambles and scrub. He also found the dense vegetation along parts of the riverbank a distinct advantage.

Johnny sat at the tail end of a large pool, concealed among a patch of bushes, weeds and undergrowth which hung down over the river. In one hand he held a thin shaft of hazel, which had a metal tip. While peering into the shallows of the clear water, he tapped the shaft on his boot toecap. He disliked waiting in daylight hours, and rarely ventured forth on his expeditions until darkness. But this new technique he wanted to try would be almost futile in the dark, and he had no option. While waiting, he overheard two English fly fishermen discuss the merits of being away from home, seemingly glad of it, and their comments about the freedom and fresh air.

He'd been in position for over an hour when he spotted the first fish, closely followed by a second. Both were no more than a foot apart and drifted slowly backward, until they were opposite and no more than six feet from where he sat.

Johnny knew he had done well to pick this spot and, while peering through gaps among the dense undergrowth, only his eyes moved, watching the efforts of the two English fishermen. Since the pool was packed with jumping, splashing fish, Johnny felt dead certain the two anglers wouldn't think one more splash being out of place or strange.

Slowly, Johnny removed his battered old trilby and, from the inside band, extracted a metal arrowhead, with a barb two inches from the tip. He deftly screwed the arrowhead into the metal tip at the end of the thin shaft. Afterward, he tied one end of a fifteen-foot length of stout fishing line to the shaft, just behind the barb. From the deep pocket on the inside of his greatcoat he withdrew a sturdy catapult, and placed the arrow between the prongs. He drew back the catapult tongue and, with good aiming, released it.

The arrow sliced clean through the water and pierced the fish, just behind the gills. The fish rose out of the water, somersaulted once and fell back where it lay; only its tail showed any signs of life.

Johnny had no idea how much fishing could be squeezed in during the remainder of that season, or how long he might continue in forthcoming ones, but for the moment he felt happy. He was a poacher once again.

Reeling in his prize, he slipped the fish in a black, plastic bag and, as usual, slung it over his shoulder, under the greatcoat. The arrowhead he tucked inside the Trilby and shoved the slender shaft in his deep coat pocket.

By that time evening was approaching, and mist spiralled up from the river pools, as it often did during this season. He strode along the path, and decided to return to the village by way of the stone bridge. He'd nothing to hide, looking just the part he wanted others to believe: an old soldier returning home after a hike.

On reaching the bridge, Johnny felt troubled again. He gazed along the trail on the other side of the bridge, longing to fish again at his favourite patch, when he noticed in the distance policemen with long poles, poking around in the vegetation. Worse still, three of the men were dressed in white, plastic suits.

He frowned and wondered what was going on. He walked close to the hedge and trees so they wouldn't see him, continuing his journey down the road, eager to get home with his catch. That night, he'd dump the prize in Reg's old freezer.

He was just about to open the gate, when he noticed a package lying on his doorstep, wrapped in black polythene. He scowled at it, knew what it must be and walked down the garden path to his front door. He picked up the package and went into his house, slamming the door behind him.

After taking off his greatcoat and hanging it on its hook, he took his catch and the package to the kitchen. The strange package mildly irritated Johnny, but he knew what it was. He drew breath, undid it and saw two silver salmon, not large, but of medium size, probably weighing four or five pounds each.

Also in the bag was a little yellow poster note, inscribed: *"Keep to our agreement. Chuck."*

McGee, yer a bastard, he thought.

That evening, after he'd snacked on a frugal meal of baked beans on toast, washed down with half a mug of Scotch, Johnny got ready to make his delivery and nightly rendezvous at The Leaping Salmon. He dropped the two fish supplied by McGee into the black bag, along with his earlier poached salmon, guessing Reg would give him a hundred pounds plus unlimited free drinks.

He still felt slightly put out by McGee supplying him with fish to sell, especially as he'd not kept to his side of the agreement. But, Johnny was determined to poach more for the enjoyment of doing so. He also reasoned there was no guarantee how long his arrogant cousin would continue to provide salmon confiscated from other poachers.

With the bag over his shoulder, under the coat, he set off down the dark lane. He reached the alleyway behind the pub, and for once felt that the threat from Dinger Bell seemed strangely absent, for some inexplicable reason. Inside the ramshackle outhouse, he dropped the salmon in the antiquated freezer, locked it and hung his greatcoat upon the nail.

Then, he entered the cosy but thriving noisy public bar and made his way to the busy counter. He didn't bother to glance around the room, knowing full well who would be there, and where they would be sitting.

Apart from the few casual visitors ordering drinks while standing near to the bar, things remained unchanged in this, the main meeting room of The Leaping Salmon pub, including the favourite topic: fishing.

On entering the pub, Johnny would never look in the direction where his three faithful friends sat in the far corner, and after his nocturnal escapades he usually generally felt somewhat guilty. While in their company he often felt awkward, having almost deceived them by not sharing the secrets of his furtive rewards, gained over the years. At times, he hoped and prayed he'd never be found out. But he swore to make it all up to them one day. Though, for the present, things had to remain as they were.

As usual, Johnny ordered a large whisky and a pint of heavy. He downed the whisky in one go, hoping the solitary swift movement went unnoticed by his friends. Then, he swung round and leant against the bar, grasping the pint glass in his right hand, and surveyed the noisy room.

He noticed Big Jock McGill present but, talking to no one in particular, he seemed to be deep in thought, and appeared rather unhappy. Jock was a bit of a loner, a man who kept himself to himself, and much preferred the company of his dog and that of his two sons, when they returned from working on the oil rigs. There was big money to be made working on the offshore oil rigs; his sons were believed to be the richest young men in the village.

Jock was a good fisherman; he always tied his own special flies. It was this that made Jock a good fisherman – great, some folks thought; the best around, others declared. It was common knowledge that, if asked, he would willingly give his precious flies to anyone who asked. In his spare time, he was always to be seen on the banks of the river, doing what he did best: fishing.

At the other end of the bar, opposite where Johnny stood, a group had gathered. They did so every Friday night: the same people, in the same place, for the same purpose. They included the village policeman, the butcher and Bert Russell, who owned the only garage for miles around. Also, a couple of farmers of sorts and a jobbing landscape gardener joined in the crowd, hoping to catch everyone's attention. Adding his tuppence worth to their trifling small talk, Reg McGuire, the pub's landlord, would join them for a spell, eager for local gossip and probably hoping they'd order another quickie before departing.

Of course, that group only turned up to show their faces and, after several rounds, would leave to meet wives or girlfriends in the more salubrious surroundings of The Grouse in the Heather. That was the type of place where they could drink well into the night, looked after by the host landlord, Mr. Nigel Shreeves. If the gods were with them, the duke would make an appearance, if only a brief one.

Amid the group, being the centre of attention in whatever company he kept, the local village character Ken Newton was known to all. He often amused others with his wacky tales of past incidents and funny jokes, though he often exaggerated facts, and was also known to be a bit of brag. No villagers ever believed a word he said, though he carried on, even when his wife Joy tugged his jacket sleeve, sighing in embarrassment. Whatever his attire, he was always welcome at The Grouse, even in the company of the duke. Ken was a man who would do anyone a good turn, and never an ill deed. He was no fool, either, despite giving the appearance of being one, and remained of a sunny disposition, always appearing to have no shortage of the readies. It was known that the duke had once said of Ken that, when his time was up, God would judge him by the size of his heart, and his place in Heaven was as good as booked.

On noticing Chuck McGee at the centre of the crowd, Johnny was much surprised and rather concerned. McGee, being the duke's head bailiff, had earned himself the reputation of being the most despised man in Glenstone, and nobody loathed him more than Johnny.

Before Johnny could order another drink and join his friends, their eyes met across the smoky room. At that moment, Johnny knew he was the reason McGee had turned up that night, and felt troubled.

Johnny ordered his second pint of heavy and intended to join his friends, who appeared to be impatient for his company. No doubt they had news and, judging by experience and the current situation in Glenstone, it would not be good. And it wasn't.

He sauntered across the room and sank into his usual chair, as

Tom got his pipe going and a plume of smoke spiralled to the ceiling. His friends seemed perturbed.

"Ya heard the news, Johnny?" asked Bobby, squirming excitedly on the edge of his chair.

Johnny glanced at him, for a moment thinking his friend had suddenly got piles. "Cannae say that I have. What news?"

All of his friends cast dark looks, and he wondered what they had heard.

"Been a murder down on river, there has," exclaimed Bobby, before the others could utter a word. "Pollis were out there all day, rakin' over riverbank."

Johnny felt a tingle of shivers run down his spine. "Yer jokin', surely?"

"It's true, every word of it," stated Ben, calmly.

"Sweet Jesus," Johnny muttered. "Where and who?"

Bobby rubbed his nose. "Some young bloke. It weren't anyone in't village."

"Apparently the body was found washed up on a shingle bank, nearly four miles downstream," added Tom. "It could have happened anywhere."

"Bugger me," Johnny exclaimed. In all the years he had fished and poached along the river, never once had a corpse turned up, though with the rough gangs of poachers arriving, he was surprised something like this hadn't happened long before now.

Ben coughed. "You realize the coppers will be calling round, asking questions? They always do the usual house to house job, grasping for clues."

"Have they any idea who did it?" Johnny asked, supping the heavy to calm his nerves.

"It seems not. At the moment, anyway."

"I'll be damned. This'll give the local folk somethin' ter chew over fer years ter come."

"Aye, an' it might draw in the crowds, too. Curious folk always turn up at a murder scene. Well, local copper had no idea about it," commented Bobby.

Johnny fingered the beermat, trying to work out the implications. Was it a local job, or something that got washed down from miles away? "Could be some city killing, just dumped there for convenience," he stated.

"Maybe; nobody seems to be certain right now," Ben answered.

Johnny glanced around the bar and noticed someone missing. "Where's yer niece?"

"She's been called away to Dumfries. A bit unexpected, too. She drove off this afternoon. I expect she'll be back. So, how goes it with ye?"

Johnny thought of his afternoon's work. "Fine, everything's fine – ticking along nicely, in fact." He drained the pint, sighed and got up to go to the bar. From amid his crowd of associates, he noticed McGee stare at him again. Johnny scowled.

"Johnny, another pint, I take it?" asked Reg.

He nodded and slung a crumpled fiver onto the bar, remaining silent.

"How's things?" enquired the publican, with a glint in his eye.

"Brilliant. Threefold, I could say," replied Johnny, with a

knowing nod.

Reg beamed. "Isn't life wonderful, knowing I can keep the dainty on the pub menu?"

"Ter be sure; kind of looks like sweetmeat supplies are almost unlimited now, too. Anyway, enough o' that. What's this I hear about a murder?"

Reg's face darkened. "That's a right rum do, eh? It might pull in a few extra punters, though."

Johnny smirked. "True enough. Have ye heard anything, though? Who was the poor sod that copped it?"

Reg shook his head. "No idea, but I reckon we'll find out soon enough, eh?"

Johnny picked up his pint and nodded, returned to the table and stroked his chin, speculating on the recent turn of events. Now he knew why the police were out raking along the riverbank that afternoon.

"Hey, just had an idea," uttered Bobby: "suppose it's got somethin' ter do with Dinger? He was goin' ter poison the river."

Johnny narrowed his eyes and peered at him. "Not so bloody daft, are you?"

"Possible, though, ain't it?"

Johnny was about to answer when he saw McGee beckon to him. Tom noticed, too; "What's that bastard want?"

Johnny's brow furrowed. "There's only one way to find out." He got up and walked across the room toward his cousin, now standing at the door.

"Outside, Johnny, if you don't mind."

The two men stepped through the doorway of the pub.

He huddled near to the wall and scowled at McGee. "What the bloody hell is it now?"

His tweed-suited cousin drew a sharp breath. "This morning, the duke had a visit from Detective Superintendent Wallace, who just happened to be in the vicinity."

Johnny felt his patience waning, rapidly. "Bloody good. Now, what's that to do wi' me, eh?"

Unruffled, McGee ignored the sarcasm. "Look, Johnny, it seems that someone might have been murdered by the riverside last night. The duke isn't happy about it; this sort of thing could easily discourage his paying visitors from coming. With the season drawing to a close, naturally he's keen to, shall we say, maximize on the last remaining weeks."

"Aye, I bloody bet he is."

McGee fidgeted with his deerstalker. "I take it you had nothing to do with this incident?"

Johnny glared at his cousin. "You miserable, stinkin' toe-rag! How could you possibly think that?"

"You've been a soldier, Johnny, don't forget."

"What of it? I dinnae go round knockin' people off just fer kicks."

"I never said you did. I just wanted to be sure you had nothing to do with—"

"Bollocks, I've nae more ter say wi' the likes o' you. Yer a scumbag, McGee – a scumbag. Nae more and nae less."

"Johnny, I didn't mean…"

He strode away, then suddenly turned. "Bollocks, I'm done wi' you. Get it? Done."

Johnny stormed back into the bar, ordered a shot of whisky from Reg, downed it in one and cared not an ounce whether his friends noticed or not. Feeling slightly placated by the liquor, he returned to the table.

"Everything alright?" asked Tom, concerned by McGee's sudden appearance.

"It is now," Johnny answered, quietly. "Do yer know what he wanted? He came round here to check if I'd anything ter do wi' that murder. Can yer believe it?"

"Always said that one were the devil," commiserated Bobby. "Shame someone don't cosh him."

Johnny burst into laughter. "We could nae be that lucky."

"All the same, it's a damned cheek," added Tom, fiddling with the pipe. "Well, I hope this little rumpus knocks a hole in the duke's moneymaking scheme."

Johnny supped on the heavy, darkly contemplating on whether his outburst against McGee had suddenly wiped away any chance of further packages turning up. Then he shrugged. *If it has, to Hell wi' him. I got me own way o' getting salmon,* he thought.

After Reg's nightly serenade of "Drink up now," Johnny hurried back home along the lane, chewing over the clash with McGee and the murder. He'd no idea who the victim was, or why his cousin should even think he was involved, but he felt slightly unnerved by the fracas. Having given Reg three more salmon, he decided to give the nightly jaunt, or the new daytime ones, a miss the next day, just in case the police were still out searching alongside the riverbanks.

As ever, he slammed the door then topped up the fire, before settling in his favourite chair to catch the late-night weather forecast. *Might as well plan ahead. See what's in store.*

And, with that thought he dropped off, and missed the cheery lady presenter tell of a calm spell for the following week.

CHAPTER 26

Forensic

WHILE JOHNNY AND his friends chewed over the latest mishap in The Leaping Salmon, Detective Sergeant Doherty weighed up the sum total of the day's efforts. And, funnily enough, he was pleased for once; the forensic team had found lots of flattened, scuffled grass beside a small stone bridge and, what's more, traces of blood. "Obvious some sort of a struggle went on here," he recalled the forensic officer commenting.

They found little else, except for the indication that something had been rolled over, into the riverbank – something heavy. Then, while searching along the track toward Glenstone, they'd found a seven-pound tin of deadly toxin called cymag, among the undergrowth. How it got to be on a riverbank he'd yet to work out, but it was a valuable lead.

That very evening, the pathologist was going to do the autopsy. He'd been invited to attend in the viewing gallery, but declined; he'd seen more than enough of the bloody, staved-in head, and didn't fancy watching Storie prodding around with surgical probes or blades.

But, the details he'd already gained from forensic confirmed his suspicions: blunt instrument, they hinted, though Storie's investigation would neither confirm or refute their theory.

D.C. Turner burst into the investigation room carrying four bags, and the aroma indicated he'd grabbed takeaways from the Indian restaurant down Frith Street.

"Spare ribs and curry," announced Turner, grinning wickedly.

"Cracker," replied Doherty.

They were now on overtime – time and a half – and he was in no hurry to go home. They'd been allocated a corner of the investigation room, but everyone else was absent that night. Turner cracked open a can of lager.

"Kind of looks like that poor sod got done on the riverbank near the stone bridge."

"Forensic are dead certain of that, sir. They've taken loads of shots."

"How come that can of poison turned up along the river, too?" asked Doherty, pointing at the tin with a rib he'd been gnawing.

"Guess some poachin' bastard dropped it, or hid it. I've seen that before; collared one o' them city gangs handling the stuff, some years back."

"Right, assuming that tin was connected with the killing, then maybe a poaching outfit is responsible. It's a possible lead to follow."

Turner tore off the foil cover on a tray of rice. "No doubt about it. Only question is why didn't the poachers use it? And, who were they? Forensic found no clear fingerprints on the container; anyone could have handled it."

Doherty sniffed. "Maybe it had something to do with that van parked near the bridge." He flipped through his notepad. "Yeah, that SEPA lot monitor the environment or something, don't they?"

"Yes, sir, and they've no qualms about taking enforcement action against polluters."

"Are you thinking what I am?"

"What's that, sir?"

"I'll bet you the victim of this terrible murder had something to do with that van – maybe the driver. Get onto Dumfries police station tomorrow and find out if SEPA are missing an employee."

"Will do, sir. Anything else, while we're at it?"

Doherty got stuck into the curry. "Yeah, we've got to get this killer. If we don't, I've been informed a career in double-glazing is on the cards. See what I mean?"

"I don't quite follow, sir."

Doherty smoothed out a paper napkin. "If we catch this killer, I get to be a detective inspector; naturally, there's going to be an opening for a promising detective sergeant. Grasp the nettle now, Turner?"

"Bang on, sir. But, how do we know where to begin looking?"

"Poachers are behind this, I'll bet."

Just then the phone rang. Doherty flinched, not wanting to get sidetracked by a mere burglary or assault.

"Answer that bloody phone, please."

Turner grabbed the receiver and answered. "… Ah, right, I get the picture… Okay, tomorrow it is… Yes, we'll be there." He dropped the handset on the hook.

"That was Storie. He's determined the cause of death and also found something rather odd. He wants to see us tomorrow."

Doherty grinned. "Small bloody wonders. Right, after we've finished eating this lot we might as well bugger off home, then."

The following morning, Doherty and Turner paid a flying visit to the mortuary at Rosstown. Doherty hated entering the building, and even more loathed having to go into the examination room, with its foetid air and stainless-steel tables. But, on this morning, curiosity overcame his sense of repugnance.

Doc Storie obviously loved his environment. He moved around the stainless-steel stretchers with an air of authority. These cadavers belonged to him.

Doherty entered the bleak room. It stank of powerful, industrial-strength disinfectant, mixed with rotted flesh and death. He gazed across the room and saw the riverside victim, lying face down on a steel table, partially covered with a shroud, except for the cranium.

"Let's hear it: what was the rumpus about last night?"

Storie was a short, bald man, with a few wisps of grey hair and knocking on for retirement. He was dressed in his surgical outfit. "Doherty, good of you to drop in. I won't mess about with the details. In a nutshell, this young man suffered severe brain damage due to the injuries he sustained, as you can see."

"I don't need to be told that. What happened?"

"I would hazard a guess he was struck on the back of his skull – several times, at least. However, with the amount of shattered bone, it's impossible to be exact. In all my years, I've never seen anything as barbaric."

"Forensics says a blunt instrument was used."

"Yes, a heavy object with lots of swing to it; some kind of long club, for instance, would fit the bill. I'm only surmising here, but it's well known for these poaching gangs to use such weapons. Also, I've been unable to find any trace of foreign matter, such as tree bark, so I'd rule out the use of a branch or similar item."

"Makes sense, I suppose. Did the bloke have any I.D. on him?"

"No, just a little money: some coins. In his coat pocket I found a hand-torch."

"Really? Now, why should a man need a hand-torch while walking along a river?"

"Maybe it was night and he was tracking someone?" suggested Turner.

"That's the picture I'm getting," commented Doherty, turning to the pathologist. "How long was the body in the water? Any idea?"

Storie fingered his chin. "In my opinion, seven or eight hours, though it might be longer. But, that's not all we found."

Doherty's eyes turned to slits. "I'm all ears."

The pathologist placed a small sample bag on the table next to the dead man. "We found this in his right trouser pocket."

Doherty picked the bag up, unable to comprehend the object. "It's a bloody coat button."

"Yes, seems odd, doesn't it? Why should anyone pocket a button, of all things?"

"Maybe it fell off his coat," answered Turner.

"I'd believe that, except for one thing: the victim was wearing a black duffel coat, with wooden toggles, not buttons. It doesn't match his garments."

Turner grinned. "Maybe it was a lucky mascot, or a souvenir off a lover's coat."

"For my money, I'd say that button came off a man's coat. It's also badly worn, and there are tiny scratches on it."

Doherty held the bagged button up to the light. "Dead right; there is. Perhaps the guy was a homosexual – alone at night on a riverbank?"

Storie shook his head: "Examination of the genitals proved negative on that point."

"Bloody mystery, ain't it?" muttered Doherty. "I'll keep this, if you don't mind."

"By all means. We'll put the corpse on ice, pending further investigation."

Doherty nodded. "Weird, isn't it? An unidentified man, who may or not work for SEPA, walks along a riverside path carrying a bloody button and a torch, then ends up dead."

"I think we're looking at this the wrong way, sir. Suppose he pocketed the button just before he copped it."

The detective sergeant nodded, slowly. "Like he wanted to provide a clue to the attacker's identity?"

"Highly possible, though one button wouldn't stand up in a court of law to get the felon convicted. Besides, we don't know who the culprit is."

"I might have a lead, sir. Yesterday, Wallace went to see the duke."

Doherty squinted. "Duke? What, that poncey landlord?"

"Yeah. And what's more, one of his minions – a man called Davidson – complained about men prowling along the river at night. He actually dropped a name, too: Johnny Mason."

"Did he now? Then, it looks like we've got to pay a call on this Mason bloke. I want to speak to that publican, too; in a backwater like Glenstone, they get to hear all the local gossip."

"Right, sir, Do you reckon we got this stitched up?"

"Far from it. There are too many friggin' loose ends."

Johnny Mason slapped the kettle onto the hob and lit the gas, needing a hot drink. He felt worried, and bitterly regretted the argument with his cousin McGee. It weighed on him, and he remembered that McGee hadn't reciprocated in kind. Johnny felt he was up to something, but couldn't work out what.

He also felt slightly agitated by Rona's disappearance, and vaguely remembered her with a stranger in The Leaping Salmon bar for a couple of nights. Who he was, Johnny had no idea.

When the kettle screamed, he made a mug of tea, savoured the warming liquid and was about to make some toast, when the doorknocker pounded.

Bloody McGee again, I'll warrant. Bastard. The last person he wanted to face that morning was his cousin.

Ready to give his cousin another mouthful, he opened the door, to see Doherty and Turner standing there. His mind flashed back to the nightmare he'd suffered, which now seemed a hundred years ago.

Doherty flashed a warrant card under his nose. "Johnny Mason?"

"Aye, what's this unexpected call about?"

"I've a few simple questions that need answers – good ones."

Johnny rubbed his temple. "Ya best come in."

The detectives entered his drab hall. Doherty noticed the greatcoat hanging on the hat-rack: khaki with silvery buttons, hardly matching the one he'd got in the bag.

Doherty twitched his upper lip, as if to emphasize his Hitler moustache. "I presume you've heard about the incident along the river?"

"Whole village is blabbing about it," remarked Johnny. "Be the talk of Glenstone fer years."

"No doubt. I take it you weren't out along the riverside that night?"

"Now, why on Earth would I be out there at that hour?"

"I can think of one or two reasons," answered Doherty. "And, perhaps it's a profitable one, eh?"

Johnny's eyes narrowed. "What do yer mean?"

"Let's not play games. Were you out there or not?"

"No is the answer."

"Good. Can you verify that? Can anyone back your story?"

Johnny sneered. "Ask anyone down at The Leaping Salmon; they'll all tell yer I was there."

Doherty sucked his teeth. "Don't worry, we will. Now, let's try another tack. Have you noticed anyone suspicious, a stranger, perhaps, who may have turned up recently?"

Johnny stroked his chin. "Aye, I have, as a matter of fact. There was a young bloke in pub the other night – well, a couple of nights, actually."

"And, what was this man doing?"

"Talking to one o' me friends' niece, Rona Cullen, ter be exact. Dunno who he was, though."

"Can you describe this man?"

Johnny sighed. "About five-eight, probably in his twenties and, ah, he wore one o' them yellow safety jackets."

"Are you certain?"

"Sure as I'm standin' here."

"Have you ever heard of a thing called cymag?"

The question caught Johnny unaware and he flinched. "Cannae says I have. What's that? Some sort o' dirty magazine?"

Doherty stared at him, knowing he'd lied. "You've heard that name before, haven't you?

"Maybe I have, but cannae remember exactly what it was."

Johnny felt tempted to inform on Dinger, since he'd planned to use the cymag, but decided against it. For all his vile ways, he was a Glenstonian; one of them: a local.

Doherty sucked his teeth again. Johnny hated the sound and wished he would go away.

"It seems quite a few people have different reasons to visit that river during dark," stated Doherty. "The duke's gamekeeper, as far as I gather, is getting a tad weary of it."

"You amaze me. Maybe it's a romantic setting, fer courtin' couples ter indulge in a bit o' the old hanky panky?"

"Don't try to get clever with me, sunshine. I'm not interested in your pissing little riverside antics; I'm out to nail a bigger fish, and it's not called a salmon."

On hearing those words his blood froze. How had the detective guessed his little secret? He thought perhaps Davidson might have said something.

"Aye, then yer might try and land a pike, eh?" he commented, trying to sound jocular.

"Could you put a name to that pike?"

Johnny squirmed. He felt really uncomfortable, as Doherty applied the heat right up to gas mark five.

"Really, in a village like this, one gets ter hear all sorts of tittle-tattle. Half o' it dinnae mean a thing, and the other half malicious gossip, mostly."

"So, you've no idea who might want bump off a stranger, one dark night along the riverside?"

Johnny shrugged. "Nobody in Glenstone springs to mind. Still, there's a lot o' them wild sorts in Ravencroft, yer know. Savages half o' them be, by all accounts."

Doherty sniffed, glanced around at the hallway and, for all his furtiveness; decided Johnny was not the person he sought.

"For the moment, I'll wrap it up, but may need to call again at a later date. In the meantime, I wouldn't contemplate taking a sudden holiday in Rio or Bogota."

"Have nae got the money," Johnny answered back.

Doherty glared at him for a moment. Johnny opened the door.

They departed and he slammed it shut.

"Fucken' duke! I might o' known."

Although it was only ten-thirty in the morning, he felt the need for a strong drink, and half-filled a mug with Scotch, sipped and contemplated. "Aye, it's a wee complex mishmash, right enough."

The detectives next paid a visit to The Leaping Salmon and questioned Reg about his various customers. Reg adopted his *know-all, say-nothing* stance; the sinless publican.

"And what can we get you, sir?" he beamed at the two men.

Doherty flashed his warrant. Reg stopped smiling.

"I'm Detective Sergeant Doherty. This is Detective Constable Turner. Now we've got the introduction done, let's get down to it."

"Fire away."

"Being a publican, you must get to hear loads of gossip?"

Reg nodded. "No more than most. What's the trouble?"

"Murder, in case you'd not heard. Now, let's not fart about here, I want to know if any strangers have called lately."

Reg frowned. "Don't take stock of everyone passing through. I mean, we often get parties of ramblers stopping off. We depend on tourists, as well."

"Don't give me that guff. I mean a patron who might have been here for a night or so, who had contact with the regulars."

Reg could see there was no fluffing the details; this detective was as sharp as a tack. "A couple of nights ago, there was a young man I'd not seen before. Apparently, he was a colleague working with Mr. Furness's niece. She works for SEPA, doin' all sorts o' funny tests along the river, searching fer pollution, as far as I been told."

Turner nudged his boss. "That fits; we found the SEPA van, too."

Doherty nodded. "What's this woman's name?"

"Rona somebody or other. Mr. Furness would know."

"You're sure this woman works for SEPA?"

Reg nodded: "Definitely. Comes in here wi' a laptop. She and this youngster were fiddling about wi' it a couple of evenings."

"Then what happened?"

"Last time I saw him, he sidled up to the bar while we was busy, bought a bag of crisps then suddenly left out the back door. Never saw him again. Next day, Rona disappeared, too. Mr. Furness said she'd gone back to Dumfries for some reason – dunno what, though."

Doherty grinned. "Thank you very much; that's a great help. By the way, was Johnny Mason in here last night?"

Reg grinned. "He's in every night. One of my regulars. Never fails to turn up."

"What time does he arrive?"

"Usually anytime around eight to nine," Reg answered, omitting the occasions when he came in an hour later, after a riverside expedition.

Doherty nodded and sniffed.

Outside the pub, Doherty and Turner chewed over the details.

"Kinda looks like she done it," stated Turner, flatly.

"Don't be an arsehole. What'd she gain?"

"Sorry, sir, it just seemed obvious, disappearing like that."

"A judicious call to SEPA might be in order, I reckon."

"Right, sir. I take the hint."

That afternoon, Turner called SEPA at Dumfries and spoke to Liam. The SEPA chief told him about Adam's sudden disappearance, and that being the reason Rona had returned, along with delivering some river-water samples.

"See? She's on the level," Doherty smirked.

"Yeah, right, sir. I blew it."

"Ah, don't worry, sonny. I got an e-mail from Dumfries police station: this Rona Cullen and her boss Liam Findlater were dead worried about Adam Burk suddenly vanishing, and went to missing persons. She's at a loss to explain what could have made the young environmental officer take flight the way he did."

"Seems obvious, in hindsight," muttered Turner.

"True. Now, here's the cherry on the pie: Rona informed Dumfries police and her boss that she got wind of a nasty git called Bell planning to poison the river, shortly before the young bloke went missing.

"Right? What's the connection?"

"Bell had a seven-pound tin of cymag, no less. All so bloody clear, ain't it? Apparently, he and his mates were poachers – big surprise. But they never got a chance to use the poison, 'cos that young officer disturbed them. Poor sod paid for it, too, with his life."

"Why did he do it? What for?"

"She and Adam had arranged for the Scottish Salmon Strategy

Task Force to send their bailiffs out, along with two policemen, to nab them. Apparently, the kid had a digital camera on him – no guessing as to why. Unfortunately, on the way to the prearranged rendezvous, the bailiffs got sidetracked: they found a gang of poachers from the city netting a chunk of the river, and assumed them to be the culprits."

"Jesus, so that environmental officer stood no chance?"

"Sadly, that was the case, but his presence was the only thing that stopped Bell dumping the can in the river."

"I've heard that name before somewhere: 'Bell'. I'm sure it's in the files."

He snatched the phone and called the local policeman in Glenstone. Minutes later, he dropped the receiver.

"Christ, listen to this: apparently, Bell, or 'Dinger' Bell, as he's commonly known around Glenstone, was convicted for poisoning the river just over two years ago. What's more, the local judge, A.G. Buchannan, recommended a Crown court hearing. He went down for two years."

Doherty snapped his fingers. "That's our man, then. Crackin' stuff."

Turner scowled. "How are we going to nail him? We've no proof, apart from the button. It's not enough; we've got to find something else."

"With a bit of luck, we just might find the murder weapon."

"You reckon, sir?"

"Be optimistic, for Christ's sake."

"You mean like you are, sir?"

"Very witty. Get a search warrant and a reliable forensic officer; we're going house searching. And, while we're at it, I want two constables along – burly ones. Bell might be armed and probably dangerous."

"Right, sir, leave it with me."

"I want him out of the house while we're searching. Let's get him in for questioning."

"Shame his fingerprints weren't on that tin."

"That'd make no difference. We got to find something concrete: evidence to tally with the button."

CHAPTER 27

Local gossip

LATER THAT DAY, Johnny called at The Leaping Salmon to collect his payment for the latest delivery, and find out if the detective had been nosing around. The one person Johnny trusted, apart from his three friends, was Reg. He strode into the bar and saw his friend ready to pull a pint.

"Heavy, Johnny?"

"Aye, might as well."

Reg placed the brimming pint on the bar. "It's on the house. Ah, yes, for last night..." He dropped a hundred pounds in used tenners on the bar. Johnny immediately snatched the notes and stuffed them into his coat pocket.

"I had a visitor earlier," commented Johnny, sourly: "Doherty, of all people. He questioned me about that river doing."

Reg hunched over the bar near Johnny and spoke quietly: "Detective Inspector Hitler called here, too, asking all sorts of questions about me patrons and their business. Apparently, that young man your new ladyfriend was knocking about with was the murder victim."

Johnny squinted. "Don't say?" he mumbled, wondering what Rona's part in this macabre web of deceit might be. "Seems ya cannae trust anyone anymore." He glanced at Reg. "Well, almost anyone.

"When that detective questioned me, he let it drop that he knew about my little expeditions to the river. He claimed to be disinterested. Now, how the hell did he find out?"

Reg scowled. "Obviously someone blabbed. Apart from McGee, who knows about you poaching?"

"I hate ter say this, but a man called Davidson who works for the duke. Maybe even His Lordship knows; I've nae way of tellin'. But I don't like it."

"Not good for the salmon trade, is it?" Reg joked.

"It is nae a laughin' matter. I had a fracas with me cousin the other night."

Reg smiled, kindly. "As I see it, McGee can't do anything. If he's supplied you with confiscated salmon, you got him over a barrel. He'd not dare open his trap, in case you rap on him."

"Aye, that's a point. I cannae see why McGee was so keen ter get me to quit poachin', though. What the hell's he after?"

"How many times a year does the devil cut his toenails?"

"No idea? What does it matter?"

"That's my point: if you knew the answer it would probably make no sense at all."

"I dinnae like that detective, though,"

"I wouldn't worry about him. I've come across his type before: miserable sods, eaten away by ambition."

"Motivated by what, exactly?"

"I'd guess promotion – it was written all over his face. He won't get far by booking one lone, small-scale poacher; he'd be a laughing stock in his profession."

Johnny looked at his friend and felt relieved of a burden. "Reg, yer have a bottomless well of assurance, I gi' ye that."

Reg beamed. "Just as well; you got an endless supply of the river dainties, so we're both happy. How about another pint?"

CHAPTER 28

New revelations

THE FOLLOWING DAY, Doherty had secured the search warrant and wasted no time organizing an incursion on Dinger's house. By midday, he pulled up in the Vauxhall Astra, with Turner in the passenger seat. A panda car with two burly constables tailed them, accompanied by the forensic officer.

He stared at the slum dwelling known to be Bell's address: one half of a filthy, squalid cottage, with roof tiles missing and the garden a riot of weeds. He noticed the front gate – a dilapidated wooden thing – had long ago fallen off its hinges, and lay propped up on a nearby shrub.

"What a pigsty, eh?"

"Yeah, the forensic guy should have a wild old time," replied Turner.

"I hope not. I want this damn thing sewn up, pronto."

Doherty waited on the pavement, until the panda pulled up and the constables got out. The forensic operative slipped on a white plastic suit and carried a case full of gear.

Doherty took a deep breath. "Let's get on with it."

He strode down the almost non-existent path to the front door and whacked the doorknocker, as the place appeared to have no bell. A lean woman with a whopping purple bruise on her jaw answered.

"Yes?"

"Is Mr. Bell at home?"

"Aye, what dae ye want wi' him?"

Doherty flashed his warrant card in front of her face. She paled and the purple welt stood out more vivid than ever. "I've a few questions to ask and am required to search the premises."

"Whit's goin' on?" grated Dinger, striding into the hall, wearing nothing more than a pair of trousers. He glared at the men on the doorstep.

"Pollis," was all Morag managed to utter, while hanging onto the door like it was a prop.

"Piss orf," retorted Dinger, dashing to get his clothes.

Doherty scowled, then twitched his moustache and waited for a moment or two. Tackling Bell clothed, he thought, was better than the alternative, so he waited.

"I take it you're Mrs. Bell?" asked Turner.

The bruised woman nodded but kept silent.

"Nasty bruise you've got there," commented Doherty. "How did it happen?"

"Slipped and fell," whispered the scared woman, fear showing in her eyes. Doherty took the hint, knowing the man called Dinger had been responsible.

Bell reappeared dressed in his ragged attire, resembling a gypsy from the 1950s. "Whit yer staring at, woman?" he snapped at Morag.

Doherty's patience began to wear down. "Mr. Bell, I have a

warrant to search these premises."

Dinger glared at the detective as though he were a piece of dung by the kerbside. "Ye whit?"

"I've good reason to believe you're involved in a nasty incident along the riverside, two nights ago."

The two constables stood at the garden path, or what was left of it, and Dinger knew he was trapped inside the house. "Whit yer goin' on aboot?"

Doherty sniffed. "I have to ask you to wait outside for a moment."

Dinger slung his newly laundered coat on and smirked at the detective. "Dae ye the noo? A' whit right hae ye ter order me around in me hoose, eh?"

"I'm conducting a criminal investigation here. Now look, sunshine, you can wait outside or down at the police station, it's all one to me, get it?"

"Aye, ootside it be."

Doherty nodded his head sideways to indicate he wanted the forensic officer and Turner to enter and begin searching. "Methodically; don't miss a thing."

Morag appeared as though super-glued to the front door, and Doherty decided she might as well remain there.

"Whit are ye lookin' fer? Maybe I can help," Dinger quipped.

Doherty narrowed his eyes and saw Dinger's coat was missing a black button, but kept silent; he didn't want to panic the man. Not yet.

"Do you ever play baseball?" he asked the scruffy reprobate.

Having burnt the bat, Dinger sneered at the detective. "Whit ye goin' on abert? I dinnae play any sports. Have nae the time."

Doherty glanced at him. "Really? Not even a spot of fishing?"

Dinger frowned, unsure where this cat and mouse conversation was leading. He thumbed his jaw. "Maybe just a bit noo an' then."

"With a rod and line, of course?"

Dinger felt the conversation sliding out of his depth and smiled, sickly.

Turner dashed into the hallway and beckoned his boss.

The detective sergeant turned to Dinger. "Wait here with these nice, friendly constables." Doherty followed his assistant into the kitchen, where the forensic officer was busy probing around.

"We found something," he exclaimed, pointing to the kitchen cupboard where, not so long ago, Dinger had slung the bloody bat.

Doherty peered at the dark cavity. "Yeah, what is it, exactly?"

The forensic officer grabbed a pair of surgical tweezers, reached into the far corner of the cupboard and lifted out what appeared to be three matted fibres, held together with dried blood. "Give you one guess what this is."

Doherty peered at the find. "Not bleedin' fishing line, is it?"

Turner gazed at the strands held in the tweezers. "This looks to me like human hair. I do sometimes get things wrong, but not this time; this is definitely human hair."

"Bag it and get it to the forensic lab. We will search the whole house, in case something else crops up. I reckon we've got the bastard good and proper. And don't forget to keep your eyes skinned for a baseball bat."

"Do you reckon that hair comes from the murdered man?" Turner asked.

"I'd bet fifty pounds on it. Still, a routine D.N.A. test should confirm that point, either way."

"What are we gonna do in the meantime, to stop him absconding?"

"Take him in for questioning. Let's hang it out a bit, long enough to get the D.N.A. test result – save us having to hunt him down later on. After all, we're operating on next to no resources. Detective Superintendent Wallace will probably hit the roof, if we use up too much petrol while chasing down wanted murderers."

Turner grinned at his boss's joke. "Yeah, then we've just got forty-eight hours."

"Don't I bloody know it? Still, it just might be long enough."

Doherty strode back to the hall doorway, relishing his role. "Mr. Bell, I'm going to have to ask you to accompany me to the station, and not for a train, either."

"Whit? Are ye serious? Whit fer?"

"Routine inquiry," lied Doherty, with a surly smirk. "Nothing at all to worry about, sir. And, what's more, we'll even dish up a free cup of vending machine tea."

Forty minutes later, at Lochbridge Road Police Station in Rosstown, Doherty and Turner, along with the beefy constables, arrived with their extra special passenger, Dinger Bell. They led him along the corridor to an interview room. Dinger glanced around the stark room, saw a table and four aluminium folding chairs, along with the inevitable recording equipment.

"Sit down," stated Doherty, removing his coat. "Now, I've a few pressing questions begging for answers."

Dinger glared at the man and said nothing.

Turner entered the interview room, carrying a tray with four plastic beakers of vending-machine tea and some sugar sachets. He placed a cup in front of Dinger. Doherty paced around in front of the table, while a constable grabbed another of the teas, watching the proceedings.

"Do you often visit the river?" Doherty asked, suddenly.

The scruffy man reached out for the beaker. "Most folks in the village do."

"I'm not remotely concerned about the other villagers. Did you frequent the riverside?"

"Aye, I might o' done."

"Three nights ago, you went to the river with a party of mates, didn't you?"

"Maybe," replied Dinger, toying with the plastic cup.

Doherty signalled Turner to leave the room and he followed, leaving Bell with the constable. In the corridor, he sucked his teeth. "Obviously, the bastard's not going to be overly co-operative. Has that forensic officer whipped the hair sample to pathology? I want results, and fast."

"Yes, sir, he's on his way."

"I want to be absolutely certain about this before we charge him, got it? One cock-up and it's bye-bye promotion. Oh, another thing, where the hell's the digital camera that young bloke had disappeared to?"

"We found no camera of any sort in his place. Doubt if he'd know how to use one, let alone a digital model."

"That figures. Maybe it's lying around on the riverbank somewhere."

"I'll check into that. Doubt if it's still out there, though; forensics were pretty scrupulous."

Doherty blew breath. "A thing like that'd easily get flogged at some boot fair, I guess."

"How many of them were in on that escapade?"

The detective shrugged. "The SEPA dame said a 'gang'. That salmon taskforce lot sent out four bailiffs, accompanied by two policemen. Suggests we're talking about four bad bastards at the very least."

Turner nodded in agreement. "What about the cymag?"

"I'll get round to that in due course. Did you get an official statement from the SEPA woman at Dumfries Police Station?"

"Done it already; they faxed a copy over."

"Brilliant, things are looking up."

"Had an idea, sir: he must have regular cronies in the village – I reckon one or more were with him that night. I'll check the records of previous convictions; a name might crop up."

"Good, but if the D.N.A. on that hair sample matches the victim's, we've more than enough to book him."

"A squealing informant would reinforce our case, wouldn't it?"

"You're dead right."

Doherty returned to the interview room.

"Sorry to keep you waiting, Mr. Bell," he sneered. "How'd you like to tell me all about that river and the things you find in it?"

"What sort o' things?"

"I believe the textbooks describe them as fish, salmon being a prominent type."

"Whit's salmon ter dae wi' me? I go fer a walk along the path noo an' then."

Doherty drummed the edge of the table. "Look, sunshine, we know all about your previous poaching escapades. I also know you were caught in possession of a canister containing toxic gas, and you used it on the river. Went down for it, too, didn't you?"

"Ach, that were a long time agoo; ah turned over a noo leaf since."

"Don't mess me about. I've spoken to the local judge."

Dinger licked his lips, squirmed and sunk on the chair. "Bad mistake that was, and I'm ashamed o' it the noo."

"I'll bet you are. So, we come round to the fact that you were along the riverside again, three nights ago. What for?"

Dinger flinched, felt trapped and racked his brain for a feasible story. "Look, ah were only out ter net a few fish, just ter pay orf a debt, like."

"Really? Who did you owe money to?"

"Ah cannae remember the feller's name the noo."

"Amnesia brought on by the stress of travelling over here in police company, no doubt?"

Dinger stared at the floor. "Really, ah cannae recall the name."

"Fair enough. How were you going to catch these fish?"

"Wi' nets. Whit else?"

"What sort of nets?"

"Just nets, fer Christ's sake."

"The following morning, four fisherman's landing nets and a large quantity of stout polypropylene bags were found near a little stone bridge, two miles or so south of Glenstone."

"Aye, whit of it?"

"Strikes me that's an awful lot of gear just for a few fish," Doherty stated.

Dinger shrugged, unable to provide an explanation.

Doherty continued to press. "That gear wasn't the only thing to turn up."

Dinger didn't want to hear the rest of it, and concentrated on the plastic beaker of lukewarm tea, fearing the worst.

"A dead body was found in the river that same morning, earlier on, as a matter of fact. I suppose you know nothing of that, either?"

He glared at the detective. "Cannae say I dae."

"Are you absolutely certain? It was beached about four miles downstream of the village. Now, either somebody is telling porkies here, or we have a classic example of a genuine coincidence."

Dinger scratched his filthy neck. "Aye, all sorts o' funny things end up in rivers. Whit's this body ter dae wi' me?"

"I thought you might know something about it."

"Nae, maybe some poacher from the city knows more aboot it."

Doherty's eyes narrowed. "Could be, and perhaps the city poacher planned to poison the river, too?" The detective suddenly snapped his fingers in mock astonishment. "Dear me, here's another coincidence: a seven-pound tin of cymag turned up along the riverbank, roughly half a mile from the village bridge. It must have been quite a busy night along that river, don't you think?"

The scruffy villain sneered. "Ah heard there are clashes between rival gangs noo and then. Nae often, but it happens."

Doherty was getting warmed up and closing in. "Yeah, and sometimes clashes happen between poachers and bailiffs, or employees from official organizations like SEPA, for instance."

On hearing that name Dinger scowled, and felt the conversation was gradually turning into an ominous threat.

Doherty grinned. "Here's the biggest coincidence of them all: it just so happens a SEPA Transit van was parked at the edge of the field, beside Glenstone's bridge. What do you make of that?"

"Cannae account fer it. Mystery, ain't it?"

Doherty suddenly shot up off the chair and sped from the room, irritated by Dinger's evasive answers.

In the investigation room, he snatched the copy of Rona's statement and pored over it. Turner entered and sat down, sporting a big grin.

"That slimy bastard's not going to crack. So far, he's wriggled out of every question like a fucking eel."

"Never mind, sir; pathology is working on that sample now. Told them the big cheese is pressing for closure. Also, I found out from the police records that a guy called Seamus O'Shaig was involved in that gassing fiasco two years ago. What's more, he lives in Glenstone, too."

"Good work, Turner. Now, let's apply a little pressure and make the bastard squirm."

"How we going to do that, sir?"

"The key is here, in Rona Cullen's statement. She acted on receiving information from one of her uncle's mates – a Bobby Burgess, to be precise. Burgess overheard Dinger and another bloke planning to poison the river, in that pub's bog."

"Bet the other person was O'Shaig, right, sir?"

"Sounds like it. I want to make this case watertight. That wife-bashing bastard's going down for this."

Doherty glanced at his wristwatch and saw it was seven p.m. "We ain't got much time. Look, you keep Bell busy with the old interrogation routine, while I get over to Glenstone. I want a signed statement from Burgess, and I know exactly where to find him."

"Right, sir, and here's O'Shaig's known address."

"Cracker. We'll get them stitched."

"Who were the others?"

"We'll find out soon enough."

After a forty-minute drive, Doherty stormed into the cheery, busy public bar of The Leaping Salmon and glanced around. He saw Johnny Mason and his three friends seated in the far corner and strode over.

"Which of you fine gents is Bobby Burgess?" he asked.

The four friends glared at him, wondering what was going on.

"Don't all answer at once," snapped the detective.

"That's me," answered Bobby, glancing at his friends.

Doherty grabbed an empty chair and pulled it up to the table, took a deep breath and sat down. "Right, I've no time to mess about; I want fast answers. Now, I gather from a certain young lady that you, Mr. Burgess, overheard a conversation while frequenting the little boys' room, a few nights ago. The topic being discussed was poisoning the river with a tin of cymag."

Bobby frowned. "Yeah, that's right. I heard every word, too."

Doherty smiled; he looked like Hitler when he was happy. "Good. Now, who were the speakers?"

"One of them was a bad man, Dinger Bell; well-known round here, he is. Often beats up his wife."

"So I gather. Who was this Bell bloke talking to?"

"Dunno," replied Bobby, "but he seemed scared. I think Dinger called him a weasel."

"Why didn't you call the police after hearing this?"

Bobby suddenly felt nervous. "Didn't know what ter do. Then Ben's niece turned up, so I told her all about it. She's takin' lots o' river water samples for pollution, and all that."

"Rona Cullen, I take it?"

Bobby nodded. "I thought she might know what ter do about it."

Doherty glanced at him. "In that case, I'd like a signed written statement from you, if you don't mind. And I'd like it now."

Bobby looked at his friends and frowned. "I ain't done anything!"

"We know that." Doherty shoved a blank sheet of Rosstown Police headed notepaper across the table and glanced at Johnny.

"Take your time, sonny, and just write down all that happened. I'm sure Mr. Mason here will feel a lot happier knowing his friends have assisted with a police inquiry."

"Anyone got a pen?" asked Bobby.

Ben handed one over and helped him with the spelling.

Johnny glared at the detective. "What exactly is goin' on?"

Doherty watched Bobby slowly writing. "I'm out to catch a fish, a slippery one, and with that statement it's going to fry like fish fingers. I take it a man called O'Shaig is one of Bell's acquaintances?"

"Yer guess right. A weaslin' wee bastard he is, too."

"I don't doubt it. Since you're all here, I may as well have it signed by a witness, too. Any volunteers?"

"Pushy, aren't you?" commented Ben. "As Rona's my niece, I'll sign the damned thing."

Doherty sneered and glanced at Johnny. "Splendid. I knew I could count on Glenstone's fine, law-abiding folk. After all, folks intending to poison rivers and poach the livestock deserve all they get."

When Bobby eventually finished writing, having made one or two spelling corrections, Ben scrawled his name beneath his friend's signature.

Ben handed the paper to Doherty. "There you are, signed and sealed."

The detective glanced over the wording, folded up the paper and slipped it into his pocket. "Yes, thanks for your co-operation."

Doherty got up, glanced at the four companions, then walked out of the bar without looking back. Outside, he smiled, clapped his hands and decided to pay a flying visit to O'Shaig.

It was nearly ten o'clock when Doherty strode into Rosstown Police Station again and dashed into the incident room.

He saw Turner and one of the constables munching portions of a mozzarella and tomato pizza. He dropped the signed document on the desk.

"Bloody bingo! Got the statement," he announced, then grabbed a slice. "I also called on that rat, O'Shaig, while in the village. He's small fry by comparison to Dinger, but we'll nab him later if need be."

"Was he involved?" asked Turner.

"He was there, but was dead against everything Dinger did. Stupid sod thought they were out to make a financial killing that night. According to that runt, they expected to earn in excess of eight grand. Then, it all went wrong when Burk showed up."

Just then, the phone rang. Turner answered, scribbled a note then replaced the receiver. "That was pathology; the D.N.A. from those hairs matches the victim to a tee."

"We got him! Get a constable to retrieve that sample, would you? I want to see that bastard writhe."

Doherty and Turner strode into the interview room, where Dinger fidgeted with another half-drunk cup of tepid tea. He glared at the detectives, but kept silent.

Doherty pointed at Dinger's coat. "Your overcoat appears to be missing a button."

Dinger glanced at him. "Aye, what of it?"

The detective dropped the bagged button onto the table. The scruffy man glared at the object, realizing then that it was the missing element – the thing which had nagged away at him since he returned home.

Doherty sneered. "No guessing where that's come from, eh?"

"Whit? Er, I cannae understand. Where'd ya find it?"

"Funnily enough, the pathologist found it in a dead man's pocket. A man that you happened to kill in a mad, drunken frenzy, brought on by getting thwarted in the river poisoning scam."

Dinger suddenly rose from the chair and sent it toppling backward. "Yer a fucken' liar! Yer planted it on him."

Doherty smirked and answered a knock at the door. Dinger saw a constable enter and hand the detective something in a small plastic bag.

"Perhaps you'd care to explain how this ended up in your kitchen cupboard?" He held up the bagged fragments of Adam's hair.

Dinger suddenly exploded in rage. "Yer got fucken' nothin' on me? If yer so fucken' clever wheer's the murder weapon, eh? Answer mae that?"

Doherty grinned at the dishevelled man. "I'd guess you buried it or burnt it. Either way, it don't matter; your coat button in a dead man's pocket and his hair in your kitchen... well, things don't look too rosy, do they?"

"Yer a bastard. A wily, schemin' bastard."

Doherty smiled. "Funny you should say that; my missus says

exactly the same thing often enough."

He glanced at Turner. "Book him."

CHAPTER 29

Keeping it in the family

MEANWHILE, IN DROITWICH Spa, a young man, hunched on a riverbank peering into a green light beam, pondered over his friend's little-known cousin. While tickling the trout, or whatever else turned up in the river, he was more certain than ever that Johnny Mason was a poacher – a successful one, too. And, the thing was, over the past few days the intrigue deepened.

He wanted to know how the old man caught the fish, what techniques he used and whether he'd ever been caught out. And, if he'd never been found out, how did he manage to keep his furtive activity secret? The more he thought, the greater the sense of mystery.

When he mentioned it to Will, he seemed astonished. Obviously, the two cousins never discussed such matters. Then again, Will was new to fishing. Perhaps Will might take them back to that pub they'd frequented?

It was now just gone mid-October, and the salmon-fishing season would soon be over. Andy had already booked the four of them on another week's fishing holiday in Scotland, to the very same cottage they had occupied before. As Andy had already said, it was the very last chance before the following spring. In a couple of days' time, they'd be heading north toward the border once again, and young George Martin couldn't wait to set forth.

In the thriving but cosy bar of The Badger Inn, landlord Les Hopkins dropped a steel platter, adorned with a large, eight-pound silver salmon, onto the tabletop. Will and his friends Andy, Tom and George gazed at it, awestruck by the creature's great beauty. Only George knew where the prize fish had come from, having caught the specimen the previous night, using his green light and rabbit snare. Earlier that night, Les had paid him, and with ninety pounds cash in his pocket, George was probably the most contented man in Droitwich Spa – at least for a brief spell. All agreed it was a fine catch.

Andy and Tom assumed that George had used a rod and line. Will, on the other hand, knew better, after he and the youngster had the discussion about poaching, while drinking Coke to recover from their celebration party at The Leaping Salmon.

Until now, Will had thought little of George and his poaching activity, but, seeing how profitable the venture had been, he now felt rather intrigued. How was it done? He couldn't imagine, but he began to find the idea of getting something for nothing from a river, with minimal risk, rather attractive. And, the thought of danger and excitement washed away the anguish of living with a nagging wife, which got worse with every passing day.

It was the night before they were due to set out for Scotland again, and the four friends gathered to make plans, having pre-booked their little cottage. Les joined them for most of the evening, being a keen fisherman also, in the few spare hours he got from his publican job. "I wish I were coming with you," he commented, with longing.

"Maybe next season, then," suggested Tom. "You're the boss; you've nobody to answer to."

Les nodded. "True, but can you imagine leaving Eva to manage things here? She'd make a right cock-up of it! And what if the taps ran dry? She's not a clue about cellar work; only my main barhand Raymond Bedford is any good at that. As for the two casual barmaids I employ, I despair; they're more interested in polishing their nails and chatting up the young fellers."

All commiserated with Les. He worked hard at his job and seldom got any recognition, except from their little group. They were his main patrons and almost kept The Badger in business, and for that Les was grateful.

The sight of the salmon on the plate made Will long for the Scottish river, the chance to cast his line once again and become the centre of the universe, while landing a whopping, twenty-pound fish. He finished off the last of his ale.

"I reckon we ought to go and say howdy to Will's cousin again," George suddenly exclaimed. "I reckon the old bod might be kinda getting lonely up there, in that wee village."

Will gazed at the youngster, astonished, but realized he might be up to something. He couldn't think what made George suspect Johnny was a poacher, but was equally curious to find out if he was right. Then Will also wanted to know a bit more about poaching, too. If Johnny did poach river fish, would he perhaps show them how it was done? Will didn't even dare think the old man might take them out one dark night, on a furtive expedition.

With another round of drinks, they planned and decided to leave early, get to the border by nine o'clock at the latest, and squeeze in every available hour to fish. Except, this time, darkness would be closing in earlier, now the year was in decline.

The following morning, after setting out from Droitwich Spa, they reached the Scottish border at nine o'clock, and everyone cheered.

On arrival at the cottage, Will got a snack going on a portable, gas-fire barbecue griddle, managing to char some burgers, sausages and sliced, organic beefsteak tomatoes, purchased along the way. The others dumped their gear in the cottage and joined him outside. Feasting on the barbecued goodies, and washing all down with canned beer, they rejoiced.

Afterward, Will stood on the bank of the river, soaking up the scenery, and felt glad to be back. Under the slate sky, the slow-moving river, wide and flat, snaked across the land like an ebony ribbon, tainted with blue. Light, olive-coloured trees were now coloured with tan hues, the shadows between dark jet, while the distant hills appeared emerald. Although overcast, it was calm. A rainfall the previous night had made the conditions just right for fishing.

Tom came over and handed him his carbon-fibre rod of fifteen feet, which proved ideal for fishing in small rivers. Will knew some of the fish during the autumn months were right monsters, often weighing in excess of twenty pounds, and longed for such a catch.

Andy decided to have a go casting with a fly, instead of bait. He used an "Ally's Shrimp" – a reddish fly – but brought along a "Yellow Ally's" and another called a "Cascade", to try them out; all were reputed to be excellent for salmon fly-fishing. Andy brought the bait container over, full of squirming, reddish worms from his dad's compost heap, as usual.

Having cast his line upstream, Will watched it slowly drift with the current, hoping the hook wasn't going to get snagged. Just being there was the thing, drifting like the water which flowed past. He relished this place, and felt content at one with nature.

The tip of his rod bent; was he into a fish so soon? He dared to hope it was. The line drifted downstream and he smiled. If the line was downstream, he knew playing the fish was to his advantage, as the salmon would expend much effort struggling against the current, to swim upriver.

Andy and George noticed and raced over. Will held the rod near-vertical, keeping the line taut while playing the unseen fish. By now, he knew full well a slack line would enable the fish to throw the hook and escape. He applied a little side-strain to deter the fish from seeking a sanctuary, and felt it in the rod he held. He reeled in a little, to keep the line taut as a drumskin.

George raced over with the landing net, and positioned it so Will could manoeuvre the prize into place. The fish briefly rose to the surface – it was not large, but Will thought worth landing. He reeled in a little more, but not too much, fearing the line could snap at any minute. He drew the line toward the positioned net and George deftly caught the fish. In the net, it struggled.

Will saw he'd got a medium fish, around five pounds, but he felt glad to have landed the first fish on their new break away. He whacked the salmon.

Andy grinned and planned its fate: "Chargrilled salmon steaks for supper, perhaps?"

"You done well there," commented Tom, admiring the catch. "You're a proper fishing sportsman now, eh?"

Will just smiled and basked in his friend's accolade.

That afternoon, when the sun broke out, the four friends caught another two small salmon and were in high spirits. Will also knew they had overstepped the legal boundary of rod fishing, as catches were supposed to be limited to two salmon or sea trout per day. Whether that was per person or per group he couldn't say, but he worried not; next day, they might catch nothing more than a clump of waterweed, so it would all even out anyway. The four friends agreed it had been a good start to their holiday.

"Hey, let's go and call on Will's cousin tonight," suggested George, with a strange glint in his eye.

"No arguments," said Tom.

Andy sighed. "Okay, then," he replied, knowing he faced another round of half ales, as he'd be driving.

Will thought what a nice chap Reg the landlord of The Leaping Salmon was, and how welcome his wife Margo made the customers feel. He was looking forward to the comfortable surroundings of the public bar. Yes, a visit to The Leaping Salmon sounded great. But, he said nothing. Instead, he speculated on what the evening might bring.

While Will and his friends fished far downstream of Glenstone, Johnny decided on another daytime foray of his own. He craved to go poaching again, and thought enough time had passed since he saw the police searching the riverbank.

A little after midday he set out on what he called a daytime shift, with his barbed arrow and catapult. He also wanted to check on his gear, now safely stashed in a new hiding place. He'd chosen an abandoned rabbit burrow, beneath a sprawling gorse bush, beside an old log. The place looked ideal: secret, and he'd not have to worry about unearthing buried objects.

After walking through the allotments and the overgrown paddock to the north of Glenstone, he carefully approached his latest hideaway. On the patch of tangled waste ground, roughly half a mile from the river, he stopped by the gorse bush, pulled out a football-sized plug of dried grass from the entrance to the burrow, and peered inside. Box, gaff and net were all safe. He replaced the plug and sighed, convinced that not even the prying eyes of Davidson could spot his new depot, as he thought of it.

He turned and looked around, saw no one about and headed toward the river, where thick vegetation swamped the banks and made for his little daytime den.

Feeling happy, he snuggled down among the thick undergrowth, tapping the stem of the shaft, lightly. He noticed a red admiral butterfly basking in the autumnal sun, its wings opening to soak up warmth. For some inexplicable reason, the scarlet bands on the black wings made him think of Rona.

From inside the battered, shapeless trilby he drew the barbed arrowhead, screwed it to the shaft and tied on the stout fishing line.

Glad that no fishermen were along this part of the river, Johnny savoured the peace and thought about events. All of a sudden, he seemed to have a lot of adversaries. He mused over Davidson, McGee and Detective Doherty, each with their dark designs, and all three knew that he poached. For a moment, he wondered if any other folk knew he went poaching. But McGee worried him more than the others; why his cousin wanted him to stop poaching he couldn't work out.

The deep pool was full of splashing fish, perhaps drawn by the warmth of the afternoon sun, or maybe by swarms of midges, which hovered over the water surface. Before long, a healthy, silvery salmon swam into view, leapt, then dived and swam toward the bank.

Grabbing the catapult, he drew back the sling, keeping the thing taut, and aimed. He let go, and the arrow cut through the water, right into the salmon's flank. Gingerly, he reeled in the line, snatched the struggling fish and swiftly rapped it behind the eyes with a sturdy hazel stick. Being a nice size, he judged it weighed all of nine pounds.

Content with the one fish, Johnny unscrewed the arrowhead, slipped it inside the trilby, rewound the line and shoved the slender rod into his deep greatcoat pocket. It had, he felt, been a rewarding afternoon. *Heh! Sixty pounds yer owe me, Reg.*

He dropped the fish in a sturdy black bin liner and slung it over his shoulder, held in place by a harness under his greatcoat. Then, making sure the coast was clear, he emerged from the thicket.

Walking casually along the riverside track toward the stone bridge, he savoured the late afternoon sunshine. Already the sun had a golden hue, and he knew that before long the first frosts would strike, the permit fishermen would be gone and the salmon free to complete their cycle, unhindered. Johnny felt mighty glad to see no policemen along the river, on the other side of the bridge.

He stepped onto the tarmac road and noticed Rona sitting on the low parapet. Unsure whether to approach while carrying the goods, he frowned, then abandoned caution. He looked at her and guessed she'd been crying – rather a lot, too.

"A right fine afternoon, ter be sure," he said, cheerfully.

She turned and glanced at him, then gazed south toward the trees along the riverbank. "Heavenly, isn't it? Peaceful, too." She wiped her cheek, as if brushing away a tear.

Johnny sat near her on the parapet, unsure what to say next, and kept quiet.

"How could it have happened?" she whispered.

Johnny shrugged. "I can't say, but it did, more's the pity."

"Who could have been awful enough to kill Adam like that? It's just unspeakable. He was only twenty-six, for Christ's sake; he'd got his whole life ahead of him."

He nodded. "Aye, it's tragic, if ever. I've seen the likes o' such things before."

She stared at him. "You're an old man; what could you know about it?"

Johnny coughed. "Believe it or not, once I was a young man – in the Army, too. I've seen death more times than yer can imagine: comrades slaughtered in their prime, far younger than yer poor colleague was. I'm still sorry to hear of his death."

"Sorry, I didn't mean to insinuate—"

"Dinnae worry; no offence taken."

"It's all my fault: I should never have asked him to come out here. I feel so responsible and guilty about this."

"You weren't ter know what could happen. It's one o' them cruel twists of destiny, I guess."

"Poor Adam. He loved this river and the countryside around it." She smiled. "He even wanted to get a nature reserve established."

"Sounds like he were a right admirable chap."

Rona nodded. "Yes, he was a bit of an ideologist and a dreamer."

Johnny fell silent, unsure what to add. "I'm surprised ter see you come back, actually."

"I had to; my work here isn't finished." He noticed the skin on her forehead suddenly tighten. "I'm going to get that damned salmon fishery near Rosstown prosecuted, if I can; they've been flushing Deosect into the river. I owe Adam that much, if nothing else."

"Excuse me ignorance, I know little of pollution, but I tell you, this river once teemed with fish, far more than now."

"Really? When was that?"

"Long ago, before you were around. I was born in this village, grew up here. Folk living here were happy then, and helped each other. Villagers had free reign to fish and take from the river what they needed. Now, money-grabbers have moved in and deny ordinary folk basic freedoms, and sell those rights ter them English sods."

Rona smiled again. "Adam said as much. Elitists, he called them."

"Aye, he were right, an' all."

"Are you going to that pub tonight?"

"I've not planned ter visit the Tower o' London instead."

She laughed. "Ben's fortunate to have you as a friend."

"He's bloody lucky ter have a pretty niece. Me, I've only got two sons, both in the Army, fighting fer freedom and democracy in foreign lands."

"You must be proud of them."

"I am, in a way. But what good is freedom in a faraway country, when we don't have it here? It all seems kind o' mixed up."

"I suppose it does, but freedom doesn't extend to polluting the environment. It's all we've got left."

"That it certainly is."

"Can I give you a lift back to the village?"

Caught unaware, Johnny envisioned struggling in and out of a car with a nine-pound salmon dangling down his back. If it slipped, what would the pretty girl make of it? He couldn't guess.

"Kind of yer, but I promised ter look in on a neighbour."

They got up and she walked across to her Nissan, parked in a bay. "See you again sometime."

She waved then drove off, leaving him to amble down the road on his own. He felt saddened not accepting the lift, but relieved in case she discovered what he was carrying under his greatcoat: his stolen fish. He'd no idea how she might react toward a lone poacher, who only took the odd fish now and then.

Back at home, Johnny admired the salmon lying on his kitchen table, while swigging half a mug of Scotch to celebrate catching such a prize. Then, he shoved a steak pie in the oven and a saucepan of baked beans on the hob. While his supper cooked, he stoked up the fire, added a log and switched on the T.V., to catch the news and weather. So far, the weather remained calm, and he hoped it would last until the end of the season. The jaunty lady weather presenter mentioned the fine spell would last for another week or so. Her news cheered him, and thoughts of Davidson and McGee were banished.

That evening, at around eight, Johnny followed his usual routine: alleyway and outhouse visit, to dump the fish in the freezer. He entered the public bar through the internal door and sidled up to the bar, where Reg and Sally chattered behind the counter.

Sally looked flushed and eyed up McGee, dressed in his tweed outfit. "What a smasher. Wouldn't mind a rub against that."

Reg frowned at McGee and turned to his daughter: "You steer clear of him – he's a bad 'un; bring you nothing but heartache and sorrow, you hear?" Then, he noticed Johnny. "Same as usual?"

Johnny nodded and glared at McGee. "What's that bastard doin' here?"

"Getting me daughter all steamed up. Ain't right; he's old

enough to be her dad, almost."

Johnny laughed. "Aye, make it a quick shot o' whisky first."

Reg plonked the chaser on the bar. In one quick swoop, the old man emptied the small glass, sighed then supped on the heavy.

"How's thing's then, Johnny?"

"Tickin' over nicely, and there's a dainty in the pot."

"That's what I like to hear. By the way, news has buzzed all around the village."

"What news?" Johnny asked, leaning against the bar.

"It seems Dinger got himself arrested, charged with murder, too."

"Glory be! Dinger Bell finally comes a cropper, eh?"

"Yes, and that soddin' detective nailed him."

Johnny tugged his nose. "I cannae get over that. He'll be out of the way fer some time, then."

Reg shook his head. "Reckon Doherty got his promotion."

"Worst luck, the bastard."

He grabbed the pint and ambled over to the far corner, where Tom, Ben and Bobby sat.

"Take it you heard the gossip?" asked Tom, filling his pipe with some fresh tobacco.

"In a potted version," replied Johnny, glancing toward the other side of the pub, wondering what his cousin was doing sitting in the public bar. He was chatting away to a crowd which usually dropped in for a quickie, before dashing off to The Grouse.

Bobby spoke: "Bastard was in here earlier, trying the come on with Sally. If he lays a hand on her, I'll—"

"Do what Dinger did?" commented Johnny. "I don't think yer

got it inside, sonny, and just as well, too."

Bobby smarted. "He's a smug git."

Johnny tried to change the subject and turned to Ben: "Saw yer niece this afternoon, down by the bridge. Is she alright, after all this?"

Ben placed his glass on the table. "Adam's death came as a dreadful shock. Ever since, she's got this personal crusade against that blasted salmon farm; it's fast turning into an obsession. Her boss in Dumfries is all for a prosecution, apparently."

"Doesn't look too good for the salmon farm then, eh?" replied Johnny, grabbing his glass. "I gather they've been draining a chemical into the river."

"Yes, in SEPA's eyes polluting the river is a capital offence; death penalty, no less. Culprits are all shot at dawn."

Johnny glanced at his friend. "Are yer having me on?"

Ben laughed. "Maybe that's a slight exaggeration."

Johnny drained the last of his pint and sauntered to the bar for a second. He saw McGee laughing, while chatting up a frivolous, snobby woman who regularly frequented The Grouse.

"Another heavy?" asked Reg.

He nodded in agreement. "Now, tell me, why is that bastard cousin turning up here like this?"

Reg furrowed his brow. "He's almost getting to be a regular, and I don't like it one jot."

"Do yer reckon he's plotting something?"

"Like what?"

Johnny shrugged his shoulders. "Like I said, he knows I been supplying you with the dainties."

"What can he do about it? If he says anything, he'd only incriminate himself. After all, he gave you those packages."

"I dinnae trust him, not an ounce."

He snatched the pint and returned to the others. Every so often, he peeped across the room and felt uneasy. Just before nine, McGee departed with the posh crowd, and Johnny was glad.

He was about to pass a sarcastic comment, when Will and his mates strode into the bar. Johnny almost dropped the pint of heavy, unable to believe his other cousin had suddenly returned. Tom and Ben also looked astonished.

"I'll be damned. What brings yer up here?"

Will gave the old man a hearty smile. "Is that a friendly way to greet your cousin? We're on a fishing holiday – last of the season. Just thought we'd drop in and say howdy, like."

Johnny rubbed the corner of his eye. "That's very thoughtful of you. Yer might as well grab a pew."

Tom and Andy grabbed the vacant table next to Johnny's party, and sat down. "Right, what's everyone having?" asked Andy.

"Pint of best ale, I reckon," stated Will.

"Make it that new Dutch lager, if they got it," added George.

"Are yer not suppin' heavy, then?" Johnny commented, smirking at Will and his friends.

"Cousin, after last time, heavy is out – way out. Jesus, I nearly died."

"Aye, takes a man to drink a man's drink."

Will shook his shoulders. "Fine if hangovers are your thing; not for me, thanks. Anyway, I landed a fish this morning: a five-pounder, no less."

Johnny smiled, wryly. "Did yer indeed? And some wily sod landed a nine-pound salmon. I cannae guess who he was, though."

George glared at him, immediately seeing through the old man's cryptic remark. A wave of admiration swept through him. He wondered if he dared carry out a plan he'd formulated, to trick the old fellow into divulging his secret.

When Andy and Tom returned with the drinks, George took a long swig of lager and decided there was nothing to lose. He put the pint down and took a small, postcard-sized envelope from his anorak pocket. He got up and handed it to the old soldier.

"Here you go, Uncle Johnny. Happy birthday."

Johnny started and glared at the young man. "What yer playing at? It ain't me birthday yet. That's months away."

George grinned knowingly, but flushed slightly – not with embarrassment, but guilt.

Johnny's eyes narrowed to slits and he tore the envelope open. He felt mystified, and saw not a card but a sheet of blank paper. Pulling it free of the envelope, he opened it and read the scrawled message: *"I know you go poaching."*

Johnny blinked hard and stared at the message again, hoping he'd misread the notation. He hadn't. Without uttering a word, he slipped the paper into his pocket, dashed to the bar and ordered a bottle of Scotch, requesting three glasses. Then he returned to the table, to the amazement of his friends.

"What's going on?" asked Ben, looking puzzled.

"Never you mind; this is family business." Johnny turned to face George and Will, and wagged his finger at them. "Right, I want ter speak with you – both of you – but not in here; out the back. Come on."

Will had never really seen Johnny angry before, and wondered if George had kicked a hornets' nest. He and George followed the old man along the narrow corridor to a door marked: *"Private"*. Johnny grabbed the door handle and they entered the outhouse.

Inside his one and only sanctuary, Johnny thumped the bottle down on the top of the freezer in the corner, then placed the three glasses alongside. Taking a deep breath, he unscrewed the lid, poured three measures and handed the glasses to Will and George. He glared at the young man, and George felt the stare burn right through him. Then the old man spoke out, sternly:

"What the friggin' hell's goin' on between you two? What makes yer think I go poachin', eh?"

George shuddered, regretting the little trick, which seemed to have backfired. He downed the hard liquor in one go and, after a minute, felt more confident. "Last time we were up here, you dropped loads of funny remarks. I just kinda got to thinking."

Johnny glared at the youngster with loathing. "Did yer now? And you'd know all about poachin', wouldn't yer, eh?"

Unsure what was happening, Will downed his Scotch in one and cheekily placed it on the freezer, as though asking for a top-up. Johnny obliged. He also refilled George's glass. George downed the drink almost in one and, feeling bolder, squared up to the old soldier.

"Yeah, I do, as a matter of fact."

"Dinnae try an' take the piss out o' me, sonny. Aye, I do go poachin' if yer must know – it seems everyone else does."

Will stared at his cousin, unable to say anything. George had been right all along. George grinned at Will; "See? I bloody told you so."

Johnny squinted. "Are yer treating this as a bloody joke, or what?"

George breezily helped himself to another Scotch. "No, actually I was just curious. Back home I go poaching, mainly for trout. Good it is, too; I got ninety quid from the local publican the other day for a salmon."

Johnny sneered at the youngster, almost dismissing his claim as a wild boast. *What could a young upstart less than half my age know of the sport?* he thought. "Aye, I suppose yer a fucken' expert then?"

George downed the drink, then casually sat on top of the freezer. "Yeah, not half; I've been at it for around five years."

Shocked by his off-hand statement, Johnny nearly sent the bottle crashing to the floor. He'd been poaching for more than a decade, and here was a kid that knew all the tricks, seemingly. He poured another drink and downed the measure in one. This startling new revelation made his head swim. How much Will had known he'd no idea. Johnny began to wonder who else might know of his furtive trade.

"Since the beans – or maybe I should say river fish – have been spilt all over this fucken' flagstone floor, what the hell do yer want?"

George gently rapped the side of the freezer with his heel. "Aw, don't worry, we ain't after your money. Actually, I kinda thought you might show us how you hooked the fish."

"Yer what? Are you bloody jokin', here?"

"No, I thought a sort of camaraderie existed between poachers, like. After all, it's only like an extension to rod fishing, kinda, without a permit."

Johnny blew breath. "Jesus, sonny, yer got some bloody gall."

George shrugged. "No matter; I ain't pushing. It's a free world an' all – so them lying politicians make out."

Johnny paced around the room, totally flummoxed by the turn of events.

Then, he thought about McGee, and how Davidson and the duke seemed hellbent on snaring local poachers, even those working alone. It suddenly dawned on him that he'd been offered a way to fight back. Will and George turning up like this seemed like a golden opportunity to give the duke and his minions the finger. And, if things came to the worst, he could always shop McGee for supplying confiscated salmon. He eyed up his cousin and the youngster.

"Aye, alright. If that's what yer really want, then I'll oblige."

Will gazed at his cousin in awe. "Really? Christ. When?"

"Dinnae piss yer pants. Poachin' needs plannin'; yer don't just go charging off to the riverside." He turned to George: "But Mr. Smartarse here already knows that, eh?"

Will couldn't believe his cousin had agreed to take them on an illicit fishing trip, and felt the thrilling tingle of anticipation. All the bitter recrimination he'd taken from Dot over the past years was suddenly swept away.

Johnny topped up the glasses again, then tapped his finger on the edge of the freezer lid. "Make it tomorrow night; there's a clear sky, no moon and calm weather. But, I'll only do this on my terms. You and yer friends better make for that little stone bridge outside the village. Then, yer want to walk half a mile along the track, heading northward – I'll meet yer out there. I have a secret way out of the village and want ter keep it that way. Agreed?"

Will and George nodded. "Yeah, no problems," George replied.

Johnny sniffed. "An' wear dark clothing. No point in advertising to the duke we are in fer a spot o' poachin'. Got it?"

George sneered. "I know that much already."

Johnny narrowed his eyes. "Aye, yer no' so bloody green, are ya?"

"Never said I were."

Johnny ignored the wisecrack. "I have ter say, a party o' five men is goin' ter look mighty like a poaching gang. We get scores o' them up here, netting the river: wild they are, and not beyond murder, too. In fact, one happened the other night."

George and Will stared at the old man. Will already felt a newfound admiration for Johnny and his knowledge of local poachers. Everything had turned out to be far darker than he'd ever envisioned, yet the thrill of going out poaching was something not to be missed.

"There's just one other little thing: we operate between eight and ten; I never work after one, ever. That way, I avoid running into them gangs." Then, he remembered the clash before Davidson had caught him. "Well, usually, that is. Set out from the bridge around eight."

"Yeah, right, agreed," enthused Will.

Johnny stared at the two men, then grabbed the Scotch bottle and hid it behind a pile of stacked beer-bottle crates. "I've no more to say on the subject tonight. Another thing: in the bar keep yer traps shut. Silence on such matters is the key to success."

Will laughed. "Don't worry, cousin, our jaws are locked tight."

He led them back to the busy bar, where Reg glanced in their direction, mystified by the odd shenanigans. Johnny went to the bar for another pint of heavy.

"Is everything okay?" Reg asked.

"Aye, it is now," replied Johnny, unsure what he'd got himself into. "Ever get the feeling yer little kingdom gets rumbled by an earthquake?"

"Frequently, but I don't let things ruffle me. In my job, I can't afford to."

Johnny nodded in agreement and returned to his friends. Ben and Tom were curious about his sudden exit.

"What's going on?" asked Tom, tapping his pipe on the ashtray.

Johnny sighed and suddenly felt tired. Everyone, it seemed, wanted to know other folks' business, and he was sick of it. The latest discovery had come as a shock. "Just a family matter, that's all," Johnny lied, hoping his friend would let the matter drop. It had been a long night, with McGee, then Will arriving with his blasé friend. Johnny felt rather glad when Reg called last orders, and wasn't heartbroken to bid Will and his friends goodnight, either.

Having left The Leaping Salmon via the outhouse, he returned home feeling shattered. He'd not felt this way for a long time, and wanted his favourite chair, with the log fire crackling away.

At home, he settled, left the lights off and relished the cosy glow from the hearth. He thought of McGee, Davidson and the recent murder. Then, Will and George had brought a new aspect to an increasingly complex web of lies, deceit and intrigue surrounding his little poaching venture. Everything seemed to be mushrooming out of control, just like the explosion from an atom bomb.

He sipped some more Scotch from the mug, then drifted off until the small hours, and the desperate need to call at the toilet. Afterward, he fell into a slumber on his bed.

CHAPTER 30

Johnny shares his secrets

THE FOLLOWING EVENING, Johnny peeked out the front door, noted the clear, dark sky and sniffed for signs of rain. He only detected the mild damp of rank vegetation.

Slipping on his greatcoat, he shoved the tightly-rolled bin liner in the left pocket and stubby candles in his right, along with a box of matches. From the cupboard under the stairs, he withdrew a small pair of binoculars – a recent purchase from a thrift shop in Rosstown; they'd cost him all of twelve pounds, and made up for his confiscated telescope. Proper telescopes like the one he had were difficult to find, and he decided binoculars would serve his intended purpose just as well, if not better. He hung the strap over his neck.

Quietly, he closed the front door and sidled to the path leading to the allotments, and the abandoned, overgrown paddock, now almost as familiar to him and his old haunt near the duke's domain. At the end of the paddock, he skirted around a field and eventually arrived at the scrubby heath, where the gorse bush flourished over the empty warren. He stood in the lee of the bush, hidden but able to see the river. He peered through the binoculars and saw four men hiking along the river – for once, he knew they were friends.

He drew the grassy plug from the mouth of the rabbit tunnel, and extracted the small wooden box and his gaff. He looked at the net, but with Will and his three friends along, decided squatting under the net would be a pointless formality. Shoving the box and gaff in the deep pocket, he carefully replaced the plug and slung a handful of autumn leaves in front. Satisfied that all looked natural and undisturbed, he set out for the river.

In fact, Johnny was really chuffed to have found the warren, as it saved all the digging and burying of his equipment. He reminded himself he must adopt a similar strategy, when the time arrived for him to return to his old poaching haunt. He was sure it would happen one day.

On reaching the river, he paced along the path, backtracking slightly, as they'd arranged to meet half a mile north of the bridge.

They were huddled there, under a tree. George seemed perfectly at ease, Will was obviously excited, while Andy and Tom looked decidedly out of place.

Johnny smiled and realized that young George must have been telling the truth, after all; he was obviously no stranger to slipping along riversides at night. He beckoned to them, but silently. Will nodded and pointed toward the old man.

Will and the others had arrived along the path from the bridge. To avoid attracting attention, Andy had left the Fiesta at The Leaping Salmon car park, and they'd simply walked down the road; four friends out for an evening stroll would seem harmless enough, and if stopped and searched they had nothing to hide. Will really couldn't believe they were on the verge of doing something totally illegal, and the thrill of becoming a "lawbreaker" felt electrifying. He was also really curious as to how his cousin snared the fish. He couldn't imagine him messing around with lines and hooks, as he'd read of in articles about poachers. Nor could he see him wielding a net.

"Right, now, listen here," Johnny whispered: "follow me, single file, and keep yer traps shut."

George smiled at the old man's advice – the same tip he'd often given to his friends, while poaching in Droitwich Spa.

Andy and Tom scowled, uncertain about the venture, knowing nothing of poaching or other furtive occupations. Andy even thought a policeman or some gamekeeper might suddenly emerge from behind a tree and get them arrested. He'd seen such things on T.V. dramas, and that was as far as his experience extended.

Johnny led them another mile and a half along the river, a little farther on from his daytime hide among the undergrowth. The place was ideal for the catapult, but hardly suitable with his other trick, nor accompanied by the four men. He chose a site, in a little dell beside a riverside pool; in the dell, they'd less chance of being spotted. George was obviously impressed by the old man's choice of location, and would have sought out a similar spot.

Motioning the party to remain silent, as George knew was the golden rule, Johnny extracted the gaff and box from his deep coat pocket. He shoved the two stubby candles on the nails inside, then affixed the string tether to the hook on the side. He lit the candles and gently eased down the lid. Then, he set the box afloat on the water's surface, and secured the other end of the string to a small aluminium peg, stuck into the ground. Then, clasping his gaff, he lay alongside the bank.

The four men squatted along the incline of the dell. Before long, George inched forward and huddled, as he usually did on his expeditions. He wanted to see what the old man did.

Johnny kept his eyes on the flickering light which emanated from the slits in the box, hoping for a decent catch, or maybe two, and put the little upstart in his place. The box bobbed along gently on the water's surface.

Before long, the first fish of the evening rose to the surface. It wasn't a large one; he guessed it weighed four or five pounds. Being a silvery colour, Johnny knew this fish had only recently returned from the sea it entered three years earlier as a smolt, and now sought to complete the endless cycle of reproduction.

While the small fish circled the box, the flickering light drew in a white moth. It hovered about, then finally ended up on the water's surface, held fast. Though the juvenile salmon ignored it, Johnny already knew the moth's life was almost done, and he was right: moments later, the trapped insect was swallowed by a passing brown trout. He thought the trout must have enjoyed such a tasty morsel.

While poaching with the tethered box, he'd watched hundreds of fish rise to the flickering lure, and rarely missed hooking a good specimen, though his heart always raced while doing so.

This time, a large salmon appeared from the inky depths of the pool and approached the box, its mouth slowly undulating as though breathing, and its eyes dark discs surrounded by gold circles, staring at the wavering light. Almost entranced by the beauty of the salmon, Johnny imagined the distance and perils it faced, to reach the spawning grounds near the head of the stream.

Waking from his reverie, he noticed the fish swim to the far side of the floating box. He cursed softly under his breath, for not striking when the salmon was within easy reach. Another, larger fish had chased it away.

Unfortunately, the new fish was not nearly so attractive, and he never generally bothered with such a fish, as they had little commercial value. Johnny knew even the permit-paying rod-and-line men, when hooking such fish, automatically threw them back into the river as a bad job. These larger salmon were dubbed "resident" fish, since they inhabited a deep pool for several months and lost all their silvery sheen, instead turning a nasty, dark shade. What's more, Johnny had discovered these less favourable fish rarely accepted any fisherman's bait, not even prawns.

The old poacher knew exactly how to deal with these ugly fish, having encountered them before. His answer was dead simple: he leaned out over the river and, with the gaff handle, struck the offending fish just in front of its tail fin, where it would do no lasting damage. Such unwanted fish quickly slipped back down to the depths of their pools.

Luckily, that night Johnny did not have long to wait before his prized salmon returned. This time he didn't hesitate, and with one smooth, swift action, swung the gaff and hooked the salmon from the water, with amazing speed. George was astounded, never suspecting the old man had either the strength or the agility. Johnny sighed with relief, pleased to have got the ten-pound salmon after all, and in front of his little band of spectators.

Johnny was not greedy but, wanting to underline to the young man from Droitwich Spa how effective his poaching method was, decided to hang on for a second fish to turn up.

Before long, one surfaced and swam toward the flickering light within the box. After a while, it shoved the box forward a little, seemingly hypnotized by the candlelight.

Johnny's eyes narrowed. He judged the distance to the entranced creature and struck without hesitation. He hooked the fish onto the bank and, like the previous catch, a quick rap from the gaff handle made the creature lie motionless. This second fish weighed around six pounds.

George couldn't believe what he'd witnessed, and nor could the others. Will felt that what his cousin had accomplished seemed to be magical; he made the task appear to be dead easy.

To Johnny's cousin, the strangest thing of all was that the time had flown by. It was now getting on for nearly ten o'clock, and that would leave more or less just an hour and a half in The Leaping Salmon.

Without speaking, Johnny signalled it was time to go. He dunked the box under the water's surface, grabbed it and shoved his gaff down his coat pocket. The two salmon he slipped into the black bag, then affixed it to his harness under the greatcoat.

Will was really amazed by how his cousin appeared to be so organized and methodical. *Perhaps that comes of being in the Army,* he thought. That was partly true, but also the case was that Johnny had pursued this sport for years.

Johnny traipsed along the path, followed by Will and George; Tom and Andy brought up the rear. Andy, though impressed, was less enthusiastic about the venture, which seemed not so sporting as fishing with a line and rod.

Within half a mile of the road, Johnny stopped and decreed that they continue to the village without him; he wanted to stash his gear away first. Will and George agreed, and they would meet up in the public bar of The Leaping Salmon.

Johnny strode off toward the scrubby heath. At the gorse bush, he uncorked the burrow, stowed the gaff and box away, then plugged the aperture once more, adding a handful of autumn leaves, as before. Johnny wondered why he hadn't thought of that idea before now.

Content that all appeared safe and sound, he trudged across the paddock, then walked across the allotment gardens, where nobody was ever present during those late hours. A quick hike along a gravel path brought him out to the tarmac road and home.

He nipped indoors for a quick Scotch, before striding down the road to the tavern, once more.

CHAPTER 31

Party rift

IN THE OUTHOUSE, he dropped the bag of salmon into the freezer, then shed his greatcoat and entered the lively, busy bar.

Alas, the first person he clapped eyes on was McGee.

Johnny was determined not to let his cousin spoil a rewarding evening, ignored him and sauntered to the bar. Reg placed a pint of heavy and a chaser on the bar. The whisky lasted all of ten seconds then, supping the heavy, Johnny turned around, cast a glance over the room and saw Tom, Ben and Bobby seated in the corner. At the next table sat Will, Tom, Andy and George. Johnny sighed. *Home team's all here, then?* he thought, and grinned.

"Take it things are okay?" Reg asked.

"Fine. Just dandy, in fact," commented the old soldier.

Reg took that as meaning: "Another salmon in the freezer."

Johnny sat down on his usual chair and watched the others in the room. He wasn't sorry to see McGee leave, with a party heading for The Grouse.

Will, on the other hand, felt ecstatic and full of adventure, dreaming of the time when he might try his hand at poaching. He'd felt electrified earlier that night, and thought it would counterbalance all the wretchedness he suffered living with Dot. He got drunk as the evening progressed, and surmised that, if he went poaching, the activity might, as his friends and neighbours had already insinuated, save her skin.

George was also in his element, and wanted to go on another venture with the old man. He suspected the old-timer had several methods for snaring fish, and wanted to know them all.

Andy, being less enamoured, insisted that they have a boozy barbecue at the holiday cottage the following night, and would then be able to get plastered. He'd now put up with two nights of his holiday supping on halves of light ale, and was getting cheesed off. Tom agreed with him. Reluctantly, Will and George capitulated, to keep the peace.

To Will, it suddenly seemed they'd become a party split: he and George eager to go on these illicit outings, while Andy and Tom just wanted to let their hair down after a day's legal fishing. Were storm clouds gathering on the horizon? Will hoped not.

After Reg declared drinking-up time, Will sauntered over to his cousin. "It's been a great night. Like to do this again some time."

Johnny nodded. "Aye, I bet yer would. Maybe fancy having a go too, eh?"

Will grinned. "Rather! Do you reckon I'd be any good at it?"

The old man shrugged. "Who could guess? Yer mastered line fishing, so anything might be possible. Aye, until next time, then."

He bid Will and his friends goodnight, disappeared through the back door to the outhouse, and casually walked down the dark lane, to home and his roaring fire, favourite chair and late sup of Scotch, while gawping at his girlfriend presenting the weather forecast.

CHAPTER 32

Lone crusader

THE FOLLOWING MORNING, Johnny paid a flying visit to Reg at The Leaping Salmon, to collect his illicit payment and grab a quickie or two. At eleven o'clock, the public bar was almost empty, Reg was busy replenishing bottles on the shelves, and Sally polished the tables.

He stopped on seeing Johnny, and furtively dropped sixty pounds on the bar, before plonking a brimming pint on the beer mat. Johnny snatched the notes faster than he swung his gaff and pocketed the money.

"I must say, for all the aggravation, you keep bringing in the goodies," commented Reg, cheerfully. "I'm starting to build up a regular trade for the dainties, too."

Johnny nodded, knowing his friend was selling the fish under the counter, without pestering the taxman. "Aye, it's a small bloody wonder, what with McGee nosin' round and all."

Johnny glanced around the room, supping his first free pint of heavy. He saw Rona sitting in her corner, playing with the laptop, occasionally sipping from a mug of coffee. Feeling the need for some company, he approached her. "Mind if I join yer?" he asked.

Rona turned from the laptop and smiled, just like Annie used to do. *So long ago,* Johnny thought.

"Hi. You're Johnny, aren't you?"

The old man nodded. "I ain't bleedin' Prince Charles, that's fer sure."

Rona laughed. "You've a way with words."

"What yer doin' with that thing?"

"Compiling data. I'm building a case against that salmon farm. With a bit of luck, Liam will send it onto the European Union Environmental Agency, in Copenhagen."

"Aye. Really, farmed salmon's rubbish; tastes like shit. Ends up in all those tins in the supermarkets."

She stared at him with those big, hazel eyes – Annie's eyes, almost. "Tell me something I don't already know."

Johnny squirmed and supped the pint. "Ain't just the salmon farm that's muckin' up the river; that blasted duke never does a damned thing for the watercourse. He just issues permits and gets them English sods ter fill up his hotel rooms. Never gives a thought to feeding the fish, or clearing the banks of debris and managing the land."

"Sounds a right cad. Has he been polluting the river?"

"I've no idea, but he don't give a fig about things unless they make instant profit."

She looked at him. "You must obviously know an awful lot about the river?"

Johnny shook his head. "Aye, I suppose it's been a big part of me life; I know it like the back of me hand. And, by God, I've seen some changes."

"Adam said this river was particularly rich in wildlife."

"He was right." Johnny suddenly had an idea to help the girl: "If yer like, I could show yer the river one night; point out how that bastard is ruining the place."

She looked at him. "Thanks, it'd provide a useful insight to a habitat that could be in danger."

"How about goin' out there this evening? I've nae much ter do, and the weather's goin' ter remain calm."

She smiled again. "Fine by me."

Johnny supped more beer. "See yer at the little stone bridge, around eight."

He got up and returned to the bar for a word with Reg, then went home, looking forward to the evening.

Just after eight, Johnny strode down the lane toward the bridge, and got a shock on seeing Rona's Nissan parked in the bay. She stood beside the gap in the hedge where, not so long ago, Adam had left the Transit van.

"Didn't think you were coming," she said.

"I wouldn't miss this fer the world. Few outsiders show an interest in the river fer what it is. Come, I'll show yer me favourite patch."

Johnny planned to frequent his beloved pool and show her how magical the place was at night. He also wanted to check up on his favourite haunt, as he'd not been there since Davidson had confiscated all his poaching gear.

They strode along the path used by anglers and sheep, and a few odd poachers now and then. Johnny soaked up the sounds of the night, listening to the gurgle of the river and the occasional screech from a barn owl. He wondered if the little owl still frequented the woods where he'd once stashed his gaff and net, and assumed it would.

The simplistic beauty of the place entranced Rona. "How could anyone with a love of the countryside view this as a money-making enterprise, and nothing more?"

"If yer mean that lousy duke, I don't think he's ever been out here and seen what there is. He views the river as a way ter robs them English folk desperate to play the fishing game. The laughable thing is that half o' them couldn't catch more than a clump o' weed. It's sad."

"Sounds like a wasted resource, if ever."

"Aye, but it's the damage these anglers do ter the riverside, constantly trampling along the banks; some of these paths are starting to resemble dirt tracks. In parts, the embankments are collapsing. In winter, great chunks of earth and grass topple away with the floods, the ground being weakened by the numbers that flock here."

"Surely this landlord repairs any damaged banks?"

"No, he just leaves the river to wash away the debris."

"That amounts to mismanagement of the river," stated Rona.

"You got it, but he doesn't care. Neither do any of the other landowners that are in league with him. They're all the same."

He led her toward the waterfall and the head of his favourite pool, and heard the gushing water. Johnny thought it sounded almost like music, and realized he'd sorely missed his old hangout. Suddenly, an intense hatred of Davidson and McGee welled up inside him. What right had they to bar him from this riverside paradise, which should be available to all people who respected nature, he thought?

Rona watched the water cascade over the rocky fall, to end up in the foaming depths of the pool.

"This stretch of the river is certainly exceptional, like nature has sculpted the land for all to enjoy."

"That's why I brought you here. Now, is it fair one wealthy egotist has the right to call all this his own, eh?" Johnny smarted.

"If they've been neglecting this river, I guess questions need asking."

"Aye, but who is going ter raise the issue?"

"I can think of one or two people. You've given me an idea."

They strode farther along the river path, to the spot where Adam had expressed enthusiasm to get the location designated as a special site of natural interest.

"This place really ought to be cared for more than it is now," stated Rona.

"That'd be all good and well, providing the villagers have free reign to come and go."

Rona nodded in agreement, then spotted a tangled mass among the reeds. She lifted up a wad of discarded fishing line, with a small lead weight. "I suppose this was discarded by one of those permit fishermen?"

"It might have got washed downstream," said Johnny. "I've seen all sorts of discarded gear: bits of line, litter and even a Wellington boot, once."

Rona frowned. "Them careless anglers are endangering the very thing they come to visit, and that's not environmentally sound."

"They're not adding anything ter the scenery, that's fer sure."

"I didn't mean that," replied Rona. "Such items could provide temporary refuge for sea lice, and possibly the G.S. fluke, too. I'm not kidding, this menace is a real threat. Why is it these fishermen fail to comply with the angler's code? Don't they realize what could happen?"

Johnny sighed. "I guess few people know of lice or flukes. And that arrogant landlord wouldn't take any damned notice, either. Not even it smacked his fat face."

Rona bagged the discarded fishing line and scowled. "Right, this gives me something else to work on."

They headed back to the stone bridge, admired the tranquillity of the river, and Johnny made up his mind, there and then, to return to his pool, duke or no duke.

Rona spoke: "I haven't seen much in the way of warnings. Why hasn't anyone bothered to display notices about clearing away their mess?"

Johnny shrugged. "Like I say, the environment doesn't worry that greedy parasite."

"You've certainly opened my eyes tonight. Obviously, action has to be taken. Perhaps you could help me with another venture, as you know all about this river?"

"Aye, I'd be glad to. What have yer in mind?"

"If I painted a picture of this locality, and depict the risk it faces, I just might be able to get the European Environmental Agency to take action, or at least implement measures laid down by their *Habitats Directive*, and safeguard this place.

"Can yer do that?

"Of course. Look, can I call on you tomorrow, say around two?"

Back at the bridge, Johnny agreed to her request, but partly for his own selfish reason. He enjoyed Rona's company, as she vividly reminded him of Annie.

After she drove off in the Nissan, Johnny wandered down the road and, for the first time in many years, suddenly whistled "Auld Lang Syne".

CHAPTER 33

Johnny tells all to Rona

NEXT AFTERNOON, RONA called on Johnny, having obtained his address from Ben. Hugging her laptop, she rapped the doorknocker, wondering if the old man knew as much about the river and surrounding countryside as he claimed.

He answered the door and led her to the kitchen. Rona smiled at the dishevelled workshop and obviously realized a woman was absent from his life, but held her tongue.

Johnny smiled. "Glad yer came. I were makin' tea. Care fer one?"

She nodded: "Please. Look, I've had an idea, but can't promise any results. However, nothing ventured…"

"I know the rest," Johnny replied, grabbing the steaming kettle and filling two mugs, hoping she wouldn't go over to the fridge for the milk: he didn't want her to see the bin liner package he'd found on his doorstep that morning.

"So, what can I do fer ye? How can I help?"

She sat down at the pinewood kitchen table, opened up the laptop and pressed a few keys, whilst sipping tea from the mug. "Basically, give me a rundown on all you know about this river. If I can paint an idyllic picture of this region, and how it's being abused, chances are I can get legal action taken against the perpetrators. That bloody salmon farm, for instance, has been flushing Deosect into the water."

"That much I gather," replied Johnny. "What of it?"

"Deosect is harmful to aquatic life, and wild salmon not least of all. About a year ago, another salmon farm along the Spey was found illegally administering sea lice treatment chemicals – notably emamectin benzoate – which had seeped into the river. Consequently, they were fined three-thousand pounds for polluting the water course."

"Sounds a lot fer getting' rid o' a wee bit of waste."

Rona laughed. "Not at all; far from it. Listen, the Scottish Government's Fisheries Research Services estimates that sea lice leaking from various salmon farms are killing Scottish wild salmon. The F.R.S. also maintains the problem is getting worse, in spite of prosecutions, and is costing the industry thirty-million a year. Of course, the impact on wild fish is hotly disputed."

"Aye, sounds like them politicians and money folk dinnae want complications."

"You got it. But the sea lice that feed on the skin of salmon have become a major problem for the industry. The lice can exist without a live host for up to three weeks, and are easily transferred from the farms to the rivers. It would only take one careless angler to wipe out the salmon from an entire region. That's why I got angry about the discarded line last night."

"Seems like a major problem here, but one I know little of."

"It is significant, but wild salmon near these farms are far more susceptible to lice infestation than those elsewhere – especially the juvenile fish, yet to develop a thicker skin and scales. But there's another side to the problem: poachers are also responsible for the spread of these sea lice."

Johnny's face clouded. "Is that a fact?"

"Yes it is, and they probably have no idea of the danger. Have you ever seen a salmon affected by lice?"

"Can't say that I have."

"It's awful; lice feed on the skin. Some days ago, Bobby and I found a near-skinless salmon farther along the river. I had a dreadful idea this G.S. fluke might have been responsible. The G.S. fluke is far more terrifying and invincible than the lice are, believe me."

"Not exactly a cheery prospect, is it?"

"No, and the polluters and poachers are mainly instrumental in all this widespread environmental and economic damage."

Johnny sipped his tea quietly, wondering what her reaction would be if she ever found out he'd poached more fish over the years than she'd scoffed ice creams. He glanced at the fridge door, knowing the dark secret that lay on the other side: a little present from his shifty cousin. He felt uncomfortable.

"Right, so, with all this knowledge, what can I possibly add?"

"You know about the river, and how it's got into such a sad state. That landlord, for instance, obviously isn't helping matters, as far as I saw last night."

"That blasted duke and his minion bailiffs have been a sore point with the villagers for years. Treats it like his own property, he does."

Johnny told her about the river as it was during his childhood, and how local folk used to revere the watercourse, even up to the post-war years. He explained how the duke's father began his small fishing permit enterprise, and how the present duke expanded upon it and, having built a hotel on his grounds, played host – though an avaricious one – to the scores of English fishermen who flocked to the shores. While he recalled the battles between the landlord and the villagers, Rona typed the information into the laptop, with all the dexterity of a news reporter, pausing now and then to ask the odd question. Naturally, he left out all the bits regarding his riverside antics, as Doherty had described it. By now, Rona had a clearer image of how not only the duke, but also poachers and the fish farms, had defiled the river.

By four o'clock, Johnny felt ready for a drink. "Care fer a wee dram?" he asked.

Surprisingly, Rona nodded while checking the copy.

"This account fills in loads of details. Gee, I can't wait to file my report to H.Q. That ruddy salmon farm's going to face a claim for damages."

Johnny plonked two glasses on the table and poured the Scotch. "Aye, I'm glad ter hears it." Johnny had little idea of salmon farms, and the havoc they'd wrought, but realized that Ben hadn't exaggerated Rona's infatuation with the subject.

He raised his glass. "Here's ter the sinking of the duke and that salmon farm, then."

Rona burst into hysterics, and began to appreciate his casual witticisms.

Just then, Johnny heard a cheery musical serenade. Then, it

sounded again. Rona drew her mobile phone from a jacket pocket and answered. Johnny smiled. He'd never bothered about getting one, as they looked too complex and fiddly. Besides, he'd have no use for such a thing.

"Hi, Liam… Great. Listen, I've almost got a case against Rosstown Salmon Farm. Bear with me for a couple of days; I don't want to dash in without hard evidence… Okay, speak soon." She hung up and dropped the phone on the table. "That was my boss. I'll have to go to Dumfries soon, but need to finish what I set out to achieve."

"Has all this got any bearing on that young man getting murdered?"

Rona squinted at him. "You're very inquisitive. The guilt weighs heavy." She drained the glass. Johnny topped it up.

"Are you trying to get me drunk?"

Johnny smiled and, for a fleeting moment, saw Annie sitting there, like she had done so many years ago. "No. Whatever gave yer that idea?"

She smiled. "Age-old ploy, isn't it?"

Johnny flushed at her suggestive remark, grabbed the empty glasses and dumped them in the sink, wiping his hands on a towel. He threw it onto the tabletop. "Dinnae be daft."

Rona smiled again, folded the laptop and slipped her jacket on. "Thanks for all the info. Really, I mean it. Just maybe we can get something done about this state of affairs."

"What, against that duke? Heh, that'll be the day."

"Be optimistic."

"Aye, right. I enjoyed our sojourn."

He saw Rona to the door, deeply happy and slightly sad; it had been a long time since he'd spent the afternoon speaking with a woman. Will's wife had been no comfort when they'd turned up for Annie's funeral.

Rona waved once, then departed in the Nissan.

Johnny closed the door, glad she'd not discovered the latest delivery McGee had made. He took a quick peek at the fish, a medium one of roughly four pounds. Right then, Johnny decided to make another riverside excursion that night, while the calm weather lasted, to top up the freezer in Reg's outhouse, and his cash jar on the mantelpiece.

CHAPTER 34

Johnny's discovery

LYING BENEATH HIS camouflaged net on the riverside that night, and watching the wooden box bob gently on the calm water, he mused over Will's ambition to have a go at poaching. Johnny could understand why the idea had hooked him: poaching fish from the river was like taking a powerful drug; it was a job to stop. Not even McGee's offerings could sway him to pack it in.

It crossed his mind to let Will try his hand with the gaff – if nothing else, he might get a good laugh. He thought of the confident youngster called George. Johnny knew it was dead obvious he was an old hand at the game, and hated to admit it. Perhaps the kid was right: maybe some sort of comradeship existed among poachers, just as between anglers.

After a spell, he noticed a familiar shape swim into view, entranced by the yellowish, flickering light. The salmon was of medium size; he judged its weight to be five or maybe six pounds. With two medium-sized fish he should get sixty pounds in cash, and he smiled at the thought.

The fish swam right up to the box, seemingly to nudge it along, but it never got the chance to do so: faster than a river rat bolting into its burrow, Johnny hooked the salmon from the river in a flash. He wondered if Will could wield a gaff with equal skill. He gave the wriggling fish a quick rap, extinguished the candles and dropped his gear in the net; as usual, the salmon went into the bin liner down his back. Happy everything was in order, he strode along the bank to return his gear to the rabbit burrow.

Then, almost by chance, his right foot struck an object: something soft, lying on the path. He stooped and picked up a dead fish, roughly four pounds in weight. Somehow, it felt wrong, but he knew it was a salmon. Deciding to keep the find, he stopped and unloaded his bagged salmon. He tore off a strip from the bin liner and re-affixed the bag to his harness. The new, strange fish he wrapped in the torn-off plastic and, on return to the burrow, would carry it home in the deep pocket. For some reason, his instinct told him to keep his catch and the odd fish separate.

Having stashed away his gear, he headed for the stone bridge and strode down the lane. First, he called at home for a quick Scotch and to collect McGee's fish, before going to The Leaping Salmon.

In his kitchen, he dumped his catch and drew the additional fish from his coat pocket. Curious as to why it felt odd, he undid the bundle and stared at the greyish, glistening, skinless salmon. The eerie spectacle made him shudder; it even made the ugly, dark, pool-dwelling salmon look attractive.

He knew it was just the sort of thing Rona needed for her case against the farm, it being probably the work of the lice. But, try as he might, he couldn't find any lice, and guessed they were either microscopic or had left the host. He wrapped it back up in the plastic sheet and placed it in an old tin, inside the fridge.

Johnny washed his hands, drank more Scotch from a mug, then

stuffed McGee's present and his latest catch in a new bin liner. Peeking out the door to make sure nobody was around, he slammed it and departed for the pub.

Having dropped the salmon in the freezer, Johnny entered the public bar and walked over to the counter.

"Heavy, Johnny?" asked Reg.

He nodded. "Aye, and a chaser first. I kind o' need it."

The chaser he downed in one. Grasping the pint, he eyed over the crowded bar. He saw McGee seated at a table, greeting casual callers in for a drink, before continuing to The Grouse.

"Johnny, do join me," garbled McGee.

The old soldier could see his cousin had drunk more than the usual quota. Johnny sat down and supped at his pint of heavy. "What the devil are yer playin' at now, fer Christ's sake?"

McGee slouched and rubbed his neck. "Be fair, I was only trying to be civil, cousin. You… you always suspect things; never see any good in others."

"See good in you? Dae me a favour. Ye make me sick. What yer after this time?"

McGee slumped forward. "I'm not after anything, Johnny, 'cept perhaps a bit of solidarity now and then. We're cousins, goddamn, but you never treat me like one."

Johnny squirmed away from his drunken cousin and noticed Reg leaning forward on the bar, grinning. He turned back to his cousin and shook a finger at him. "You got some fucken' nerve! Treat yer like a cousin? Like yer treated me, I suppose? Because o' you, I lost me gaff, net and daren't visit the river. And, fer that I'm supposed ter treat yer like a bloody cousin? You make me want ter spew."

"Johnny, please, I'm only trying to save you from getting caught. The duke's determined to squash all the local poachers. And he will, you know. One day he'll stamp on you, and grind his heal into the ground. He's like that. Don't you understand?"

"Aye, and if I get caught, then you go down wi' me. Never threaten me again, cousin. Dinnae forget you supplied all those wee fishes! That wouldn't look very good in Davidson's book, would it, eh?"

"Johnny, surely you're not thinking to shop your own cousin?"

"If I did, I'm bloody certain the Supreme Being would forgive me fer it."

"I only wanted to help, that's all."

"Yer sloshed, McGee, and I've nothin' more ter say." Johnny picked up his pint and strode across to Tom and Ben.

"What's he ranting on about?" asked Ben.

"Whole load o' crap, as usual," Johnny replied.

"The bastard was slobbering over Sally earlier on. Wonder Reg didn't slug him one," commented Bobby. "If he does it again, I'll whack him when he goes outside."

Johnny narrowed his eyes. "Do I detect a wee jealousy here?"

Bobby flushed. "No way. He just ought ter back off, like. Anyway, she's too young for him."

Johnny smiled and rubbed his temple. While his three friends chatted away, he thought about the grisly find on the riverbank – the skinless salmon – and how it could have got there in the first place.

Then, the small matter of Will and the kid – who claimed to be the best poacher of the year – intruded into his thoughts. Johnny badly felt the need for a second heavy, and strolled to the bar. After another chaser, he supped the pint and almost drifted away, while the others talked.

After last orders, he returned home, had another peek at the sinister-looking fish, and decided to inform Rona about it the following morning. He shoved it back in the fridge, washed his hands and, on grabbing the towel, unearthed a strange object lying on his kitchen table: he realized it was Rona's mobile phone. He shrugged and decided to take it along to Ben the next day.

He settled in his comfy chair, beside the roaring fire, and contemplated on McGee's latest outburst. Why was his cousin so keen to warn him about the duke and his gamekeepers?

He dozed off, then woke with a start at the sound of the front-door knocker pounding. *Fucken' McGee again,* he thought, as he glanced at the clock and saw that it was gone eleven.

CHAPTER 35

Johnny's trip to Paradise

CAUTIOUSLY, HE CREPT to the door, wondering who was calling at this hour, convinced it was McGee – and drunk, too. Instead, he saw Rona standing on the doorstep, dressed in a scarlet, strapless frock, with a short coat draped over her shoulders. Awestruck, he remained lost for words.

"Hi, I think I left my phone behind. Sorry about this."

He then noticed she carried two bottles of wine. "Yer best come in."

She smiled, stepped into the hall and took off a pair of stiletto shoes. "Feet are killing me. God, I hate those damned things."

Johnny staggered slightly, with the heavy and chasers he'd downed. "Aye, yer phone's in the kitchen. While yer here, I found somethin', too."

She followed him into the kitchen, plonked the wine bottles on the pine table and rubbed her bare arms. "Sounds mysterious. What, exactly?"

Johnny drew the old tin from the fridge and unfurled the plastic, to reveal the grisly salmon.

"Jesus!" exclaimed Rona. "Where did you get this?"

"Found it on the riverbank tonight. Just lying on the grass, it was."

She placed the fish on the tabletop, peered at it, then sighed. "Looks like a sea lice casualty, if ever. It's far worse than the other fish I found, too."

"Yer weren't kidding about the threat, if that's what happens."

She shuddered. "God, I need a drink." She uncorked a wine bottle and Johnny proffered a glass. "Join me?"

He shrugged; "Might as well."

"That dead fish caps the evening, it really does."

"Yer look mighty radiant tonight. Have yer been anywhere special?"

Rona grinned, wickedly. "I've actually infiltrated enemy territory. There happened to be a party on at The Grouse, so I kind of gate-crashed. I only went along to sus out the villains, though."

"I'm amazed."

"You didn't miss anything. God, what a load of snotty-nosed morons; not one of them could talk any sense. And that host publican, a man called Shreeves, is an insidious ogre."

Johnny smiled and nodded. "I could have told yer that. Now yer know the sort of folk that defile the river, in the name of democracy."

She drained the glass and poured another, then topped Johnny's glass up.

Johnny never drank wine and, on top of the heavy and numerous chasers, began to feel woozy in a way he'd never experienced. "I expect the duke were there, too, eh?"

Rona nodded: "Unfortunately, and those people think the sun shines out his arse."

Johnny was mildly surprised by her reaction. "I did try ter tell yer."

Rona suddenly burst out laughing. "Never mind. The E.U. *Habitats Directive* has been totally disregarded by that lot, and they're in for a few shocks before long."

She suddenly got up, waltzed around the kitchen and switched on Johnny's small, battered transistor radio on the windowsill. "God, I've had rather a lot to drink. Like a dance?"

Johnny nodded, staggered over and clasped her hand. "Haven't done this fer some years; I'll be a bit rusty, like."

The best Johnny managed was a sort of jig, but Rona seemed not to notice. For a very brief spell, the kitchen took on the dimension of a ballroom in some shoddy hotel. Then he sat down, laughed and realized Annie had come home.

He led Rona up the stairs to his bedroom. As they kissed passionately, she slowly fell back onto his bed. They undressed with trembling hands, and Johnny felt he was in off into Paradise.

Johnny woke the next morning, his head thumping away, and saw Rona lying beside him. Suddenly, the full impact of what he'd done crashed down like a ton of bricks.

He slipped out of bed, donned a dressing gown and crept downstairs, desperate for some black coffee.

He felt numbed, guilty and electrified, all in one; a mixed bag of emotional turmoil. He sipped the black coffee, while the whirling universe inside his head slowed down. He took a deep breath. It had been many years since he'd felt the heat and tightness of a woman climaxing.

He also felt ashamed. She was half his age and he'd not been thinking of her at all; he'd been fantasizing over his long-dead wife, Annie.

For the first time since his internment in Korea, he cried.

Johnny was unsure how much time elapsed, but the coffee had grown cold when he saw Rona standing in the kitchen doorway, with the bedspread draped around her like a sari. She looked decidedly sheepish.

"Hi. Er… God… I don't usually make a habit of picking up old men, but you are exceptional."

"Aye, I suppose not," croaked Johnny. His mouth felt dry. He got up and lit the hob to reheat the kettle. "I guess yer need a coffee? A black one? Are ye okay about this?"

Rona shrugged and drew a breath. "It happened. We were both dead drunk. Accept it."

Johnny placed two steaming mugs on the table. "Aye, I've never been able ter cope wi' wine. Never."

Rona sat down and sipped the coffee. "God, you must think I'm an awful slut."

Johnny sniffed. "No, I dinnae think that at all. I was in the Army, remember?"

She glanced at him. "There have only really been three men in my life. Poor Adam, the only thing I did for him was taking his virginity."

Johnny shook his head, knowingly. "Kinda guessed that much. Is that why he went out along the river that night? To try ter impress you?"

"I guess so. Liam's the only one I want." She laughed. "He's nothing much to look at; in the street, you'd think he was an aged hippie or a drug pusher, but he's not like that at all. He respects all living things, whether it's a cow in a field or a dragonfly basking on a reed stem. That's what I love about him."

"Aye, I bet yer both get on well." He stared at the tabletop, racked by a deep sense of guilt. "I got something ter confess: I deceived yer. I weren't thinkin' of you, but another woman."

Rona frowned, puzzled by his unexpected statement. "Oh! Can I ask who?"

Johnny got up and sauntered to the cutlery drawer, from where he withdrew a photograph in a faded, tatty wooden frame. "Aye, it was me wife, Annie. She's been gone fer more than a decade now, God rest her. Cancer, it were. Bloody awful way ter go, too."

Rona reached out for the photo and saw an image resembling herself. "Oh, God, I'd no idea. I'm sorry."

"Don't be. There are times when I still miss her, very much. I just hope yer can forgive me fer it."

She slid the photo back to him. "Under the circumstances, I guess so. What's the point of doing otherwise?"

"Are we still friends?"

Rona laughed. "After what we've done, it'd be stupid to become enemies."

"I'm glad. I'm just sorry for misleading yer."

"Don't be."

Johnny fretted. "Did yer mean all that about them poachers?"

She scowled. "Of course. The risk element regarding the fluke and lice is too great."

Johnny toyed with the mug. "Yer might as well know: I go poachin' fer salmon, but nothing large scale; just snatch the odd fish every so often."

The girl stared at him, unable to believe his disclosure, and blew breath. "This is turning out to be a right morning."

"Aye. I been supplying the pub landlord wi' salmon fer years. I'm only doin' it ter supplement me measly Army pension; I could nae survive on that."

She gazed at his seedy kitchen curtains for a moment, then faced him. "By rights, I should report you to the S.S.S.T.F. I'll overlook it, but I don't approve."

Johnny smiled, tiredly. "I'm only doin' what generations o' folk have done before: just takin' what I need from the river, and never greedy with it. Not like that bloody duke and his lackeys; they're the real thieves."

"All comes back to this landlord, doesn't it?"

"Aye, unfortunately it does."

"Okay, it's obvious two issues require addressing here: one, the salmon farm, and two, this presumptuous landowner, right?"

"I couldn't sum it up better myself. But, how? That's the big question."

Rona frowned. "Salmon farm first; that's the priority. I've

worked out a strategy and could do with some help. Would young Bobby like to help me?"

"I'll have a word with him. I expect so."

"Great, then we've a target to aim for." She looked at her watch. "I've got to get going."

She went off to get dressed.

Johnny replaced the picture of his dead wife back in the drawer, face down, took a deep breath and got dressed.

Waiting in the hall, he thought about his luck last night. She was young, beautiful and just what he wanted. He would look forward to their next encounter, wherever it may take place – even by the river, at his favourite poaching spot.

"Jesus, I'd better take that dead fish for analysis," came her voice.

Johnny handed her the package and her mobile phone. She kissed his forehead, then dashed out the door to the Nissan and drove off.

He stood and stared at the hedgerow opposite his gate and, for a brief moment, a ray of sunshine pierced through the thick foliage. Johnny thought it might be Annie, saying that all would turn out to be fine.

CHAPTER 36

Salmon-farming trouble

THAT AFTERNOON, RONA and Bobby ambled along the bank of the river toward the salmon farm, not far from Rosstown.

He pointed out the effluent pipe from the tanks. "That's where all the water gushes from," he stated, knowingly.

She frowned. "Really? Those sods are flushing the stuff direct into the river? I'm going to need samples of the discharge. When does it happen?"

"Dunno as it's regular, but usually afternoons I see it. Sometimes it's all foamy, like."

Bobby dumped her bag by the verge and withdrew some small, plastic sample jars. "I guess we play the waiting game now."

He grinned. "What are you gonna do with the samples, then?"

"Hand them over to my boss. We'll get them analyzed and then, if the results test positive and the Deosect is dangerously high, we alert the E.U.'s Environment Agency."

"Sounds right complicated, don't it? All those officials and that."

"Not really. I think the case is cut and dried."

"You're right clever. I wish I was, too."

"I've studied ecology for years, don't forget."

Rona took numerous shots of the riverbank where serious erosion had taken place, then a couple of the salmon farm, through the mesh, chain-link fence.

"It's not ideal, but it'll do: visual evidence in a court of law these days is everything."

After forty minutes, Bobby recognized the familiar sound of rushing water. "The flow is gonna happen any minute now."

Rona dashed to the pipe, and lined up her camera for an incriminating photograph or two. Foamy water spurted out of the pipe and she took several shots, then quickly dropped the camera beside the bag, slipped on a pair of latex gloves and picked up a jar. Leaning over the side of the bank, she scooped a jar full of the effluent, screwed the lid tight and quickly repeated the exercise for a second sample.

"That should do it. We won't know the outcome until these have been tested at H.Q."

Bobby stood transfixed while watching her, then smiled. "Yeah, now I have seen a pollution fighter in action."

"It's all part of my job."

The gushing outflow subsided rapidly. Rona leant over the edge again, scraped some algae from the inside of the pipe and placed it in a jar. She took further samples from along the riverbank. "It's possible that traces of harmful chemicals have been absorbed by this weed."

"Why do they do this?" asked Bobby.

"It's probably plain laziness or economy. Either way, they're going to find they've made an expensive mistake."

She labelled up each of the sample bottles and placed them in the bag. Then, she and Bobby looked along the shoreline for traces of the fluke, or any dead fish. They found nothing untoward.

"We're not done yet," stated Rona, suddenly remembering a promise she'd made to Johnny.

They returned to her Nissan, parked in a layby at the front of a field. She drove back toward Glenstone and pulled up near the stone bridge. "Let's hike along the riverside, near the duke's patch. I want to get shots of the damage he's been so careful to overlook."

Bobby followed her along the narrow path, eager to help someone determined to put down the duke. A few anglers staying at The Grouse were out along the river, with line and rod. While they walked past, a few fishermen voiced their objections at her and Bobby traipsing along the path.

She ignored them and continued to snap images of crumbling banks, litter and, on occasions, anglers wading in the river unnecessarily, splashing around and causing havoc to the gravel bed. She also noted two of the visitors had dogs, which were free to roam around.

"Things are not looking good for that lousy aristocrat, Bobby – not one little bit."

Bobby nodded. "Then he gets everything he deserves."

Rona glanced at him. "I know, but loathsome though he might appear to be to the villagers, he is providing work for local inhabitants, too. There has to be a fine balance."

"What about all the things he *hasn't* done. No, I reckon he's done more damage than good. I say we snitch on the bastard."

"Okay, but there's no guarantee we are going to achieve anything."

"Better than not bothering, though," commented Bobby.

Rona agreed.

"Come on, I'll give you a lift back to the village. It's getting late."

CHAPTER 37

Build-up of evidence

THAT EVENING, RONA sped along the A75 to SEPA H.Q. in Dumfries, triumphant that she'd got enough evidence to get the salmon farm fined for discharging Deosect into the river. She also had high hopes Liam would back a case for legal action against the pompous landowner at Glenstone, for failing to comply with relevant standards stipulated in the *Water Framework Directive*, and therefore, in theory, breaking the law.

Along with all the water and weed samples, she also had the dead salmon Johnny had found: more evidence of the perilous hazard which might lie on the horizon. If the G.S. fluke had attacked the salmon, it could be the first of many such cases.

She felt an overwhelming sense of urgency and planned one last, major task: the "biggie", as she thought of it, was to alert local and regional authorities, angling associations, landlords and all folk with a vested interest in the fishing industry to the potential threat, and for more stringent controls to be set in place regarding the sea lice menace. Whether it would all work she dared not contemplate. Everything was a desperate gamble and, if it failed, she knew that the salmon, both wild and farmed, were in grave danger of being decimated. In the wake of such destruction would come hardship, redundancies and social deprivation. The risk was incredibly ominous, and for that she was glad to have the backing of the Scottish Salmon Strategy Task Force.

There was another, less important objective, too. Ambitious, but she wanted to try and get Scottish Natural Heritage interested in managing the stretch of river Johnny had shown her, as a site of special scientific interest, and with any luck perhaps an educational centre established, too. It was a strange, ironic situation, as the S.N.H. generally worked in co-operation with regional landowners and local authorities. If the Glenstone nobleman refused to grant permission, the venture might fail.

Eventually, she saw the skyline of Dumfries come into view and speculated on what Kay and the lab staff might discover. Everything hung by a thread, and Rona almost felt as though she was the one person that held the key to preventing a major ecological disaster erupting across Scotland, and perhaps all of the U.K. as well.

CHAPTER 38

Three cousins

WILL LANDED ANOTHER fish that afternoon – a seven-pound salmon – to the amazement and envy of all the other anglers along the riverbank. The fish had actually put up a bit of a fight, but with the skills he'd recently acquired, and George netting the fish, he now felt he was an old hand at the fishing game.

One thing that Will really wanted to do now was go poaching again. The thrill of it made up for his years of torment, from a wife who had no interest in his activities, or any real love for him.

At the end of the afternoon, he suggested having a slap-up meal in The Leaping Salmon, partly to see Johnny and partly to enjoy a change of menu. Excellent though Andy's culinary skills were, everyone was getting a bit tired of salmon steaks. Besides, Will wanted to keep his catches in order, to supply Les Hopkins at The Badger Inn and gain some tax-free cash in hand.

Andy remonstrated: "Getting in with that cousin of yours is heading for trouble. Big trouble."

Will grinned, not wanting to cause a rift in their happy party. "We'll just go an' see him. No harm in that."

"If we're caught poaching and reported, getting a fishing permit up here is going to be near-impossible. I mean it, we'll be finished. I ain't keen to take the risk."

"We won't get caught," replied George. "Lighten up for bloody once."

Andy looked from George to Will, then blew breath, realizing they were not going to be dissuaded. But he felt uneasy. Perhaps the grilled steak supper would make up for the disquiet.

Will couldn't get over Johnny's little bobbing wooden box of flickering light, and thought it a unique way of drawing in the fish. The idea was dead simple. He had never done drugs or indulged in addictive habits, but after one taste of poaching he was hooked – rather like the salmon Johnny had snagged with his gaff.

"Huh! Married to a lowly wrongdoer! The shame of it!" he heard Dot screaming at him. He shook the awful mirage away, grinned and decided she wasn't ever going to hear about it.

George was dead keen to go out along the river in the dark again, and wanted to discover if the old man had other methods to snare the fish. He guessed his approach using a green light and rabbit snare would be pretty difficult to beat, but was open to new ideas. He knew that, like all good ideas, the simplest ones were usually the best. Besides, in daytime his method was simply not practical.

That evening, the four friends arrived at The Leaping Salmon to arrange another expedition. Will warned them that Johnny would never take a party out along the riverside on spec, which George already knew, as planning was the essence of a successful venture. Only the amateurs went out willy-nilly, and usually got nabbed by some bailiff or gamekeeper.

Johnny wasn't surprised to see his cousin arriving at the tavern and smiled, quietly amused at how quick the furtive pastime had gripped him. "Will, grand ter see yer again."

He sat down at Johnny's table, while Andy and Tom went to the bar for drinks. "How are you doing?"

Johnny's eyes narrowed. "Are ye asking after me, or how fortunate my enterprise has been?"

Will was often amazed how sharp his cousin could be, and nodded. "Kind of both, to be honest."

"Aye, I'm doin' fine. Feel hail and hearty so far, and I'm in the black. And that's all I've ter say on the subject in here."

George leaned over Will's shoulder and muttered to him: "Golden rule, see: no blab and no one suspects."

Johnny glanced at the younger man and nodded in agreement, supping on his pint of heavy.

Andy and Tom Richards ambled to Johnny's table. They commandeered the adjacent table and sat down.

Ben smiled at the party from Droitwich Spa. "Reckon you'll not be up here much more. Salmon season's almost done, as I understand."

George swigged the Dutch lager, then burped. "Yeah, maybe. We might try our hand with a spot of fishing, over at Dumfries. Along the River Nith, salmon season doesn't close until the end of November. Have to see what the others think."

Tom Furness got his pipe going again. "Ah, yes, Dumfries. Nice place. Friend of mine went angling there a while back – in winter, too. Apparently, fishing for grayling is permitted long after salmon season's done."

George frowned. "Grayling? No thanks, they ain't worth the

effort."

Johnny coughed. "So, how long are ye up here?"

Andy glanced at him. "Only 'til the end of the month. The owner offered us two days extension at the cottage for free. Being the end of the season, he'd no one else wanting to rent."

"Aye, I guess yer want ter book an appointment fer another wee outing, eh?"

Will stared at his cousin. "How did you guess?"

"I'm nae daft, seeing how you and the young 'un got enchanted wi' me activity that night."

"It'd be really great if we could visit that place again."

Johnny nodded slowly and stroked his chin, playing them along. "I dare say it would, too. Now, what makes yer think I'd fall in with that idea?"

Will sipped on his pint of best ale, before answering: "I just thought you might oblige, for old times' sake. Besides, you must know the kick it brings is mighty powerful."

"That I do indeed. Make it two nights from now, same time and place. I dinnae want ter be leading a mob through the village; it might look a tad suspicious."

"Agreed," answered Will, without hesitation.

Andy and Tom muttered something, but Will didn't catch their conversation.

"Make sure yer not followed. Dark characters lurk around this place, and some would think nothing of grassin' fer less than twenty pounds."

Will shook his head. "I get the hint."

A thin smile oozed across Johnny's face.

Will couldn't believe they'd fixed up another illicit venture so easily.

"Are we ordering?" interrupted Tom Richards, waving the menu card, impatiently. "I'm starved."

The four friends agreed on steaks, chips and all the trimmings.

For the rest of the evening, Will and his friends enthused to the others about their fishing holiday, and often added boasts. Will half-heartedly joined in with the conversation, but he drifted away, thinking of the floating box, and how the old man judged when to strike. Just maybe his cousin would let him have a go.

There and then, Will decided fish was his future: supplying Les with illicit goodies and coining in the fat profits to be made. It was a dream that had come true, after years of self-denial, for the sake of placating his harridan of a wife.

That evening, when Andy drove them back to the cottage along the dark lanes, Will felt incredibly light-hearted. He'd secured the one thing he wanted most to complete their fishing holiday, and was sure the next illegal expedition would change his life forever.

On returning home that evening, Johnny also felt more positive than he'd been in a long time.

He stoked up his fire and switched the T.V. on, to check if his ladyfriend, the weather presenter, bore good news. She did: the fine spell was due to last up to the end of the month, and that made his kind of fishing ideal. Funds in the mantelpiece jar were more plentiful than ever, so he had no real pressing need to go out poaching. But, he realized it might be a temporary reprieve, since bad weather would surely arrive, as November followed October.

He thought of Rona, and now looked upon her as a friend – a powerful one, with connections in high places. Was it really possible that she could help him, Johnny Mason, bring the duke crashing down from his pedestal? It was a question he dared not hope to answer in his favour. The fact that she'd dismissed his poaching activities enhanced his conviction.

Then, lastly, he thought of his cousin, McGee, scourge of the village and friend only to the parasite that preyed upon those foolish enough to squander small fortunes in his hotel, bar and grounds. He'd not clapped eyes on McGee for a day or so, and was glad.

Another idea struck him: was McGee really in with the crowd at The Grouse, as he made out. And, did he have any clout with the duke? Suddenly, almost overnight, there were all sorts of intriguing possibilities – and, for once, not all stacked against him.

Johnny poured half a mug of Scotch, settled in his favourite chair and felt contented; all was well with the world. Before long, he dozed off.

CHAPTER 39

Poaching party

TWO DAYS LATER, Will enjoyed another day of line-fishing, along the river near the holiday cottage, Andy having served a full breakfast of bacon, sausage, tomatoes and mushrooms, washed down with tea. In spite of landing another salmon, of five pounds, the thing that made this day special was the thought of evening – the secret outing only they would know about – and he couldn't wait.

While Andy drove them to The Leaping Salmon, Will got the impression he was in some sort of a dream. Yet, his awareness of things seemed heightened; small details he'd never noticed before caught his attention. While walking down the road to the stone bridge, he detected furtive little movements in the thick hedgerow – obviously mice, or perhaps shrews, about their nocturnal business. The smell of the country seemed more prominent than it had before: the rank odour of wet, decaying leaves and half-rotted vegetation. Every so often he caught the scent of turpentine, from the thickets of pine trees.

Andy followed behind, but all day he'd been pensive, almost withdrawn. He'd agreed to go along with the rest of them, but the idea of losing the right to purchase fishing permits obviously weighed heavy on his shoulders, rather like a dead albatross, Will thought.

By the bridge they halted briefly, and Will noticed the dark river gurgle, as it flowed through the arches. To make sure they weren't followed had been Johnny's advice. Will peered around in the dark, trying to detect any sign of movement. A few villagers had been wandering about when they'd left Glenstone, but now they had the road to themselves; there was not another soul about, so far as they could tell.

"Okay, head up the path, then," said Andy.

In single file, they traipsed along the slightly muddy track, careful to remain quiet and avoid trampling over twigs, to alert some gamekeeper half a mile away. In spite of having been a fisherman for a short time, Will detected seasonal change had arrived; no longer did the air of summertime carry the sweet aroma of grass and cut hay. Instead, he sensed the raw, sour odour of damp, decay and wet, dying bracken.

They headed along the path, eager to reach the place where Johnny would meet them. Before long, they came to the large tree and stood under it, as before, though what kind it was Will couldn't tell, having no knowledge of such things. But, he liked the thought of it providing shelter, while taking a breather.

Johnny, as ever, peered out of his front door before setting forth on one of his nightly undertakings, to assess whether the weather-lady had got it right, and check on any prying busybodies who might be peeking over walls or through hedges. He saw nothing adverse. The evening, being calm and clear, proved ideal, though without the moon's presence. Johnny felt glad about that: although romantic, the moon was no friend to a river poacher, only to the bailiffs and gamekeepers.

Snatching his binoculars from under the stairs, and with bin liner and candles stuffed in his coat pockets, he pulled the front door to and set forth.

He sidled down the little track to the allotments, through the paddock, entered the field and skirted round the edge, to reach the scrubby heath. Seeing no evidence of anyone about, he headed toward the gorse bush sprawling over the empty warren. He hid behind the thicket and peered through the binoculars toward the river, saw four men walking toward the agreed rendezvous and smiled.

Then, he retrieved his box and gaff from the tunnel and headed toward the river, confident that the night would be profitable and perhaps entertaining. He envisioned his cousin making a complete hash of hooking a salmon with a gaff, having never handled such a thing before.

On approaching the river, he signalled them to join him, before they strode along for another mile and a half, in single file, to the dell.

Johnny motioned them to settle and Will stood on the edge of the bank, watching. The old man removed box and gaff from his deep pocket and, having tied on the string, shoved the two candles onto the nails inside, then lit them. Will watched every move his cousin made, filled with admiration, and mentally noted down everything he did. Johnny set the box afloat, and tied the other end of the string to an aluminium peg stuck in the ground. He then slouched along the edge of the bank, grasping his gaff, ready to strike.

Before long, the first fish turned up, drawn by the flickering light emanating from the slits in the box. Johnny waited until it was slightly upstream of the box and let it get nearer. He knew the fish would find his wonder light irresistible. Will took in every move his cousin made, with avid interest.

Like lightning, Johnny swung the gaff and hooked the salmon in, snagging the fish an inch or so behind the gills. He laughed quietly, something he rarely did on his exploits, and rapped the fish with the handle.

Johnny handed his gaff to Will and whispered: "Let's see you try, eager cousin."

Will couldn't believe he'd got the chance to be a poacher. With a trembling hand, he held the tool of the trade: a real gaff. He took a deep breath, followed Johnny's example and lay by the bank, hoping the next fish might be larger than the first.

George squirmed in envy, dying for a go. Tom and Andy watched, too, crouched against the side of the dell, but had little enthusiasm for the illegal activity.

Johnny sat back, a cynical smile spread across his face, sure his cousin would fluff it. A dorsal fin moved into view – obviously another salmon – closely followed by a second. Will couldn't see the fish all that clearly, but noticed the fin moving close toward the gently undulating box. "Dinnae mess about now, but take it slow," he heard Johnny say.

Will swung the gaff into the water beside the box, made a terrific splash, and hooked nothing more than a few drops of water.

Johnny's smile became a broad sneer. "Aye, see? Ain't as easy as yer thought."

Will declined to answer, and rolled back over to face the box, flushed with anger at his cousin's cynical overtone, and mad as hell that he'd made a total cock-up of things in front of his three friends.

The larger of the two fish had taken fright, but the smaller returned and gently nudged the box toward the bank. His heart pounding away, Will desperately wanted to snag the fish, but it was on the far side of the box and impossible to reach. He swore softly under his breath.

He couldn't believe it when the fish swam round to the nearside. Faster than he'd planned, Will swept the gaff where the fish was and, convinced he'd got something, almost wept on seeing the gaff-hook without a fish. He suddenly thought the entire thing was pointless and futile.

"Yer not judging it right," Johnny remarked. "Yer have to feel the fish is there, but in yer mind, like."

Will flinched, thought of Dot and gripped the gaff, tight.

"That's right. No use holding on ter the thing like it's a stick o' candy floss," Johnny commented, softly.

Will slouched onto the bank again. He desperately wanted a fish. In front of the others, he had to hook a salmon, or he'd never hear the last of it, especially from George.

A small salmon came into view, drawn by the light, and swam in on the box, its angle and position just right. Will concentrated only on the fish, imagining how it must see the box from just below the water's surface, and felt its presence there. Drawing a deep breath, and not taking his eyes off the fish for an instant, he swung the gaff and hooked the salmon free of the water.

Will stared at the three-pound salmon, unable to believe he'd actually done it. Then, suddenly, he noticed a figure standing on the lip of the dell.

He struck the salmon quickly, then hid it behind a grassy tussock and glared at the man, obviously a gamekeeper of some sort. The gamekeeper strode into the dell.

"So, that's how you do it?" the stranger declared.

Johnny spun round. All his worst nightmares had come true, as McGee stood there, almost motionless. He sighed, softly.

"Dear me, I told you to stop. Why didn't you listen?"

"McGee," whispered Johnny, his eyes drawn to slits. "How the hell did yer know I was here?"

"Easy, Johnny: I saw your friends in the pub, put two and two together – or perhaps I should say four and four, to be more exact."

Johnny slowly exhaled. "You're a crafty bastard."

"Johnny, please, can't we sweep aside all the bitterness of the past?"

"Why did yer follow us? Who stands ter gain from this, apart from you?"

"Nobody, I… I just wanted to be a friend, that's all. Be part of this."

Will pointed the gaff at the tweed-suited man. "Who the bloody hell is this, for Christ's sake?"

Johnny smiled, wryly. "Ah, Will, meet me cousin, Chuck

McGee."

Will scowled at him, trying to work out the implications. He cast his mind back, and had a foggy, vague recollection of his parents paying the odd visit now and then to an Aunt Jean and Uncle Donald, living in Newcastle. That was long ago – he was only at junior school – but the memory came flooding back. His relatives had a kid: a right pugnacious brat called Chuck. Was that the stranger before him? He stood there and blew breath. He'd all but forgotten about them.

Johnny paced around, waiting for the penny to drop. "Ain't families wonderful, eh? Relatives yer loathe or love, or leave well alone?"

Will still found it hard to believe the tweed-suited man was his cousin from the distant past. But, even if he was, what was he doing here? A thought suddenly struck him: "If he's followed us, can we be sure that no one else has?"

Johnny spun on McGee. "Answer the man: is Davidson on the prowl?"

"That bastard? No, I shouldn't think so. He doesn't suspect me of anything – why should he?"

Johnny worried his brow. "You've been supplying me with all those packages, remember? Just suppose he cottoned on? More to the point, does Davidson know what happens to the illicit goodies I landed?"

McGee frowned. "I don't think so. At least, *I* never mentioned it to him."

Johnny stroked his jaw, weighing up the situation. "Aye, then just consider that if I get caught out, you've jeopardized yer livelihood."

"I'm prepared to take that chance. Everyone in the village hates my guts – I know that much."

"You got that bunch o' snobby cronies at The Grouse, though."

"Oh yes, and a fine upstanding bunch they are, too, forever bickering and backstabbing. Competition to win the duke's goodwill is intense. He likes things that way; maintains it keeps the staff on their toes."

"Does he, now? So, he treats his employees like his bailiffs deal with poachers, eh?"

McGee sighed. "That sums up the situation."

Will spoke up: "How can we be sure this fellow won't snitch on us?"

Johnny shrugged. "Ask him, not me."

McGee turned to Will: "Long lost cousin, I love doing my job, and wouldn't risk that for the world. It's just the people I have to deal with and work with... you've no idea. At times, the tension is like a taut cheese-wire."

Johnny laughed, softly. "And yer thought a spot of poaching would wipe away all the pressure?"

"No, I just craved after the sense of companionship. There's precious little genuine friendship in the duke's domain, I tell you that."

Johnny sighed. "I don't know what ter make of you, McGee. I don't indeed."

"I'm not asking you to. And, it wouldn't hurt to call me Chuck, just now and then."

Andy and Tom stalked over. Andy stuck his hands deep in his anorak pockets, appearing clearly disgruntled. "I knew this would bloody happen," he snapped.

"It ain't Johnny's fault," retorted Will.

"Thankee cousin; that's a fucken' comfort," muttered Johnny.

Will glared at him. "Look, it's just that my two friends over there think they stand to lose any right to buy fishing permits, if this all comes to light."

"Permits? Jesus Christ," scoffed Johnny.

Andy sniffed and stared at the old man. "Never bought a fishing permit in your entire life, have you?"

Johnny gave him a sunny smile. "Never needed ter, thanks all the same."

Andy snorted and stalked off, closely followed by Tom.

"Jesus, man, I thought we'd come here to snatch some fuckin' fish, for crying out loud!" exclaimed George. "You lot are actin' like a bunch of bleedin' old tarts." He snatched the gaff from Will and squatted on the riverbank, watching the box. He turned around. "Now, for Christ's sake, you lot belt up."

Johnny smiled at the kid's tenacity. McGee scowled, but said nothing.

Before very long, another salmon had swum out from a deep pool and snapped up a midge, which must have noticed the bobbing box and swam across. Instead of holding the gaff mid-shaft, George grasped the end of the handle and swung it round, like he was twirling a lasso. Johnny watched, mildly amused.

The salmon edged round the corner of the box, its flank exposed to the riverbank. George brought the gaff crashing down to the water's surface… and hooked out a ten-pound salmon with ease.

Johnny gazed at the kid, flabbergasted. He'd never seen anyone wield a gaff in such a casual manner before, and seemingly with no effort.

George bashed the creature dead. Will raced over, peered at his catch and snatched Johnny's gaff, determined to try again. Like George, instead of lying on the bank, as Johnny had done, he hunched and held the handle at the end. Will and George glanced knowingly at each other, as much as to say: *Let's show these clever bastards what poaching is all about.*

Will thought the gods were with them that night, as a large salmon swam in from the opposite bank, obviously drawn by the flickering illumination. Mustering patience, he waited for the fish to swim around the bobbing box, so its side was almost parallel to the riverbank. After a few minutes, the fish submerged and Will thought his chance had gone. Then, miraculously, it reappeared. Without thinking, and almost acting on instinct, Will swung the gaff and hooked the salmon clean from the water. He found the momentum of the swinging action made it easy to land the fish. It was around nine pounds. He whacked the salmon.

Then George snatched the gaff and hunched near the box, ready to strike the minute another fish should swim into the right position. He didn't have long to wait. George thought this flickering box was almost as good as his bicycle lamp, but wondered about its viability in windy weather. With the approach of another salmon, George grinned, knowing this was going to be a pushover. On landing it, he and Will would be the poaching kings that night. George eyed the fish and waited until it swam into the right position for a strike. When the salmon was side-on, George swung the gaff, fast and with expertise, landing the fish onto the bank with dexterity that Johnny found difficult to believe. He rapped the fish.

George stood up, snatched a deep breath and slowly exhaled.

Johnny stalked over. "I'm impressed, sonny. Really."

George grinned. "Told you I'd been poachin' before, but you didn't listen. Still, best not to go round braggin' about it. Anyway, Will and I are done. One thing: we keep our fish, right?"

Johnny nodded. "If yer get caught carrying them, I know nothing, understand?"

George grinned again. "We ain't goin' to get caught. You got any other techniques for poaching then, old-timer? How do you manage with the box in windy weather?"

Johnny smirked. "Me little box has never let me down. Let yer into a secret: I make me own candles, wi' an extra-thick wick. That stops them blowing out so easily."

"You right crafty old sod."

Johnny smiled at the kid. "Aye, sometimes I go fishin' wi' a barbed arrow on the end of a thin shaft, and a bit o' line tied on; fire it from a catapult, I do. Only good fer working in daytime, though; it's totally useless at night."

"Poaching in daytime's dead risky. I'd never, ever be tempted."

Johnny glanced knowingly at the kid. "Very true, but up here, near the end o' the season, few folk are around. Yer have ter find a good, camouflaged spot ter work from. You, being an expert poacher, could probably better the lot, eh?"

George grinned. "Actually, it's similar to your box. Use a green light, I do, made from an old bicycle lamp, and a rabbit snare to nab the fish. Works wonders, especially for trout."

"Heh! Trout? Almost coarse fishing, that is."

"Where I come from, trout poaching is right profitable, almost as much as salmon."

"Ah, down in England I suppose it would be. Give yer a bit o' advice: lone poaching works best, never be greedy and keep yer trap shut, except wi' whoever yer deal with. That way, nobody gets any the wiser."

"Yeah, I already know that much. And I'm prepared, too."

Johnny nodded. "Aye, that much is obvious."

From his coat pocket, George pulled out a black bin liner, and slipped in the four fish he and Will had caught that night. He handed the gaff back to the old man. "Thanks for the loan of not a bad tool. I never actually used a gaff before."

Johnny smiled, and wondered if he or Will guessed that he'd made it from a sea-angler's hook and the wooden handle off a garden fork, but declined to explain.

Johnny slipped his solitary catch into his bin liner, then strode over to McGee. "Now, I suggest yer return to the village wi' me friends here, and keep out o' me way. I've nae wish fer you or anyone else ter knows where I stash me gear. I'll not get caught out a second time."

"What if I choose not to go along with that suggestion?" asked

McGee.

"Then, friendship is somethin' yer can forget all about and, surprise-surprise, Davidson might get ter hear how the duke's head bailiff took it upon himself to give a poacher confiscated fish to sell. I reckon that'd amount ter instant dismissal, eh?"

"Okay Johnny, you win: I agree."

"That's very obliging of yer, Chuck. I'm sure we're going ter get along fine – like a house on fire, maybe."

"No need to rub it in, Johnny."

"I wouldn't dream of it." Johnny snapped his fingers; "Aye, forgetful old sod I am!" He dashed to the riverbank and plunged the box under the water's surface, extinguishing the candles. "Aye, that's better."

He shoved the box and gaff in his deep pocket and carried the black bin liner. He wasn't going to give away how he concealed the fish under his greatcoat, held in place by the harness.

George and Will were all smiles while traipsing along the path, toward the little bridge. Andy and Tom followed along behind, but remained silent and morose. Johnny and McGee brought up the rear.

"I must say, that were a right entertaining evening, dinnae yer agree, Cousin Chuck?"

McGee sniffed. "I have to admit, I enjoyed the company."

When they reached the tree, half a mile from the bridge, Johnny stopped. "Right, this is where I get off. Now, be a good cousin and follow the others back ter the village. I have me own way back home, and it's like a company's trade secret."

"I take the hint, Johnny."

"I just want be sure, that's all. Away ye go. Drop in at The Leaping Salmon afore ye go back home, if yer like."

Will gave his cousin the thumbs up. Andy and Tom scowled. Johnny smiled.

Suddenly, he felt as though he'd come up trumps against all his adversaries. Just maybe there was a fighting chance he'd topple the duke yet.

On seeing his friends and McGee far away along the path, he returned to the warren, hid the gear and aligned the bin liner under his greatcoat.

He decided to call in home first, desperately needing a Scotch before pressing onward to The Leaping Salmon. With the weighty salmon dangling down his back under the greatcoat, Johnny felt incredibly jaunty, for the first time in a long while. Thoughts of McGee, Davidson and the duke's other minions seemed nothing more than peripheral pests, like the gnats which swarmed along the thick hedgerow.

Turning off at the alleyway, he slipped into the small courtyard, dived into his sanctuary, the outhouse, and deposited the fish in the freezer. Having shed his greatcoat, he slipped through the internal door to the public bar once more, light of mind.

"You look right sprightly tonight, Johnny. Anything happened?"

Johnny grinned at Reg. "It's been a cracker of a night, so I'll celebrate wi' a chaser first and a pint o' heavy."

"Heavy and one chaser coming up," replied Reg, knowing another salmon lay in the freezer. "It's on the house."

Johnny gazed around the bar and saw neither McGee nor the party from Droitwich Spa present.

"Those English friends of yours not calling tonight?" asked the publican.

"Seemingly not," remarked Johnny. "I thought they might be here. Still they rent a cottage down the hillside."

Reg nodded.

Johnny thought for once that the bar looked incredibly sparse. The usual mob heading for The Grouse hadn't turned up, either.

Grabbing the pint, he ambled to the far corner where Ben, Tom and Bobby had gathered.

Tom filled his pipe and lit up. "It seems the shit is going to hit the fan in one or two establishments, before very long."

Johnny supped the heavy and leant back in his chair. "Now, tell me, would one of those places be The Grouse in the Heather?"

Tom blew a plume of smoke at the ceiling and nodded. "The other is a salmon farm. Bobby had a right wild old time with Rona the other afternoon, didn't you?"

Bobby grinned. "Helped her, I did, gatherin' up all them samples. Then, I showed her all the bits of riverside the duke let fall to bits. She wasn't half put out. Said she's gonna get them in hot water, and serve them right."

Johnny looked round. "Where is Rona, anyway?"

Ben stirred. "She's taken all the evidence to Dumfries. She'll be back later."

"Maybe she's done us all a favour, eh?"

Ben placed his glass of heavy on the table and glanced at him, purposefully. "Perhaps, but if folk lose their jobs through this, things are not so good."

Johnny squirmed, felt slightly guilty and wondered what his friend would say, if he'd known of Johnny's brief liaison with his niece. "I dinnae think that falls into the equation."

Bobby spoke: "Rona said them sea lice is goin' ter wipe out all the salmon."

"*Might,*" corrected Ben, adamantly; "until they get the tests, all is mere theory."

"I wouldn't be too sure about that," Johnny muttered, remembering the grisly, skinless fish.

Tom stirred, as if to change to subject; "How's your cousin, then?"

"McGee? I dinnae reckon that bastard's goin' ter set foot in here much."

"I meant your other cousin, the one with that fishing party."

"Ah, Will. I guess he's found a new vocation in life."

Ben and Tom looked puzzled. "He obviously enjoys fishing, then?"

Johnny grinned, wryly. "That he does. More than yer can imagine."

That evening at The Leaping Salmon was one of the happiest Johnny had experienced for a long time and, after four pints of heavy, and on hearing Reg's nightly request for glasses to be drained, he slipped to the outhouse for his coat, fearing nothing and nobody. He felt incredibly free of an oppressive burden, and almost began to wonder what all the apprehension had been about.

Back at home, he settled in his chair after stoking up the fire. It was his favourite place in the entire world, except for his patch along the river. On that note, he plotted and planned to return, to reclaim what was rightly his, passed down to him from Uncle Furgus. No longer was he going to be banished from his beloved, salmon-rich pool.

But first, the small matter of Davidson had to be dealt with; he was the real barrier between Johnny and his river. Quite how he would overcome that obstacle was, for the moment, a complete and utter conundrum.

Meanwhile, down the hillside from Glenstone, Will felt ecstatic, and knew that he'd arrived at a new turning point. Gone were the days of capitulating to Dot and her constant hectoring. He had mastered rod fishing and indulged in poaching, and now felt ready to alter the course of his life. Already, he planned to rent a small, cheap flat, as near as possible to The Badger Inn – not as a place to live, but merely as a base to operate from, and stash the proceeds of his new cash flow gained from poaching. He'd still live with Dot, to keep the neighbourhood pretence going, but had little worries about deceiving her. He knew now that she wasn't really worth a damn. He envisioned frequenting different places with the same aim in mind, and perhaps George would assist.

George was also full of jubilation, and told Will he estimated that

Les Hopkins would give them a round three-hundred for the four salmon they'd poached that night, and maybe more for the all others they'd caught legitimately in the river.

With hunger gnawing away, the party desperately needed supper. To use up all the leftovers, Andy set about making Scottish dish stovies. Tom peeled then diced and boiled the spuds, while Andy fried chopped onions, added a dash of pepper, then shredded burgers and chopped sausage into the mix. He cracked open a can of best ale, supping while he cooked.

While dining in the open-plan lounge, the four discussed their last day of fishing, and decided to have a final cast along the river in early morning, if the weather held, as they didn't have to vacate the cottage until noon. All scoffed the meat-rich, greasy potato dish, served with chunky, crusty bread, washed down with cans of ale or bitter and Scotch. They decided to empty the cottage supply of liquor and beer, if they could.

Before long, their conversation drifted to Will's cousin and his riverside habit. Will was rather proud of his wily cousin, and defended his activity: "He's barely got sod-all up there in that village, for Christ's sake. On a miserable Army pension and a bit from his time in the police force, he needs a little extra income. I say bloody good luck to him."

"It's iniquitous," stated Tom, flatly. "Downright immoral. Little better than pimping, if you ask me."

Andy nodded. "I want no part of it. Next season, when we come, I stick to legal rod-fishing, but want nothing to do with foul-hooking."

George sneered. "Scaredy-cat. What's lifting a salmon or two now and then? Jesus, man."

"Don't get bloody flippant with me. It's just stupid and pointless to risk losing the right to get fishing permits, like I said."

Tom nodded. "Dead right: not worth the risk; too much at stake; get a criminal record, too. No, thanks; that's the slippery path to self-destruction."

Seeing the situation among his friends, Will decided to keep quiet about his plans. Perhaps he and George might indulge in a few side-trips later on.

The following morning, Will stood on the riverside shingle beach. He was now and would be forevermore a fisherman, and all the jubilation he felt last night was still with him.

The weather had dulled slightly, but it mattered not; by noon they'd be gone, back to England, and for a spell not return – unless, as George had suggested, they try a fishing break along the River Nith. Will thought it worth a try, now craving to go fishing.

And, perhaps, a bit later on, he thought, *poaching as an extra.*

CHAPTER 40

Downfall of the duke

THE FOLLOWING MORNING at eleven, Johnny strolled down the road to The Leaping Salmon, eager to collect his illegal earnings and sup a pint of heavy. He felt incredibly cheerful, for some unknown reason, and aware of change in the air. He entered the bar and saw Rona at the corner table, complete with laptop, as ever. She smiled at him. He waved, then strode over to the bar, where Reg was about to pull a pint of heavy.

"Usual, Johnny?"

He nodded. "Everyone seems jolly this morning. What's going on?"

"Good news all round, seemingly," replied Reg. "Your friend over there got a victory over that salmon farm at Rosstown: face a hefty fine, they do; eight-grand, no less."

Johnny blew breath. "She did nae waste any time."

Reg casually dropped eighty pounds on the counter. Johnny snatched the money faster than a speeding bullet, and stuffed the notes in his pocket. Reg leant forward on the bar. "What's next, eh? Maybe that duke's going to come a cropper?"

"Could the Almighty grant us that?"

"Possibly, but your friend says feathers have been ruffled in Copenhagen – environmental ones, too."

Johnny supped on the heavy, then strolled over to Rona. She seemed highly animated. "How are things going?" He noticed that her eyes sparkled.

"Hi, Johnny. Jesus, we must talk; everything's worked out far better than I ever thought possible! Kay at the lab found exceptionally high levels of cypermethrin in all those samples I took. What's more, she found the algae and waterweed has absorbed the stuff. Liam reported all my data and her findings to the European Environmental Agency. On that alone, my case against the salmon farm has been accepted – in fact, they are going to prosecute."

"So I just heard. Eight big ones, eh?"

She nodded. "Might amount to more. I've also informed Scottish Water about what's going on and, believe me, they weren't the least bit happy about discharges entering the river. In turn, they could be fined for failing to follow the *Water Framework Directive*."

Johnny smiled. "All seems like a kind o' game, does it not? Everyone's out ter fine whoever they can."

Rona laughed. "True, I guess, but at least the polluters are put in their place."

"I reckon yer done well."

"That's not all: I filed a case against that obnoxious landlord and the E.E.A. pounced on it, almost at once."

Johnny narrowed his eyes. "What does that mean, exactly?"

"That magnate is suddenly going to find he's made an expensive mistake. The E.E.A. is already going to prosecute him for failing to comply with their *Habitats Directive*; he's neglected that river for years and it's going to cost. But they are also considering further charges against him, for failing to conform to E.U.'s river management guidelines, ignoring stipulated conservation measures laid down by Copenhagen and, lastly, flouting the *Water Framework Directive*. Chances are, all tolled, he'll end up with a bill topping sixty-thousand pounds, plus costs."

Johnny whistled. "My, that's a tidy wee sum."

"Less than he deserves, really; the E.E.A. should have sued, but they don't work that way."

Johnny swilled on his pint, hardly daring to think that the pretty ecologist had achieved what the villagers had wanted for years: to slap the duke where it hurt – namely, his wallet.

"I have ter say I'm right surprised and, if I may say so, yer done us proud."

"Thanks, Johnny. Alas, all is not good news."

Johnny's smile melted away. "What's the problem?"

"Remember that skinless salmon you found?"

"Aye, what of it?"

"Kay examined the fish and deduced that sea lice weren't responsible for its condition; she said that far too much skin tissue was missing. However, she failed to detect any sign of the infamous G.S. fluke, so it's still a mystery. I'd hazard a guess it was lice and the skin rotted off afterwards, but I could still be wrong."

"Eerie it was ter look at, I have ter say."

Rona nodded in agreement. "On that find alone, the E.E.A. has put all the fishery concerns across the U.K. on red alert; first sign of the fluke and we're ready to act. Already, contingency plans have been drawn up to implement buffer zones, to prevent the spread of this deadly pestilence."

Johnny scowled. "Is this thing dangerous ter us?"

Rona smiled. "God, no, it can't harm humans, only the salmon. But the economic and social impact will be devastating."

"Aye, that seems kind o' equally bad."

"At least we've got things moving. The E.E.A. have already despatched two senior inspectors to go over the landlord's grounds, partly to back my case and partly gain substantiating evidence to present, when the hearing is reviewed in Brussels."

Johnny grinned. "That bit of news is worth another pint. Would yer like a drink?"

"Thanks, I'll have a coffee if you're offering."

"Ben must be proud of you."

"He's sort of impressed, but he really doesn't understand all the details."

Johnny strode to the bar again, hardly daring to believe that his enemy, the duke, was about to fall.

"Same again, Johnny?" Reg asked.

"Aye, and a coffee for Rona."

"One coffee coming up, along with another pint of heavy, on the house."

"Very kind ye."

"Reckon our friend got all this done just in time. I saw the weather forecast; it's not good, seemingly: rain is on its way."

Johnny envisioned the river in flood, oozing over the banks and into the fields. "Is that so? Thanks fer the warning."

He took the beer and coffee and returned to Rona. "There ye

go."

"Cheers. I've one last little snippet of info."

"Have yer now?"

She smiled again. "I've actually managed to get Scottish Natural Heritage interested in that delightful patch of river. They show great interest in the site."

"What would they do with it?"

"Manage the site for its special wildlife value. Perhaps even establish a centre where people could visit. It's what Adam dreamed of."

"Make yer day that would, eh?"

Rona stared at the tabletop. "If they did that, it would be as good as a memorial."

Johnny knew how she felt about the subject. "It would that. But, alas, the duke looks upon that part of the river as his property."

"The S.N.H. work along with landowners, so hopefully there won't be any problem."

Johnny squinted. "Surely, if the duke gets a whoppin' fine, he'd be smartin' rotten, and never co-operate wi' anyone."

Rona fondled the laptop. "Possibly. Then again, if he wants to recover some of his costs, he might be prepared to sell off that part of the river to a third party. With funding from the E.U., and other sources, S.N.H. might be able to acquire the site. Still, that's all hypothetical right now; nobody's made any firm decisions."

Johnny swilled on the pint and thought. "All rather like a jigsaw, ain't it? Piece by piece, things fit together."

"I hadn't thought of it that way."

Johnny smiled. "Just recently I've come across a few startlin' revelations and surprises – things I never dreamt were possible. It's made me kinda look at things from a different perspective."

"New discoveries often change one's personal outlook. I know mine has, and in a big way."

"How long are yer stayin' here?"

"A few days yet. I've got a few loose ends to tie up."

"I'm glad o' that. I'll have ter get goin' now. Glad things worked out." He drained the glass, left it on the bar and waved to her.

Then he strode down the road, savouring the aroma of the heavy, mixed with the fresh, light gust which blew from the southwest. All of a sudden, Johnny thought life was good. He was happy and felt ready to plan ahead. Just one tiny thing stood in his way, and it was called Davidson.

That evening, Johnny tuned into the news and weather, to find out if Reg was right. The cheery forecaster did indeed predict rain, due in three days' time. Johnny looked at his funds jar, now almost overflowing. He really didn't need to go out again, but if the weather turned nasty and the river flooded, he'd be starved of income. How long would the bad weather last? That was anyone's guess.

Reg had also hinted he'd got a market for the dainties, and not just for the pub menu. Johnny finally decided to do what the local farmers often did: harvest their crops while the fine weather lasted.

He sniffed the air while standing by the front door, and saw it was another fine night, though slightly overcast. He nodded to himself; the season had changed and winter was approaching.

Johnny went through his usual routine, stuffed bin liner and candles into his greatcoat pockets, then grabbed the binoculars. With a glance around to ensure all was clear, he pulled the door to.

He strode along the path, to the allotments and the paddock. This time, he felt certain it was the right thing to do, to make provision for the lean times ahead, though he knew Reg would tide him over when weather conditions made poaching impossible.

Lying under the net in the dell, he recalled Will and George having a go with the gaff. He'd been surprised at the kid's ability to wield the thing.

Before long, a medium-sized salmon slipped into view, drawn by the bobbing, flickering light. He waited until it was on the near side of the box before striking. He hooked a five-pound salmon into the bank with ease, almost like lifting a packet of frozen fish out of a supermarket freezer.

For a moment, he briefly thought of Will and his fixation for poaching, speculating on whether he'd continue to engage in illicit expeditions, and concluded that he would. The addiction was simply too strong to resist.

To make the trip worthwhile, Johnny decided to wait for a second fish, and was glad to have done so. After ten minutes, a much larger salmon appeared; he judged it to be around ten pounds, maybe more. Biding his time and never taking his eyes from the target, he waited until the fish moved to the front of the bobbing box; it was always best to have the fish's flank facing the bank, thus maximizing the overall area for hooking. He swung the gaff, hooked the salmon free of the water and gave it a quick rap.

Without any messing about, he dropped both fish into the black polythene bag, and the gaff and box on the net. Speed was of the essence on poaching ventures, just as much as alertness. After leaving his gaff, box and net in the warren, he strode along the riverside path, glad to have been out, but longing to venture to his other patch, temporarily off-limits.

He decided to call home first, partly to leave the binoculars behind, and also because he felt the need for a quick Scotch.

Ten minutes later, he hiked down the road. Everything seemed to be like it was before Davidson had nabbed his gear and warned him off. He flitted through the dark alley, then across the courtyard. Safe inside the outhouse, he dropped the two salmon in the freezer and, for a moment, recalled the argument he'd had with George and Will, smiling at the memory.

Shedding his greatcoat, he entered the thriving bar and saw the crowd of frivolous socialites, due to frequent The Grouse.

At the bar he ordered a chaser and pint of heavy, caring not who saw him down the short. Grasping the pint glass, he swung on the bar and noticed his three friends in the corner, accompanied by Rona. She blew him a kiss. He hoped he'd caught it.

Then he saw McGee, sitting alone at a table, with his back to the entrance. Johnny supped on the pint, watching him, trying to work out why he wasn't mixing with the in-crowd intending to visit The Grouse. It was unlike him, and Johnny felt slightly wary.

"Been like that all night, he has," Reg muttered from behind the bar. "I reckon he's a bit sloshed."

Johnny turned around. "Has he, now? What the hell's that bastard playin' at now, do yer reckon?"

"No tellin' as far as that one's concerned."

Johnny sniffed. "I still dinnae trust him."

"Nor do I. Is it something to do with the dainties?"

"I cannae be certain," he replied.

When the frivolous crowd departed for The Grouse, McGee didn't join them, but remained seated. It was then that Johnny realized his cousin had been drinking, heavily. He sidled up to McGee's table, then sat in the opposite chair and took a deep breath. "What the bloody hell are ye playin' at?"

McGee pulled greedily from his pint glass and looked coolly at him. "I'm drowning my sorrows, and you can't blame me: I've been sacked. Can you believe it? Sacked from the job I adored, and an instant dismissal, too."

Johnny sneered at him. "How the mighty fall. Yer brought it down on yerself, McGee; you've nobody ter blame but you."

McGee snorted and glared at him. "That's not true, Johnny, and you damn well know it. Bloody Davidson was responsible for this. He found out I'd been supplying you with confiscated salmon and informed. The duke went spare."

"My heart's bleeding already. What of it?"

"Dammit, Johnny, that bastard's ruined me!" snapped McGee.

Johnny saw his three friends look in their direction, seemingly intrigued and puzzled, their attention drawn by his cousin's outburst.

"What the hell am I going to do now, eh?" he bawled. "I've been given two days' notice to quit my pay-house, lost the use of my Land Rover and God knows all the perks. Fucking forty-five and I've not a stinking thing to show for it." He thumped his fist on the table in frustration and fumed. Then, he slumped forward and spoke quietly: "I'm ruined. Ruined, Johnny, and I can't see any way out this goddamned mess."

Rona strode over and casually pulled up a chair. She gazed at him sternly, then sat down. "You must know an awful lot about the rivers, poachers and the way these and other unlawful people operate?"

McGee rubbed his eyes and peered in her direction. "Yes, I suppose I do, but a fat lot of good it'll do me now, though."

She drew a sharp breath. "With all of that knowledge, and your gamekeeper skills, the organization I work for could use somebody like you."

McGee mopped his brow with a handkerchief. "Are you offering me a job?"

"I'm not asking you to join the dole queue, honey."

McGee stuttered: "You are serious, aren't you?"

"Of course I am. However, there is one condition."

McGee squinted. "What's that, if I dare ask?"

"I'd like you to testify against the duke, when his case comes to the European Court in Brussels."

"Are you joking?" screamed McGee. "You must be insane."

Rona stared at him. "Okay then, you go washing windows in Glasgow when it's pouring with rain, and good luck."

McGee smarted. "You can't threaten me like this. I mean, that's bribery."

Johnny interrupted: "McGee, for once in yer miserable life, listen ter someone else. She's offered you a way out on a silver platter, fer Christ's sake. Snatch the opportunity, man. Ya dinnae owe that fat bastard duke anything; he's just sacked yer. Wake up."

McGee scowled and rubbed his lower lip. "Alright, I'll accept your generous offer. You're right: that lousy bastard's done me a wrong turn."

Rona smirked. "I've one more little piece of advice: get rid of that ridiculous Victorian outfit; nobody goes round in knickerbockers and deerstalkers anymore. I suggest black jeans, a tee-shirt and SEPA will even supply the yellow safety jacket."

"You're really enjoying this, aren't you?"

"Get used to it, honey. In our organization everyone mucks in, rank is out and everyone's an equal, more or less."

"Does my outfit really look that daft?" asked McGee.

"No comment."

"Yer bloody lucky, Cousin Chuck; you should thank the Supreme Being fer this chance. You'd get few others elsewhere, and I should know – that's why I go out to the river. Only, yer were too bloody full o' it, and high an' mighty to realize it. I hope yer realize it now, 'cos I haven't done wi' me little ventures, and neither you or Davidson, or anyone else, is gonna stop me. Yer hear me?"

McGee drew himself forward, as though trying to remember something important, and then it registered. "Never mind all that. Before I got the bad news, two sinister-looking inspectors paid the duke an unexpected visit, that very morning – from the European Environmental Agency, they were. Naturally, the duke was livid."

"Aye, I can imagine," muttered Johnny.

"They'd got warrants and everything. They were very thorough: combed the estate and found loads of what they called 'anomalies', took notes of all the procedures and questioned the staff. They also found traces of poison, which our groundsman used to get rid of the vermin. They weren't too happy about that, either, since it was cymag."

Johnny whistled. "Now, where have I heard that name before?" Johnny and Rona looked at each other.

She pursed her lips. "Are you thinking what I am?"

Johnny's eyes turned to slits. "Be too much of a coincidence, wouldn't it?"

"I wonder if there was a barcode on that tin?"

"More to the point, how did Dinger come by that poison? That bleedin' detective never found out."

Johnny turned to McGee. "So, who had access ter the stuff?"

McGee shrugged. "Anyone could have entered the storeroom, where all the toxic material was kept, but the key always remained in Davidson's office; all staff had to get permission from him to enter the store."

Johnny whispered to Rona. "Bloody obvious, ain't it? Someone lifted that tin."

She nodded. "But, who?"

"I've no idea, but I might know of somebody that could provide the answers. I'll pay the rascal a visit tomorrow."

Johnny and Rona got up. He felt the need for another pint of heavy, and was about to go to the bar, when a furtive man sidling around the far end of the room, near the corridor, caught his attention. He cautioned the girl: "Wait here."

He spurted toward the scruffy man and shoved him into the corridor.

"Hey, whit's goin' on?" he expostulated.

"Ye know very well. I want ter speak wi' yer."

Johnny pushed O'Shaig into the gents', closed the door behind them and the small man slowly backed away, suddenly looking very scared.

Johnny wagged a finger at him. "Now, I ain't messin' around here. Where did Dinger get that tin o' cymag, eh?"

"Whit's it ter ye? That's all finished and I know nuthin' more aboot it. Lemme goo."

Johnny sighed. "Me patience is wearin' mighty thin, yer weaslin' bastard. All I want ter know is how your pal came by that tin, that's all."

O'Shaig looked ashen. "Yer sure that's it?"

Johnny nodded.

The weasel sniffed. "A lowly gardenin' assistant – a git called Scobie – got hold o' the stuff. He planned ter sell it an' make a few bob, that's all. When that bruiser bastard took his lunch break, Scobie lifted the key, nipped ter the storeroom and snatched the tin. He replaced the key long before that gamekeeper bastard returned, havin' wiped it clean o' fingerprints, first."

"How much did this Scobie feller get fer it?"

O'Shaig shrugged his shoulders. "Twenty pounds ah think; nay very much fer all that risk. Bloody daft, if yer ask me."

"Is that all? Did this heavyweight bastard get wind o' what happened?"

"Dinnae think so. If he did, he kept quiet aboot it."

Johnny smirked. "Thankee, that's all I want ter know."

Johnny grabbed the door handle and departed from the gents', happy he'd been saved a bit of extra legwork the following day.

Minutes later, O'Shaig sidled out of the gents' to the back of the bar, watching but feeling unnerved. He badly needed a double Scotch and a strong lager. His little world had come crumbling down since the fracas with Dinger and, feeling shunned by all, he made a plan, there and then. With renewed confidence, brought on by the Scotch, he decided it was time to leave Glenstone for good and head north – maybe to Alloa, or perhaps even Oban.

Johnny returned to his friends in the bar, after ordering another pint of heavy. "A right fine evening this has turned out ter be."

"Anything wrong?" asked Ben.

"No, but I just need to tidy up a few loose strands, that's all. It seems the duke ain't so bleedin' perfect, after all."

Rona frowned. "What happened?"

"Apparently, that Dinger bastard got the poison off a humble gardener workin' on the duke's estate, fer a wee sum. Bloke's name was Scobie."

"If that tin had a barcode, maybe we can find out if it's the same one. Who's got the tin now?"

"That bleedin' clever-dick detective has, as far as I know."

Rona frowned, whipped out her mobile phone and called Rosstown Police Station. "Hi. Yes, can I speak to Detective Sergeant Doherty, please? … Yes, it's Rona Cullen, and it's urgent – very urgent."

Johnny's friends all bore puzzled expressions, wondering what drama was unfolding before them. Johnny sat back and watched his cousin, sitting alone and looking dejected. After a few minutes, Rona hung up and smiled.

"What did Detective Hitler have ter say?" Johnny asked.

"He sounded very cheerful, and up for promotion by the way. Apparently, there had been a serial barcode affixed to the tin. Whoever lifted the can tore it off; there was only a shred of label left. But, that's neither here nor there. Doherty also told me that, under intense questioning, Bell admitted to gaining possession of the cymag tin from a man called Scobie, and paid him twenty pounds for it."

"Aye, then that detective's answers tally very nicely with our discovery, eh? This little episode makes Davidson a guilty party, too – guilty of negligence, that is, if nothing else."

Rona sighed. "It's only a tiny misdemeanour, though. Hardly crime of the century."

Johnny smiled. "True, but I'll bet anything you like the duke won't see things that way. After all, a tin of poison off of his estate finding its way into the hands of a felon and, as it turns out, being involved in a murder, isn't good publicity. Now, do you suppose Cousin Chuck here has cause ter celebrate?"

"He won't know if you don't tell him."

Johnny and Rona got up and sat at the despondent ex-head bailiff's table. "Cheer up, Cousin Chuck. We got some crackin' news."

Bleary-eyed, McGee stared at him. "Really? I got sacked and hired all in the space of one day – what more is there to hear?"

Johnny placed his pint on the table. "It seems that Davidson got a wee bit careless doing his job. Hardly a major felony, but his boss might not agree."

McGee sat upright on hearing of Davidson. "What? That bastard's never been slack on the uptake."

"He was on this occasion. A tin o' poison from the store went astray; it ended up in the hands of Dinger, who was planning to poison the river. And, if yer didn't already know, it did nae end there: a young feller got murdered trying ter stop him."

"Yes, I remember that. I didn't know about the poison, though."

"Cousin Chuck, yer missin' the point: in the duke's eyes, surely Davidson is guilty of failing ter carry out his job properly. See what I mean? Yer got some ammo ter shoot him down, should yer choose ter do so."

McGee suddenly appeared to sober up, rapidly. "Yes, I do see now, Johnny."

"He grassed on you, got yer sacked. If yer feel inclined toward a wee spot o' vengeance, yer could always shop him. He's done yer no favours, dinnae forget."

"That action might make things tricky for me."

"You've nothin' ter lose: Rona's offered yer a secure job; you no longer work fer him."

McGee stroked his temple, turning over the new idea. "You're right there, Johnny. I suppose a letter to his lordship might not go amiss."

Johnny smiled. "Chances are, if Davidson messed up over that episode, he might have done so with other little procedures."

"Yes, Johnny. And now, I suppose, I owe you a big one in return."

The old man smiled. "Aye, perhaps. Just forget about me riverside ventures, and pretend yer never heard about the place the goodies end up. Good enough fer me, that is."

"Seems I've no choice. Alright, Johnny, I suppose that's fair enough. I'd be totally wrecked, otherwise."

Johnny smiled and decided to push his good fortune. "And, I'm bloody sure yer goin' ter feel a whole lot better fer informin' on that bastard."

McGee stared at him, took the hint and said nothing.

Johnny smiled, glad to have found a way to sink the last major barricade between him and his beloved river. "Now, if yer excuse us, our friends are kind o' anxious ter speak wi' us."

Johnny and Rona returned to the corner table, happy with their evening's unexpected detective work. The old man leant back and supped his heavy, hardly daring to believe he'd almost single-handedly brought down his major opponent, providing McGee held to his word. Johnny was sure his cousin would, being filled with resentment toward Davidson betraying him.

Ben, Tom and Bobby remained mystified.

"Is something going on that we should know about?" asked Ben.

Johnny suddenly wearied of all the intrigue. "Ye could say it were a family matter. It seems me cousin has, er, had a sudden change o' career."

Tom tapped his pipe on the ashtray. "Really? How astonishing."

Johnny drained his glass and turned to Rona: "Fancy a top-up?"

"Please. House red, thanks."

Johnny ambled to the bar and ordered another heavy and a glass of red wine.

"What was all that about?" asked Reg. "And that weasel turning up, too? He looked mighty shaken up after you spoke to him."

"I reckon you're suddenly goin' ter find this bar is short of one or two patrons before long, and I'll nae cry over that. And, as fer our wee enterprise, I think it's safe ter say the trading embargo has been lifted – if it ever existed, that is."

"I'll go to the devil," muttered Reg.

"I hope not; I cannae see myself supplyin' dainties ter yer wife."

Reg grinned. "Nor can I, for that matter."

With Reg's call of "Drink up, now," Johnny felt over the moon with the way things had turned out. Nothing, it seemed, could go wrong. Having departed via the outhouse for his greatcoat, Johnny walked down the road, more content and at ease than he'd felt in a very long time. Before long, McGee would be out of his life, Davidson sacked, with luck, and all worries regarding a salmon blockade crumbled to dust.

Only one factor added a touch of sadness: Rona was leaving, to return to Dumfries, and tomorrow was her last day in Glenstone. To mark the occasion, the four friends decided to have a farewell drink, the following evening.

When Johnny tuned into the T.V., after stoking up the fire, he was glad of that, as within two days rain was due. Even the weather presenter seemed depressed by the forecast. But it wouldn't rain forever, and Johnny began hatching plans to frequent his old haunt again. This time, he was going to do things properly, and not mess about wasting time burying and unearthing tins containing his gear. The rabbit warren had made a big impression on him. He decided it was a brilliant strategy and, being a natural feature of the landscape, would not draw undue attention from prying eyes. He knew no portion of the river would ever be free of bailiffs or, for that matter, other poachers, but felt that, from now on, things were going to be far easier.

Next morning, as was usual after making a delivery the night before, Johnny called at The Leaping Salmon. He liked to arrive at around eleven, before the bar had filled with patrons, have a quiet word with Reg, collect his earnings and down a pint and a chaser or two, which usually came free. This time, Reg dropped ninety pounds on the bar. Johnny never left the notes there for more than two seconds, before stuffing them into his coat pocket.

"Here's ter happy times again," stated Johnny.

Reg smiled. "You can say that again. I gather that cousin of yours is moving out today."

"Aye, he found himself a wee flat in Dumfries fer now. His new job's down there."

"Sorry, but I can't say that I'll miss him."

Johnny smiled grimly, realizing that, if McGee had kept his promise, the duke would receive the informing letter about Davidson before the day was out. By then, of course, McGee would be far out of reach. He'd planned everything to a tee. For that, Johnny warmed slightly toward him, but only just. At least he was now out of the way.

After a second pint of heavy, Johnny returned home and made another batch of stubby candles for his little floating box, more to while away the afternoon than anything else.

That evening, Johnny decided he need not go poaching, as the funds jar was filled to the brim, and he had to keep the rest of the cash in a polythene bag, stashed away behind the bookcase, full of mouldering volumes he never read. Besides, as Rona didn't approve of poaching, he thought turning up to see her off after such a venture would somehow tarnish the evening. He respected her too much for that. There would be plenty of other dark evenings.

Johnny remembered to do one other little thing – not that he was really a sentimental type, but Rona had touched him in a way that had changed his outlook, and in return he wanted to repay her. He'd very little to offer but, with deep emotion, went to the dresser Annie had always used, drew out a small, crimson box and opened it. The one thing of Annie's he couldn't bear to clear out, after she passed away, was her jewellery box. He fingered through the trinkets and brooches, mostly just paste, and picked out one particular item: it was a brooch in the form of a golden fish, though what species it was supposed to represent, Johnny hadn't a clue. He stared at it and smiled. It would be perfect.

That evening, at around six o'clock – much earlier than usual – Johnny strode down the road to The Leaping Salmon, happy yet slightly saddened, too. Instead of the bagged salmon swinging under his greatcoat, his right hand clasped the little cardboard box containing the gold fish – a salmon, he thought to himself.

He sidled through the alley to the courtyard and entered the outhouse – not to drop a fish in the freezer, as he'd so often done, but for a crafty quickie, before the emotional farewell in the cheery bar. From behind the stacked, empty beer-crates he withdrew the half-empty bottle of Scotch and, without any glasses, swilled from the bottle, feeling the liquor scald his gullet. The last time he'd touched that bottle was when Will and George had their heated discussion. He smiled at the memory.

Johnny Mason, yer getting ter be a right sentimental bastard, he thought. He swilled again, almost to banish such thoughts, and screwed the cap on, placing it behind the crates. Remembering to drop the brooch into his jacket pocket, he glanced once at the freezer rattling away in the corner, and headed for the door, opening it.

Entering the bar, he saw Ben, Bobby and Tom in the corner with Rona. He went first to the bar for a beer.

Reg smiled. "Usual tonight, Johnny?"

"Unless yer got the elixir o' life, I reckon the heavy will do. And make it a chaser, an' all."

Reg pulled the pint and placed it on the bar. "All on the house tonight – I reckon you deserve it. I got news, too; unexpected news."

Johnny's eyebrows rose. "Really? Now what the bleedin' hell's happened? Don't tell me, the duke had a cardiac while receiving a whopping bill fer damages?"

Reg grinned. "Not quite. That heavyweight bastard Davidson stormed in here earlier, looking for McGee."

Johnny's eyes narrowed. "Fat chance. He's away."

"Just as well! Apparently, Davidson had a set-to with the duke."

"Suddenly looks like he's made other plans, then?"

"I never felt anything for McGee but, Jesus, I'm glad he weren't here; I reckon if they'd clashed it'd come to blows."

"That bad, eh?"

"I'm not kidding you. Anyway, he stormed out of the bar like a black tornado. Hope that's the last I ever see of that one."

"Funny, isn't it, how one tiny thing leads ter another, then before ye know it, everything falls ter bits and a new way o' life begins from the ashes, like?"

Reg laughed. "Ah, you're right. Scholars call it history, I think."

Johnny downed the chaser and walked across to his friends.

Ben looked up. "You made it, and just in time, too."

Johnny sat down, supped the beer and slowly placed the glass on the table. "What do yer mean?"

Rona smiled at him. "My work here is done; there's nothing more I can do. I just wanted to say goodbye to you all in this place." She stroked Ben's hand. "Thanks, Uncle, you've been a saint putting up with me."

Ben flushed. "Rubbish. You're me niece, for goodness' sake."

She sipped from the wineglass, then held it up. "Here's to the four of you."

The four friends raised their glasses and cheered. "To Rona, and everything she's done for us," stated Bobby.

Johnny placed his glass on the table and squirmed, being unused to this sort of thing. "Aye. I, er, have a wee parting gift fer ye." He fumbled around in his jacket pocket, withdrew the box and handed it to her.

Totally surprised, she opened it and stared at the golden fish. "Johnny, I'm speechless, really."

Johnny blushed and smiled tentatively. "Memories, perhaps, of the river, and the life that lives in it, that you fought so hard to save. God bless you an' Liam with a happy future."

She closed the box, placed it in her shoulder bag and glanced at her wristwatch. "Hate to say this: I really have to go."

Outside the bar, Ben, Bobby and Johnny stood to say farewell. She hugged Ben. "Thanks for everything."

"Anytime. Call again, if you like."

She turned to Bobby, standing on the other side of Johnny, kissed his cheek and whispered to him: "Thanks for all the help along the river."

Finally, she turned to Johnny, kissed his forehead but just smiled.

Then, she walked quickly to the Nissan, got in and drove off down the road, while the three friends stood in silence, watching the car disappearing into the distance.

Just then, it started to drizzle slightly, and Johnny thought it fitting, in a strange way. "Goodbye, Rona," he muttered, softly.

Back in the bar, the four friends returned to their table.

Johnny sagged at the table with a second pint of heavy, briefly wondering what Will would be doing, then leant back, listening to his friends. He also made new plans to reclaim his territory.

Bobby was about to go to the bar for another beer, when he noticed Sally saunter up to her dad. She spoke to him, seemingly in earnest, and he looked at her, almost as though shocked. "Something's up," Bobby mumbled.

Johnny glanced at him. "Find out soon enough, I reckon."

He did, too, when ordering his third pint that evening. Reg looked quite amazed – taken aback, in fact. "Hey, Johnny, you won't believe this. Sally told me a while ago that bruiser Davidson had done a runner. Can you believe it?"

"How did she find out?"

"Her best friend Lucy told her. She'd know, working at The Grouse. She said he had words with the duke – lots of them, in front of his guests – then buggered off. He's gone to the States, apparently."

Johnny stared at the public bar's ceiling for a minute, then suddenly burst out laughing. "Jesus, all me prayers have been answered; the way has been cleared. Make it a chaser ter celebrate, eh? And another heavy, too."

Reg looked at him. "Are you okay there, Johnny?"

"Aye, I am. Never felt better."

Much later that night, after the usual "Drink up now," Johnny strolled back to the bar.

"Reg, can I ask a favour of yer?"

"Yes, anything; fire away."

"Would yer be wantin' that chunk of glazed drainage pipe in your outhouse?"

"Jesus, takes it, by all means; I'd be glad to see the back of it. Damn thing was left over when we had the drains done."

"Thankee, I'd dae just that."

He departed to the outhouse for his greatcoat and grabbed the two-foot section of glazed stoneware pipe. Rather conveniently, Johnny noted it had a bore roughly resembling the same diameter of a rabbit burrow. Johnny was ready to put the next part of his great plan into operation.

The following evening, Johnny ventured to the field he'd not skirted since Davidson impounded his gear. He risked carrying the pipe and had a trowel in his coat pocket. Determined to get the chore finished before bad weather set in, he knew it was necessary to move fast. Although pleased to enter the woods again, he felt strangely aware that eyes could be watching, but it bothered him not.

Standing under the ash tree once again, he surveyed the river through his binoculars and saw nobody, except for three sheep. Satisfied all was in order, he dug a trench three feet deep, on a small bank not far from the lookout post. He made sure the pipe lip was set a few inches back from the side of the embankment. Pleased with the work, he then set about making a plug for the entrance with dried grasses, just as he'd done with the tunnel at the warren.

Happy all was in order, he returned home for a quick Scotch, to fuel the immediacy of the task at hand.

Afterward, he set out for the rabbit warren to retrieve his gear. His heart pounded and he moved swiftly, like a fox about its nightly business. He had one thought only, and that was to get set up before the heavy rains came. For a moment, he wondered if it was wise to remove his stuff from the second fishing spot, but the desire to frequent his own pool erased all doubts. It was the place that had been unofficially passed down to him, and since Davidson had flown, he was now free to reclaim it.

Less than an hour later, Johnny returned home, to break the journey from the warren to his favoured pool – that way, nobody could possibly have followed him from one hidey-hole to the other. He also wanted a quick breather and another drink.

An hour later he'd returned to the familiar woods, almost looking forward to meeting the little owl again, and felt sure he would before long. With the gear safely stashed away, he felt incredibly euphoric. He, Johnny Mason, had conquered all adversity: the duke, Davidson, McGee and the nosy detective.

All done and dusted, Johnny called home again, to catch the evening weather forecast and gloat at the prediction of much rain, knowing he'd achieved impossible feats. He swilled half a mug of Scotch and smiled.

Then, donning his greatcoat, he departed for The Leaping Salmon. Suddenly, it had all become a game and he loved it. Inside the outhouse he hung his coat on the hook, glanced at the freezer and smiled, imagining filling the thing with bag after bag of salmon.

On entering the bar he found Ben, Tom and Bobby in the usual corner. He ordered a chaser and Reg pulled a heavy.

"On the house" was a commonplace phrase in Reg's vocabulary now, and Johnny knew it was going to be even more familiar.

He downed the chaser and, grasping the pint of heavy, felt on top of the world, knowing McGee was never likely to set foot in the bar again.

Johnny spent the evening in the cosy tranquillity of the bar with his friends, downed five pints of heavy, and Reg only charged him for one.

On hearing Reg's recommendation that everyone empty their glasses, Johnny retrieved his greatcoat from the outhouse and strode down the road, the happiest man in all of Glenstone.

Indoors, he stoked up the fire, switched on the T.V. and settled in his favourite chair to catch the weather forecast. The rainy spell would not last for long, and afterward Johnny knew he would be out fishing by his pool again. With that thought he laughed, and was soon dozing off.

THE END

Glossary

B.A.: A degree; Bachelor of Arts.

BOD: Biological Oxygen Demand; a measure of oxygen consumption in water samples.

BOD count: As above, but a specific measure.

Cast: To throw a fishing line.

Civvies: A term used by military personnel to describe civilians.

Cymag: A mix of sodium cyanide and magnesium sulphate used as vermin poison.

Cypermethrin: A deadly chemical found in Deosect, also used in sheep dips.

D.C.: Detective Constable.

Deosect: A toxic chemical used to kill parasites on horses and poultry. Occasionally used illegally on salmon farms, to eradicate sea lice infestation.

D.S.: Detective Sergeant.

Eco: Ecological.

E.E.A.: European Environmental Agency.

Enzyme: A catalyst in organic lifeforms, generally produced in digestive tract.

E.U.: European Union.

F.R.S.: Fisheries Research Services.

Fry: Young fish, fresh from the spawn, or a first-year salmon.

Gaff: A stick with a metal hook at the end, used by anglers to land fish.

Glasgow kiss: A headbutt.

Grilse: A young salmon that returns from the sea, usually in its second year.

G.S. or *G.S. fluke:* Gyrodactylus salaris, a deadly parasite of salmon measuring 0.5mm.

Howking: Dredging river pools with treble hooks fixed to a stout rod or line.

P.H.: Usually spelled pH., a scale to measure acidity or alkalinity of water or soil.

Ph.D.: A degree denoting a Doctor of Philosophy.

S.A.S. 22nd: Special Air Service regiment.

Sassenach: A Scottish term to describe a Saxon or Englishman.

Sea lice: A parasite of salmon which generally attacks younger fish.

SEPA: Scottish Environmental Protection Agency.

Smolt: A young salmon in its second year, when it acquires silver scales.

S.N.H.: Scottish Natural Heritage.

S.S.: A nickname used by Glenstone villagers to describe S.S.S.T.F. bailiffs/personnel.

S.S.S.T.F.: Scottish Salmon Strategy Task Force.

Stovies: A Scottish casserole of onions, meat and potatoes.

Supreme Being: God.

W.F.D.: Water Framework Directive.

Dialect

Aboot: About

Agoo: Ago

Ah: I

Ah'm: I am or I'm

Dae: Do

Dinnae: Do now

Gi': Give or get

Gie: Give

Hae: Have

Nay: Not

Noo: No

Oot: Out

Ootae: Out of

Pollis: Police

Shite: Shit

Tae: To

Tay: To

Ter: To

Tew: Two or to

Un: One (as in young 'un)

Utinnite: Out tonight

Weer: We are or we're

Wheer: Where

Whit: What

Whit noo: What now

Wi': With

Ya: You

Ye: You

Ye'll: You will

Yewait: You wait

Acknowledgments

The publishers and authors would like to thank Russell Spencer, Matt Vidler, Susan Woodard, Leonard West, Lianne Baily Woodward and Laura Jayne Humphrey for their work, without which this book would not have been possible.

About the Publisher

L.R. Price Publications is dedicated to publishing books by unknown authors.

We use a mixture of both traditional and modern publishing options, to bring our authors' words to the wider world.

We print, publish, distribute and market books in a variety of formats including paper and hardback, electronic books, digital audiobooks and online.

If you are an author interested in getting your book published, or a book retailer interested in selling our books, please contact us.
www.lrpricepublications.com

L.R. Price Publications Ltd,
27 Old Gloucester Street,
London, WC1N 3AX.
020 3051 9572
publishing@lrprice.com